FORTUNES OF THE IMPERIUM

BAEN BOOKS BY JODY LYNN NYE

View from the Imperium
Fortunes of the Imperium
The Grand Tour
School of Light
Walking in Dreamland
The Ship Errant
Don't Forget Your Spacesuit, Dear

License Invoked (with Robert Asprin)

With Ann McCaffrey

The Ship who Saved the World
The Death of Sleep
The Ship Who Won
Planet Pirates (also with Elizabeth Moon)

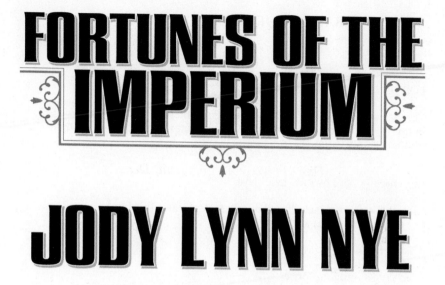

FORTUNES OF THE IMPERIUM

JODY LYNN NYE

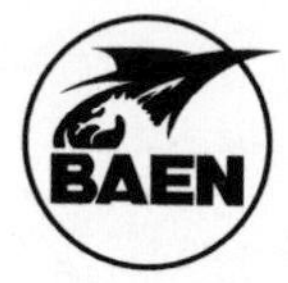

FORTUNES OF THE IMPERIUM

A Baen Book

Baen Publishing Enterprises
P.O. Box 1403
Riverdale, NY 10471
www.baen.com

ISBN: 978-1-4767-3672-3

Cover art by David Mattingly

First printing, September 2014

Distributed by Simon & Schuster
1230 Avenue of the Americas
New York, NY 10020

Library of Congress Cataloging-in-Publication Data

Nye, Jody Lynn, 1957- author.
Fortunes of the imperium / by Jody Lynn Nye.
pages cm
ISBN 978-1-4767-3672-3 (paperback)
1. Science fiction. I. Title.
PS3564.Y415F68 2014
813'.54--dc23

2014019715

Printed in the United States of America

10 9 8 7 6 5 4 3 2 1

FORTUNES OF THE IMPERIUM

PROLOGUE

Standing at the vending machine wall with her eight-year-old son, looking at the selections available, M'Kenna Copper felt hopeless frustration. She leaned her forehead against the blue glass. Pepper Papardelle. Nougatine Pie. Rare T-bone Steak with Potatoes Duchesse. Wild-caught Filet of Salmon. Peanut Butter and Jelly Sandwich. No matter what they called each of the entrees and snacks, none of it was really what it said on the label. All of the food was made up from a vat of nutritious glop inside the wall. Flavorings were added as the pre-measured quantity hit the mixing tray, and texture came from cooking, or whipping, or frying, depending on what the customer ordered. Nothing tasted natural, and it certainly wasn't high quality, not out here on the edge of the Imperium where only spacers and traders passed through, and usually stayed only for the least amount of time possible until their documents were checked through for the Uctu Autocracy.

M'Kenna sighed. That was the problem. Their family-run trader, the *Entertainer*, had been held up there on Way Station 46, for no good reason anyone could give them, for over three months. The distributor awaiting the goods they were carrying had sent them dozens of cranky messages, escalating in irritation and threats of cancellation with every further delay. Her husband, Rafe, had argued back, as patiently as he could, that he couldn't make the government move any faster.

The Coppers weren't alone in their misery. Four other trading ships had been mired even longer than they had. In spite of warnings the five of them put out over the Infogrid, seven more had arrived and become stuck in the bureaucratic spider web since then. Worse yet, none of the ships heading back from the Autocracy into the Imperium were held up. They pulled into the airlocks for a brief inspection of their manifests, and zoom, they were on their way. No one had any reasons for why there was a one-way bottleneck. Rafe and all the other captains had sent appeals to the Core Worlds, all of which were answered by prerecorded vids of a pleasant-looking Human woman who reminded them that the Autocracy was sovereign space and its laws had to be obeyed. M'Kenna and the other traders were eager to obey the laws, if only they had the chance!

And she was so sick of the food on the space station she could have cried. So were her four youngsters. But they had to eat. She chose an entrée at random on the projected display and started to tap in the code.

"No, Mama," Lerin said, grabbing her wrist and dragging it down to his level. "No, no, no, no. I hate tofu chili! No!"

M'Kenna held herself back from snapping at him. They were all on edge. She was the adult. She had to hold on to her temper. Their troubles weren't his fault. She knelt down beside him and stroked his thick black braids.

"Lerin, you have to eat something. The others all chose already. They're back in the ship, eating. You can't starve."

He folded his arms and stuck his chin out in defiance.

"I'd *rather* starve. When are we getting to Partwe? I like the food there."

She sighed again.

"Soon, honey."

His nose and ears showed red under his walnut-brown complexion that was just the same shade as hers. He broke away from her caresses and threw his hands in the air.

"You always say soon! It's never soon! I want to get out of here!"

"So do I, honey," M'Kenna said. In desperation, she decided to try bribery. "Look, we'll go for one of the premium meals today. It comes with a game download. They have Asteroid Tag. I know you wanted to try that."

"All right," Lerin said, his eyebrows rising in anticipation. Disaster was delayed, at least for the moment. He picked the fanciest sandwich on the list, mock-chick baked in round puff bread with cherry mustard globules and crisp cheese stars. He tapped the image. They both watched the animation of a happy-faced robot chef putting together the ingredients. He tossed them a cheery salute with his long spoon. His image disappeared, replaced by a scannable code. Lerin held up his blue-framed tablet. A shrill tootle from both the vending machine and pad indicated the download was completed. The screen on his small device lit up and music blared from the audio output.

"Great!" he said, jabbing at the controls with his thumbs. The hatch on the front of the vending machine slid open to reveal the sandwich, cut into half-spheres, on a stiff, recycled-fiber plate.

"No playing until you eat your lunch!" M'Kenna ordered, reaching for the pad, but it was no use. Lerin eluded her grasp and ran into the ship.

"Hey, I got Asteroid Tag!" he shouted.

"Lerin, your sandwich!"

M'Kenna groaned. This happened at least every other time she had bought one of the kids a premium meal. She had pleaded with the station authorities to delay the games from opening for at least twenty minutes so kids would eat half of their meal. They argued that it was unfair to make adults wait. In the official release, the authorities suggested that parents ought to install controls on their children's tablets. M'Kenna and her husband had done that a dozen times, and each time the children had unprogrammed them. Until people started having dumber kids, it wasn't going to work.

No sense in wasting food. She layered the crunchy cheese stars in on top of the mock-chick and took a bite. The premium meals did taste a little better than the cheaper choices. The tart cherry mustard livened the bland mock-chick flavor considerably. Until the food touched her tongue, she hadn't realized that she was hungry, too. She finished one half in six bites, and licked the mustard off her fingers.

The overhead speaker in the corridor blared out its pseudo-trumpet call, demanding attention. M'Kenna looked up.

"Crew of the *Entertainer*, report to the port manager's office."

At last! She grabbed for her own pad and signaled to her husband Rafe.

"Honey, did you hear that?" she asked, as soon as his narrow, oblong face appeared on the small screen.

"Yes! Can you go? I'm changing Dorna."

"No problem," she said. She put the pad back in her hip pouch. No longer hungry, she glanced around for a disposer to take the rest of the sandwich. The only hatch in the vending wall flashed the message "Out of Order" in insistent blue letters. She couldn't just drop the food. Video pickups were everywhere, and the penalties for littering on the station were ridiculously high. She dashed up the ramp into their ship and tossed the plate into the disposer just inside the double airlock doors. She wheeled on her heel and hurried off to see the port manager.

"And you are . . . ?" the Liberated Artificial Intelligence in the doorframe inquired, though M'Kenna knew it had already identified her biometric information via the bulbous lenses and sensors just below eye level.

"M'Kenna Copper, navigator/owner, ship *Entertainer*, tail number Beta Ni Gimel 5466G."

"Welcome, Navigator/Owner Copper. Enter. You are ninth in line to see the port manager."

She groaned. Another wait! But when the door zipped open, the waiting room was empty. The receptionist, a Croctoid with gleaming teeth and scales, waved her toward the door to the inner sanctum.

"Good midday, M'Kenna," said Rothem. "Join the group. The meeting will begin when three more arrive."

"Three!" she exclaimed. "What's going on?"

If the Croctoid had had shoulders, he would have shrugged them. Instead, he blinked his small eyes rapidly. "A meeting."

"Good news?"

This time Rothem showed all his teeth. There were lots of them. "It's hopeful, for a change."

M'Kenna slid into the small office. In spite of the importance of the port manager's function, his chambers were no larger than those of a planetbound clerk. Such were the strictures of an atmosphere-preservative environment. Almost every trader that had been trapped on Way Station 46 was present, so whatever was going on concerned all of them.

Tall though she was, she couldn't see over the furry shoulders of the three-man, or rather, three-Wichu crew from the *Sword Snacks IV*, one of the ships from a large-scale specialty foods importer. They had been grousing to anyone who would listen that their cargo was no more than a week from spoiling. M'Kenna was only marginally sympathetic; she and Rafe had carried fresh food into the Autocracy once—only once. The import licenses were the least of their problems. The smell of the refrigerated food was what drove the Coppers crazy. The fruit the lizard-like Uctu preferred was the stinkiest growth native to the Imperium. By the end of the trip, M'Kenna had been ready to jump ship and go live in a biological desert.

She tapped the Wichu captain on the shoulder.

"Nuro, what's going on?"

The Wichu turned huge, round purple eyes to her. He showed his upper gums. That meant he was happy.

"They're talking about letting us leave!"

"They are? What was the holdup?"

"Shut up," Nuro said, suddenly. The Wichu had a crude manner of speaking, even to their friends. "Big Mouth is talking."

That was everyone's nickname for Port Manager Denzies FitzGreen. M'Kenna strained to hear.

". . . So, the *Faroe* arrived this morning at 0530," FitzGreen said. He was a big, red-faced man with a wisp of white hair stretched unconvincingly from side to side over his head. "They're clearing customs. As soon as they've finished with the Ag inspection, the Autocracy has said all of you can leave with it."

M'Kenna felt outrage rising in her gut. The *Faroe* was their fiercest competitor on the Uctu run! She pitched her voice to carry over the massed voices in the low-ceilinged room.

"The *Faroe*?"

"Yes, ma'am," FitzGreen said. He moved until he could make eye contact with her in between the shoulders of the others in the room. "You can untie as soon as they're ready to pull out."

"Why do they get special treatment?" M'Kenna demanded. "Why do they get priority?"

FitzGreen shook his head. "I'm sorry, I have no idea. The Uctu inspectors sent an advance copy of the *Faroe*'s manifests to Nacer. They got word just a few minutes ago. You all leave together, ASAP. Look, do you want to get out of here, or not?"

M'Kenna joined the unhappy muttering of the crowd.

FitzGreen took that as assent. He smiled and flicked a hand at them.

"Good. I was getting tired of seeing your ugly faces anyhow. Go pay your tabs, clock in with Flight Control, and get off my station!"

"But what about preflight?" Derward Rissul asked. "I've got to recharge my atmospherics, and there's a couple of circuits in my main cabin portals need replacing!"

FitzGreen put on a sympathetic expression that fooled no one.

"Well, Rissul, no one lifts unless all of you do, so ask your fellow pilots what they think of further delays. All of you have had weeks . . ."

"Months!" an annoyed voice rang out from the other side of the room over the collective moans.

". . . Well, yes, months, in some cases," FitzGreen said. "You should have taken care of that when you had the chance. Can it wait to your next transshipment point?"

"It had better," Nuro bellowed. "I'm not waiting one microsecond longer than I have to. As soon as *Faroe* clears, I am leaving! Anyone who delays me is getting rammed."

No one got rammed. In fact, every one of the thirteen ships exited Way Station 46 in record time.

The passage through the frontier and the jump that followed seemed to take only minutes instead of the hours that the chronometer said it did. M'Kenna kept her eyes on the tank display as soon as they broke into real-space.

"Well, thank all deities, there it is," M'Kenna crowed.

Rafe Copper bent his long back to look at what his wife and navigator was so happy about. His odd-colored eyes offered an unspoken question.

"Edge of Partwe system," M'Kenna said, slapping her hands on the console. "I thought we'd never make it."

The blue-white beacon, the size of a small moon, flashed its lights in a sequence that she and Rafe knew so well. Their trading ship, the *Entertainer*, had made the journey over forty times since they had teamed up and married. Almost invisible from this distance was Partwe's sun, more orange in color than that circled by the Core Worlds or most of the Human-inhabited systems, but plenty warm to sustain life. Partwe 3, otherwise known as Nacer, the second planet out from the star, was one of the most lucrative of trade worlds in the Autocracy. The system lay between the closest Imperium outpost and the Autocracy's home system, Dilawe. Partwe 3 was home to innumerable distributors and small businesses who acted as middlemen for the traders who poured over the frontier every year.

To Rafe Copper's infinite annoyance, the *Entertainer* was forced to stay amid the convoy that had left Station 46. M'Kenna knew how much that irked him. Their sublight engines were his pride and joy. They could kick an extra .2 gees more than any other ship in the group. They could have made orbit around Nacer and dumped their cargo hours before *Faroe* got there. But, no. FitzGreen had been adamant. Everyone had to travel together, or no one left. Still, flying so close together, they had company. Rafe spent all his time grousing with the other captains in near-real time. Their children played games and exchanged messages on the Infogrid with children on other ships.

Not far inside the orbit of the outermost planet, the Coppers' elder daughter, Nona, their communications officer in training, picked up the first beacon. It overrode their audio comm channels and started spewing the laws of the Autocracy that pertained to visitors, immigrants, tradespeople and diplomats. It was repeated again and again, in ten or twelve different languages, including Imperium Standard, Kail, Wichu and Trade Union patois as well as the native Uctu. On their first trip to Nacer, the Coppers had let it run uninterrupted just to see how long it went on. By the time they made orbit, it hadn't repeated a single statute.

". . . Item 54H, clause the second, the punishment for those who are found in possession of dangerous narcotics not strictly prescribed to a member of the crew and without an import license is death. Item 54H, clause the third, the punishment for smuggling dangerous foodstuffs that are not strictly for the use of a member of the crew and without an import license is death. Item 54H, clause the fourth . . ."

"Turn it off, honey," Rafe said. "Just acknowledge that we accept the terms, same as always. Then it'll quit blabbering."

"Is there anything that isn't punishable by death, Dad?" Lerin asked.

"I haven't heard of anything," Rafe admitted. M'Kenna laughed.

At least she had the satisfaction of clocking in to the trading station orbiting Dilawe 3 ahead of the *Faroe*. The officials took their manifests by electronic transfer while the ships were still en route. With a little pushing, Rafe managed to find out that they were second in line to check in behind *Sword Snacks IV*. That cheered M'Kenna. The moment Rafe had the ship secured and popped the airlock, she ditched her emergency gear, jumped down the ramp and headed for her distributor's office, physical manifest in hand. The custom was a throwback to the ancient days of transport, when waterborne ships powered by wind reached their ports of call on Earth, and had never been rescinded, though powers that be knew the traders tried. Even though it was the middle of the night, station time, at least one executive with the power to accept her shipment would be on duty.

She heard footsteps pounding the deck behind her. She opened up her long stride and poured on the hustle. No one was getting past her!

Every door on Dilawe Station was made to withstand an internal or external blast equal to five megatons, but most of the businesses installed a window that looked out on the corridor, completely negating the safety measure. It meant that M'Kenna could see a low-intensity blue light in the window of Wittlock Enterprises. She slid inside and palmed the door locked. The slim, redhaired man behind the counter looked up from his keyboard.

"Hey, M'Kenna. Glad to see you."

"Here," she gasped, thrusting the chip with the files on it plus a sample of the dry goods to him. He timestamped the chip by inserting it into his console, then handed it back to M'Kenna. The manifest lit up on twin screens, one facing him, and one built into the counter M'Kenna leaned upon. Wittlock scanned it, looking for expiration dates. M'Kenna knew perfectly well he wouldn't find any.

"Nice work. We can still accept a hundred percent of what you brought in."

"Excellent," she said. But Dale never made it that easy for her, not even on an unobstructed run. "And the price? What we agreed on before we left the Core Worlds?"

Wittlock put on a crafty expression. "Well, no. We can't really do that. You were late. . . ."

"Do not try that on with me," M'Kenna snapped, aiming a finger at his nose. She knew her eyes were flashing. By the expression on the executive's face, he didn't want to tangle with her, but he was a bureaucrat. He couldn't help but try.

"I'm sorry, but Wittlock Enterprises has had to deal with delays and complaints . . ."

"Every one of which we have heard about for three months!"

". . . So in light of the expenses we've had to incur, we're assessing you a penalty of two point five percent."

"Of net?"

He chuckled, as if she had made a great joke.

"Of course not. Gross. Deducted from your payment."

The frustration of the entire journey came pouring out of her. " *One* percent," she said, her voice echoing off the perforated ceramic ceiling of the office. "That is my first and final offer. You need our stuff. The powers-that-be alone know when you'll get another shipment, considering how screwed up things are at the frontier crossing!" M'Kenna mentally crossed her fingers, hoping that the *Faroe* wasn't carrying the same mix of goods on board. But it didn't matter. She had arrived first.

Wittlock pursed his lips. "All right. One percent. But off the top."

"Fine." M'Kenna entered her private code on the contract. Her image appeared on the document along with her biometrics. Wittlock added his, and a red disk lit up between them. Signed, sealed and delivered.

"Thanks," Wittlock said. "Always a pleasure. You folks are the best."

"And don't you forget it," M'Kenna said, but she was so pleased she winked at him.

M'Kenna was able to relax at last. In fact, she strutted back to the ship, passing on the way the frantically racing crews from *Sword Snacks IV*, *Faroe* and all the others.

With a triumphant flourish, she opened the hatch of the *Entertainer* and stepped in with her palms raising an imaginary roof in the multipurpose room that acted as dining hall, entertainment center and whatever else was not a bunk or bath.

"A little applause, if you please. We have full acceptance of cargo, signed and sealed, and that space-weasel Wittlock only took one percent!"

Her entire family, Rafe and all four children, sat huddled together on one of the long bench seats that folded down from the bulkhead. The tank display was blank except for a body-sized image of the Uctu's green and yellow Autocratic Seal. Rafe looked as if he was in shock.

"What's wrong?" she asked.

"We're in trouble."

"What happened?"

"The authorities have put us under arrest. They're accusing us of smuggling."

"Smuggling what?" M'Kenna asked. "Our ship was searched when we reached Station 46. We couldn't have brought in an orange peel."

"Smuggling a skimmer-sized warship. An armed scout."

She gawked at him.

"That's impossible! There isn't one unaccounted-for crate in our cargo bays!"

Rafe shook his head as if trying to convince himself.

"It isn't in the cargo bay. It's in our waste tank. They're not lying. I saw it myself."

M'Kenna felt for the nearest bench and sat down. Her two smaller children came and nestled into her arms. She clutched them tight, though inside she felt numb.

"But how? How could it get in there?"

"I don't know."

Lerin, huddled against his father's side, was wide-eyed and sober. "We're all going to die."

CHAPTER 1

I crept out of the Taino Central Constabulary with, I believe, a creditable chastened expression on my face. Very little can bring one so low as the walk of shame in broad daylight, except if it should be in the company of one's own conscience brought to life and embodied. My aide-de-camp, Commander Parsons, held my upper arm as if to prevent it removing itself from the rest of my torso and fleeing. I rather wished it could, and take me with it. I am very tall, but Parsons is somewhat taller, with remarkably dark eyes, and possessed of an austere expression that would cause even an angel to search its heart for any sins it might have committed. Parsons is also an old family friend, so I have beheld that expression more often than I care to think about.

"Perhaps you will reveal the reason that you flew your racing flitter in between the pillars of the charity art exhibit, Lord Thomas?" he asked.

"Well, my cousin Xan rather dared me," I admitted. "In fact, he dared me to the fifth power. It was a challenge I hardly liked to ignore. And," I added, with a hopeful look added to the shame on my face, "he went first. I wasn't the only one to crash into the sculpture. Several of us impacted with it."

The austerity of his countenance did not soften.

"It was a tribute to the Emperor's late mother."

"I know! It didn't look a thing like the old girl, though. In fact, it looked like a wad of yellow sponge, magnified three or four thousand times. Modern art is an insult to one's intelligence. If you don't guess correctly as to the artist's intention, then you are ignorant. If you just happen to be right, you probably commit illegal acts of art on your own time."

I glanced at Parsons in search of a twitch of amusement, but in vain. No continental shelf full of ice could have been more glacial. I looked away, seeking something more pleasant to behold. The sunlight caused my pupils to contract painfully. I had noticed before how bright natural daylight appeared after a night's incarceration. Something about the illumination in the cells, perhaps. My head pounded so loudly that I feared I was yet again disturbing the peace. I massaged my temples with shaking forefingers. My chest and thighs had been bruised from forceful impact against my flitter's comprehensive safety harness, and I had a purple lump on my forehead from the crash itself. This edema felt tender to the touch. Perversely, of course, I could not help but probe it now and again to confirm. To distract myself, I gazed at my surroundings, trying to convince myself they had become more beautiful overnight.

And yet, the city of my birth needed no public relations specialist to enhance its attractions. Taino, capital of the Core Worlds of the Imperium, lay in a natural, high-sided valley surrounded by wind-and-water-etched cliffs of white and rust sandstone. As if to add that pop of color so beloved of decorators, muted green moss had been daubed in streaks, stripes and swags all over those cliffs. Above all hung a marvelously clear sky of the most enchanting blue with the faintest hint of turquoise. Here and there, a white cloud dawdled, and I could see the contrails, also white, from the morning arrivals and departures from the Taino spaceport downriver. I inhaled a great gust of air, still cool before the burning heat of a summer day descended.

"Here, my lord." Parsons steered me toward a hovering skimmer. I glanced with a measure of hope at the controls, but they were locked into a thick cylinder twinkling with small lights and gauges.

"I suppose the robot won't let me drive," I said, with little hope. "It's such a beautiful day. I'd adore a quick zip over to the Highclerc Cliffs and having a look out over the spaceport."

"Your ban on operating a motorized vehicle took effect at midnight last night," Parsons reminded me. "It will last for the next sixty days. SK902 will be your chauffeur until the ban expires."

"Well, that's dreary!" I declared, but I swung into the rear passenger seat. Parsons, with more dignity, ascended and took the place beside me. The skimmer lifted off. With gratitude, I watched the looming building of the Constabulary disappear behind me. "Where are we going? This is not the way back to the Imperium Compound. I had hoped to change out of these clothes. They are less presentable than I wish them to be."

"We have a different destination. Your mother is disappointed in your lapse of memory."

"Oh, no," I chided him. "That is impossible. I have all important dates and facts listed in my viewpad." I patted my hip, to which my pocket secretary had been returned by the warder on my departure from custody. "It's not her birthday, nor my father's, nor their anniversary, nor the natal days of myself, my brother or my sister. It is not Accession Day for my cousin the emperor, or any other day of importance. It was, in ancient times, the feast of the shoemakers Crispin and Crispian, but according to my star chart, that is a lucky day for me."

"That is not what you have forgotten, my lord."

"Then, what?"

"The dignity of the Fleet."

I sighed, a trifle derisively, if I am to be honest.

"Oh, *that*."

Parsons's tone did not change one iota.

"Yes, that."

"Why should that enter into the equation? Half my cousins were behind us on air scooters."

"Because none of them is the son of the First Space Lord. None of them is still a serving officer. And they are not escaping the exploit unscathed. I believe that Lord Xanvin's father retrieved him from the cells shortly before I arrived."

"Ugh," I emitted, with sympathy. "That probably means a few days on his hands and knees cleaning out whisky vats with a toothbrush in the family's fabled distilleries." It was his father's favorite punishment. That led me to realize my own fate had not been revealed. "Er, Parsons? My mother didn't hint at a penalty for me, did she?"

The hoped-for twinkle made a brief cameo appearance. "No, my lord."

I blew a gusting sigh of relief. "Well! The shoemaker patrons are looking out for me!"

"No, my lord," Parsons repeated. "There was no *hint*. She stated your punishment outright. You will start today on habiliment therapy for Uctu environmental hazards. You will be leading a small but important diplomatic mission to the Autocracy, to commence within two weeks."

"Really?" I asked. I beamed. That sounded like an honor, not a punishment. The shoemaker patrons had indeed come through. I leaned back in the skimmer seat, well pleased with life. "Lead on, Commander!"

It seemed only two hours later that I was walking through the streets of Taino at a sixth of my former size. There had, in fact, been an interval of four days—a discreet blackout, if you will. I had just emerged from a medically-induced coma to spare me some of the more heinous side effects of the inoculations, vaccinations and other treatments I required on my first visit to the Autocracy. Those which I retained upon waking were gruesome enough that I wondered how much worse were the ones that occurred while I slept. With every step, I experienced a wave of nausea and giddiness that swamped most other sensations. My head swam so that the landscape around me tended to wash up and back in my vision like ocean surf. It was difficult to tell if the buildings were actually rushing toward me or not.

It was fortunate that my crew—I liked to refer to them as my crew, though they were only assigned to me when a mission called for my specific involvement, as now—had decided to accompany me on my first outing from the travel medicine facility. Ensign Miles Nesbitt, a large and stocky fellow with beetle brows that I would have sworn were walking impatiently to and fro on his forehead, held onto the arm on the side of the wayward buildings. My other side was protected by my good friend, Ensign Kolchut Redius, an Uctu with coral-scaled skin whose parents had immigrated as youths to the Imperium.

The most curious of the side effects was the difference in size I had undergone. I kept glancing up at my compatriots. I hadn't realized from previous encounters how large the pores were in Ensign Miles Nesbitt's skin, nor the intricacy of each of Redius's scales, nor how gleamingly white were the teeth of First Lieutenant Carissa Plet or the fur of Indiri Oskelev, ensign, Wichu and demon pilot. The latter, in fact, steered us up the street, as Lieutenant Philomena Anstruther stayed behind us, possibly to catch me if I fell.

"Why, or perhaps I should ask, *how* did they manage to shrink me? And why are your arms so long?" I asked, in a querulous tone I would more usually associate with my elderly great-uncle, Perleas.

"No longer than before," Redius said, with the breathy squeaks his species used to indicate it was laughing. "Perception yours!"

"I suppose you don't have to go through the same treatment,"

Oskelev snorted. "We already have, Lieutenant."

"It's part of basic habitation," Anstruther said. "We have all undergone treatment to prevent ill effects from the biomes of major space-going races. You never know whose ship you might have to board without working hazard suits . . . sir."

This final sentence faded down to silence as I regarded the speaker with admiration. The final member of my coterie was a shy girl with thick, dark hair and startling dark blue eyes. Her skills in information technology probably rivaled my own, though her retiring personality undoubtedly would hold her back from otherwise well-deserved promotions. I had taken it on as one of my responsibilities to ensure that her efficiency and innovation would come to the attention of those of higher naval ranks. No sense in wasting extremely competent personnel when I so seldom made use of them myself.

"Thomas, please," I said. "As long as you are so much taller than I, it would be a friendly gesture if you would dispense with naval formality."

She reddened, a charming trait of hers. "Thomas."

"How long will this proportional dystopia last?"

"It took me three days," Nesbitt admitted. I let out a cry of protest. "The doctors said it was longer than usual. You shouldn't be more than a day. We'll look after you, my lord."

"Well, thank all powers for that," I said, with genuine relief. "In gratitude, allow me to take you all to lunch. I know a very smart new café with excellent food not far away. . . ." I glanced up the street, which seemed to be ridiculously longer than I remembered.

"Which one?" Oskelev asked, impatiently, holding out her viewpad, always the pilot.

"Social Butterfly," I said. Picking up on my voice, the graphic appeared on the enormous vid screen. Oskelev pointed ahead and to the right. Her arm stretched forward into infinity.

"Six hundred meters. You'll make it."

My team sounded as if it had faith in me. I wish I shared it. I hesitated as I reached an intersection. The signal changed so that the ground-level vehicles wafted to a halt, leaving the way clear. Yet, I did not dare to step off the curb. It seemed to be dozens of meters high. Intellectually I knew it was less than the depth of my boot. I hesitated, one foot hovering over the abyss.

"Come on, my lord," Nesbitt coaxed me. He held out an enormous hand that filled my vision. I reached for it. To my astonishment, my hand seemed almost as large as his. I could have covered my entire body with it. Together, we stepped into the depths. My boot sole hit the pavement long before I thought it would. The force of it landing sent juddering vibrations up my leg and into my hip. Somehow we managed to cross the street. Every bump in the terrain took on epic proportions. I stumbled as I attempted to dodge a huge pink monument obstructing my way. My friends righted me.

"When did they erect that?" I asked, appalled. "It's nearly as ugly as the sculpture they dedicated to my late great-somethings-aunt!"

"That's just a piece of gum, sir," Anstruther said.

I glanced back over a clifftop that was my own shoulder, and realized that the wad of pink had receded to a spot miles below me. When I swung my gaze back, I was daunted by the approaching wall over which a cascade of giant feet descended.

"May I, sir?" Plet asked, in a tone of understandable exasperation. She elbowed the giant Nesbitt out of the way, and placed a vast hand over my eyes. Kindly darkness descended. I felt myself relaxing for the first time since I had emerged from the medical facility. "All right, lift your left foot. There. You are up on the curb. Please walk forward. I will guide you."

Once I could not see, everything felt normal. I stepped forward with the utmost caution. Shortly, Oskelev took my shoulders and turned me sharply to the right. I heard the *swish!* of a door opening, and the temperature dropped precipitously as we passed inside and were enveloped by the atmospheric controls of the building. I was steered over a smooth floor, onto a deep-piled carpeted riser, and made to stand still while I heard the squeak of a chair being pulled out for me. Together, Oskelev and Nesbitt maneuvered me into it and pushed me down. I sat. Only then did Plet remove her shielding hand.

I gazed down a table as long as the carpet to my imperial cousin's throne. My friends, rendered giants, stared down at me. I was, indeed, inside the walls of Social Butterfly, though I viewed it as perhaps no one else ever had, except for the health inspectors. I could see every detail of every wall, chair, table and decoration.

"What a relief!" I exclaimed. "How did you all manage this perilous landscape following your own treatment?"

"Mostly confined to barracks," Oskelev said. "I had to be blindfolded until the effect wore off. Lucky that I could smell the head without having to see it. Everybody brought me food. I listened to music and dictated my Infogrid updates. I got along fine."

"Opposite reaction mine," Redius said. "All too small. Doorways size my snout."

I chuckled. "If you were a cat, you could pass anywhere your whiskers went."

The gigantic face of the Uctu wrinkled, his people's way of showing amusement.

"Not standard issue."

"Alas," I agreed.

"Uctu Syndrome passes swiftly. No worrying."

The surface of the table, which resembled cobalt blue glass, shimmered with light. Before each of us, the menu appeared. Holographic representations of each appetizer and entrée spun into being as one touched the name on the bill of fare. I cupped my hands around the display, causing it to render into a space that I could read without having to turn my head from side to side.

"Please, have anything you like," I said. "I won quite a bit from my cousins for coming in first in the skimmer race."

"And how much was your fine for damaging the sculpture?" Plet asked.

I waved a careless hand. "Probably twice that. It was worth it."

"Nice, that," Redius said. "Tridee most entertaining."

Though I possessed the highest noble rank of the group, I deferred to Lieutenant Plet, whose military rank surpassed even my recent promotion. She perused the menu with the same serious concentration that she devoted to every task. At last, she raised an unfeasibly long finger and touched the menu.

As host, each of my guests' selections was forwarded to my console for me to indicate whether I needed to veto any. In such manner could impecunious swains decrease the impact of a date upon their pocketbooks, and, much more importantly, parents had the ability to naysay ridiculous impulses by their offspring. My mother had used that tactic on me and my siblings many more times than I would readily admit aloud. But I clicked on "permit all" at once. In fact, noticing that Plet had chosen an open-faced sandwich that I had often ordered, I added two bottles of a white wine that I knew went well with it. That choice was reflected around the table for all to see.

That action freed the others to make their decisions. A roboserver arrived with the wine, uncorked it and presented it to me for my approval, then served it to everyone but Oskelev, who held up her hand.

"Got a nav test scheduled later," she said. "No caffeine, either."

"I respect your skills," I said. "I am certain you'll have no trouble with the test."

"I know!" the Wichu said. Her kind were notoriously impatient with elaborate manners or social niceties. I understood that, and took no offense.

"I have a gift for each of you," I said. I attempted to reach down into the pocket on the front of my right thigh, just above my knee, but it was simply too far away. With some embarrassment on my part, Plet retrieved the small parcel contained therein. I dispensed the contents, each of which had been labeled with their names. "One for each of you, specially designed by me from ancient drawings."

"But, what is it, sir?" Anstruther asked, turning hers from side to side.

"It's your lucky circuit," I said. "It gives off waves of light, sound and heat that are particularly fortunate for you."

"It does what?" Plet asked.

"It helps bring you good fortune," I explained, to the enormous face that turned to me wearing an expression that denoted disbelief.

"Is there any scientific basis to support that claim, sir?"

I smiled at her ignorance. "While it is impossible to influence random events in one's favor, lieutenant, the makers of these circuits employ quantum theory that certain elements, sounds and other input help crystallize unspoken wishes."

"It's very pretty," Anstruther said, examining hers. "It looks like a piece of jewelry."

"I am pleased to hear you say so," I said, most gratified. Of all the ones I had had made, hers was the smallest, only the length of the first joint of her forefinger—a most harmonious and fortunate dimension —but the most colorful. Nearly invisible wires had been bent into configurations that I had found in a divination booktape eight or nine thousand years old in my family's archives. At key points, miniature diode lights were affixed, as well as one speaker no larger than the lights. For her age, height and planet of birth, the book had demanded deep reds, one tiny white and three of deep ochre and one of teal blue. It emitted a low but soothing hum that would be perceptible only to the person wearing it.

I would have thought that Oskelev would be openminded about such a gift. I had been surprised at how much royal blue light was dictated by the time and date of her birth, along with a single green light, a scattering of white and a few light blue lights. The sound it emitted was a form of pink noise, conducive to deep thought or relaxation. She examined it carefully, held it to her ear to check the aural portion, then put it into a side pouch of her harness, all without changing expression. Most Wichus I knew were much more outspoken than she was.

Nesbitt's circuit was more visible and the lights less obtrusive. A peridot-green LED sat at the center, with radiating spokes reaching out to nine points of tiny white light, one blue and one orange. Rather than a sound, the speaker created a subsonic vibration that tickled my fingers when I activated it. Nesbitt had the same reaction. His hand jumped nervously away from the device at first, but shyly crept back to it, as it became evident that the sensation was enjoyable. He beamed at me, the smile almost bursting his large jaws.

"Handsome," Redius said, evidently pleased with his rust-orange, gold and deep purple lights. Since the crew was not in uniform, he hooked it into the breast of his tunic. "Pleasing in many dimensions."

"Keep them with you," I said. "They should always bring you good fortune."

"Thank you, my lord," Plet said, hastily putting hers away. I understood her reticence. The designs were rather personal. She might have felt I was exposing her psyche in ways that she felt were none of anyone else's concern.

Our meals arrived. I inhaled deeply to better appreciate the aroma, and my head spun around. I expected to catch sight of my spine during the rotations. I caught the edge of the table with my hands.

"Are you all right, my lord?" Nesbitt asked, concern writ overly large on his expanded face.

"I wish the medications that they used on me would settle into my system!" I said. "I have given them every opportunity, and the doctors set me loose upon the general public with the assurances that I was ready."

"Not drugs," Redius said. "Nanites chiefly."

"Really?" I asked, my eyebrows climbing my forehead. "How many of them are there? It sounds like an entire platoon of the little characters, and they are all playing different music."

"The feeling will pass, my lord," Anstruther said. "Really."

"Thomas, please!"

"Thomas." Her face reddened, and she dropped her eyes to her lucky circuit. "I . . . I can explain more if you would like."

"Yes, I would," I said eagerly. Anstruther's specialty was technology. "This is your wheelhouse, and I would be obliged if you would show me around."

I saw a peep of iris appear through her eyelashes.

"As you wish, my lord . . . Thomas."

I waved to the others.

"Please, don't let the food go cold, or the management will never allow me back in here," I said.

The hour being a bit late for lunch, my guests needed no encouragement. They tucked into the gigantic repasts before them. Anstruther took minute bites of her food, but unlimbered her viewpad and linked it with the circuits in the table so I could see the file she had opened.

"Well, sir," she began, "the Uctu settle on planets with a higher concentration of chlorine in the atmosphere than humans and Wichu are comfortable with. The process is necessary so it doesn't harm our tissues."

A professional-looking graphic appeared, showing an extreme

closeup of a tiny, round, smooth-bodied machine equipped with pairs of pointed mechanical feet. It toddled into the center of the screen. The rounded back opened up to reveal a nugget of red, then closed again. It was joined by a few more, which showed the payloads they bore: chemicals of several colors and textures, or complex machines still tinier than they were. Hundreds and thousands of objects just like them increased the ranks. The "camera" pulled away to display serried ranks of nanites, more and more until they were a seething mass of silver.

"Are these genetic changes?" I inquired, warily. I knew from previous private briefings I had undergone that it was imperative that my genes remained intact.

"No, sir. About sixty billion nanites have been introduced into your system to process the excess input. They occupy your kidneys and liver, as well as a few in your lungs and brain to prevent any contaminants from crossing the blood-brain barrier."

The animation displayed a thin gray wall against bright green waves that washed against it in vain.

"None shall pass," I said, in a jolly fashion. "So I become a cyborg?"

"Um, in a way."

"Is that what causes the magnified vision?"

"It is, sir. The nanites occupy a small portion of your retinas, to protect them against infrared glare. Uctus prefer suns that are slightly cooler than Humans do, so the solar profile is on the red side of the spectrum. Exposure can be dangerous. Some early visitors went blind later in life."

"I don't want that at all!" I said. "But if that's all, and I will feel larger in the next day or so, I will cease to be concerned."

I attempted to tackle my food, but even taking into account my knowledge that the magnification was artificial, I couldn't seem to fit a bite onto my fork or, once there, into my mouth. A discreet tap on the menu brought the serverbot to my side.

"It smells irresistible," I told it, "but it's all too large. I couldn't possibly finish what is here. It would be a shame to waste it."

"What would you like me to do, Lord Thomas?" it asked me.

I noticed Nesbitt's hopeful eyes above the receptor unit of the serverbot.

"I'll help you, my lord," he said.

"There, that's the answer," I said, relieved to have a good alternative. "Divide and conquer. Serve me half of this delightful treat, cut into bits small enough for me to eat. I would like to share the other half with my good friend."

The serverbot put my plate into its large, square hatch, big enough for a shuttle craft to land in, and assumed a huddled stance as though it was about to lay an egg. I heard low humming from within. In a moment, a tiny *ping!* sounded. The hatch opened to reveal two identical plates, in area one-half the size of the original dish. On one, huge hunks that would have served a Tyrannosaurus rex. On the other, bite-sized pieces I could actually picture eating.

The first bite was the worst. I had trouble maneuvering my hand toward my mouth, but once I accomplished the feat, I found the bite delicious, if much smaller in fact than in anticipation.

"You did it!" Anstruther cheered, as I chewed.

"I knew it was possible," I confided to her, once I had swallowed. "My daily stars told me that I was going to feel small and humble."

"Feeling not to last!" Redius chuckled.

I smiled at him. I took his teasing in good part, because it was good to feel humility once in a great while, so one knew what one was missing the rest of the time. But it was also good to feel humility among friends, who, while they would not allow one to rise too high, neither would they permit one to sink too low at the other extreme. I appreciated their company and their friendship. I applied myself to my lunch, feeling deeply contented with life.

CHAPTER 2

Lingering over beverages at the end, we chatted about this and that, always deferring to the austere Plet. It had been too long since I had seen them, and I realized how much I had missed the camaraderie. To be among my cousins was to feel at home, but to be with my friends was to open up a new and delightful galaxy the extent of which I had yet to fully explore.

"And where have you been since I last saw you?" I asked. "I keep up with your public Infogrid pages, but I am aware that such things can be fudged when Imperium security demands it."

"Nothing fancy, my lord," Nesbitt said, clenching his coffee cup with both hands.

"We are still serving aboard the *Shahmat* with Captain Calhoun," Plet said. "He sends his regards to you and your mother."

"Very good of the captain," I said, with a polite nod. "I will so inform the maternal unit. She'll be pleased. Anything to take her mind off my transgressions is a welcome distraction. Is the *Shahmat* in orbit?"

"No, sir. We were transferred here with some personnel who were going on leave."

"So you are enjoying a holiday?" I asked.

"Not a chance," Redius said. "On administrative attachment to the Admiralty until departure. Doing errands, running security shifts, debugging files, cross-referencing Infogrid files."

"Sounds tedious," I said.

"Not really," Oskelev said. "It's nice to be in the Core Worlds for a change."

". . . And what about you, my lord?" Nesbitt asked, after shamefacedly pushing away both plates, well scraped. "What have you been up to since we saw you?"

"Well," I said, pleased to have a chance to enlarge upon my latest enthusiasm. I leaned forward upon my elbows. "You might already have perceived that I have become interested in how random phenomena impact upon one's daily life. I am a student of the occult, that which remains hidden to the casual observer."

I received a fleering snort from Oskelev. "You know all that is a pack of hooey, Thomas?"

"Is it?" I countered, gazing at her enormous, white-furred face. "You have to admit there can be a case made for causality when two phenomena occur at the same time, or one immediately ensuing upon another."

"Could be. But there's no proof! *Scientific* proof."

"The possibility of proof under scientific rigor is not possible, because a person's fortune is as individual as one's genes," I argued. "What happens to one person, in one lifetime, will likely not correspond to another. Experience is personal and subjective."

"Then why are there only twelve zodiac signs?" Anstruther asked.

"Oh, that one actually makes a degree of sense," I said. "Factors that can be associated with the season are something that every baby born during that period have in common. Babies born in winter will perforce have less exposure to sunlight and therefore a lower concentration in their systems of vitamin D."

"Then why keep paying attention to horoscopes after infancy?" Plet asked, in spite of herself.

"For the fun of it!" I said. "And that sense of belonging which herd animals such as ourselves crave. You might feel a kinship to others born under the sign of the Space Traveler." As this was Plet, I added, "or perhaps not."

"Not," she confirmed.

"But consider this," I said. "Whether or not one believes the daily horoscope, why does it not add to one's luck to take its counsel into consideration when planning one's activities for the day? Suppose your fortune read 'be cautious with money dealings today.' Should you approach an unfamiliar situation in which money is involved, you will think back to it, and perhaps give yourself a chance to think more carefully about the details. Chances are, if a good thing happens, you'll simply disregard what you read, since it didn't apply. As random as life can be, any fortune you read is only a guidepost, not a command."

"Those fortunes are purposely vague," Plet said.

I nodded eagerly. "Of course they are! If you will allow me, I would be willing to tell your fortunes right here and now." I reached into a concealed breast-pocket pouch for the ancient cards I had brought with me. They felt unusually heavy. I feared I might not be able to lift them or my friends' hands to read their palms.

"Most fortune tellers are charlatans," Plet said, dryly.

"And I am the most sincere charlatan of them all," I said. "I offer my findings for entertainment purposes only. I promise to tell you one thing that makes you feel good about yourself, and two dire warnings that will not come to mind until they are needed."

"Maybe later," Nesbitt said, his cheeks turning red, although I could tell he was interested. Other diners peered around to look at us. The others looked a bit embarrassed, as if I might find out secrets about them they would prefer not to have revealed.

"Fear not," I said, fanning the cards between my hands. They flew in a twinkling, colorful arc. I had practiced for a month to create that effect. "If I learn anything, it will be as though I was your doctor. All matters remain confidential between us."

"*Not here*, my lord," Plet said. I read urgency in her voice.

I scanned my crew's faces, and recorded the apprehensive expressions thereon. In my eagerness I was being insensitive. I put the cards back in their silk-lined repository.

"My apologies," I said, truly chastened. "You're right. It's best done in private. When we have the chance, you shall sit in the marvelous silk tent that I have had made, and wait until you see my robes! They were made for me by the imperial tailor. He told me he had not had so much fun in years! I have also considered robes for seekers, those who come to me to have their future foretold. Not much historical documentation is available as to appropriate wear for querents, but there's little as satisfying as starting a new tradition."

"Have you read your briefing about the mission to the Autocracy?" Plet said, interrupting me in full spate.

I was not troubled by her abrupt change in subject. Humans born under the sign of the Space Traveler were apt to multitask.

"I fear not," I said. "At the moment every word seems to spread across my entire field of vision. There wasn't time to listen to audio transcription before all of you rescued me from my medical cocoon. What does it entail?"

Plet frowned.

"Perhaps you should review it when you can focus."

"Give me the overview," I pleaded. "I hate waiting."

"Reports from the frontier between the Imperium and the Autocracy indicate that the Autocracy is blocking groups of ships from entering the jump points, often for weeks or months, then suddenly granting permission. There is no reason given for the sudden change in policy, though it came only a matter of months after the installation of the new Autocrat, Visoltia, two years ago. Our ambassador consults frequently with the Autocrat, but the impasse remains in place. But there is a more troubling matter. At Way Station 46, the most direct frontier crossing from the Core Worlds, a spate of smuggling was reported. Nine ships that were granted leave to enter were all found to be carrying contraband. Ordnance and ships."

"Really?" I asked, astonished. "All of them?"

"So it would seem."

"How very odd that they would not think they would be suspected. They are all incarcerated?"

"Awaiting trial," Plet said, then hesitated. I picked up on her natural distaste for mentioning the consequences.

"I am aware of the penalties for smuggling weapons of war," I said. "It is a terrible shame."

"The traders plead that they are innocent," Plet said, "although the evidence is overwhelming that they did commit the crime."

"But how was it that their smuggling was not detected, in spite of their spending months on the customs space station?" I asked.

"If we knew that, there would be no need to investigate," Plet said.

"How right you are," I said.

"Speaking of investigations," Anstruther began, then blushed crimson as we all turned to her.

"Do go on," I said, gently. "I have been out of touch long enough in my medical confinement!"

She glanced from me to Plet, as if asking permission to continue.

"Well, from the news reports, two crime syndicates that are known to be operating in the outer systems had a gang war right there on Keinolt!"

"Very troubling," I said, although I fancy my avid expression gave the lie to the austere statement. "What was the outcome?"

"Broken up by law enforcement," Redius said. "Nothing."

"But that isn't terribly interesting," I said.

"One gang had a run-in with a number of civilians in Taino," Nesbitt added.

"Tell me everything!" I commanded them.

"Well, it happened on Sparrow Island," Anstruther said, with the awed expression of someone who had never been there. "Some aristocrats were threatened by the criminals. Alleged criminals," she corrected herself.

Sparrow Island was a favorite haunt of my relatives. This sprawling resort was constructed as a playground for the moneyed and highborn. The management catered in particular to the nobility. Some of the restaurants, bistros, pools and suites were reserved for our especial use. I had most recently secured a season's pass for a four-room cabana on a rocky promontory overlooking a booming wave pool. Woe betide the interloper who tried to make use of it in my absence, something of which the management was well aware. It occurred to me, though, that it might be fun to bring my crew there—on an evening when none of my cousins were around, of course.

"What exactly happened?" I asked, torn between alarm and delight. "If anything serious had happened, you wouldn't be so keen to discuss it, would you?"

"Well," Nesbitt said slowly, but, I believe, honestly, "we might."

"It wasn't too serious," Anstruther said. "There wasn't a fight."

"Pish tosh," I declared, priding myself on an archaicism that I doubted few of them had heard. "Then what? An exchange of fleering glances? A fight over an attractive mate? Some primeval chest-beating? An indecent proposition?"

They looked at one another. At last it was Plet who retrieved the most detailed news item to be had, and forwarded it to my viewpad.

"A Very Refined Brawl," said the headline.

I read through the brief notice. Some newcomers to the city had reserved a few of the exclusive venues on Sparrow Island, but upon arrival yesterday had found them not as they had hoped. As the management was, as I knew, eager to please its clientele, it attempted to find them something suitable that was unoccupied at the moment. But it seemed words were exchanged among other important guests who shortly thereafter arrived on site, and some maneuvering had to be accomplished to accommodate all of those who arrived. Mr. Sted Banion, the manager of Sparrow Island, was quoted by at least one member of the press.

"We always strive to give our guests the very best experience possible. We did not stop until all parties were satisfied with their visit."

I rather doubted that all parties were satisfied. The bandied adjective "important" meant relations of the Emperor. It might not be so stated, but was understood by society reporters and those who loved to read them.

I also checked the links to the numerous cross-postings on my cousins' Infogrid files. It appeared that five of them were among the civilians who were threatened. The intruders in question withdrew immediately, though not without harsh words for the management and the nobility who had confronted them. The nobility, in their turn, harangued the management for ignoring some of their own reservations in favor of the newcomers, thereby putting them into harm's way. The management apologized in seventeen different positions of increasing humility. I fancy that a good deal of choice food and drink was offered to assuage the injured feelings and twisted limbs of my cousins. I would have expected no less of a venue that wished to remain on our list of favorite haunts.

Those of the ruffians who could be captured were followed to their lairs and taken into custody, pending trial and, I hoped, deportation, though as citizens they were permitted to visit, even live on Keinolt, even if I wished they wouldn't. The ringleaders had slunk away, not to be seen again. They had not left the planet, as far as law enforcement could detect. I spun a coin on my viewpad screen. No, they were still on-world. Of that I was certain.

I posted my divinitive finding, suggesting that the search continue, and got a derisive message back from my cousin Xanson, who was skeptical about my newfound enthusiasm for superstitions. I sent a suitable pithy retort, which immediately garnered many thumbs up signs and smiles from our various friends and readers, and another sour reply from Xan. I riposted with what I felt was a palpable hit.

"What a pity I was not there," I said, swiping a hand to silence my viewpad as it tried to display for me all the posts that poured in following my latest entry.

"Just as well you weren't, sir," Nesbitt said. "Honor of the force, and all."

I winced.

"You have hit upon a spot that is still tender, my friend," I said. "Honor of the force is and heretofore shall be my priority. Now, if anyone will help me to return to the Imperium compound, I shall meditate toward my recovery and prepare for our departure."

Oskelev rose first.

"I better go, Thomas. No way I'm going to be late for my exam."

I raised both hands to her in benediction. They seemed slightly smaller already, though as large as leaf rakes compared to their normal size.

"Good fortune follow you."

The Wichu snorted, the nostrils of her pink nose curled. "The harder I work, the luckier I am. See you later."

But I noticed that she tucked her lucky circuit carefully away in a chest pouch.

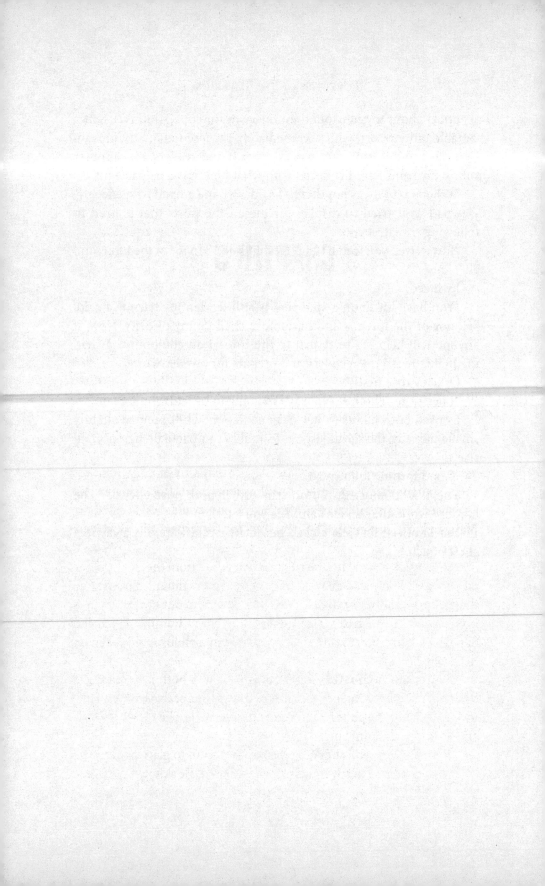

CHAPTER 3

Nile Bertu leaped out of the covered flitter as soon as it landed, bursting out of the hatch as if he was escaping from prison. His expensive suit, a shimmering example of the latest fashions anywhere in the Core Worlds, was creased and stained. He ripped the jacket off his broad chest and threw it to the side of the landing strip.

"Better to go naked than to wear it now!" he snarled.

His sister, Skana, emerged calmly in his wake. A more slender version of her brother, she had the same rusty-brown curly hair, the same short-lashed hazel eyes, and the same short, thick fingers. No one would ever call them beautiful, but no one would dare to call them plain in their presence. The penalties for disrespect like that were severe.

It had taken several hours to fly to their estate from the center of the city. Nile had bounced all over the interior of the flitter, until she had dialed up a sedative for his next drink. It kept him out until just a half hour ago. Then he had started screeching about humiliation again. Skana had had hours to think about it, and put a philosophical spin on her feelings.

Their majordomo Tuk, a Croctoid who was both secretary and head of security for their organization, extended a scaly paw for Skana to hang onto as she pulled herself out of the vehicle. She rolled her eyes and picked Nile's tunic up from the floor.

"It can be cleaned," she said. Her brother spun to glare at her.

"I never want to touch it again!" Nile shouted. He skinned out of the matching trousers and tossed them in the direction of the cool, shadowy grotto that housed their elegant in-ground pool. Skana started toward the pants, but a small cleanerbot shot out of a niche in the wall and gathered them up. It rolled over to her. She dropped the tunic on top of it, and watched as it fled into the warren of service tunnels that lay within the walls of their compound to be laundered.

"So it didn't go well," Skana said. "We'll do it again another time. But after I talk with that manager."

"He won't *be* there next time," Nile said, his brows drawn down. "I'm sending a team after him right now. They won't even find the pieces."

"No, you don't," Skana said. "Your temper tantrum is what got us thrown out of there in the first place. I'll override anything you order. So it wasn't what we expected. We got a full refund."

"Half our guests were arrested!"

Skana raised an eyebrow. "They should have known better! All of them have outstanding warrants. They didn't have to get involved. All they had to do was to stay in their places and let me handle the situation. No one was going to ask any questions. The staff was coping."

"Up until *she* got involved!"

"Well, what did you expect from a noble?" Skana said, flipping her hands over. "They're overprivileged pains in the ass who go wherever they want and do whatever they want."

Nile stopped punching the air and stared off into space.

"She was so beautiful," he said, forlornly. Then he stormed into the house.

Skana sat down at her little table beside the pool. Another 'bot brought her her afternoon cocktail. She arranged the skirt of her ridiculously expensive dark orange dress around her knees, and felt terrible that there was no one around to see it except their employees. She had wanted to show it off on Sparrow Island. Skana longed for people to admire their style and have them guess how much money they had. She wanted them to look at her and think she was somebody important. She knew it. Nile knew it. The hundreds of employees they had in teams spread out across fifty planets knew it, but society had no idea.

She did feel resentment for their treatment, but not for the lords and ladies. She couldn't blame them. They acted like they owned the planet because they *did* own the planet. Everyone else had to take second best in social situations. That was just the way things were, and had always been. People on Keinolt understood that.

What shouldn't have happened was for the stupid *resort* to double-book their reception rooms and the private bar that Skana had gone to so much trouble to choose. She had heard that the Double Rainbow gazing salon was a favorite of the aristocracy. That was why she shelled out absurdly large amounts of money on a deposit. It was up to the management to make their experience as wonderful as they expected. As they had paid for.

She and Nile hobnobbed with the aristocracy at numerous events, such as fundraisers and charity showcases. They were part of the uppermost edge of society that stood just below the tier occupied solely by the Imperial family. The lords and ladies always treated her well, even recognizing her when they met again, but she knew it wasn't as if they accepted her as one of their number. She was among them but not of them. That exclusion really bothered her more than it bothered Nile.

He saw his ego being bruised in more ways than she could count, but each wound was shallow. For her, it cut deep. She could never be one of the real aristocracy, and *they* weren't going to pretend otherwise. She and Nile, like others, had to make their empires where and as they could. As she and Nile had. As their grandparents and more distant ancestors had. They might not be as well born, but she would have bet they were richer than most of the lords and ladies. Far richer.

The Bertus had a heritage of their own in which they took pride. The Bertu Corporation had been formed by their own great-grandfathers and great-grandmothers. Their primacy simply wasn't based on, well, being the face of government, the uniting principle of the Imperium. It had fulfilled needs as and when they arose. Skana knew their income was illegal—most of it; they were branching out into legitimate enterprises—but the stuff that paid the bills and got them the best cars, the fastest ships, the fanciest jewelry, hangers-on, power and land, lots of land, was outside the law. It still had to be treated like a business and run like a business, or they were just as pathetic and small a concern as the aristocracy treated them. Since the death of their mother, they had taken over the empire left to them, and made it prosper. Both she and Nile had good sense and the tenacity to find opportunities and exploit them. Neither of them gave ground out of pity. They were rich and feared, but respected . . . ish. Occasionally they needed to issue a reminder to those who defied them. Skana never attacked without provocation. Nile was another story. He was hot-headed and occasionally impulsive. He had been known to take personal vengeance on rivals. It put him into danger of exposure. Being publicly humiliated in the courts would weaken their hold on those who were in thrall to the corporation. They could not afford that.

She was worried, and with good reason, what Nile would do next. He had fallen in love at first sight with a *noble*. That was understandable, but stupid. He had tried to kiss the lady. That was absurd, but forgettable. He had threatened her, which was criminal. The impulse could be put off as being said in the heat of the moment, but so many witnesses couldn't be silenced. If the matter went to court as an assault, too much would come out in discovery regarding their business.

When the authorities were called, Skana had bundled a protesting Nile into their limousine and ordered the driver to take off. Nile had raved, wanting to go back and reason with the lady, beg her to forgive him and accept him as her true love. Skana wanted to put poison in her wine. Something that took a long time to take effect, so no connection could be made between a very unfortunate incident and . . . a very unfortunate incident. It wouldn't be much trouble. She had had to dispose of one or more of his girlfriends in the past. Nile usually had rotten taste in women. This time, he had chosen a winner, but one he had no hope of wooing, let alone bedding. Better if there was no chance of a second meeting.

Never mind; she had other responsibilities to take care of.

"Have we received the deposit from Otimbo yet?" she asked Tuk.

The Croctoid extended his oversized viewpad for her inspection. Hundreds of items awaited her attention, but she was interested only in that one. She found it at the top of the list. Tuk was the best administrator they had ever had.

"The deposit came while you were in transit. I sent a message with the details."

"I was taking a nap," she said. "Nile wore me out with his nonsense."

Tuk curled his scaly lip. He understood.

"The money has been allocated. Party drug Blute ready for shipment to the Leonines on your word."

"Give it," Skana said.

Tuk made a note and touched an icon. The word had been given.

Fortified by another drink, Skana went through entry after entry on Tuk's viewpad.

"I didn't know we were doing so well with the low-income housing on Paradil," she said, approving of the bottom line.

"It works that way when you use other companies' materiel to build your stock," Tuk observed dryly.

"It was a steal," Skana said, with a bark of laughter.

It wasn't her business to inform another concern that *their* employees were ripping them off. That was the problem with operations that had centralized offices too far away from the action. If a company had no one on the ground to make sure that shipments were going where they were intended to go they tended to stray, often one piece at a time. Nile would never make a mistake like that. He kept an office with a team of enforcers on every world that contained a Bertu Corporation project. Sometimes he liked to go and oversee a punishment himself, but word spread quietly. He rarely had to.

"The rents are scheduled to go up in two years unless the cost of living index on Paradil drops," Tuk said.

"Put in a reminder for me for twenty months from now," Skana said. "I want to review it at the same time I look over the factory receipts. No sense in letting too much of that profit go offworld. I have a lot of other projects there the rent money is intended to fund."

"Yes, ma'am." Tuk entered a few gestures on the screen. It filled with graphs. The tips of Tuk's sharp, curved claws tapped in squares too small for Skana's fingertips.

The next item made Skana frown. It was surrounded by a red frame, an indicator of extreme urgency.

"What's the problem with the goods Enstidius ordered?" she asked. "Didn't they get there safely?"

"Yes, ma'am," Tuk said. "One of the main pieces was intercepted. It was confiscated by Customs." The viewpad displayed a rotating image. "So were some of the small pieces. Eight ships were compromised."

"So what?" Skana asked, impatiently, dismissing it. "We have people in place to take care of that. Didn't you notify them?"

"Enstidius did at the time it happened," Tuk said, showing her the decoded copy of a sent message. "They are doing what they can to make the merchandise disappear from the Banned Goods warehouse."

"It'll be fine. So why the red frame?"

"He is afraid he will not get the value of the goods. He's afraid the planned obsolescence will kick in before they make their attack."

Skana snorted. "Enstidius has nothing to worry about. I promised him the program won't fail. I guaranteed it with my life. I promised that the goods will remain intact as long as they're needed, and I mean it. I have that much faith in them. Has he put the deposit in our account to download the destruction codes when he wants them?"

Tuk checked the records, and scrolled down the list of receipts. "No."

Skana shook her head. "His problem, then. When he starts a coup, how he gets rid of the evidence is his smallest problem. His last shipment's going to be the big one, though. He'd better be ready to act when it arrives. Craters! It'll be big news all over the *galaxy* when it happens!"

"He is looking forward to having you witness his triumph, ma'am," Tuk said. "If your plans to accompany the shipment have not changed."

"I wouldn't miss it for the world," she said. Tuk's expression changed to one of concern. Skana peered at him, trying to guess what he was thinking. "What am I missing?"

"There is one more matter. All the traders who carried in your merchandise will be tried under the laws to prevent smuggling. If they're found guilty, they'll be executed."

"Isn't there a way to speed that up?" Skana asked, impatiently. "The longer they're around, the more likely it is they'll talk to someone. We definitely don't want an investigation, not when we'll be right there."

"Sorry, ma'am. There are protocols that must be followed. The merchants are permitted a fair trial and the right to appeal. It could take months."

Skana moaned.

"Months! That's too long. How about a bunch of 'unfortunate accidents'?"

"Ma'am!" Tuk sounded shocked. She frowned. It wasn't often that Tuk questioned one of her decisions.

"What's the problem? Everyone knew there could be collateral damage."

"There are several children involved, ma'am."

"So?" Tuk was silent. Skana clicked her tongue. "What am I paying you for?"

"I will see what I can set in motion."

"Take care of it before we get there. You know I hate loose ends."

"Yes, ma'am." He tapped away at his screen with his claws.

Skana stretched her arms, trying to ease the tightness in her shoulders. The orange silk rasped against her skin. Enough business. She needed some light entertainment. She turned back to Tuk.

"How many jesters are there in the house at the moment?"

"Just the one, ma'am. Murrye from Tomlin Pharmaceuticals. He has failed to make this quarter's projections."

Skana peered at him. "By more than twenty-five percent?"

"Twenty-seven. An abject failure."

"Then why are we keeping him?"

"He has been a good CEO. He swears it was just market pressures and it won't happen again."

Skana beckoned. "Bring him on. Can he juggle fire?"

"Not yet, but he's learning."

CHAPTER 4

I opened my flattened hands across the lofty fibersilk-filled pad that supported me, trying to rid my body of weight and substance. My eyes were softly shut, my jaw just slightly ajar with my lips barely touching. Every joint, tendon and organ I possessed lay slack. I even urged my nose to relax. My meditation chamber was redolent with an earthy essential oil mix that contained vetiver, white truffle, oak gall and musk ox hair. All lights were extinguished, the doors locked and the curtains closed.

I had attempted to recede from the earthly form that had gone through such contortions and changes in size in an effort to bring it under control. As my crewmates suggested, the distortion was fleeting, but it was an uncompromising nuisance not to know what dimensions everything had from moment to moment. My studies repeatedly informed me that size, as well as time, space, other beings, every object and what I thought I could see from my own eyes were all illusion, a whim of creation that we sparks of energy all shared. If that were indeed the case, I mused, it was a pervasive and complex illusion, one that I could not dispel without a great deal more practice at mind control than I had yet accomplished. I just wanted my body to go back to the size and shape it had been before the treatment, so I could go on attempting to escape from it.

I had hoped that I might be able to achieve astral projection, but had not yet managed it. Day after day, at the hour appointed by my quotidian stars, I had put myself into a comfortable position from which I could lift my astral body and tour the stars. I must confess that the only part of me that went wandering was my mind. Every time I began to feel truly relaxed, I thought of other things I could be doing. I suppose my astral self was quite busy during those times. I discovered it was best attempted when planetside, particularly in a non-technically-furnished domicile. Even the slightest little buzz seemed to distract me, let alone the ambient noises of a working warship. But if one has already found peace in a very quiet place, why would one have to seek further peace? It was already there around one. I realized that I might be missing the point. To be able to achieve a meditative state when all around me was chaos was the intended goal. I took on an instructor for meditation, but as I kept checking to see if he was meditating, and how it looked different than my meditation, I realized he was more distraction than help. I offered my thanks but did not renew his contract. I think he, too, was relieved.

Instead, I began personal studies into the various methods of achieving higher consciousness. For the first week or so, I had fallen asleep each session, only waking when the temple bell was sounded by one of the house valetbots, which had approached my couch as if on little cat feet and retreated afterward. By this time, several weeks into my studies, I was much more proficient. Wakeful mindfulness was my watchword. I still had difficulty removing my mind from my surroundings, but I was getting better. Meditation was, as the experts decreed, most restful without having to resort to sleep.

My difficulty was in preventing my thoughts from becoming occupied by plans. I was fascinated by the thought of exploring Uctu space. My mother had been there several times, first as a young officer, later as a captain, then as First Space Lord. She had not gone since before my elder brother did his two years' obligatory military service. I found my mind casting after her into the unknown—a far more intriguing journey than any the astral plane seemed to offer. I imagined that I could see her on the bridge of her flagship, though she looked rather younger than she did now. Not that time had been unkind to her. She was often mistaken for a decade, sometimes two, younger than she was.

"My lord," came the softest of inquiries from just inside my sitting room door. Parsons had entered, ignoring the DO NOT ENTER sign on my suite's outer door, not to mention the five locks and intruder-apprehension system active within the anteroom. I didn't bother to guess how he had done it; most likely even my wildest imaginings were too tame to account for his proficiency. I peeled open one eye to behold him, as serene a presence as any lama. In truth, I was furious.

"Have I forgotten an appointment?" I asked, with a hint of asperity. "For no other reason, Parsons, could I imagine that you would interrupt my hour of serenity."

He was unmoved by my ire. He did not even trouble to lift an eyebrow.

"I regret to discommode you, my lord, but a matter has arisen. I thought it best that you hear it accompanied by the background information that you will not obtain along with the request you will shortly receive."

No meditation was possible following such an exciting prologue. I unwound myself from the double-lotus position and rose eagerly to my bare feet.

"You have engaged my curiosity, Parsons," I said, slipping on a pair of silk-lined sandals. "Please, join me. I enjoy a cup of gen mai cha after my attempts at meditation." I gestured to the low table at the end of the room. It had been placed there once I had become interested in the contemplative cultures. On it was a line of three small cups, an earthenware pot painted with a frieze of bamboo leaves, a jar with matching bowl, a scoop, and a straw whisk.

I waited until Parsons had seated himself in the guest position at the head of the table. I sat at the foot. My chief valetbot, an LAI designated as OP45-AE7, rolled forth and extracted from his central cabinet a steaming cast iron kettle of hot water and three more small cups.

I made the tea, and poured the first of three small cups for each of us. To my chagrin, Parsons already knew about the number and method of drinking each one. I could never surprise him. The brain that pulsed against the expressionless forehead contained more knowledge than the entire Infogrid, plus all the lost libraries of humanity. Still, I enjoyed the ceremony greatly. In no other circumstance could I picture Parsons slurping anything, but it was the custom with this tea. I made a private recording of the moment, which I assumed he would cause to be erased the moment I turned my back on him.

"Good fortune favor us," I said, lifting my own cups in turn. When the third ceremonial cup was drained, I produced two larger cups of handsome dark blue ceramic that could be filled as often as one pleased. I pushed one toward him. "Go on, then. Tell me about the request! Am I at last to have a meeting with the mysterious Mr. Frank?"

Parsons regarded me with a glance that I would have called pitying. I was surprised, because I assumed he would admire my perspicacity. After all, we were fewer than ten days away from our mission. He decanted a sufficiency of tea and pushed the pot toward me.

"No meeting with Mr. Frank is scheduled at this time, my lord. It is unnecessary."

I allowed my eyebrows to climb my forehead.

"Then what is the request?" I asked. "Or should I inquire as to from whom it will come?"

"I predict that you will hear from Lady Jil Loche Nikhorunkorn very soon."

I lowered the brows.

"Jil? What does she want? How may I help?"

Parsons took a moment to sip tea thoughtfully.

"Perhaps you have seen on the local news a negative interaction between locals and visitors of importance?"

I recalled the conversation I had had with my crew. "If you mean the brawl that ensued on Sparrow Island, I did hear something at lunch. When I looked it up, I found numerous links to postings by my cousins in their Infogrid files. Organized criminals, or some such thing?"

"Some persons of less-than-savory character, sir. The press does not wish to state the condition outright without a court conviction to fall back upon to prove that the persons in question are criminals."

I waved my hand to dismiss journalistic delicacy, which never seemed to be employed when it came to my personal hijinks being publicized.

"But what has this to do with Jil? How is she involved? It would never occur to anyone of our class even to associate with such pond scrapings."

"She insulted them, my lord. They were occupying a favorite table of hers, and she told them what was in her mind upon beholding them there."

"Well, of course! Any of us would have. We are the best customers Sparrow Island has."

"But perhaps it was not the most tactful course to take. She could have enlisted the assistance of the management."

"Didn't, eh? How like Jil."

"She embarrassed the visitors," Parsons continued.

"Oh, dear," I said, and I meant every syllable. "Never embarrass little people. They will kill you."

"Precisely."

I rose to my feet more gracefully than I had in years. Tai chi and yoga had done wonders for my muscular control. I began to pace.

"She'll have to lay low for a while. She won't like that."

"No, sir," Parsons agreed.

"Well, what has it got to do with us?" I asked.

"She is accompanying us to the Autocracy."

I halted and permitted myself to goggle. I had improved greatly on the expression since I had taken up meditation, allowing the joints to relax, and so on. A half-raised eyebrow from Parsons indicated to me that the expression was effective.

"What?" I demanded, throwing myself down beside the table. This concept called for more tea. "What about our mission? She'll get in the way!"

"Of suspicion, perhaps," Parsons said, verbally laying a finger alongside his nose. I nodded several times as the notion soaked into my brain.

"Ah! She will provide cover for us."

"In a manner of speaking, my lord."

"But the mission!" I pressed him. "What of our mission?"

"I am not at liberty to disclose the confidential details at this point," Parsons said. "Your assignment is similar to ones that you have undertaken in the past. You are an envoy of his Imperial Majesty, Shojan XII. As such, you are to visit his most august sister, the Autocrat, in her residence on Nacer, the capital world of the Autocracy, and present his compliments."

"As well as several gifts, I fancy. I shall have to check with the Chancellor and see what cargo we are taking on board."

"Indeed, sir. Along our way, we have a few matters to investigate more closely, also on behalf of the throne."

I nodded. "I had heard that some of our ships have been caught with contraband. Bad practice, I say."

"At the very least, my lord. But both our nations believe firmly in the presumption of innocence until guilt is proven. There does seem to be a case for believing the protests in that direction from some, if not all, of the affected ship owners."

"I look forward to finding that out," I said. "I have been intrigued by the case. Why did those pilots believe they could slip goods past the scrutiny of the Uctu customs officials? I can scarcely sneak an extra bottle of wine by ours."

"It is one of the matters on which we will make enquiries, sir."

"And the others?"

"My lord?" Parsons inquired, rising to his feet in one smooth motion. I stood up as well. I was not going to allow him to escape that easily.

"You have still given me no information regarding the rest of my responsibilities! I suppose nothing I can say can shake you on this point?"

"Nothing at all."

"Then how am I to prepare?"

Parsons allowed a small smile to play about his lips, no doubt under strict adult supervision.

"If I may suggest, my lord, prepare in your inimitable fashion. You will need to be in excellent physical condition to withstand the rigors of the change in gravity. Your system already has been equipped with modifiers to prevent damage to you from the atmosphere, water and food. Continue to fortify yourself with information on the culture and the people you are shortly to meet. I have forwarded to you a detailed biography of the Autocrat. If you study it closely, I believe you will find insights that will give you an advantage in strengthening the friendship between two great houses."

I was delighted by his confidence in me.

"I could ask nothing better, Parsons. Then I will cast the bones to see what portends for us. I'll let you know what precautions we need to take."

Parsons nodded. I escorted him to the door.

My mind was of such clarity following my meditation that I felt it was the perfect time to look into the future. I had various devices that

I had purchased or had made to use with the assorted methods of divination that I was studying.

My favorite device was the crystal ball that I had had shipped in from one of the outer worlds of the Imperium. The perfect sphere was carved from eye-clear rock crystal, colorless, cool and surprisingly heavy. Though I saw little more than my own hands on the underside through its depths, it was a marvelous item with which to play.

It occupied a table near the bow window that looked out upon my mother's garden. I had of late taken to erecting my soothsayer's tent beside the iris bed, to allow the reflection of the handsome purple flowers to reflect in the clear depths of the sphere until such time as my mind filled it with other visions. From a distance it looked as if I kept a severed head underneath a cloth. More than one visitor had jumped in startled surprise. Once in a while, it caught me unawares as well.

Not troubling to put on my fortune-teller's robes or bring out the tent, I sat at the small table near the window and whisked the covering away. The globe looked back at me like a colorless eyeball on a socket made of ebony wood.

I set my hands underneath it and looked into its heart.

I stared for what seemed like hours. Condensation formed between the pads of my fingers and palm. I implored the universe to favor me with an insight regarding our enterprise. How would I know the truth when I saw it?

My eyes ached with the strain of gazing. Then, to my surprise and delight, a tiny thread of cobalt-blue light arched from the mound of one thumb, crossed the arc of the globe to the tip of my left forefinger, where it exploded into minute sparks. Fireworks!

It must be a reflection. I was not so deluded as to believe I had suddenly acquired the ability to see complex illusions like skyrockets exploding. I looked up. The blue sky was clear but for a few whipped-cream clouds and the tapering contrail of a departing spacecraft. But where had the vision come from?

I was not going to get answers from cudgeling my own brain. It had only seen what my eyes had. But I took the image for inspiration for the near future. I was going on an adventure. The next step, naturally, was a going-away party!

I spread the silken cover over my crystal ball and retrieved my viewpad from its charging cradle on my desk. I fell back into my favorite armchair to gather inspiration. Fireworks, first and foremost. Then, food and drink. Next, other entertainment, including musicians, magicians, and a palmist I knew to be reliable and discreet. Decorations! Prizes, to be randomly distributed, according to rules that I would make up on the spot. Then, the guest list, the people I wished to come and enjoy it all.

Pro forma, my cousin the emperor was first on the top of the page, though he never attended any of our parties. Shojan had far too many official events and functions to attend. I didn't expect him, but all due homage would be paid if he did show up. I made arrangements for the portable Chair of State to be present, under its own marquee in the colors of his coat of arms, with a royal blue ribbon stretched across the arm rests to prevent anyone else sitting in it and taking mocking pictures for their Infogrid files (it had happened; I possessed images taken of many violators. Though it might not be creditable, I was never one of them.). The rest of the guests would be those with whom I most enjoyed being. Ah, the fun of it!

When I finished constructing the theme of the party and assembling the vendors, stationers, and entertainers, I felt rejuvenated. My soul soared. My body was full of energy. My mind kept racing ahead, anticipating the delight on my guests' faces and the joy in my own heart. I tapped away on the viewpad, enjoying myself more and more as I went along.

Meditation truly was good for one's morale.

CHAPTER 5

When I was finished making the list of those I wished to attend the party, I ran up and down the small screen. To my chagrin, I realized that there was a gaping hole in the number of invitees. How could I have failed to include my crew? Hastily, I keyed in all of their names. Parsons, first and foremost, must be asked, though he might show up anyhow, to ensure that I did not drink myself paralytic and end up on the launch pad in an unfit state. But I thought with deep pleasure how my crew would respond to the kind of entertainment that my family was accustomed to enjoying.

The cards arrived within an hour from the imperial stationer, who was used to spur-of-the-moment parties within the compound. Each of the thick, cream-colored envelopes was embossed with the name of the invitee. With the mailbot waiting, I sorted out those meant for my crew and kept them. I decided that I must deliver those invitations in person. I wanted to see the happiness on all of their faces.

The reality, though, was a trifle different than I anticipated. My crew, gathered together in the common room on base, received their invitations with some bafflement and disbelief.

"You're inviting us?" Nesbitt said, his ruddy skin flushed to brick redness. "You want us to serve drinks or something?"

"Only to yourselves," I assured them. "I want you to be my guests. We are setting out as a company for parts unknown. Therefore you must attend my gala."

"It's the night before we launch," Anstruther said, reading the date.

"Can you think of a better time to schedule a going-away party?" I asked.

"Well, we have to be up pretty early the next morning, sir," she said.

"Then depart from the festivities when it seems appropriate for you," I said. "But if you don't come, I will feel as though I have cheated you out of an experience that you deserve."

"That's really nice of you, my lord," Nesbitt said, his ebullient voice hoarse with emotion. "I dunno . . ."

"I think it'll be a blast," Oskelev said, flipping the card up so it cartwheeled in the air. She caught it. "It's a yes from me."

"Me also. What garment style?" Redius asked, the coral-red scales on his forehead glowing with interest. Like me, he was a bit of a dandy. I admired the clothes he wore while on leave. "New tunic favored with decorative tail accessory bought."

"Dress uniform, of course," Plet said, severely. The others looked deflated.

As one, they turned to look to me for guidance.

"Alas," I said. "She is right. You are on active duty."

"I don't mind," Anstruther said, pulling her suddenly drooping shoulders erect. "We couldn't compete with your relatives anyhow."

"No, indeed, you can't," I said, with an expansive gesture. "You are useful members of society, and they are not."

Leaving the others to buzz over the antique style of printing and the quality of the cardstock, I pulled Plet aside. Though my crew members were immune to the charms of me and my family, I still needed to protect them from my cousins' sometimes harsh sense of humor.

"I have prepared a dossier on my cousins, with a list of their most frequent hijinks that they pull in the presence of those who do not belong to our genetic blueprint," I said. We touched viewpads, and the file on mine transferred to hers. "This will help you counter their inevitable jokes on newcomers. For the more egregious attempts, find me or Parsons. We will deal with my cousins from a different level."

"Thank you, sir," she said.

I breathed a sigh of relief as I was able to check two more responsibilities off my list.

"Very well!" I said. "I will see you four days hence!"

⁂

My crew looked trim and professional in their dark blue dress uniforms, though I had to admit they did seem a trifle out of place in the Edouardo V garden of the Imperium compound. Though I brought them in past the gate personally and introduced them to several acquaintances and friends, such as my personal tailor and the wonderful woman who ran the local public archive, they clung together like waifs. It broke my heart to see the normally ebullient and self-sufficient spacers of the Imperium navy uncertain as to what to do.

The arrival of my mother changed all that. When she was announced by the steward at the gate, Plet's back straightened like a yardstick. The others, taking their cue from her, stood to rigid attention.

In glided Admiral Tariana Kinago Loche. Since my prepubescent years, I had been a good foot taller than she, but I would never match her in formidable presence. Not that she seemed dangerous, something that her foes had found to their dismay upon encountering this small, slim, youthful-looking lady with her fresh, peach-kissed complexion, her sea-blue eyes, and her marvelous caramel-colored tresses. Tonight, those tresses were arranged high in a waterfall of waves and ringlets, just brushing the shoulders of an impeccable dress uniform. Her pale blue trousers bore a stripe down the side that was not white for an admiral, but platinum for the First Space Lord. Some had mistaken the two to their deep and pathetic sorrow. To crash upon the rocks of my mother's asperity was indeed to break up and sink without a trace.

The maternal unit approached. I feared for the worst, but she pulled my head down and kissed me on the cheek.

"Well, my dragonlet," she said. "Is this in an attempt to make up for your outrageous behavior?"

"I am afraid that would take several lifetimes of expiation," I said.

"So true. Have you been to see your father to say goodbye?"

"Yes, I have," I said. "I brought him a model of the *Rodrigo* that I made myself. It is a proper poppet of the ship, since I included a shaving of metal from the underside of the captain's chair. My chair," I corrected myself. Mother nodded approvingly.

"That is right, Thomas. You are not a captain yet. Commander Parsons has the highest naval rank of your company. You lead by courtesy. Please do not forget that. I don't want to have to read another report of you usurping his position."

"We work together!" I protested. "Parsons himself will tell you that my ideas are sound ones."

I stopped to cross mental fingers. But my mother had always been adept at reading my mind.

"But you would rather seek forgiveness than ask permission."

"There never is time to ask permission," I said, with all truthfulness. "Every time I went against his wishes on my last mission, it had been in the heat of battle, so to speak. It was act or be acted upon."

"That is the risk you take when there is a chain of command. Don't assume you know everything, Thomas. In fact," she added, with a twinkle in her sea-blue eyes that was the physical trait we shared most closely, "don't assume you know anything. It will keep you out of trouble more frequently than it will put you in it."

"I will carve your words upon my heart, mother," I said, leaning over to kiss her again.

"See that you do. And have pity upon young Captain Naftil. He is not as immune to our charms as most. It is his only flaw as a commander. He has a long future in the navy, and I don't want my own son preventing him from attaining promotion."

"I will treat him with the respect he deserves," I said. "You have my solemn promise."

Mother sighed and shook her head.

"You will treat him as the captain under whose authority you travel, my dear. Don't forget that. Now, will you make me known to your crew?"

I made the introductions with all due propriety. Mother advanced her hand to shake first with Plet, who had gone so rigid I feared she might implode, then to the others in turn.

"This is such an unruly crowd," Mother confided to them, with the ease she always showed nervous recruits. "I'm afraid they may topple me off my feet! I would greatly appreciate it if you would accompany me. My escort has not yet arrived." It was a white lie. I knew she hadn't brought an escort. After all, she was my mother, this was my party, and she was related to over eighty percent of the guests. But the excuse served to electrify my crew.

"Yes, Admiral, ma'am!" Plet exclaimed, dashing a fierce salute. "Oskelev, Anstruther, right flank! Redius, Nesbitt, left flank!"

"Aye, lieutenant!" they chorused. They took their positions, one fore and aft on each side of Mother. Plet rammed herself into place at the head of the group.

"To the drinks tent," Mother said, gesturing forward.

"Ma'am, yes, ma'am!"

Together, they marched off. Throughout the evening, I would see them in much the same configuration. The First Space Lord treated them as if they were a flock of chicks and she their mother hen. Gradually, they began to relax, and even enjoy themselves.

I sincerely hoped they would. The chef was the finest I knew, hired away from Sparrow Island for the evening at colossal but reasonable expense. The food was a feast for the eyes long before its aroma touched the nose or the flavors and textures the tongue. A raft of pastries that I hoped would be sufficient for the growing throng came from a bakery that I had discovered in a part of Taino frequented most often by commoners. The secret was out, though, since the baker had pleaded with me to allow her to use her branded doilies and platters for the evening. Wines and spirits had come from the Kinago cellars. For those who knew good vintages, I needed to say nothing more.

As for music and entertainment, the Edouardo V garden was large enough to accommodate three musical ensembles with audience seating, plus smaller venues for close-up magic, acrobats on trapezes, and comedians.

Of the original three hundred people I had invited, I estimated that roughly six hundred and fifty had come. I was not in the least surprised. My cousins and I generally felt free to bring along whomever we wished to a casual event. Formal parties, such as weddings or diplomatic soirees, were considered inviolable, but a going-away bash had very elastic sides. I had purchased food and drink for a thousand, and prepared the Imperium staff to fetch more from selected vendors if necessary.

At times like these, I missed my cousin Scotlin, but he had recently moved to the Castaway Cluster with his wife and children. We still corresponded as copiously as of old, but it wasn't the same as having him there where I could clap him on the back. I cheerfully greeted our cousin Erita, who sniffed her way past the commoners in the crowd to offer me a fishlike hand. My great-aunt Nestorina sailed in. Behind her were her grandson, my cousin Nalney, and Nestorina's fourth husband, Gorokomo. Goro was only two years my senior, but he, like everyone else, struggled to keep up with my energetic aunt.

"My heavens, auntie," I said, submitting to a fierce kiss on each cheek, "you look younger every year."

She smirked.

"I should, silly boy. I've had every rejuvenation treatment known across the galaxy. Look at this complexion!" I surveyed a cheek as smooth as a debutante's. "Three weeks of Dr. Salm's special diet, and my skin is back to the same state as when I was twenty. You should try it."

"I was thinking of trying one to make me look older, auntie," I said. "No one takes me seriously at this age."

She laughed. The nearest server swooped in upon her and offered a choice of colorful beverages. She chose pale orange. I turned to my next guests, a Wichu couple wearing brightly polished formal harnesses on their white-furred shoulders.

"Ah, Ambassador!" I said, offering her a deep bow. "And your mate. I don't believe I have met him before."

A thread of dance music met my ears from the most proximate of the bandstands. People from all walks of life—well, several walks of life; I did draw the line somewhere—were hopping and gliding together to a famous band just returned to Keinolt from a multi-world tour. I recalled that the ensemble had had their breakthrough performance at a birthday party here in the compound.

"Thomas!"

A stout man with a tonsure of black curls hailed me. Donel was my first cousin thrice removed on my mother's side. He came over with a group of his friends, none of whom I recognized.

"Thomas, I can never get a story right the way you can. Tell them the one about the malfunctioning flitter."

I bowed. "It would be my pleasure." I made conspiratorial eye contact with each of my newfound audience in turn, and began. It was rather a long story, but it built up toward the conclusion a satisfying giggle at a time.

I heard a familiar shriek, and glanced toward the gate.

My cousin Jil arrived amidst a gaggle of ladies whom I did not know, but I did not mind. She acquired friends like a butterfly hunter amassed a collection, and a small thing like their failure to be invited to a private event would not stop her bringing them. She preferred colorful acquaintances to drab ones, but learned every detail of their lives, personalities and preferences. If there was an obsessive love of learning in the Kinago heritage, that is where it manifested itself in Jil. She was not threatened by a friend being prettier or richer than she, though there were few on Keinolt who fit that description. Jil was tall, very slender, with a golden complexion that set off her deep blue eyes and caramel hair that was not dissimilar to my mother's.

I waved to Jil, making a note to compliment her upon her blue-green gown, which floated upon the evening breeze like a distant melody. She had not yet notified me as to our mutual travel plans, but it would not surprise me to have her wait until the last minute, the better to prevent me from refusing. But, forewarned was forearmed, and I knew that I had Parsons's approval to allow her to take ship with us.

She broke free of the pack and, in a thoroughly businesslike manner, cut me out of the circle of friends, but not before I finished my joke.

". . . And he said, as he picked himself up, 'You see? It wasn't so far to the ground. Just one little step.'" My audience laughed appreciatively. When the arm hooked around my neck and dragged me backwards, as if removing me from a vaudeville stage, I had had my applause.

"Thomas, dear," Jil said, low in my ear. "I need to speak with you."

"You have my entire attention, cousin," I said, theatrically clutching my abused neck. "But all you had to do is beckon to me. My throat may never be the same." I signed for the server to bring drinks. Then I remarked upon the unfamiliar apprehension in her eyes. Teasing her, which she surely deserved, could wait. "How may I help?"

"Thomas, I . . . I hate to ask."

"Then don't frame it in the form of a question," I said. "Tell me a story."

She pushed me. I staggered melodramatically backwards. The little pantomime broke the tension.

"Thomas! I need to leave Keinolt for a little while."

"Do you need to leave tonight?" I asked, in all seeming innocence. "Then it was very kind of you to come to my party at all."

Her eyes went wide with dismay.

"No! I mean, I need to go away somewhere far."

I frowned. "How far?"

"Well . . . as far as the Autocracy sounds rather good at the moment."

"What a coincidence!" I said, all jolliness. "My mother is sending me on a diplomatic visit tomorrow morning. Do you want to come along?"

She gripped my forearm with both of her hands. Her painted fingernails, half as long as the digits to which they were attached, dug into my skin through the fabric of my sleeve. I did my best not to wince.

"May I? It would save my *life*."

"Of course, cousin. I think it would be great fun to travel with you. It has been a long time since we went on a long trip together."

I was able to sound sincere because I was. Jil was good company. She exhaled, as if she had been holding her breath for hours.

"Thank you, Thomas. I am very grateful."

"We depart from Oromgeld Spaceport at 0900," I said. "I know it's an awful hour. I shall have to have all the valetbots haul me out of bed and dress me. Can you be there on time?"

"Oh, yes," Jil said, then hesitated. "But it isn't just me."

"Oh?" I inquired. Parsons had not mentioned a companion. "Would you like to bring someone with you?"

"Yes, if it isn't too much trouble."

"I am sure that it isn't. Who is it?"

Jil beckoned. The gaggle approached.

"Which one of them?" I asked.

"Thomas!" Jil said, with an expansive gesture. "I want you to meet my companions! They are all wonderful people, and I know you will come to love them as much as I do."

"All of them?" I asked, in disbelief, peering from one elegantly clad lovely to another.

"Of course, all of them! Banitra Savarola Wilcox, Hopeli Asmudov, Marquessa Royode, Sinim Nikhorunkorn Torm, this is my cousin, Lord Thomas Innes etcetera etcetera Kinago. I am sure he will tell you to call him Thomas. Thomas, these are my very dear friends. We are all looking forward to traveling with you."

I bowed, giving the most elegant of gestures with my right arm, while my mind went through deeply complicated contortions to accept what I had heard.

"Ladies, it is my deep pleasure to make your acquaintance. I hope that we will all become good friends. Jil is correct. Please do call me Thomas."

They giggled.

I described her companions collectively as a gaggle, though once they separated into disparate examples of humanity I found elements of interest in each one of them. Two of them, Banitra and Sinim, were minor members of the nobility, though they were untitled, but meaning that they were very distantly related to Jil and to me. Banitra was attractive, with warm, tawny skin, very dark eyes, and with the molded brow that distinguished all Wilcoxes, including the current minister for industrial development. Like him, I perceived that she took in her surroundings with those bright eyes, filing away interesting facts for later. By her surnames Sinim shared several ancestors with Jil, though her skin was more bronze than gold, and her cheekbones more prominent. She was shorter of stature, and draped her curvaceous frame in swathes of turquoise crepe silk. Her long, black hair was gathered in a complicated plait.

The other two were commoners. One could distinguish that condition by their very faces, which were asymmetrical to a dismaying degree. Since I was surrounded nearly all the time by my close family, all of whom were of Imperial blood, on beholding ordinary human beings, I sometimes found myself trying to urge their features into a more harmonious line by furtive movements of my shoulders or body, as one seeks to influence the arc of a ball one has already thrown. The action did no good in either case. Marquessa had dimples, a pointed chin, and thick blonde hair that waved upon the shoulders of a gown of excellent design and expensive cream-colored fabric. Teak-skinned Hopeli had a frame so slight I feared she would fly away, but she moved with admirable grace. All four ladies were charming and attractive, and seemed to be interesting conversationalists, as subject gave way to subject without hindrance or hesitation.

My viewpad buzzed on my hip. I did not need to look at its screen to know what it said.

"It is time for the toasts," I said, offering Jil my arm. "Come along with me, ladies. This is the sole official event tonight."

CHAPTER 6

Precisely on schedule, serverbots were constructing a small dais in the center of the garden, immediately between the (unused) throne and the ornamental fountains. A trio of narrow pylons had been erected and draped with bunting that twinkled with tiny lights sewn throughout the fabric. I stepped into the center of the round stage, where my voice would be picked up and carried by the speakers concealed in the pylons and at numerous points around the massive garden. Another server, human this time, appeared at my elbow with a tray containing tall flutes of sparkling wine. I served them to my cousin and her entourage, then secured one for myself.

"If I may have your attention, my friends," I announced. I held up my glass, and waited for silence. The hubbub gradually died down. I looked out over the sea of faces, both familiar and unfamiliar, some rather the worse for drink, even though midnight had not yet struck. "Thank you all for coming to my party. It is such a pleasure to see you all enjoying yourselves."

"Great food!" shouted the Wichu ambassador, waving a plate in the air.

"I quite agree," I said. "I have no idea how I'm going to fit into my pressure suit—there's no time to have it altered. For those of you who don't know the reason for the celebration, such as if you did not receive an invitation directly . . ." I peered out at the crowd, pretending to be gruff, and received the expected laugh. ". . . tomorrow I proceed from here to the Uctu Autocracy! It is my first time making the long crossing. I shall be accompanied by a highly competent and efficient crew," here I gestured toward my friends, who had pitched up close to my dais in the company of my mother, "on an official visit on behalf of his imperial majesty, the emperor, Shojan XII. To the emperor!" I held up my glass.

"To the emperor!" chorused my guests and all the servers. I threw out my free hand in Jil's direction. She held up her hands to stop me, but the spate of my eloquence could not be stemmed.

"My dear cousin, the Lady Jil Loche Nikhorunkorn, is coming along with me, to make certain that no store or goods emporium within the borders of the Uctu Autocracy will remain unshopped!"

Loud cheers erupted, along with some fleering comments from our closest relatives, who knew Jil's propensity for clearing shelves. In spite of her worries, Jil made a face at me.

"Why you?" cousin Erita shouted from beside the drinks pavilion. "The emperor has plenty of other relatives, not to mention diplomats with actual experience. I mean, what do you plan to do, tell the Autocrat jokes? Do you want to undo all the ties that have been formed between us in the last thirty years?"

I held an innocent hand to my chest.

"I am the very person to bring Imperium humor to the Autocracy, cousin," I protested. "Even as we speak, my computer system has been gathering, sorting and analyzing humorous stories guaranteed to bring laughter bubbling to the lips, er, mandibles of our dear neighbor. I will have routines ready for every occasion! No event will find me unprepared."

My mother came to my rescue. She stepped out of the protective circle of my crew and held up her hands for silence.

"Thomas is going on this mission because he is *my son*, and I plan to get what use I can out of him. Since he is still seconded to the navy, I can order him to make a diplomatic visit to the Autocrat. The rest of you," she sent a mock-baleful eye around to my relatives close enough to receive the glare, "have retreated out of my reach."

Howls of laughter rose. I even received some looks of sympathy.

"It is true," I said, assuming my most chastened expression. "My brother and sister successfully made it out of the navy. Mother simply did not get her hands on them in time." I looked suitably sheepish and put upon, which caused another laugh to go up. I signaled to the servants to bring more champagne and sweets to the guests. When they were so furnished, I raised my glass again.

"A toast to my lady mother! To the First Space Lord, the most honored Admiral Lady Tariana Kinago Loche!"

We drank the toast. My mother abstained, since it is discourteous to drink to oneself. Instead, she looked quietly dignified. I adored her. She always knew the right thing to do.

"Now, if I may have everyone join hands in a circle, or several circles," I said, stepping down from my stage. The servers moved in to collect the empty glasses. I took Mother's left hand and reached for Plet's right. She shied away from me like a startled horse.

My crew looked rather nervous, but two of Jil's ladies, Banitra and Sinim, took pity on them and herded the entire group between them, forming our own small ring encircling the dais. I realized that though the ladies were accompanying me with an entirely unwelcome task in mind, they seemed to be kind and inclusive. They would not be so great a burden as some of my cousin's friends.

"Let us concentrate our mental strength so that our trip to the Autocracy will be a grand success! May the universe lower all barriers to friendship between our two peoples, and make the bonds between us stronger than ever before."

I squeezed my eyes shut and focused on channeling the energy I knew must be building around me to bend fortune to my will. I heard some giggling and moaning from the assembled, casting aspersions on my efforts, so I added, "And when we return, may our hands be filled with gifts to share among you!"

A loud cheer went up for that latter wish. I knew I would have no trouble making them concentrate upon gain. I felt an inward rush of positive energy, which I directed toward the power of good by lifting my hands heavenward. If that didn't add luck to our enterprise, I would be greatly surprised.

Dance music began afresh, and the circles broke hastily. The servers moved in hastily to offer fresh drinks to the guests, who retreated into smaller groups to discuss my small ceremony. I would ask my staff later to let me know what they had overheard. I was always curious what people thought, but they did not always share their honest opinions. But my family tended to talk without reservation in front of the servants.

My cousin Xan came over to slap me hard on the back. He was a man of my own height and age but far handsomer and possessed of thick, dark curly hair and a sculpted and muscular torso that sent a primal thrill through many women's brains. Xan had two young lovelies with him, one hanging on to each arm. He detached them carefully and leaned close to have a private word with me.

"Be careful," he whispered. "I heard Great-Aunt Sforzina say that two of Jil's girls are prospects for you."

My eyes narrowed at the warning.

"Of the nuptial variety?"

"In what else is Aunt Sforzina interested?" Xan countered. "She cannot seem to see any of us without picturing our future offspring. The last time I went to have tea with her and Uncle Perleas, she told me I should have six children, four boys and two girls, and she knew just the wife who would manage me properly."

The serenity I had been cultivating all the way through a rather successful party retreated, leaving me feeling like a chastened schoolboy.

"Confound it!" I declared. "I have to fly all the way to the Uctu Autocracy with a quartet of girls who are angling to become my bride? That is going to put an immense strain on my, er, shopping trip!"

"Just don't buy any of them a ring," Xan said, with a cackle. He winked one sapphire-blue eye. "But I fancy two of them only are prospects. The others are commoners. Even Aunt Sforzina, in her zeal to put you on the wedding path, would not tie you to anyone who is not of noble blood."

"Very true," I said, buoyed partway up again. "That halves the threat, but still leaves me with two problems I did not need. Thank you for the klaxon, cousin. I am in your debt. Curse all meddling aunts!"

"You owe me a bottle of Uctu brandy. They grow a very odd variety of grape that makes the most marvelous fortified wine in the galaxy. I have had only one stingy taste from my uncle Radyion, who guards his cache fiercely. That will expiate the debt. Two bottles will put me in yours."

"Gladly," I said. I added Uctu brandy to the growing list of requests from various cousins. My little scout ship was going to have its own gravity well by the time we returned.

Jil came rushing to me, followed by her ladies. The women all seemed to be having a wonderful time, but Jil wore a look of terror.

"He's there," she said, pointing frantically toward the gate. "How did he get in?"

"Who? The man who threatened you?"

"How do you know about that?" she asked, astonished.

"I heard about your encounter. Is it he?"

"Yes. He looks like he could murder me!"

I took her hand and marched in the direction she indicated. Parsons, whom I had not seen before during the evening, shimmered into existence at my side and walked with us. I turned to him.

"My cousin, Parsons, has had a fright."

"I know, my lord." He turned to her. "You are safe, Lady Jil. Please remain with me."

"Oh, Parsons!" she wailed, grabbing his arm. He stood stalwart as she melted onto his shoulder and wept.

I summoned my door wardens, faithful retainers who had served the emperor's family all their lives and were experts in keeping the compound secure. With a mere flick of his forefinger, Parsons sent a full description of the alleged perpetrator to their viewpads.

"Have you seen this man at all tonight?" I asked. "The Lady Jil said that she just saw him."

"Here?" asked one guard, disbelievingly.

"Just here, just a moment ago."

"No, my lord!" the chief guard exclaimed, her square face full of concern. "We've been monitoring security all night long. No one came in without your invoices, or accompanied by an invited guest. We ran every single person through Infogrid, sir. This man hasn't been here. How would he get into the compound anyhow?"

"Run a security audit immediately," Parsons said. "This person has access to technical capabilities that may compromise the systems."

"On it, sir," said the sub-chief. He hurried back to the console in the gatehouse. The rest of the doorwardens scattered to their various stations. The sub-chief returned in a moment with an oversized viewpad in his hands.

"No, sir, no man of that description has entered here tonight."

Parsons and I exchanged concerned expressions.

"Then what did she see?"

"I couldn't say, my lord, my lady," the sub-chief said, though Jil kept her face buried in Parsons's immaculate collar.

Suddenly, an explosion of sound erupted at the far end of the party lawn. I turned to run in the direction of the noise. Parsons clasped my shoulder firmly.

"No, sir," he said. "It will be handled."

I subsided. Parsons detached my cousin and urged her into my arms. Her ladies surrounded her like a pastel-colored wall, their backs to her in a protective shield. Parsons glided away into the heart of the crowd. We waited.

Security guards, some human, some LAIs, appeared on the scene. I spotted my mother in the midst of a cluster of concerned guests. I could tell she was doing her best to reassure them. An officer in door warden uniform approached my mother. She listened closely to him, then nodded. A word from her sent my crew running in the direction of the disturbance. Even in their glad rags, they did their duty to defend the emperor's domicile.

I heard the distant sound of a flitter taking off, but it was so far away I doubted that the occupant could have been where Jil said she saw him. Unless he had some kind of other small vehicle or propellant pack, and we would have heard *that* in the aftermath of the alarm. It would also have set off a host of proximity sirens and security responses. I wondered why they had not sounded when the charge was set. The system in the compound could detect traces of thousands of volatile compounds. A couple of these very door wardens had confiscated a couple of my essential oils only a week ago until they could be analyzed and found harmless.

Plet appeared at my mother's side and threw a crashing salute. She spoke in a low tone close to Mother's ear. The maternal unit nodded sharply and gestured toward me. Plet marched in my direction.

"No sign of an intruder, sir," she reported. "A small parcel was caught on a security eye falling from a height and detonated by remote lasers. Anstruther is analyzing the video to see if we can detect what vehicle it came from."

"There shouldn't be anything flying over the compound but one of ours or a licensed delivery vehicle," I pointed out.

"I know, sir," Plet said. "Security is investigating."

"Thank you, lieutenant," I said. She saluted with an efficiency of movement, and returned to my mother's side. I patted Jil on the shoulder.

"Never fear, cousin. Tomorrow we depart. No threat can harm you."

Jil raised her face. Her eyes were huge. Tears stood in them, prepared to overflow.

"How did he get into the Imperium compound?" she asked.

"It happens, now and again," I said, deliberately casual. "A detector failed, perhaps. Maybe the man wished to apologize to you. An unfortunate coincidence of events. It's all over now. You have nothing to worry about."

I signaled for a drink. One of the hired servers approached with a small salver on which was a tumbler filled with pale green liquid. As I hesitated to take the glass, Parsons appeared. He handed it to my trembling cousin.

"This will help to calm your nerves, Lady Jil," Parsons said.

She seized it and drained half its contents. I could smell celery seed, a pinch of cardamom and other soothing herbs, spices and oils. I approved.

"Come on, my lady, let's go," Banitra said, putting her arm around Jil's waist. "We need to get some sleep if we all have to be up by that awful hour. I want to go through my luggage one more time to make sure I haven't forgotten anything!"

"Me, too," added Hopeli. "My mother wanted me to call when I got home from the party and tell her all about it. She won't believe how wonderful everything was!" The blonde woman shot a grateful glance at me. I bowed slightly in thanks.

As they made for the gate, accompanied by two door wardens and a trio of securitybots, I leaned conspiratorially toward Parsons.

"Have we anything to worry about between now and launch?" I asked.

"No, sir. The investigation will continue. Lady Jil will be watched until then."

I was certain he would see to it, but I would have been a poor host if I had not made certain. I had a quiet word with Plet, who had Oskelev attach herself to Jil's party. Until my cousin and her friends reached her rooms, she would be well looked after.

That settled, I went back to full-scale hosting. The grand finale of the evening, a battle of the magicians, was about to begin, and I didn't want anyone to miss it, most especially me.

CHAPTER 7

I know I was a trifle bleary-eyed the next morning when I reached the launch pad on which my scout ship, the *Rodrigo*, stood, but I knew that something was amiss.

My crew made busy in and around the ship. As each of them caught my eye, he or she would salute me. I returned the gesture with alacrity, though my mind was perforce elsewhere. My primary interest was my luggage.

When I did not see the matching cases on the impact-resistant pavement, I went aboard the *Rodrigo* to check where they had been bestowed. Some of the cases were for long-term storage, as the contents would not be required until we reached Nacer, but the rest I required not only in transit to the interstellar carrier *Bonchance,* which would convey us to a position near the frontier jump point into the Autocracy, but aboard the carrier and thereafter. Yet an inspection of my cabin revealed that a few items I had packed were not present.

Oh, I was accustomed to Parsons going through my wardrobe and removing garments of which he disapproved. For that reason, I had brought potentially confiscatable items with me in a small floating valise, so they would not be out of my sight before launch. In any event, no garments had been removed from the collection I had packed.

No, the objects that I sought were vital to my occult studies. In particular, I could not locate my prized crystal ball. I knew that I had packed it in the flat circular case, padded by my silken robes and two round cushions I could repose upon should there be no room to arrange my scrying chair. The case in question was absent without leave.

It weighed more than other single item in my luggage, but I was dismayed and annoyed by its absence. I suspected Parsons. A quick essay with the golden pendulum I kept handy in my belt pouch determined that he was indeed the one who had taken it. When confronted, he did not deny it.

"It is not standard issue, sir," Parsons informed me.

"I insist that it be restored to me," I thundered. Unfortunately, Parsons had equipped himself with a conversational umbrella. The precipitation of my disapproval did not spatter him.

"I am afraid not, my lord. It weighs twenty-one kilos, which can be better deployed for fuel and foodstuffs."

He stopped me in my verbal tracks. Just the meaningful way in which he emitted the last word drew my attention.

"Foodstuffs?" I inquired.

"Yes, my lord. Dainties to please a discerning palate, even when far away from one's preferred providers, of quantities suitable for the length of the journey. Not to mention the devices to keep those comestibles at the appropriate humidity and temperature."

"Go on," I said, "I am listening." I kept my expression imperious. It was a perfect reflection of Parsons's.

"Sir, dantooth caviar is in season at this time. You will recall that it is sustainably harvested by law, but I took especial care in choosing the purveyor. The packaging is very fragile, and it requires constant refrigeration just above the freezing point. Variation of more than three degrees either way results in irrevocable harm to the caviar. Six kilos were harvested this season."

"You didn't obtain six kilos of dantooth?" I asked, breathlessly.

"No, sir, I am afraid that one kilo was all that was obtainable. Some wealthy patrons were placed on the list ahead of you. And your imperial cousin took delivery of the majority of the harvest."

"He would," I mused mournfully. "My cousin the emperor does maintain a superlative table. But at least I will have some of this delicacy for my own."

"Indeed you will, sir."

"And crysbort lemons?" I asked, with growing excitement.

"They are the only ones with suitable acidity and sweetness to complement dantooth."

"Naturally, sir," Parsons said.

"Capers? Blini?"

"I would not have omitted anything that is expected."

"Of course you wouldn't," I said, expansively. "I impugned you and I apologize. I cannot wait to see what my crew thinks of the finest caviar in the galaxy. But that hardly makes twenty-one kilos, let alone the weight of the case in which my crystal ball travels. And the folding table with appropriate silk velvet drapings. And my scrying chair. And my hand-sewn tent with the embroidered stars picked out in microscopic crystals and diamonds." I perused my memory. "No, wait, the tent is still there. I saw the bag in the hold."

"No, indeed, sir, it does not. I will provide you with a full manifest of the foodstuffs if you require it, but would you not care to enjoy the element of surprise as each fresh offering is revealed?" One of his eyebrows rose perhaps two millimeters on his forehead.

I weighed the notion in my mind and found proximate curiosity overwhelmed by the joy of anticipation. The way to my heart eventually finds its way past my stomach, but it needs to get past my curiosity first.

"I would rather wait. As always, Parsons, you know my mind better than I do. You will, of course, partake of these marvelous delicacies with me, won't you?"

"I am gratified, my lord. Will you please finish the inspection so we may get under way?"

I fetched a sigh of pleasure. I did love my ship and my crew.

As always, I found the *Rodrigo* as clean, ideally equipped and perfectly maintained as if it had been extracted directly from the text of the military manual. No dust soiled any surface, no lingering smells wafted from the food or sanitation systems, no odd or worrisome noises issued from life support or the engines. I offered praise to each of the crew as I encountered them. As always, Nesbitt turned red with pleasure in the ordnance and shields station. Anstruther, in her seat overseeing the last moments of maintenance on the electronics systems and communications array, had trouble meeting my eyes. Oskelev was too busy over the pilot's console to do more than wave at me. My ostensible responsibility while we were in transit was to oversee the life support station, which doubled as the hydroponics center. I stopped off to install a tiny stone carving of the Buddha, to add a touch of serenity to the already peaceful green space.

"Present as personal goods," Redius said, taking me aside as I checked in with him in engineering. He opened his left belt pouch to reveal tiny lights twinkling.

"Your circuit!" I said, in pleased surprise. I showed him the one chuckling to itself in my own belt receptacle. We shared a conspiratorial grin, and I went off to find Plet.

She was outside the shift, aft and below the tail, examining the exterior ports of the engines. To the consternation of the ground crew, she had discovered faults unobservable to the naked eye. Repairbots moved in, tweaking away at single particles, for all I knew. Parsons stood a few meters away, still and watchful as a benevolent statue.

"Good morning, lieutenant," I said, offering a friendly salute.

"Good morning, my lord lieutenant," she said. "How did your inspection go?"

"Very well," I said. "Everybody is at his or her station, and all will be ready to go very soon."

"Did your visit serve any useful purpose, or did you merely pass the time of day?"

I waggled a playful finger at her.

"Ah, you are testing me, Plet. Oskelev has updated charts, showing the debris from an exploded asteroid left in place five light minutes off the second jump point where the Minchin Mining Megalopoly demolished it in quest for transuranics. When I left, Nesbitt was checking the sonic range of the deflectors. I believe he was concerned about the microwave capacitance, but the indicators say that those are in the amber section of the meter, not red. I believe that means he has found the problem and is undertaking its correction."

She nodded, not changing expression. I believe she must have been taking lessons in stoicism from Parsons.

"Very observant, lieutenant," she said. "I have sent your viewpad a reminder detailing your responsibilities for the transit to the Autocracy. Among them is overseeing the comfort and safety of our civilian guests."

I distinctly heard the plural.

"You *know* that more than just my cousin is coming along with us?"

A raised eyebrow confirmed she had been communing with Parsons.

"Of course I do. The commander issued us Infogrid files on each of our guests five days ago, my lord," Plet said.

"You knew that we were going to have a horde traveling with us *five days ago?* You know all their names?" I asked. "I only found out yesterday!"

Plet was calm. I turned to Parsons to express my outrage. He studied me blankly, as if I were an uninteresting museum exhibit. I returned my glare to Plet.

"Naturally I would get that briefing as soon as possible, sir," she said. "With Commander Parsons acting as your aide-de-camp, I am the ranking officer of this mission. I must have information on all personnel and freight requirements. But I did forward it to you when I received it—five days ago. All that data was available on the official briefings. If you had only troubled to read them when they were sent to you, you would have had it ahead of time."

"Touché," I said. Hoist by my own petard. I lowered my head, chastened. Plet did not dwell upon her victory, at least not outwardly.

"I leave you to deal with them," she said. "Please see them installed in the quarters prepared for them."

I presented a second salute, and only just in time. The ladies were arriving.

A gigantic limousine set down just beyond the public edge of the terminal building. A marquee panel along the broad side of the vehicle displayed Jil's family coat of arms over a background of her favorite clear blue, the color of Keinolt's skies. All of the noble family was precleared for departure, and those traveling with us were required to do so as well, so they emerged on the space side of the building in scarcely more time than it would have taken merely to walk from one door to the other.

Jil bore down on me like a bad cold. She overwhelmed my senses and distracted me. I hardly need to add that her perfume filled my nostrils so that I could smell nothing else. Privately, I resolved to remove all scents from her cosmetics kit and jettison them while we were in deep space. She was clad in a rich green, form-fitting travel dress that clung to her body to the knees, then flared outward. On her feet were high-heeled ankle-high boots that would be ill-suited to traversing deck plates, but I was certain that she had footgear she could exchange for them as soon as she was on board.

Her friends were similarly attired for travel. Marquessa was the best turned out, in powder blue with leather piping, and black shoes with soft wedges that gripped the pavement with every step. Much more suitable. Sinim was swathed in overlapping thin cloths of rainbow hues. One of these had been wound into a complicated headscarf-hood arrangement, from which her small face eagerly peered. Banitra and Hopeli had suits much like Jil's, and similar ridiculous shoes.

Behind them came a robocarrier laden with eight blue crates, each the size of the bed I slept in as a small boy. On closer examination, I realized they were matching luggage, their surfaces carved in fanciful designs, and code-locked with the latest security devices.

"Welcome, Lady Jil," Parsons said. "Ladies."

"Allow me to introduce the senior officer of the *Rodrigo*," I said, "apart from myself, of course. You met her last night at my party, but perhaps you do not recall her name. Lieutenant First Class Carissa Plet."

I could tell by the wrinkle that interrupted the perfection of Plet's smooth brow that she disagreed with my interpretation of rank, but in my view the matter had been settled long ago. But she was in charge of the ship's physical well-being, which included those who traveled aboard her.

"Welcome," Plet echoed. "Lieutenant Kinago will see to your needs."

"Lieutenant Kinago!" Sinim shrieked, delightedly. "Oh, Thomas, you look so official!"

"Thank you," I said. "Your luggage will need to be placed on board at once. Have you marked each bag to indicate whether it will go in your cabin or the hold?"

"They have to go in my cabin!" Jil exclaimed. "I need all my things with me!"

"No, you don't," Banitra said, taking Jil's elbow. "Remember, I went over everything with you last night. Just the one with the blue tag is for the transit, Thomas. I believe you said it would only be a day or two until we rendezvous? The others can be stored until we are on board the *Bonchance*. Then she will just need the one with the green tag. All the others can wait until Nacer."

I blessed her for her organizational talents, not the least of which was managing my cousin. But I was caught by the obvious concept, or omission thereof.

"Just a moment," I protested. "Which bags belong to the rest of you?"

"Oh, these are only mine," Jil said, laying possessive hands on the cases. "My friends' bags haven't arrived yet."

"They will be here at any minute," Banitra said, giving me an engaging smile. "I was very stern with the cargo company to make certain they would be here before launch."

"How many bags do you have?" I asked.

"Only five. Not as big as these."

"I have six," Hopeli said, with a laugh. "Small ones. Well, comparatively."

"Four," Marquessa said.

"Just two," said Sinim. "But they're bigger than those."

I gave Parsons a sour look.

"Surely my crystal ball and its attendant impedimenta would have taken up less than a single one of these enormous receptacles."

"If I may remind you, the Lady Jil is not a serving member of the Imperium Navy, sir."

"Heavens, no! But it would seem as though a battleship will be required to carry her luggage!"

Overnight, Parsons had provided me with Infogrid links to each of the ladies' files. I studied them closely. Marquessa was a personal shopper at the local Colvarin's Department Store embassy cum shopping center. Sinim had become a correspondent with her via the Infogrid over a mutual interest in the designs of a graphic performance artist. Their acquaintance with Jil was not of long standing in any of their cases, but that did not surprise me. Jil had a tendency to form lifelong friendships on first meeting. And they had proved to be interesting conversationalists as well as good dancers. It should not be a dull journey. The addition of a group of ladies would keep Jil too busy to meddle in my mission and, as Parsons had suggested, their presence would prove a useful diversion for interested onlookers.

"It will be all right," Banitra assured me. "We have everything organized. All she has to do is enjoy the trip."

"I am in your debt," I said, sounding a bit more formal than I would have preferred. I rather liked her and the other companions. I simply had to remain perched on my toes to avoid any romantic entanglement with either her or Sinim. I had sent an early-morning message to my great-aunt Sforzina (who had also avoided attending my party, undoubtedly to forego such a confrontation), but she had not replied.

"This will be such fun!" Jil said. She stopped and surveyed me up and down. I straightened up automatically, as though my mother were looking on. "I just realized! Why *are* you in uniform, Thomas? Haven't you been separated from the service yet like the rest of us?"

"Well, you see . . . ," I began.

"Lord Thomas has been returned to active service as a favor to the Emperor by his lady mother, the First Space Lord," Parsons said, appearing at my side like my own shadow. "He proved to be of some minor use to the Imperium in the past. The First Space Lord felt that his presence on this mission would be of similar aid. He is to represent the Emperor to the authorities of the Autocracy. Therefore, official costume will lend him greater authority when he encounters those whose assistance he needs to request."

"Ah," Jil said, with a mix of spite and malice such as only she could blend, "this is your punishment for the skimmer race!"

At an almost invisible nod from Parsons I bent my head in shame.

"You need not put it exactly like that," I said. "It's no worse than your reason for taking temporary leave of Keinolt."

This time Jil dipped her countenance. I felt momentary sorrow for that thrust, seeing as it was delivered with less than perfect tact before her friends. I was about to apologize when yet another luggage carrier appeared on the scene, rumbling under the weight of its load. It had been piled as high as a mountain with bags of every color and configuration. I executed a perfect double-take, to the amusement of the ladies.

"And where is all that going?" I inquired.

"Well, wherever it will fit!" Jil said. "You can't expect my ladies to travel stark naked."

"And by 'stark naked' you mean fewer than twelve layers of clothes?"

"Just exactly," Jil said, laying a delicate hand upon my arm. "I am so glad you understand what I say, Thomas. It will make the trip much more entertaining."

What could not be cured must be endured, I mused. I turned my back on the loader.

"Gentlewomen," Plet said, inclining her head a few millimeters. "Welcome aboard. Lieutenant Kinago, please see to their comfort."

"It would be my pleasure," I said. I applied a salute to my forehead, then extended an elbow to Jil. "Please come along and see your quarters."

Jil battened on, and I proceeded toward the boarding ramp.

The cooling system was in full operation, so the ambient temperature within was several degrees lower than the desert sunshine outside. After a moment of shivering, the ladies had acclimatized. They looked around, their brows wrinkled with curiosity. I followed their glances, taking in the thin layer of the cream-colored inner hull against the steel-blue of the shielded and armored outer hull. Beside the hatch were glassteel-fronted cases containing emergency gear, each with a series of images instructing on their use. Beyond the airlock, the size of the average foyer in the Imperium compound, a short corridor led to the main passage. I was accustomed to its appearance, but I realized how utilitarian and forbidding it might seem to civilians.

"Why don't we start with a tour?" I asked. I directed them to the main corridor and to the right, where the ship's artificial gravity took hold and turned us thirty degrees. "This way is the bridge."

"Here we have the nerve center of the entire ship," I said, entering the command module with understandable pride. "You see all the screens and tanks that provide telemetry for all information the crew will need to pilot the ship and take care of its many functions. The four station chairs are for command, navigation, communications and defense, and are fitted with complicated padding and harnesses to protect the officers during launch, landing and any rough travel."

"Battle?" asked Marquessa, with a frisson that shook her delectable flesh. As she was not related to the imperial family, she had not had to go through the academy for two years' service. Instead, she had taken part in an ecology program on a planet being terraformed in Colvarin's Department Store system. I imagined what it must look like to her to enter a warship for the first time. The walls full of screens and scopes must be a trifle overwhelming.

"If need be, of course, but our first move would be evasive tactics," I assured her.

"Why are there six chairs?" Hopeli asked, pointing out the obvious.

"Well, that one is mine," I said, pointing to the one slightly behind and to the right of the center of the bridge. It had superbly comfortable padding and an enhanced sound system installed. Its extended frame was custom-fitted to my long back and legs.

"Where do we sit to watch the launch?" Sinim asked, eagerly, peering around. "I don't see any other seats."

"Not in here, I am afraid."

I led them off the bridge, past the hydroponics garden and conference room, showed them briefly the location of ladders and conveyance chutes around to the cabins and bathing facilities, storage facilities, and repair bays. I explained the spinning core that ran through the center of the ship, to provide normal gravity while in the void. I looped back briefly to the cargo bay at the far aft just behind engineering. With all the goods needed for the trip, including military skimmers and aircycles already occupying a large portion of the area, the addition of the ladies' luggage filled it up to the toes of the evac suits hanging on the walls in their individual cubbyholes. We had just room to squeeze all the way around to observe the aft airlock and back again. Our tour ended in the common room.

"This is where you will observe launch, or anything else you choose," I said. I flipped on all the lights.

The enormous chamber, thus revealed, elicited appreciative *oohs* from my audience.

"This is the entertainment center," I said, my voice echoing off the white enameled panels that were the default walls of the room. "It doubles and trebles as the refectory, tri-tennis court, exercise room, theater, party venue and whatever else helps keep the crew healthy and pass the long weeks or months that the ship may be in transit. Here is where you will dine."

I showed them the tables that rose from the floor, then operated the control to activate the kitchen.

The food service section hummed into life. It occupied a large cubbyhole of its own. A wide conveyor, self-cleaning, led to the dishwasher-cum-food recycler that all cycled down into a system that was part of life support. Dishes and utensils left the washer and stacked themselves neatly in a cabinet beside the mechanized food preparation area. Prepared meals need only be placed on the IO platform for each section to be heated or chilled to temperature.

"You are not expecting us to eat processed glop," Jil said, horrified. "I left that behind at graduation!"

"Certainly not," I said. I pointed. "Cold storage, including walk-in freezer or refrigeration units for real food, is behind this section. You have access to anything not marked with somebody else's name. I have ordered excellent supplies to see us through the transit and beyond the frontier. Rank *has* its privileges. But look here," I added. "You will enjoy this."

I opened a few of the wall hatches to show them the clever storage units concealed within. My sports equipment had been secured in the storage lockers along with that belonging to my crew. I took out my favorite tri-tennis racquet, a Williams model in black high-impact compound with electric blue and pink flashes, and swished it through the air. The ladies opened one hatch after another to have a look. They found bats, hoops, nets, balls of every size and configuration, exercise equipment, weights, variable resistance machines and so on, secreted behind panels all over the large room.

"Yes, but one does not always want to play sports," Jil said, bored already with the delights of the chamber.

"One is not expected to do so," I said, activating a control on the wall. A black glassteel panel slid up to reveal a state-of-the-art video center and music player, compact enough for one person to operate, but with extensions and connections for three dozen to use. Tri-dees, old videos, thousands of subscriptions to holographic and sound magazines and countless other media were stored for recall by anyone who had time to kill. Myriad games, with appropriate controllers and joysticks, needed only to be unlocked to be enjoyed. "Every file is available anywhere on the ship on demand. Come take a look."

Jil allowed herself to be persuaded to seat herself at the console and peruse the listed media selections. She ran her finger up and down the screen, frowning at some entries, smiling at others.

"Oh, *Ya!*" she exclaimed happily. "You have *Ya!*"

"You're a fan, too?" I asked. The video series was an import from the Autocracy, starring an all-Uctu cast. Our distant ancestors would have called it a soap opera. I had been a devotee of it for years.

"Of course I am a fan," Jil said, with a moue for my stupidity. "You *knew* that. You bought me season six for my eighteenth birthday."

"Oh, but that was so many years ago, cousin," I said. "Oof!" She hit me in the stomach with her elbow. I folded over the blow, giving her enormous satisfaction.

"What a wonderful collection," Sinim said, her eyes aglow as she scrolled down the list. "We'll enjoy all of it!"

"Yes," Marquessa said. "It won't be as bad as I thought it would be."

"Well?" I asked, waiting for the inevitable reaction from my cousin.

"Well, what?" Jil asked.

"What do you think of my ship?"

She looked around, her lower lip pushed out in thought.

"It's a trifle small, isn't it?"

"Small!" I was taken aback and said so. "How many other Kinagos have their own warship?"

"Technically, it's not yours," she said, teasingly. "It belongs to the Imperium Navy."

"Then I suppose it belongs to my mother," I said. "And you *should* be impressed. She has thousands of ships. Of every size."

"I wonder if she gives them pet names," Jil said. "I would, if they were mine. The *White Star* would become *Trinket*. How does that sound? And this one would be *Neeps*."

"*Rodrigo*," I said firmly. "It is named for my father. But I quite agree. Some of them would be the better for a nickname. They are only meant to sound fearsome to our enemies, not to the brave souls serving aboard them. I shall run us up a copy of the naval manifest, and we can rename all the ships in the fleet."

Jil clapped her hands. "That would be splendid!"

My viewpad buzzed. I lifted it to see Plet's severe face staring up at me.

"Launch in ten minutes. To stations. Countdown beginning."

With that terse order, her image disappeared, to be replaced by clock numbers tolling downward.

Jil pouted.

"Do you really have to go?" she asked.

"Plet gets very annoying when she's being officious," I said, casually. "I had better get you situated, cousin. Oskelev is the most amazing pilot, nearly as good as I am, but technical glitches can happen to anyone. I should hate to see you bruised when the event is so preventable."

I went around the room, pulling down crash couches and seeing to it that the guests were properly buckled in. The veteran of many transstellar voyages, Marquessa fastened her own harness expertly. I was glad there was one I did not need to worry about. Hopeli became intricately tangled in the padded straps, and did some most intriguing contortions to get free. I remembered from her Infogrid page that she was a fellow student in a dance class Jil took in town. The others waited for me to secure them in place. I flipped buckles and grip-pads expertly, and had them safely strapped in no time. I had learned from several hours' practice the most efficient order in which to secure the various parts of the harness. I could tell that my guests were impressed.

With less than five minutes remaining, I hurried to the bridge and threw myself into my crash couch. Parsons was already serenely fastened in.

Plet gave the order to Oskelev, who opened communications with the tower.

"Oromgeld, this is scout ship CK-M945B, ready for departure."

"*Rodrigo*, we read you. Safe journey. Prepare for launch in six, five, four, three . . ."

I braced myself against the coming thrust of engines. I always adored takeoff.

". . . Two, one!"

Oskelev planted her big furry hands on the controls. I felt the skin of my face seem to part and slide toward my ears as g-forces took hold.

We were off.

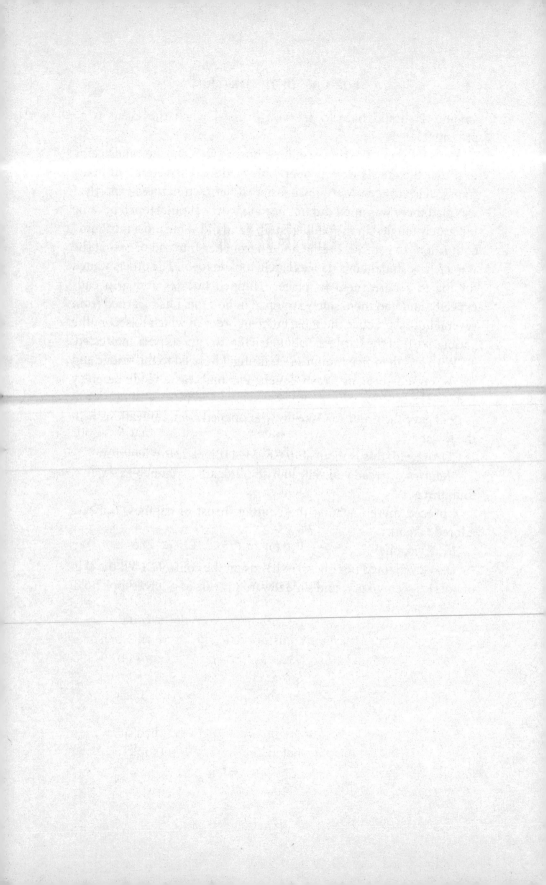

CHAPTER 8

What good was a crash couch, Skana Bertu mused pleasantly, stretching, *if it wasn't suitable for just crashing in?*

She lounged at her ease within sight of the viewtank that showed their position in space, one jump beyond the Imperium home system. There had been no good reason to stay awake during the approach to or transit through the jump point. Her custom-made protective settee was upholstered in silkskin, the hide of a rare species that was both durable and incredibly soft to the touch. For years she had thought about raising the creatures for their pelts. This new couch decided her for certain. She was going to do it.

"Tuk," she said aloud, "make a note. Silkskins. Where can we get enough for breeding stock?"

"The information is already in my records, madam." The Croctoid's voice came from a few yards away. "If you would care to peruse it while we are waiting until it is safe to unstrap, I would be pleased to send it to you."

She waved a dismissive hand, although she knew he couldn't see it in the depths of his equally custom-made but not as handsome lounger. Croctoids liked rough fabrics and lumpy cushions that would make humans writhe just to look at them.

"Later's fine. What do we hear about those prisoners? Taken care of yet?"

"No information yet, madam, but they will be handled shortly."

"All right," Skana said. She hated loose ends. "What took so long to clear Keinolt space?"

"Random inspection!" Nile's peevish voice erupted and echoed off the ceiling. Skana made a note to improve the soundproofing. It could be done at their next supply stop. "Customs has decided to search every vessel leaving the system now, instead of just coming in! Invasion of privacy!"

Skana tried not to sigh aloud.

"They've been doing that for centuries, Nile," she said. "Random inspections started before Earth's first colonies. It's purely a safety measure."

"They're picking on us! They know this is a Bertu ship!"

"They can't possibly suspect us of anything," Skana said, not bothering to try and look in his direction. "We have receipts and safety certificates for every single object on this ship. They were just trying to make sure we didn't blow up ten minutes into flight. Let it go, Nile."

"Don't be angry, Mr. Bertu," said one of the two girls who were sharing Nile's ample couch and protective harnesses with him. "Wouldn't you rather be happy? Can't I help you?"

"And me," the second girl said. "How about a shoulder massage? Would that help to relax you?"

"Well, maybe . . ." Nile's voice trailed off into a sigh.

When they had launched from Oromgeld spaceport, Skana wasn't sure if hiring the girls had been a good idea. They had both been nervous. She was afraid that their caution might rub off on Nile, but it hadn't lasted. In fact, giving him a couple companions was paying off handsomely. Alone, by that point in their journey, he would have been having fifty kinds of fit, over whether they had brought enough booze, or if Tuk had remembered to load the entertainment system with all the new music Nile craved (he had; he always did), or bemoaned yet again the temporary loss of connectivity with their businesses. Skana glanced at the viewtank again. She could see the space station that orbited near the jump point. They didn't need to stop for supplies or maintenance yet, but communications would have been reestablished. Yes, she could hear the sound of Tuk's claws on the screen of his clipboard. Any minute Nile would hook in. He'd have a happy hour or so dictating his daily messages to the hundred or so factories, businesses and other concerns. If there were any real problems, he'd probably shuffle them off to her. In the meantime the girls would keep him happy.

They were both slender and fairly tall, with golden skins and green eyes, deliberately chosen for their resemblance to the lady that Nile had picked on. Skana hated to feed his obsession, but it might keep his mind off the real thing.

Both the girls were nervous, scared that they might not make the return journey alive. Skana found their concerns neither here nor there. If they made Nile happy, they would be transported back again. Then they could resume their jobs, one a quality control manager in an orbiting factory out in the direction toward Cassobrix, the other as a receptionist at a Bertu Corporation office in the outskirts of Taino. They would be safe as long as they never breathed a word about what they saw or heard during this trip to *anyone* for the rest of their lives. That meant lovers, children, as well as the press or future biographers. Once they had accepted the assignment, Skana implanted them both with recorder chips to make sure.

They didn't have to take the job, she had pointed out. It was genuinely optional, with no strings attached to refusal. The Bertus kept their word on that. Her brother had a bad temper, yes, but he could be very generous. He was a good businessman when his emotions weren't engaged. The girls decided to take the chance, so they had agreed to the terms. Betray the Bertus, and no one would ever find the bodies. But if they survived and kept silent, they had a good opportunity to rise higher in the company, not just in Nile's bed. He and Skana rewarded loyalty with loyalty. And once the trip was over, they'd never have to sleep with him again. This was a one-off. Every girl who ever traveled as one of Nile's arm candy knew it. He probably wouldn't recognize either one a year from then. The odds were he couldn't pick either of them out of a line of similar girls now.

It wasn't like they were traveling steerage, either. The *Pelican* was luxurious and brand new. In fact, it had just floated out of the shipyard. Skana had designed it with the shipbuilder who created the Emperor's personal vessels. State-of-the-art engines purred at the rear of the long, sleek body. The repulsor array was calibrated to take out any particle up to a pretty good meteor. The cabins wouldn't have been out of place in a palace. Every single component, every piece of furniture, was beautifully made as well as durable. A few of their friends had joked about the ship's name, but the Bertus liked it. After all, it was registered as a cargo vessel, even though it would take a genius with a map to locate the storage bays from the residential areas. Oh, the customs officials had no trouble locating them . . . at least the majority of them. Little hiding places, and some not so little, occupied what would be dead space in other ships. At the moment, those were empty, and the main bay was full of crates of fine metal powder suitable for manufacturing use. The Bertus had no intention of being stopped for any infraction whatsoever. When they crossed the border into the Autocracy, they wanted to be clean as a whistle. Enstidius and his connections would make certain there were no other delays. She'd hate to be late for a coup.

A gentle chime sounded from concealed speakers and from everybody's pocket secretaries and clipboards. Noises like a pig emerging from a wallow meant that Nile was getting up. After one surprised squeak from the receptionist, probably a foot in the face, neither girl let out a peep. Skana nodded. She had chosen well.

A thick, scaly hand appeared over the edge of her couch and hit the release on her safety straps. Tuk's long snout peered down at her.

"May I help you up, madam?"

"Thanks," Skana said. "What's for lunch?"

Tuk took her by both shoulders and lifted her out of the silkskin cradle as though she weighed no more than a doll.

Good thing he works for me, she thought.

"Omelets, madam. Champagne grapes and fresh strawberries. A light fruity white wine to accompany."

"Nice choice." She smoothed her travel garments. You couldn't go wrong with a silk jersey tunic and an ankle-length skirt over ship boots. She peered at Nile's companions. They each had on a version of the outfit that Nile's crush had been wearing when they saw her on Sparrow Island: a midriff-revealing bandeau top and a petal skirt with an irregular hem that brushed the knees. And ship boots. Not so romantic, but practical.

"Thank you, madam," Tuk said. "I hope you will enjoy it. The cookbot was trained in the very finest Taino hotels."

"I suppose you're having something different."

Tuk closed one small eye.

"I will be dining with the crew so my meal will not distress the guests."

Skana had seen him eat. It didn't bother her, but she appreciated his delicacy.

"Stay in touch," she said.

After lunch, Skana settled down with a bookfile on a silk-upholstered couch in the corner of the common room. The crash cradles had been stored away. They were really comfortable, but too hard to get in and out of in the course of a normal day.

Nile took his companions on a full tour of the *Pelican*. Skana only hoped that he would remember not to show them the hidden cargo holds. The fewer people who knew they were there, the better. You never knew when you had to hide something vital.

An hour or so later, he came in alone, to flop on the matching couch against the adjoining wall to hers.

"Where are they?" she asked.

"Taking some Infogrid time," he said. "I think they were impressed."

"They'd have to be morons not to be impressed," she said, "and we don't hire morons."

"They know what they can post and what they can't, right?" Nile asked, concern giving him a more pugnacious expression than usual. "They can't talk about me."

"Yes, they can, Nile," Skana said, with a patient sigh. She put her book on standby. "You're a private citizen, going on a trip in your private vessel. Anyone who reads their postings is going to think 'lucky you.' The girls can't anticipate anything, like saying that we're going to the Autocracy until we actually get there, but they will get in trouble, and *we* will get in trouble, if they don't put up accurate posts about location."

"I know . . ." Nile looked up at the coffered ceilings. Skana was proud of those. They were patterned after an ancient Earth palace in which every side of every panel, beam, lintel, and wall throughout the building featured a different and intricate painting. When traveling between star systems, you needed plenty of new things to look at. "Nice, Skana."

"Like it?"

"I do. Almost like we were royalty ourselves. I wish . . . I wish *she* could see it."

Skana eyed him seriously.

"She's not your ladylove. In fact, she's back on Keinolt. With any luck, you'll never see her again."

"I couldn't stand that," Nile said, glancing away.

Something in the way he spoke made Skana suspicious.

"You tried to see her." It was not a question. "When?"

"Um. The other night."

Skana sat bolt upright on her couch.

"Are you out of your mind? Where? Did you try to arrange a date? Did you use any of our communications circuits? Her Infogrid public file?"

"No!" Nile protested. He waved a hand. "Never mind. I used some of the merchandise. I thought if she saw me, she would come with me and we could talk."

Skana groaned.

"You tried to meet with her in person? There was a big party in the compound last night. The Edouardo V garden."

"I know," Nile said sulkily. "I tried to get in."

"And that worked out how?" Skana demanded. "Not good, is my guess." She reactivated her tablet and ran over the Infogrid for the night before. "You were spotted. An intruder was seen just inside one of the entrances."

"That wasn't me! I never got in. I was waiting for her just outside the garden. Then there was an explosion, and I took off."

Skana knew all about the explosion. She had sent a few employees in to see if they could X out the lady so Nile would stop being obsessed by her. The bomb had been intended to flush guests out of the garden so the lady could be picked off by a sharpshooter. Too bad she had been hustled to safety in the middle of a horde of friends and security guards. Looked like neither of them had been successful at their nocturnal endeavors.

"Good thing we left town," Skana said, reading down the entries. "Ah. And so is she. She's going traveling with one of her crazy cousins. Good. That'll take her mind off you."

Nile grunted.

"She'd understand if I only got the chance to explain," he said.

"Forget about her," Skana advised. "I hear they're all as dumb as stones anyhow."

A wail burst from the hidden speakers, interrupting Nile's retort. They glanced at each other.

The ship lurched to the right and upwards, pressing them into the cushions of their sofas.

"What was that?" Skana asked. She reached for the in-ship

communications panel in the table beside her couch. "Captain Sigismund, what's going on up there?"

"My apologies, madam!" came the bell-like voice of their pilot. "The shields detected an incoming energy blast!"

"Who's attacking us?" Nile demanded, springing to his feet. The next evasive maneuver sent him flying. He scrambled to his knees and pulled himself into one of the big chairs in the middle of the floor. "Captain, is it an Imperium ship?"

"Attempting to read the signal, sir," she said.

Loud shrieks from the corridor heralded the arrival of Nile's two girlfriends. One was barefoot. They tottered in, tossed from side to side as the *Pelican*'s defense system observed the discharges from the enemy's guns and anticipated where they would pass. The sharp turns indicated the *Pelican* was being bracketed. Tuk appeared in the opposite doorway. He strode to the women and gathered them up under his short, muscular arms. Nile beckoned to him. Tuk dumped them onto his lap.

"What's happening, sir?" the receptionist pleaded.

"It'll be okay," Nile said, gathering them into the oversized chair with him. It was a tight fit for three.

"Prepare for possible impact," Tuk said. Skana swung her legs up onto the sofa and palmed the wall for the emergency harnesses. Tuk seized them when they appeared and fastened her into place.

Just as he did, the ship leaped again.

Boom!

"That was a direct hit," Nile said, his voice hoarse. The girls let out little fearful noises, but didn't scream.

"Are they nuts?" Skana asked. "Tuk, go tell them who we are."

"The pilot is telling them right now," Tuk said, touching the side of his head. Croctoids had no visible ears, so hearing devices were hidden from view, too. His brow ridges went up, and all his teeth showed. He normally sounded mild-mannered, but Skana knew that the cardiac system in his body belonged to a cold-blooded killer. "They challenge us."

"That's it," she said. "Gut them."

Tuk nodded.

"They're Paskals, ma'am! Get into the secure cabin!" He unfastened her straps again and helped her to her feet. She glared at her brother.

"Nile, Paskals attacking! Buckle down!"

Brother and sister hurried into the forward corridor. The concealed door of the safety chamber slid open just long enough for them to enter, then slid shut with a fierce hiss. Two platforms snapped out of the walls.

The crash couches in there were not so fancy, but they were of the most impact-resistant foam known to science. Skana abandoned dignity as she clambered over the deep side of the bathtub-sized recess. The harness sprang over her body like a spiderweb.

A loud grunt and the sound of fibers resonating told her Nile was safe. Then she heard pounding on the door.

"Let us in, Mr. Bertu! Please!"

"What about them?" Nile asked.

"What *about* them?" Skana echoed. "The Paskals must have found out we were traveling this week. Coming out of the jump point, we were an easy target."

"Damn them!" he bellowed. "I told you it was a bad idea to leave home."

Whirring noises drowned out the sounds from outside. Bracing struts inside the door frame turned and locked into place. Intruders could not now penetrate it any more than they could break through the hull plates beside it. The dedicated air supply that was fed by a power source embedded in the walls kicked on. The unit could be jettisoned from a ship under siege. If it wasn't detected and blown up, it and the live contents could survive for weeks until rescued. If she and Nile didn't kill each other first.

"If we just stay put on Keinolt all the time, we're just as vulnerable," Skana said. "You know that as well as I do."

"Paskals! Those scum!"

Skana reached behind the padding near her right shoulder. A projection of what the captain was seeing beamed onto the flat gray ceiling. She spotted the blips of more than one ship, all with Paskal markings.

The Paskals were a rival organization, and fierce competitors with the Bertus and other family-held corporations. Skana admired their tenacity and intelligent application of business practices, but they had resisted a merger on the grounds that anyone who had done that in the past two thousand years had ended up having their businesses picked off one at a time and subsumed. What happened to the other family members involved could never be proved, but they disappeared off the Infogrid.

"Tuk, I must have missed it in the reports," Skana said. "Have we seen somewhere the Paskals are pushing into our territory?"

"They have a new recreational drug on the market in the Leonines," Tuk replied. "PS4. No doubt Blute is cutting into their profits. Limuel Paskal probably hopes that by removing you he can profit in the entire system."

"That is never going to happen," Nile said fiercely. "I want to tear them apart myself!"

"Tuk will see to it you have a survivor to kill," Skana said, calmly, although inside her senses were in turmoil. A fourth ship joined the three she could already see. In spite of Sigismund's expert handling, they didn't stand a chance of outrunning all of them to the next jump point. One ship hovered between the *Pelican* and the return point. There was no escape that way. It looked as if the *Pelican* was outnumbered.

"They're going to attempt boarding," Tuk announced through the speaker system. Skana could hear the girls somewhere near him begging to be put in safe quarters. No time for that.

"Slow down. Let them catch up."

The *Pelican* lurched. Skana was thrown from side to side in her safety couch. The blips grew larger and larger. One of them took the lead. The others surrounded it like the fletching on an arrow.

"Magnetic beams grappling on."

Skana smiled fiercely. "Is the programming ready?"

I have activated it.

"Excellent." Skana relaxed in the cradle and let her head fall back against the enveloping cushion. "Open the hatches."

Their secret weapon was about to claim its first victim.

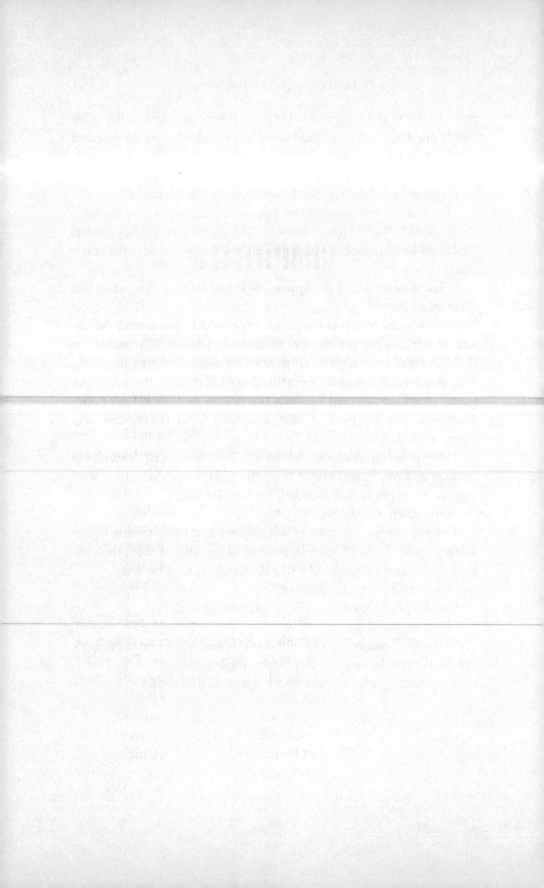

CHAPTER 9

M'Kenna Copper concentrated on the small tablet that was all the technology she or her family was allowed in their dim prison suite. Who knew they had family cells on Partwe?

She never thought in a million years she would have been arrested for any reason, let alone smuggling. They had always had good relationships with the merchants in the Autocracy. She and Rafe were law-abiding to a fault. They would never, never, never have risked their children's lives, let alone their own, on contraband.

Yet, a prison suite was their current home, and had been since their arrest. Two rooms were all they had. Temperature and lighting were out of their control. To her it always felt a little too warm and dry. The glare of the lights from the corridor drew attention to the fact that the lighting in the cells was dimmer than she liked. She felt as though she was hiding in a cupboard away from a threat. That was true enough.

The bunks the Uctu constabulary provided were comfortable enough. Their padding was made so it couldn't be pried away from the platform. It was raised at one end to make a pillow. The blanket fabric was too air-permeable to allow one to suffocate oneself, and too stiff to use as a noose. The walls were metal with a thick resinous coating on them that not only dampened the sounds from the corridor, but prevented the occupants from bashing their skulls in hopes of escape—or death. M'Kenna could see why suicide might be an alternative some might choose instead of official execution. She had looked up the methods the Uctu used. One glance was enough to make sure she code-locked the sites so the kids couldn't open them.

The children slept in one room, she and Rafe in the other. Sanitary facilities were behind an unmovable privacy barrier that prevented others from seeing what was going on behind it, although anyone could hear. They wore bright green prison coveralls day and night. They were taken from their cell for showers once every couple of days, at the same time their coveralls were replaced with clean ones, although some leeway was possible for small children not yet toilet trained. Being able to leave the confines of the cage-fronted cell with Dorna a few times a day helped M'Kenna cope, but it wasn't enough. There was no privacy at all.

Small as the living quarters in their ship were in comparison to a space station or the surface of a planet, at least they were able to stake out parts of that space for themselves, no-go areas that allowed them a morsel of alone-time. That was what kept M'Kenna in particular from committing mariticide or filicide. It was the little things, like the kids bumping into them or each other while playing, or her husband reaching out to touch her when she was thinking. Or M'Kenna stretching out her legs and kicking Rafe by accident. All of them were driving each other crazy. She needed time alone to work back through her memory of where the disaster might have happened. She had a gift for concentration, but it worked only in peace and quiet. There was little of either in the ward. She had to think. She had to!

The truth was, she was baffled. How in the explosive core of Alpha Centauri Five had that war skimmer gotten into their ship? It was impossible! The family had never been away from the ship long enough for anyone to unbolt all those hull plates, penetrate the insulation and protective bladders around that usually stinky tank, drain it, stick the flyer inside, refasten all of the layers around it and rebolt the hull, all without making a sound or setting off any of their alarms. It certainly couldn't have been done with them aboard. Anywhere they had docked ought to have detected interference on that scale.

"It could've been when we went to the circus on Vijay 9," Rafe said, breaking into her reverie. "We were gone all afternoon and half the evening."

"You are not helping," M'Kenna snapped. "In fact, you are unhelping." Her fierce look told him to back off. He did. So did all the kids. They knew when they heard 'Mommy's thinking voice,' there was no appeal. They retreated into their chamber and played together quietly. For a while.

"Let me out of here or I will tear you apart!" bellowed Nuro. He and the rest of the Wichu crew from *Sword Snacks IV* were just up the corridor. So were about half the ships that had left Way Station 46 with the *Entertainer*. They were all in the same boat, so to speak. A death ship.

At least they had been transferred planetside. The air was fresher on Partwe 3, although the chlorine-heavy atmosphere friendly to Uctus was getting to all the outworlders. M'Kenna had complained repeatedly until the warden had increased filtration in the cells. The trouble was, every time an Uctu warder or guard opened a door to the outside, they got another lungful of chlorine. It wasn't enough to kill anyone, but it made the prison smell like a swimming pool. Lerin had developed a worrisome sounding cough from it.

M'Kenna's inner noises were getting the better of her, too. Very few offenses in any nation called for the death penalty. Their court-appointed attorney, a Wichu named Allisjonil Derinket, assured them that most of the laws recited over the in-system relay were overturned on appeal. The trouble was that the crime of which she and the others stood accused was of carrying weapons of war over the borders without government license or permission. They had been caught red-handed. They had no way to prove their innocence. How long before the courts decided if they deserved an appeal? They were waiting to hear that and whether the children could be detached from the responsibility for the crime, leaving only their parents under indictment. M'Kenna would let herself be tortured to death slowly and agonizingly before a live audience if it would save her babies.

The thought of never seeing her children again made her sob out loud. She stifled the noise in the horrid green fabric of her sleeve, but Dorna, always sensitive to M'Kenna's moods, came toddling out of the other room and threw herself into her mother's arms. M'Kenna cuddled the toddler, kissing her wealth of dark curls over and over again. Something had to be done to get the Coppers out of there.

Somebody knew what had happened. She needed evidence. She needed a witness. Somebody had seen something that wasn't right. A file somewhere had the data that proved that skimmer had gone into her ship when she wasn't looking.

Rafe kept the maintenance records. They showed nothing out of the ordinary. He swore up and down that every detail was correct. M'Kenna trusted him. He was the best husband and partner she could have imagined, not to mention efficient, hard-working, shrewd and patient. When he talked her out of her job as a saleswoman for modular domiciles fifteen years before, it had sounded so outrageous to her to spend her life as an interstellar merchant, but his family had done it for centuries, millennia, even. She had been right to trust in him, to tie her life to his among the stars. At his fingertips, he had the experience to know when a ship part was starting to go. Every little wobble in the ship meant something to him, even if they all sounded alike to M' Kenna. If Rafe said there was nothing out of place on his scopes or database, he meant it. That brought her back to an exterior threat. Somebody had targeted her and some of the others.

M'Kenna kept going over the reports over and over again. When could that flitter have been placed in the waste tank? She still found it impossible. But it must have happened at some point, because there were other unexplained problems with the ship. Lerin had complained about the taste of the water. It turned out that their filtration system had gone almost completely on the fritz. If they had not been close to Nacer, they all might have died in transit of salmonella poisoning or another waterborne illness from lack of sanitation. They were all feeling pretty sick, though. It wasn't only the strain of their situation, although that was bad enough. She could not stop smelling the chlorine in the atmosphere. It was almost as if they had not had their habilitation therapy, but all of them had had it years ago. Maybe the sanitation problem had undone all the injections and things, knocked out their enhanced immune systems.

She ran the files up and back on the tablet again and again. When could someone have gotten close enough to open their tank without them detecting it? She went through Rafe's pristine logs again.

Before arriving at Way Station 46, the *Entertainer* had called in to see a few of their best customers and three suppliers, all in systems outside the Core Worlds on the way to the frontier. Normally M'Kenna would have said she could trust those people as far as she could throw them—but she could still trust them. She would also find it pretty outrageous that any of those vendors had an interest in military vehicles. Over the years she and Rafe had shed connections with people who cheated them one way or another, putting warnings on the Infogrid to protect fellow merchants, as they all did. Rising tides lifted all boats, and a hole in the tub made them all sink.

So where was the weak link? It seemed crazy to suspect any of their long-time customers or suppliers, but it was just as outrageous to suspect an ordinary space merchant family. Still, she was in jail and they weren't. She needed to find out who was to blame.

She added names and dates of last contact to the file of enquiries that needed to be made, to hand over to their attorney. M'Kenna was desperate to ask those contacts herself, to ask what she hoped were the right questions, and ask to see security videos of the docking facilities on the stations that circled those worlds. But she couldn't. She was stuck on Partwe 3. For maybe the rest of her life.

But what about the other merchants? That gave her something new to chew on. Those ships were not likely to have been anywhere together until they were all stuck on Way Station 46. *Had* they all stopped at one particular station during the last few months? She would have to see if she could compare the *Entertainer*'s logs with *Space Snacks* or the others. Or if the attorney could do so. It was such a pain in the afterthrusters not to be able to go and ask questions herself!

A movement out of the corner of her eye caught her attention. Lerin stood a couple of paces away, bobbing up and down impatiently. She forced herself to smile at him.

"What is it, baby?" she asked.

"Mama, I want to play *Dozer Ships*," he begged. "Please? I'm booooored!"

M'Kenna looked at the time in the corner of the tablet screen.

"Not now, honey. Hey! It's time for lessons."

He wrinkled his nose.

"Lessons! Why do we need lessons if we're all going to die?"

M'Kenna grabbed him and crushed him to her, bruising his nine-year-old dignity. He fought loose, but not before she saw the fear in his eyes.

"Nobody is going to die, sweetheart," she said firmly. "So you still need spatial geometry and calculus, so you can become a pilot like your daddy and your auntie Siff." She opened the lesson plan folder and locked all the others, especially the game folder. Long time since she studied the basics of calculus and navigation. Math was ideal for learning how to think logically. "Here. You get started. There's two screens of homework problems. When you're done with them, I'll quiz you. Then you can quiz me."

He went along with her effort to keep the mood light.

"Bet I get more right than you!"

"We'll see about that." But she surrendered the tablet. Lerin grabbed it and raced into the children's room.

Rafe sat on the bench that doubled as his bunk with his long legs outstretched and ankles crossed. His arms were folded tight against his chest.

"Are you awake?" she whispered.

He opened his eyes.

"Yes. Daydreaming of being anywhere but here," he said. "Are you all right?"

She stopped herself just in time from snapping. He had the long-haul spacer's gift of being able to accept long delays without reacting. Her shorter fuse marked her as a born groundling. But she was learning.

"I'm okay. I'm worried about the kids. I don't care what happens to me, but I want them safe and out of here! I haven't heard from your family yet if they can come and get them."

"Dad or Aunt Libby will get back to us. They'll probably hit the same snag when they try to cross the frontier. Better make some long-term arrangements here for the kids if . . ." Rafe didn't finish the sentence. He didn't have to. They talked the grim possibilities over and over after the children had gone to sleep.

The front of the cell lit up red. That was a signal to anyone near the barred wall to move away, or be burned by the glowing metal. It meant they had a visitor. The door slid open about a meter, no farther.

The bulky figure covered in thick white fur who marched into the cell was both a welcome and an intrusive presence. Allisjonil Derinket had arrived. Like most Wichus, he had a no-nonsense personality. He had no time or patience for pleading, begging, complaints or explosions. He was capable of exploding pretty loudly himself. He and M'Kenna had gotten into fierce arguments over the last few weeks that needed to be broken up by Rafe. She tried to keep her temper with him, since he was their court-appointed attorney. The Uctus understood that foreign defendants would find it easier to trust a lawyer who came from the other side of the border. M'Kenna would have preferred a human, maybe even a Croctoid, to the brusque Wichu. But by the remarks on the Infogrid, he was a good and savvy advocate. The two slender Uctu guards who accompanied him checked the visitor's badge on his chest, and stood sentry until the bars closed behind him.

He took a tablet, same model as their prison-issued gear, from the cross-body harness he wore over his furry shoulders.

"Got some news for you," he said.

"When will the hearing be?"

"I don't know yet," Allisjonil said, turning an annoyed glance to her. "I obtained a stay until we can investigate all your connections. You have that ready?"

M'Kenna sprang up and strode into the children's room. All four of her kids sat on the floor around the glowing rectangle, playing a game of Pin the Part on the Ship Engine. She leaned into their midst and picked up the tablet. Her four-year-old son wailed a protest and tried to grab it back.

"Sorry, kids. I need this now."

"We understand, Mama," Nona said. She gathered the two small children to her. Lerin sat like a statue.

M'Kenna brought up the file from the locked folder and transferred it to Allisjonil's computer. He opened it and scanned the text.

"Right. I'll look into these." He turned his big, round eyes to the Coppers. "Meantime, you're getting out of here."

Rafe grabbed her hand and squeezed it.

"Really? Yay!" M'Kenna cheered. "Allie, you're the best!"

"They're releasing us? They're letting us post bail?" Rafe demanded. The children appeared in the doorway, their eyes wide at the outburst. Allisjonil waved a dismissive hand.

"Go away, kids," he said sternly.

"But . . ." Lerin protested.

"Shut up," Allisjonil said. "Go away. We're still talking. If your parents wanted you to listen, they would have told you."

One by one, the children backed into their room. Lerin was the last to go, his eyes full of reproach. The Wichu waited until he was gone, then turned back to the Coppers.

"Are you stupid? You're not being released. Have you had a trial yet? You're being transferred to Dilawe. No one stands trial for a capital offense on Partwe. They don't do executions here. It raises too many questions about impartial witnesses."

"That doesn't help us!" M'Kenna protested. Allisjonil snorted impatiently.

"I can't do anything about that! You're the ones who committed the crime."

"Some attorney!" Rafe snarled. He flung himself away from them and paced the three steps to the end of the cell.

"We did *not* commit a crime," M'Kenna said, controlling herself with difficulty. "We are being framed. Set up."

"By who?" Allisjonil asked.

"I don't know who! When I can figure out how they did it, you can find out who. That's your job!"

"My job is to defend you, not investigate anything. For that, you pay extra." Allisjonil checked another file on his tablet. "You got the schedule of fees, right?"

"Yes!"

"Good. That includes how much you have to pay for me to accompany you to Dilawe. You're splitting the fare with three other groups of defendants, so it won't be too bad."

The Coppers were not satisfied with that, but there was nothing more that they could do about it, either.

"What about our kids?" M'Kenna asked.

"No judgment about that yet. I'll let you know if the appeal goes through. Meantime, they stay with you."

"What about our ship?" Rafe asked. Allisjonil shrugged.

"It's being transported, too. It'll be put into secure dock until after the trial."

"And then?"

The Wichu shrugged, making his shoulder fur flip up and settle down again. "If you win, you get it back. If not, it'll be auctioned off to cover court costs. That's the way they do things here."

M'Kenna, aghast at the feelings inside her, couldn't say a word. She sat down heavily on the berth, clutching the tablet to her chest.

"That's all you have for us?" Rafe asked, his voice hoarse.

"That's it. I'll be back when you get transferred." Allisjonil tapped the badge on his chest. The door at the end of the corridor slid open noisily, accompanied by a blast of chlorine-scented air. The two guards marched to the door. One activated a handheld control to open the bars while the other covered the Coppers with his wide-range stunner. Allisjonil squeezed out. Without a backward glance, he strode away. They heard his voice further down the hall, as he greeted yet another of his unhappy clients.

Nona appeared in the opening between the rooms. M'Kenna met her eyes. Nona had tears running down her face. She did her best not to listen when the attorney visited. Why would she? She had never heard anything good. She extended a trembling hand to her mother.

M'Kenna rose and rushed to her. Nona threw herself into her arms. M'Kenna held her close, murmuring soft words into her daughter's hair. How could anybody think that they could wrench something so precious away from her? Her eldest child, almost a woman herself but never getting a chance to have a life of her own, not yet? Nona pressed herself close, her eyes squeezed shut. The half-moons of long black lashes gleamed with tears. M'Kenna kissed each eyelid. At a small sound from the children's room, they broke apart. The younger three sat huge-eyed on the floor.

"You all right?" Akila asked, looking from one to the other.

"We're fine, honey," M'Kenna assured him, wishing it was true.

"How about a story?" Nona asked, her voice bright. She never let herself betray her fears to Dorna or Akila. Lerin had obviously heard everything. His face had gone as hard as a stone. M'Kenna went to embrace him, too, but he ducked out of reach. He retreated to the far corner and sat on the floor with his knees up. In a way, M'Kenna was glad. She wanted them to understand, even if it wasn't just or fair. But he needed to know. She wished she could reassure him, but she couldn't. She could not even promise him they would be able to stay together, because she didn't know. Better if they created their own defenses. They might need to protect themselves one day, if M'Kenna and Rafe couldn't.

She stuffed the idea down deep in her mind, underneath deliberately hopeful thoughts. They would get out of there! Soon!

"A story sounds like a great idea, darling," M'Kenna said. She offered the tablet to Nona.

"No, mama, you pick," Akila said.

M'Kenna hesitated, then decided they all needed some cuddle time. She squeezed in among them on the floor, then requested access to their ship's personal files via the tablet's one available circuit. It took a long time for the computer system to grant permission, but allowed her to open the kids' library.

"Pick a long one," Akila said, with one elbow on her thighs.

"Why not?" M'Kenna said. Scrolling along the book covers gave her a small measure of comfort. For a little while, she could pretend they were all together in the mess room aboard the *Entertainer*, sailing in between ports of call. She fought down the feelings of resentment that they *weren't* out there.

Their government ought to have their back! When she could get the unit to herself again, M'Kenna planned to send another message to every single official she could think of, trying to get an investigation going, but mainly to get them out of there!

Dorna didn't care what she read, as long as she could sit against her mother's side with her thumb in her mouth. M'Kenna chose a chapter book from among the other three's favorites.

"Voice or text," the tablet inquired.

"Text," M'Kenna said.

The age-old two-dee images began to scroll across the screen, with text in a very readable typeface at the bottom nearest her. She put the tablet out on her lap as far as she could and still see the print, so the bright pictures were visible to all of them, including Lerin.

"Once upon a time, seven bears lived in a cottage on a broad, green hill," M'Kenna read. "A royal palace was up the hill from them, at the very top, and the river was down the hill. People of all kinds came and went between them. The bears kept ten thousand bees in ten hives behind their cottage . . . ."

Before she got to the next illustration, the one that showed the bears wearing veiled hats and carrying square boxes with steam coming out of them, she felt pressure against her other side. She glanced down. Lerin had come to cuddle up next to her. She put her other arm around him.

"Tablet, voice instruction activate."

"Acknowledged," the device said, pleasantly.

"Turn the page."

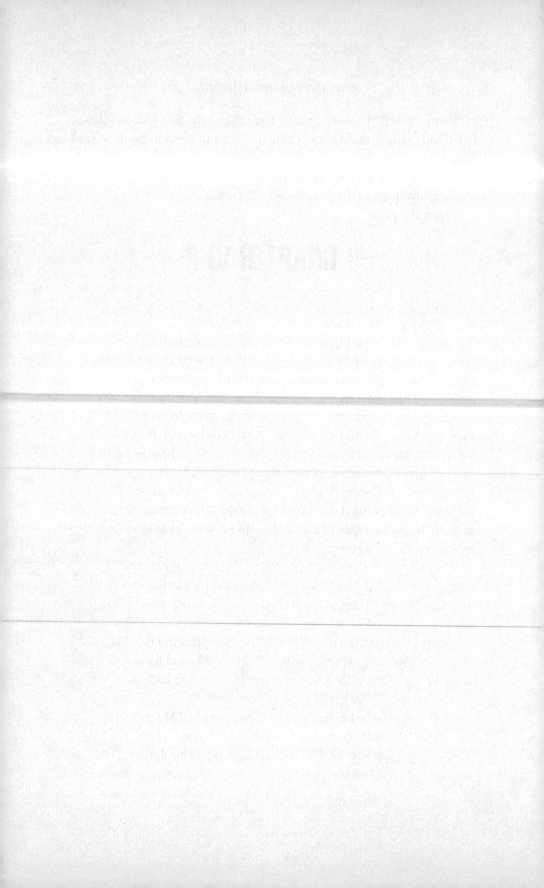

CHAPTER 10

As the *Rodrigo* was a serving military ship, accommodations were not lush. My cabin was set out as I preferred, but most of the time, when the scout was employed elsewhere by the Imperium Navy, it held two junior officers, not one. Still, I had extra storage and floor space, which cousin Jil commandeered for her excess luggage. In no manner did I expect her to leave her other bags in the hold where they belonged, but it was tedious always to be tripping over sprawling duffels full of cosmetics and fripperies. Jil even made an attempt to occupy the cabin itself, instead of the small guest quarters below to which she had been assigned, but I pointed out that I was among the serving officers, and at their beck, whereas she and the others were nearer the bathing facilities and had some privacy.

"You don't want us waking you up if there is a catastrophe, do you? I find it a bore that Mother insists that I take part in the exercises."

"No," Jil acknowledged, though grudgingly. "That would be an utter calamity. Very well."

I did point out the excellence of the soundproofing in between the cabins, so nothing except announcements intended for them would pass through the walls. On the other hand, when hatches were left open, one could hear the giggling everywhere.

I felt myself to be bridging two different worlds. My cousin and her friends represented the majority of my life to date.

Still, the addition of five women changed the dynamics of life among the crew of the *Rodrigo*. As they were civilian guests, we acceded to their choices of entertainment. Therefore, the large screens in the common room were endlessly running the latest gossip programs. Now, I am as fond of knowing who was with who and what was what, but I felt it lowered the dignity of my ship.

Still, I could not help but feel wistful as I passed through the mess hall, seeing the five of them seated at the oval table in the middle of the room, rapt upon the love life of this celebrity or that, or the current gossip regarding an affair being carried on by an 'unnamed member of the aristocracy,' as the chicly dressed reporter described, whom I deduced from context was Xan. I could have been part of this happy scene. Instead, I had *duties*. I confess I felt rather hard done by.

I ordered up a cup of coffee from the robot server.

"Good morning, Lord Thomas," it chirruped, as my favorite porcelain mug clicked into the steadying bracket placed below the dispenser spigot.

"Good morning, NG-903," I said, reading the designation on the small metal seal above the speaker port. "Shouldn't you call me Lieutenant Kinago?"

"If you wish, my lord," it replied, over the whir of its internal roaster-and-grinder combination. "But when I worked in the compound as the cleanerbot in the workshop owned by your father, Lord Rodrigo, I became ingrained in the habit of using noble honorifics. We have spoken before many times."

"You're *Angie?*" I asked, delighted to meet an old acquaintance. "What are you doing here?"

"Work exchange program," Angie replied. A stream of fragrant black liquid trickled into my cup. I inhaled gratefully. "The chance to serve aboard a naval vessel interested me, and the coincidence of finding an LAI who worked on a vessel of the same name as my usual employer made it appear as if this opportunity was meant to be. And I appreciated the chance to serve you again, my lord."

"Well, well," I said, taking the steaming beverage from the cradle. "This is nice, to come across an old friend. I fear my father will miss you."

"My locum tenens is a most efficient server," Angie said. "Lord Rodrigo may come to prefer DNS-502A to me."

"I very much doubt that. My father is a loyal soul." I glanced over my shoulder at my cousin, and dropped my voice. "Angie, I have some delicacies on board that I would appreciate you helping me to safeguard. Everyone will be welcome to enjoy them when I bring each forth in turn, but I prefer to be the dispenser of bounty rather than finding a scatter of crumbs in an otherwise empty pantry. My cousin has a tendency to fall upon such treats as caviar and exotic fruits as one of the ancient breed of locusts would, leaving nothing behind but ruin and regret."

"Understood, Lord Thomas," Angie said. "Are there perhaps two or three foodstuffs to which they may help themselves at will? That would divert any resentment that they cannot have access to it all."

"Why, yes," I said, surprised. "That is a very clever stratagem. My compliments on picking up on such a subtle point of psychology."

"Your father holds forth now and then on strategy," Angie said, placidly. A small paddle covered by a sleeve of dampened cloth smelling of cleaning fluid emerged from a slot below the dispenser. It swabbed the cup bracket clean, then vanished into its niche.

"He does? To whom?"

"To whoever is there to listen, my lord. I and my fellow LAIs are the most frequent recipients of his wisdom. He has provided me with an excellent education in understanding human nature. I owe being able to qualify for this position to him."

I was silent for a moment in admiration for my paternal unit. Lord Commander Rodrigo Park Kinago had been a most promising young officer in the navy, or so I have been told. He was a hero who performed many daring feats on behalf of the Imperium, culminating with a dangerous covert mission in which he saved hundreds of lives during a deep space battle. The father that I and my siblings adored was a sweet-natured potterer and part-time inventor who hardly seemed aware of his surroundings. The mental disconnection was a result of his injuries following that space battle. To my shame, I had been ignorant of those facts until comparatively recently. Like most of my relatives, I had come to think of him as "Poor, dear Rodrigo." It was in tribute to my father that I maintained my connection to the navy and the service of the mysterious Mr. Frank.

"The sweet-spice puffs," I said, without further prompting. "The green Leonine wines. And half of the Colvarin cheese. Hold back the rest unless I so direct you."

"As you wish, sir," Angie said. "Those will be left accessible. I shall make it look as if your cousin and her friends have sidestepped my security programming to attain them."

I laughed. "Oh, you are very good, my friend. I look forward to exchanging stories of my father with you."

In a much cheerier mood, I went to sit beside Jil at the oval table.

Banitra scooted down the bench a trifle to make room for me. She steadied my coffee cup until I was settled.

"Oh, Thomas," Jil said, as though noticing me for the first time. "Good. You can be the sixth. We want to play Snap Dragons. I thought we would have to play with one of the AIs, but you will do."

"Of course," I said. "Do you have your own cards, or do you need me to provide a deck?"

"Oh, both," Hopeli said, beaming at me. "Let's play with a double deck. Then we can invoke the alternate rules. That will be much more fun."

"I hope you will not take it amiss when I beat all of you," I said. Most of my games and sports equipment had been transferred to the caches in the common room, so I had but to open a hatch in the wall to retrieve my Snap Dragon deck and the earpieces used for private negotiation with one's fellow players. The game, part role-play, part chance, had become a craze among my circle of relatives in Taino.

"You haven't got a chance!" Jil said, laughing.

"We'll see about that," I said.

We put the cards on the table and sat back to watch them fold themselves together. Snap Dragon decks, like many of the current games, contained infinitely small dynamic engines that allowed them to shuffle themselves. I had introduced programming into mine that did not alter the core honesty profile, but did cause my half of the deck to parade itself around, trailing pairs and trios that fanned out, snapped together, arched and collapsed like a party of cardboard acrobats.

Marquessa gaped openly at their antics.

"Is this a custom game?" she asked. "Something I can order for my clients?"

"No," I said, pleased. "All my own work."

"Thomas has so many things he would rather do than useful labor," Jil said.

Momentarily stung at the accusation, I opened my mouth to defend myself. After all, what was I doing on a warship bound for a complicated investigation? But I smiled. Jil knew nothing of that, nor should she.

"Indeed, that is the case," I said, languidly. "But when I acquire a fresh enthusiasm, I pursue it with all my heart."

"Very admirable," Hopeli said.

"And is programming cards to dance your current enthusiasm?" Banitra asked, with a flirtatious lift of her long, dark eyelashes.

"Not at all," I said. I collected my hand from the table where the decks had left it. "In fact, my current studies might be of interest to all of you. I am delving into superstitions."

"What kind of superstitions?" Sinim asked, her lovely eyes alight with curiosity.

"Every kind of small behavior that a person exhibits that is intended to influence fate," I said. "There are so many. Take, for example, the stricture that one should never step on a crack in the pavement lest it cause pain to one's maternal unit. How one should affect the other is a matter of superstition, not reality. There is no cause and effect."

"Well," Banitra said, with a tiny smile, "your mother might just be hiding underneath the paving stones, and if you walk on them, you will break her back!"

"As if!" Hopeli said. "The paving stones would have done it first!"

"Exactly," I said. "But we are not looking for direct causality here, but indirect. The intervention of unseen powers appears to change one's luck, if you will, but I have not found one yet that achieves a level of scientific rigor."

"Thomas tells fortunes," Jil said.

"How marvelous," Banitra said, leaning closer to me. She turned her large, dark eyes up into mine. "Will you tell me mine?"

"Of course," I said. I put my viewpad on the table. "Open numerology program."

The small device clicked and whirred as the correct colorful graphic appeared on its screen.

"Enter Banitra Savarola Wilcox," I said.

On the screen appeared a series of numbers: 2159291 11419631 593366. A second line, then a third and a fourth, appeared beneath it:

29 + 26 + 32 = 87
8 + 7 = 15
1 + 5 = 6

"Oh, but that's just a program!" Banitra protested.

"Ah, yes, but the magic comes when I interpret its findings," I said, pointing at the first line. "There is a distinctly personal element that is part and parcel of this practice. You see, all the letters of your name add up to a total of eighty-seven."

"And what is six?"

"One of the very best name numbers," I said warmly. "It stands for dependability, wisdom and integrity."

Banitra burst into shrieks of laughter. She grabbed my hand with both of hers. She had a surprisingly firm grip.

"Imagine me, dependable! Oh, what would my father say? He never knows where I am from one day to the next!"

"Do you see?" I said. "That is why I don't rely upon superstitions."

"Then why study them?" Jil asked.

"Because they are fun to investigate," I said. "They often have striking origins. I am enjoying discovering the source of ones that have come down through the ages unexamined by those who invoke them daily."

"Me next! Me next!" Sinim cried.

"There, now," I said, smiling at them. "I have just proved to you that there's no substance in it, but you still want your turn at the mystic's table."

Sinim's name number, once I added in the rest of her noble family nomenclature, worked out to seven. She was very pleased at its psychic and magical overtones. Oddly enough, both Hopeli and Marquessa also had names that equaled seven.

Marquessa held out a trembling hand. Her eyes were huge with wonder.

"It means we were all supposed to be together," she said. "That's . . . that's amazing."

"What about mine?" Jil asked.

"What names are you most attached to?" I asked. "Like me, you have a wealth of middle and family names."

She waved a vague hand. "Just a few. It's so tedious to write them all out."

So, I instructed my viewpad to calculate against "Jil Loche Nikhorunkorn."

"Eight. The number of great wealth."

Jil looked pleased. "Well, of course it is."

"What about you?" Banitra asked. "I am sure yours is just as interesting."

I hated to reveal it, because it just came across as bragging. "Nine," I said, hoping I seemed modest when I said it. "The number of great power."

"But as you say," Jil said, wrinkling her nose. "There's nothing to all this."

"Of course not," I agreed.

"I knew it," Banitra said, tucking her hand into my elbow. "I could tell you were a man who could get things done."

Her grasp was soft, but it felt like a manacle pinioning my limb. I hesitated to move. She seemed harmless, but I felt suddenly as wary as the proverbial cat surrounded by threatening furniture. While it was not uncommon to encounter a person who communicated through tactile means, it did appear that Banitra, at least, was setting her cap for me. And while I did not condemn cap-setters in general, I objected to them being aimed in my general direction.

I began to rise and reached clumsily for my coffee cup.

"I had better get about my duties, or Lieutenant Plet will chide me," I said, in a confidential manner, though I knew perfectly well my words could be heard on the bridge through the interior communication system. Plet would be annoyed and amused at my statement.

"Oh, must you go?" Hopeli asked. "We were just going to play cards!"

"I have no wish to excite comment on my behavior," I said. "My mother and all."

"Lieutenant Plet wouldn't tell on you, would she?" Marquessa asked, shocked.

"She would have no choice," I said, with a helpless lift of my shoulders.

"Lieutenant Plet would have no reason to complain if you carried on your duties here, my lord," Parsons said, appearing suddenly by my side. I controlled myself heroically to keep from jumping. His materialization caused the ladies to burst into fits of giggles.

"Really?" I asked, with a lift of one eyebrow. Parsons retorted by elevating two eyebrows. Since I could scarcely best a move like that, I furthered my inquiry. "What may I do to keep her ire from falling upon me?" I shot meaningful looks in the direction of the ladies, particularly Banitra and Sinim, and hoped that for once his impressive powers of mind-reading would be used for good, not evil.

My silent plea was not in vain. Without changing expression whatsoever, Parsons removed his own viewpad from his belt.

"I have files for you to study before our first stop at Way Station 46," he said, "but many that must be mastered before arriving in the Autocracy."

"Bring them on!" I said, relieved that I was going to have to study. It took me out of the admiring gaze of the ladies who saw themselves as potential future mates. The fact was not lost on me that I would need to learn how to keep them at arm's length without exciting comment.

"Oh, Thomas," Jil chided me. "Reading files! That makes you look so respectable."

I lowered my head. "You needn't be so harsh, cousin."

She touched my arm. "I didn't mean to tease. Aunt Tariana must have been very angry with you."

"You don't know the half of it," I said, leaning forward to exude a confidential air. "In fact, she insisted that I . . ."

"Hem!" Parsons clearing his throat could have brought a raging waterfall to an apologetic halt.

"Well, I mustn't tell tales," I said, sitting back hastily.

"No, indeed, sir."

"And which files do you prefer that I review?" I asked, returning the conversation to the subject at hand. After all, he was saving my life, matrimonially speaking.

Parsons touched the viewpad. Images sprang up on mine.

"Regarding the Autocrat herself, Visoltia. Before we arrive, it would be prudent for you to gain knowledge of her thought processes and interests. As she holds the same office as your cousin, the Emperor, it behooves you to avoid causing distress or offense."

"I am ahead of you there, Parsons," I said, unable to prevent smugness from infecting my smile. "The Autocrat, Visoltia, posts often on her Infogrid file, though the Uctu do not seem to be as strict about required posting as here in the Imperium. I have been reading her output daily. She's a most interesting young soul. Did you know that her mother was elderly when she was born, and passed away when Visoltia was an infant? She was raised by her father. I know what that means. She was actually in the hands of a raft of servants. But I think they were good for her. She sounds quite normal, really."

"Are you reading her file in the original language?"

"Not strictly. Everything is translated, though of course I do understand fluent Uctu. My spoken language is a bit behind my comprehension, though."

"At present, you have time to work on improving it," Parsons said.

"But I have a translator on my viewpad," I protested.

"It would be insulting to Her Serenity if you did not speak fluently to her in her own tongue. Naturally, she speaks perfect Imperium Standard, but you will be in her court. Therefore, as a petitioner, you must put all effort on your side of your appeal. Otherwise, it would seem arrogant."

"I wouldn't *think* of causing a calamity," I said, chastened. I checked with my Tarot card program on my viewpad, and requested a single-card reading. The Star. A world will open up to me if I study the language. "Redius can help me to learn it."

"He will not have the facility of native speech," Parsons pointed out. "He is Imperium-born."

"What about *Ya!*" Jil asked. "That's all in Uctu."

"Marvelous idea," I said, warmly. "I will catch up on the episodes I have missed, and they will aid me in learning fluent modern Uctu. I shall immerse myself, watching as many series as I can between now and landing upon Dilawe. And you can be part of my education, Jil."

"I already understand Uctu," she protested. "I love *Ya!*"

"But you don't *speak* it fluently, either," I pointed out. "Don't let a little thing like a verbal faux pas destroy your chance to become an intimate of the leader of another entire empire." I put the matter as temptingly as possible. "And to bargain in the shops, like they do in Kotirus Street on the show? You could come away with a new dress for a single credit. Remember how delighted Fratila was when she bought that formal outfit?"

"When you put it like that, how could I refuse?" Jil said. "It'll be a contest."

"To the fluency?"

"Of course!" Jil said, going eye to eye with me. "What'll you bet?"

"What do you want?"

She smiled slyly. "Your crystal ball."

I admit it: my mouth dropped open.

"But you are not a student of the occult arts," I protested. "And besides, Parsons made me leave it at home."

Jil pouted.

"But it's pretty. I want to put it on my dressing table. I would look at it every day."

I would have missed it, so it was a good item to use as stakes. I nodded. Such a goad would make me work my hardest.

"You are on, my cousin. No cheating, no viewpads, nothing to assist you. Pure conversational Uctu. Redius shall be the judge."

I was not worried about winning and retaining my precious crystal. Jil did have a natural flair for languages, but I counted upon her becoming too bored to study. Yet, it would not matter in the slightest if she became more fluent than I. It was all in the service to the Imperium.

"It's a deal," she said. She put out a hand, and I took it.

And thus began the marathon. *Ya!* became the soundtrack of our travels between Keinolt and rendezvousing with the *Bonchance*. We watched episodes together. We watched them in our separate quarters. *Ya!* accompanied us on our physical fitness regimens and during mealtimes. The only points at which I did not have a season's worth to hand were during sleep and when Parsons chose to drop by and request a report. For some reason, my viewpad ceased to function in any useful manner when he was nearby. I suspected a devious device furnished by our friend Mr. Frank had been secreted about his person, but it was not in my remit, nor even at the reach of my most daring, to seek it out. Redius, Jil and I spent our free time poring over the transcripts of past shows and discussing the plots, our use of Uctu words and phrases increasing daily. I even began to translate my daily horoscope readings into Uctu. I made my immersion as complete as I could without compromising clarity—or interfering with my devotion to my occult studies. One never knew when a peek at the infinite might come in handy.

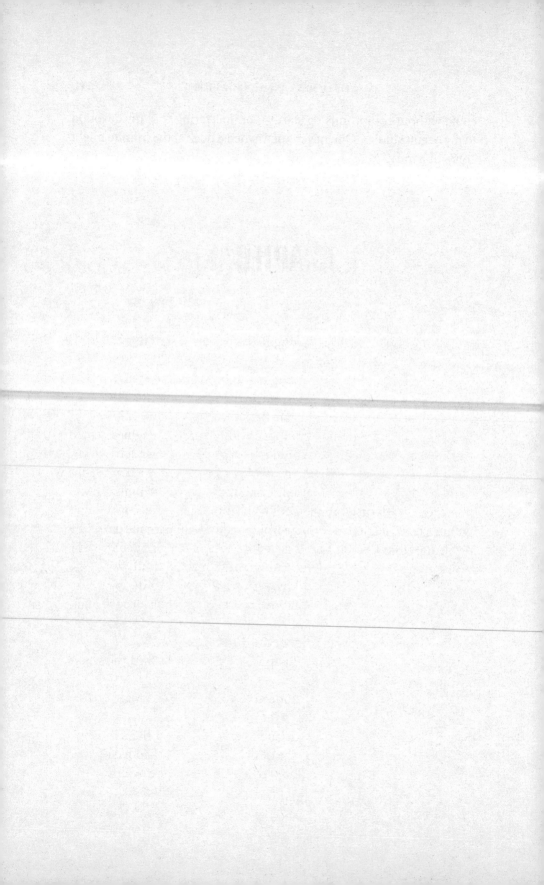

CHAPTER 11

"*Dila'entha an?*" I asked, following Redius through the crew corridors of the *Bonchance*.

"*An thale*," Redius said, pointing to a door. He switched his tail back and forth in excitement. I felt much the same emotion. It always excited my curiosity to investigate the workings of a new ship.

My small scout, though equipped with ultradrive engines, would suffer undue wear and tear should it be expected to make the journey to the border by itself. Instead, the *Rodrigo* would occupy a berth in the flight bay of the carrier *Bonchance*, and my crew would bunk in with the carrier's ordinary complement while the larger vessel conveyed us within a few days' journey to the frontier. It was almost nine days after departing from Keinolt that Oskelev settled the *Rodrigo* gently in the echoing landing bay among individual fighters, scout ships and corvettes. We were welcomed by a lieutenant commander who gave us a brisk but thorough orientation briefing and set us loose to make ourselves at home. So to speak.

I palmed the panel at the door lintel and peered in.

"No," I said. "I must have misspoken. I thought I asked you where my quarters were, not yours."

"Grammar correct. Yours indeed," Redius replied. "Mine Nesbitt shares alongside." He nodded to the next door.

I studied the chamber with a jaundiced eye. A single bunk had been made up, though I could see the outline of a second bed base folded into the wall opposite. A floor-to-ceiling hatch the width of my shoulders stood open to receive my personal possessions. But it was no exaggeration to say that I could stretch out my arms and with a single sidestep either way, touch the walls of the chamber. I admit my arms are long, but the cabin was definitely on the small side. It measured less than two-thirds the size of my cabin aboard the *Rodrigo*. My scout had been constructed with me in mind. Its quarters were more generous, along the lines of the *White Star*, the in-system vessel that I and my relatives had served aboard during our Academy training. (Since only members of the imperial house were in our class, it might be excused that we were given more comforts than the average commoners who were not used to similar luxuries.) Still, it was a shock to expect to wedge myself into so small a container.

Even more by contrast, I had just come from escorting my cousin and her entourage to their quarters. Those pleasant domiciles were in the guest area, not far from the hydroponics gardens, a dedicated break room and the nursery crèche. Each lady was given a chamber to herself, with hygienic facilities shared between each two cabins. There were no other guests on board beside them, so all the amenities were theirs alone to enjoy. Those bedchambers were easily three times the size of the cabin I was expected to occupy, in spite of being granted single occupancy instead of double. In Jil's case, and those of our distant relations, I would not have had it any other way. Still, I took it a trifle hard not to be placed similarly.

At least the bed was comfortable and the cabin spotless. I could not discern a single dust mote out of place. A sink with a large mirror stood in one corner, along with a fold-out booth containing a sonic cleanser. The latter was only to be used in need of haste or chemical contamination requiring isolation. Bathing and sanitary facilities were close by, across from Anstruther's cabin. I realized that nearly all of those in active service to the Imperium Navy lived in quarters like this, but I thought some exception could have been made in deference to my rank.

It took only moments to stow the contents of the standard case I was permitted in the closet. I spruced myself up before the room's mirror, then answered the tap at my door.

"Glad together," Redius said, showing the tip of his tongue.

"As am I," I said, heroically subduing a sigh. I consulted my newly downloaded housing chart. Anstruther and Oskelev were together beyond Redius's quarters. All of our quarters were on the same corridor. Plet had a single on the other side of mine. As if invoking her name caused her to appear, she emerged from her chamber and came to join us.

"Are you settled, sir?" Plet asked.

"Well and truly," I said. "Though it's a trifle cramped. Our last guest occupancy was on a much more spacious vessel."

"The *Wedjet* is Admiral Podesta's flagship," Plet reminded me, with the same toneless voice I might have heard from my viewpad's LAI. " It is also the newest of the destroyer class. The *Bonchance* is thirty years older and part of the carrier class."

"I do know that," I said. "I studied the floor plans. I simply had no notion that I would be disposed down here in the smaller cabins."

"But floor plans of naval vessels are not available to civilians," Plet said, then the perfect ivory of her cheeks tinted ever so slightly with red.

I smiled, a trifle self-deprecatingly. "I can't help it if my mother's passwords are so easy to guess," I said.

At the sound of our voices, our fellows emerged from their cabins.

"Where is Commander Parsons?" Anstruther asked, glancing over my shoulder as if to find my mysterious aide-de-camp a pace behind me. I offered a magnificent shrug in return.

"Where Parsons is disposed, I have no idea. For all I knew, he sleeps upside down like a bat somewhere within the ventilation system. We will see him when he chooses to allow us to see him, and not a moment before. In the meanwhile, I shall catch up on my Infogrid updates. I fear I have let them slip the last week."

"No, sir," Plet said, in that irritating fashion she had of contradicting me. "Our crew has been ordered to report to the senior officer in Maintenance. That is our duty for the duration of our passage to the frontier."

"Curse it, Plet, that's no way for a gentleman of my rank to spend my time!" I said. "Nor is it fit for my highly-trained crew to paint what doesn't move and salute what does."

"Review your instructions," Plet said, imperturbably. "You will see our rota."

I brought out my viewpad and clicked upon the message that was pulsing red with official impatience.

"Orders different now," Redius said, peering over my shoulder.

I glanced down at the entry. Was I mistaken at my first reading? My duties, listed as belonging to Kinago, T., Second Lieutenant, were to be carried out in "'laboratory, hydroponics."

"Well, that is a good deal more pleasant," I said. "I would welcome duty in those lovely gardens. Wouldn't you all prefer that?"

"Not for me, sir," Nesbitt confided, looking a little embarrassed. "I have hay fever."

In any case, Nesbitt did not need to attend infirmary for anti-allergy treatment. Ship's bells sounded, indicating that it was time for mess. Crew members wearing the insignia of our host vessel began to appear out of cabin doors and head for the lifts. We joined the throng. I realized that I had not allowed my viewpad to download the correct shiptime schedule, and followed along with the mob.

Crew on duty aboard a working warship had their day essentially divided into four portions. The first and most important was the work shift, eight hours, followed by first rest period. Formal mess was at the beginning of this period. What time was left following the meal was for personal use before the sleep shift. The fourth was the second rest period, during which one prepared for the day, socialized a trifle, and undertook personal chores. A ship typically divided its crew into three contiguous work shifts. The rest periods were designed to be sacrificed during enemy action or emergency, for greatest overlap of personnel.

I was most intimately familiar with the mess hall aboard the *Wedjet*, which featured a head table at which its master, Admiral Podesta, had sat surveying his flag crew with an eagle-like eye. The rest of the room was filled by round tables, waited upon by both serverbots and living staff. As the *Bonchance* was not a flag-ranked vessel, serverbots were the order of the day, with only the occasional spacer or ensign helping out.

A much smaller vessel meant a smaller crew and, hence, a smaller dining room. The tables were long rectangles, with the exception of an oblong board at one end of the room. A flag on a small standard flicked and waved as though caught in a breeze. To my eye, experienced as it was in picking up the nuances of diplomatic dinners, teas, luncheons and every other dining experience to fete visiting dignitaries, I deduced that must be where Captain Naftil entertained his guests. I straightened my mess tunic, adorned with my sole medal, and made for a chair not at the head or foot of the table, but modestly along one side. I took my place and stood at parade rest.

My studies of the day before we arrived had included looking up the captain on the Infogrid. Therefore, when he arrived, accompanied by his executive officers, I was able to recognize him readily. I straightened my shoulders. When he approached, I favored him with my most enthusiastic salute.

"Captain Naftil!" I said. "Lieutenant Thomas Innes Loche Kinago. I and my crew are very pleased to be aboard."

The captain was a slim Human male with the broad shoulders of a long-time space soldier. As my mother had said, he was fairly young for such extensive responsibilities, but he carried them easily. His warm ochre complexion contrasted in a striking manner with his glossy black hair and eyes. The eagerness of his expression told me that he possessed considerable natural energy and enthusiasm. I felt that we could be good friends. I had readied several topics of conversation to get to know him. Such courtesy would please my mother.

He returned my salute with a snap of his wrist.

"Lieutenant Kinago, I am glad to make your acquaintance. Welcome aboard."

"Thank you, sir."

He did not invite me to sit down. I paused for a moment to give him a chance to gather his thoughts. No doubt he was unused to having so many members of the aristocracy in his complement at the same time.

"I await your cousin, Lady Jil, and her party," Captain Naftil said, lowering his voice. "She is absolutely enchanting, isn't she?"

"I must confess, fifty percent of the time she is," I confided in him. Only I and others who occupied her company more frequently than that fifty percent knew the quirks of her personality.

He chuckled in appreciation of my quip. But we had not long to wait. Just before the second signal to mess sounded, Jil and her friends sailed into the dining hall.

My cousin was in the vanguard of the coterie of ladies, gliding forward as if on antigrav skids. I heard Naftil's breath catch in his throat. Jil overwhelmed the senses as if she were one of her own perfumes. The gown she wore would have been flamboyant at a club in the most fashionable neighborhoods of Taino. The blood-red garment occupied no more space than one of Jil's swimming costumes, except for the gory streamers that descended along her legs from the wisp that concealed her slender nether regions and a cursory strap of gold braid that rose from the brassiere to circle about the nape of her neck. Poor Captain Naftil fairly quivered in his regulation footgear. Only the very best training prevented him from the social faux pas of forgetting to greet his other guests, Parsons among them, who brought up the rear of the procession. Jil swooped down upon the captain and offered him a delicate hand.

"Captain, how generous of you to offer us your hospitality."

"I am . . . delighted to have you here, madam," he said, holding her fingers as if they were soap bubbles. "You grace us with your presence."

Jil gave a warm chuckle, laden with wholly unnecessary sensuality.

"You are more than kind," she said, though she knew full well how much of a bombshell her appearance had exploded upon the senses of the assembled service people in their dark blue uniforms. "May I present my friends?" She introduced the ladies in turn. Marquessa curtseyed deeply as the captain bent over her hand. She was a vision in deep royal blue. She made way for Sinim, in a coral gown that warmed but did not overwhelm one's vision like Jil's dress. Banitra and Hopeli both wore shades of purple and, thankfully, more fabric than Jil did.

"You look like a bouquet of exotic flowers," I said, approvingly. "Most becoming!"

"Oh, Thomas," Jil said, turning to me as if surprised to see me. "*Nee'af than de outhu?*"

I was not caught off guard at her sudden use of Uctu.

"*Salthu denau*," I said, easily. "*Ene'af than drau bedothu?*"

She shook a chiding finger at me. "You have got that wrong, cousin. You ought to say '*ene'af dan drau*.'"

"That's not right," I said.

"It is." She tossed her head. "Perhaps you ought to go and check your grammar."

The captain escorted her to the chair to the right of his seat at the head. Parsons and three of the other officers showed the others to their places. There was nowhere left for me.

"I say," I said. "I believe the table has been set one chair short."

The captain gave me an odd look.

As if in answer to my query, a serverbot rolled up to my side.

"Lieutenant Kinago?" it inquired in a mild alto. "Please come with me."

Startled, I glanced at the captain and my cousin.

"But I should be here, shouldn't I?" I asked. "We have so much to talk about."

"Your assigned seat is this way, sir. Please come with me."

I looked to Parsons for rescue, but not was forthcoming. I followed the server.

Though the room was not large, it felt as though I was walking miles through a desert. I fancied I heard scornful whispers as I went, but the sound was undoubtedly my own thoughts chiding me. Why was I not at the captain's table among others of my rank?

I noticed Plet seated at a rectangle for eight in between others wearing the same insignia. She shone among the ordinary crew like a modest gem. I spotted an empty seat not far from hers. Her eyes shifted briefly to meet mine, then returned to the officer with whom she was speaking. That was not my place, then.

"Whither goest?" I asked the server, a bullet-shaped device on rollers concealed under its metal skirt.

"The table second along the wall from the right," it said.

I glanced ahead. I spotted Nesbitt because it would have been difficult not to. He was at the table farthest to the right, gesturing to me to join him, Oskelev and Anstruther. Instead, my destination featured two humans, an Uctu female, one Croctoid, and two Wichu plus Redius. I knew from their lopsided faces that I outranked the humans present. The others, too, were unlikely to be members of their races' noble class.

I glanced back. In fact, I could not have been more distant from the head table, where my cousin, wearing a gleeful expression to complement her scanty outfit, was regaling the captain with a story that required a number of humorous hand gestures. It would be just like Jil to steal one of my best jokes and fail to attribute it to me.

Still, my upbringing had taught me the importance of noblesse oblige. I would put myself out to be as likable as possible. I slid into the seat held out for me by the bullet-shaped serverbot and smiled around at my new companions.

"Good evening, all!" I said. "Lieutenant second class Thomas Kinago. Please call me Thomas."

"Kinago?" the Croctoid asked, rolling one of its small eyes severely in its scaly socket. "Any relation?"

"The most important of relations, if you mean Admiral Kinago Loche," I said. "She's my mother."

The smaller of the two Wichus took her viewpad from her belt and beckoned to the other.

"Pay up. You said he wasn't."

Some good-natured grousing accompanied the settling of the bet. Redius gave me a humorous shrug. He introduced everyone at the table, beginning with the other Uctu, a round-faced female who, by the blue scales on her coral-colored head, was even younger than he.

"Yerbinat Nordina. Thon Delaur. Mimi Chan. Bedere Lumon. Dinas Veltov. Oresta Veltov. All lieutenants second."

Dinner began with a spicy soup. I savored the first few sips, then realized that it had been dosed very heavily with a chili extract that could not, by my observation of other diners, have been in any other bowl in the room. It was so powerful I wondered how l could hold out before I began to perspire, let alone dive for the water pitcher in the center of the table and soak my burning tongue in it. But I was a Kinago, by jay, and a son of the First Space Lord. I could take hazing. My cousins had pulled this particular jape on one another more than once.

"Delicious," I declared it. "You must have an excellent food program on board." I took another spoonful. "Really very good."

Every mouthful was more painful than the one before. I had to force my throat to swallow the liquid. It begged me silently not to torture it any longer. It would devote its life to charity if only I would go find it a bowl of oatmeal laced with heavy cream.

Chan smiled a little nervously.

"I hear you know funny stories," Lumon, the Croctoid, said, working his heavy green jaws back and forth over a chunk of vegetable. "Tell us one."

By the sixth spoonful, my mouth had gone numb, but I fought for clarity of speech.

"I see my reputation has preceded me," I said, searching my memory for a good joke. I possessed a superb collection that I had amassed over the years, a substantial half of which had come to me while I was on board the *Shahmat*. "I would be delighted to oblige. It seems that there was a young Solinian cadet who was on his first assignment planetside in a human outpost. . . ."

As I progressed through the story, my audience, as I hoped, leaned in closer and closer, not observing that I was no longer eating my soup. My tongue, in sincere thanks, put itself out to be as eloquent as ever it had been. When the serverbots moved in to replace the soup with the main course, the other junior officers hardly even noticed.

A peal of laughter interrupted my thoughts. Out of the corner of my eye, I could see my cousin grasp the captain's forearm as if in amused appreciation of a story he had related. He looked a trifle bemused at the intensity of her reaction. I could have told him that he was getting away with fairly mild treatment. A shifting of bodies at my own table told me that I had better return my attention to my audience.

". . . Well, you weren't supposed to eat the whole thing!" I concluded.

My tablemates laughed loudly. Dinas, the male Wichu, slapped a hand on the board. His sister applauded.

"Another!" they chorused.

"I'll try," I said, pointing to my throat. "But the soup, you know, it was a little . . ."

"Strong?" asked Delaur.

"Weak," I said, and enjoyed the astonished looks on their faces. I laughed. I had over the years perfected a laugh that was part snort, part guffaw, and all mine. Those who were subjected to it were invariably impressed and often intimidated, as in this case. Everyone at the table but Redius recoiled. "Pathetically weak. You want to use tarantula chilies if you really want to incapacitate a newcomer. This was cobra pepper oil in the soup, wasn't it?"

"Uh, yeah," the Wichu said.

"My cousins and I *train* with cobra peppers for such occasions as this," I said, hardly disguising my scorn. Then I allowed my expression to soften ever so slightly. "But if you'd like to hear about some really dirty tricks that we play on one another in the Imperium compound . . . ?"

"Yes!" came the general chorus.

I smiled. Now I had them in the palm of my hand. I leaned in conspiratorially. They shifted forward, their faces avid, as I began to reveal secrets scarcely known outside my family.

". . . And the filament is absolutely invisible, so if you sew it into the fabric of a garment meant to be worn against the skin, they won't realize where the shocks are coming from. At least, not for a while."

With the unstated truce in place, we began to get to know one another. They were all eager for stories of my life at court. Gossip that was readily available within my cousins' Infogrid files was easy, permissible fodder. I also regaled my tablemates with one gentle tale that included my mother as a peripheral character that only served to elevate her standing in their eyes. It didn't do any harm to mine, either.

Over dessert, an unadulterated hazelnut cake that made my wounded taste buds feel mellow, we broke into several smaller conversations. At that point, I was able to get Redius's attention. We leaned back in our seats to speak behind the back of our shared neighbor.

"Fear not use of tarantula on you?" Redius asked, his mouth slightly open to show he was smiling. The Wichu between us was arguing loudly with the two humans across the table.

"Not now," I said, with a little smile. "Tarantulas are classified as a weapon of war on a naval vessel, not a food. They will be in the armory, not the pantries. But some unlucky souls might stumble on some in their meals planetside."

"Unfortunate them." Redius studied my expression. "Expression puzzled. Trouble?"

In the course of my immersion in Uctu over the last couple of weeks, I had come to realize that his stilted command of Imperium Standard was almost a direct translation from Uctu. In his tongue, each of the words meant so much more. With every day's study, I began to get a greater sense of how well he expressed himself in spite of the shortcomings of my native language. His staccato phrasing concealed a wealth of meaning.

"Redius, I have a question of grammar. Just a few moments ago, Jil just asked me how my day went, and I told her my labors were rewarding. Then I asked what she did today, and she corrected my phrasing. Doesn't such a question begin with 'ene'af than drau'?"

"Confirmed," Redius said. "What she?"

"She told me it was 'dan drau.'"

Redius burst into hissing laughter.

"Means wasted, not spent," Redius said. "Common courtesy becomes insult."

I emitted an exaggerated growl.

"So! Jil is going to use underhanded psychological means to confuse me," I said. "We will see about that. I can play that game as well as she."

I did not, however, let the matter of my placement in the dining room rest. At the end of the meal, I cut Parsons out of the pack as the senior officers and their guests attempted to flee.

"Parsons, I have a quibble," I said in a low voice, as the rest of the diners streamed past, replete with the excellence of the cuisine that I had been largely unable to taste. "Why was I not seated with the captain and the senior officers? It is unquestionably correct that my cousin and her friends were there, but why not me? Even you were there. I was with the lowest of the low. Not that they are not all good and worthy people, but I would expect to be given a place according to my class. And I would ask that my circumstances, when I represent special operations, also to be considered."

Parsons drew me further off the beaten path, into an alcove near where the serverbots were stacking piles of dirty dishes.

"It is for the best, sir," he murmured, his voice covered well by the clattering of plates and flatware. "Your presence on the *Bonchance* is as a simple emissary from the court of the Emperor. No one except the captain is party to your actual function, and he does not know all of it. You should take advantage of that anonymity. Such placement frees you to ask for information from the *Bonchance*'s crew at large."

My eyebrows went up.

"Is there anyone specific whom you suspect of misdoing?" I asked, feeling the hounds of inquiry raising their noses in a group howl in my psyche.

"It would be better not to point out anyone who is under suspicion lest it unfairly arouse attention to that person. A rotation of crewbeings will occupy the four additional seats at your table. Use this opportunity to gather impressions. Data gathered over a shared collation might reveal more than a formal inquiry. You will be doing this captain a service by making use of your faculties of observation. You have been of assistance in the past."

He gave me a deeply meaningful look.

"So true," I mused. "Very well, I shall take my demotion in good part, although I fancy that my cousin will make much of it. She did, didn't she? You cannot deny it."

My emotions dashed against the bastion of his countenance, but made no impression.

"I would not attempt to do so, my lord. But she serves a purpose as well."

"Wheels within wheels," I said. "Although I think Jil would be mortified to learn that she had a purpose beyond her own whims."

CHAPTER 12

Rafe Copper leaned against the cell bars as the afternoon Uctu patrol went by. He stuck out an arm and waved at them.

"Hey, officers," he called. "When do we get lunch? My kids are hungry."

They weren't unkind people, M'Kenna thought, holding a very fussy Dorna in her arms. Only businesslike and aloof. They didn't get involved with the prisoners. One of them turned to the human captain.

"Not yet," the Gecko said, simply. "You will be fed later. Please be patient. It is better to wait."

"Wait?" M'Kenna asked. "Wait for what?"

"Hungy, mama!" Dorna announced.

"I know, honey. Please wait. Look, would you like to sing a song?"

"No! Lunches! Lunches please, mama! Soooo hungy."

"I'm sorry, honey. We have to wait."

She rocked her daughter on her lap. Her own stomach was protesting against the lack of food. The prison didn't give them a lot of rations, but they were served regularly. Her system and those of her children had become accustomed to the schedule. Delays frustrated them. M'Kenna even missed the phony food on the space station. At least she could go and get it when she wanted it.

As a toddler Dorna had the fewest tools for dealing with disappointment. She alternately struggled against M'Kenna's grasp and nestled close to be cuddled. M'Kenna fumed. When she got to court, she was going to give the judge a piece of her mind about making children wait to be fed. M'Kenna herself wanted the kids fed so she could go back to their mail. While she rocked her daughter, she was composing as compelling a reply as she could, to send to any one of the officials who had appended a name to their automatic replies. She had to be able to attract someone's attention. It was a wonder that their plight hadn't made headlines on the interstellar news channels yet.

The guards reached the end of the ward and turned back.

"Get our rations as soon as you can, huh?" Rafe asked as they went by. This time they ignored him. His arms sagged. "What's going on? We're not trouble, but the Wichu next door are going to eat the cell doors and the beds if some meals don't get here pretty soon."

"I don't know," M'Kenna said, worried. "They never do this when our counsel is coming. Maybe there's going to be a VIP visitor."

"Why would starving us help?" Rafe asked. "Unless they want us in a bad mood for some reason. Journalists? Some kind of news item on 'the accused smugglers'?"

The door clanked shut at the far end, out of the Coppers' sight. M'Kenna felt her heart sink.

Dorna suddenly threw herself off her mother's lap and slid down to the floor to sit with her knees akimbo. She drummed her feet.

"Hungy!" she wailed. M'Kenna dropped from the bed frame and sat down beside her.

"I'm sorry, honey. I really am."

"Stinky scaly hungy! Stinky . . ."

Suddenly, her head drooped. M'Kenna reached for her just as the toddler's whole body sagged sideways. She scooped Dorna up. The little girl had gone completely limp.

"What's happening?" she screamed, clutching the baby to her chest.

"Mama, feel funny," Lerin said. He appeared at the opening to the children's room, holding onto the open frame. His eyes closed. Rafe ran to catch him.

"Smell that?" Rafe bellowed, holding the boy's body. "They're gassing us! They found us guilty, and they weren't even gonna tell us!"

M'Kenna staggered toward the children's room.

"Nona, sweetheart, can you hear me?"

"Mama . . ." The girl's voice came weakly.

M'Kenna felt as though she were swimming in liquid concrete. Her limbs became heavier and heavier. The baby in her arms was a bag of steel weights. She reached the threshold of the children's room. Nona sat on one of the beds with four-year-old Akila draped bonelessly over her lap. Her head had fallen back against the wall. Her eyelids drooped only halfway over her dark brown eyes. M'Kenna felt tears spurting from her eyes, hot as molten glass, but she couldn't lift a hand to dash them away. It was too heavy. Her feet felt as if they were slogging through mud. They were all dying—dying! And she would never know who targeted them.

Her vision had narrowed to a round porthole. With the last of her strength, M'Kenna forced herself toward one of the beds and deposited Dorna on it. She put her cheek down on her baby's hand. The soft palm was the last thing she remembered feeling.

"Help me," she whispered to the darkness.

CHAPTER 13

If some interaction was good, more was better, to my way of thinking. At the next meal, the male Wichu had been replaced by Gillian, a lanky human female with long brown hair and pale freckles, and one of the male humans by Franklin Allen, an ensign with broad shoulders and a pleasant, open countenance. To my delight, they were also assigned to the immense hydroponics area, along with Redius, Oskelev and another human named Douglas.

That which lay between the walls of growing was the realm of Commander Diesen. This formidable-looking human woman, with wire-sinewed limbs and short-clipped white hair, had frosty blue eyes that peered out from under straight white brows. She looked like the very spirit of winter, in the midst of a wilderness of green. The sound of nutrient liquid pumping through pipes, tubes and straws all around us created a percussive and authoritative undertone to her pronouncements. I thought of recreating the effect in a lucky circuit, though I was not sure who would benefit from such a thing.

"And you, Kinago," Commander Diesen said, turning to me once she had set three of our companions to cleaning the tank beneath a broad table. "When they're finished reassembling this growing station, you will take these seedlings and place them one by one into an open pipette. Can you do that without killing every single one of them?"

She pushed toward me a broad flat of tiny plants. A narrow stem supported a fuzzy leaf the size of my thumbnail.

"Squash," I said, with interest. "What variety are they, commander?"

Her white brows went up.

"You can tell what they are at this stage?" she asked. "I'm surprised."

"I grow several varieties at home. Not squash per se, but I served a brief apprenticeship under the head gardener to learn how to care for small plants. Cucurbits are more sturdy than most other young plants, so he felt I would destroy the fewest of these while I was learning."

"Had your number, huh, Kinago?" Allen laughed.

"In several decimal points," I agreed.

"They're butternut squash," the commander said. "A favorite of the captain, so I like to make sure there are enough for special dishes."

I noted the information. One never knew when such a fact would come in handy.

Diesen stood over my shoulder as I transferred seedlings from their propagation pods into the refreshed table. The framework was sturdy enough to support the fruits once they began to erupt along the leafy vines which were also yet to come. Nutrient fluids circulated just below the surface. I took care to ensure that the tiny roots with their spiky hairs were immersed in the liquid. Once the roots got a taste of the plant food, they would grow eagerly until they rested on the bottom of the tank.

She moved me on to herbs: dill and chervil. I realized it was a test, and took the greatest care with these most fragile of plants. I slid each minute slip of greenery into its own tube, where the fluid of life would barely tickle its roots.

"Not bad, Kinago," Diesen said, in her terse manner. I beamed, knowing it for true praise.

"I grow several varieties of herb at home," I said. "A few are too delicate for anything but a hydroponic bed."

"What, a noble growing his own food?" the female Wichu asked, popping her round black eyes mockingly.

"Not for food," I said. "The gardeners would be appalled if they felt I was reduced to supplying my table by my own efforts. No, I am intrigued by the properties of some plants, most of them ancient, many almost legendary. Fenugreek, hyssop, grains of paradise, love-in-a-mist, and a number of others."

Diesen's severe face softened a trifle.

"You have access to rare species?" she asked. I realized I was in the presence of a fellow enthusiast, if not one in my own field.

"Indeed I do," I said. "I have promised half the seeds that come from my plants back to the Core Worlds Preservatory . . . ." I saw the avid light in her eyes. "If there are any in which you have an interest, I would be happy to share my bounty. Of those I am successful in growing, allow me to add. I am not an expert herbalist yet."

She recoiled, as though stung by my words.

"*Herbalist?*" she echoed, scorn coloring her voice. "Don't you dare tell me you are trying to recapture ancient hallucinogens! I've heard your class dabbles in anything that will give you a momentary thrill."

"No, ma'am," I protested. "I could only interest my relatives in what I am doing if I were to take up viticulture. Wines and spirits are our customary indulgence. Anything that will cause damage to the imperial gene pool is frowned upon."

She was unmoved.

"Huh! I'm surprised to hear that there's something you people *won't* ingest," she said. She pointed to another table with a couple of flats balanced upon it, awaiting transplant. "That's your next task. Try not to destroy everything in the garden before you leave."

She stalked into a tomato-laden archway and vanished among the trailing vines. I made a quick note on my viewpad to send her some seeds from my plants upon my return. She wouldn't ask again, but I knew in my heart that she craved the rarities I had named.

"She must be an Alchemist," I said.

"What does that mean?" Allen asked.

"Her astrological sign," the tall woman said, looking at me with new interest.

"Meticulous, not necessarily good with people, but hard-working and practical," I said. "She has the look of it, with her narrow bones and prominent teeth."

"I'm an Alchemist," said Gillian. "I never thought that Diesen and I looked alike."

"It's a superficial resemblance," I said. I studied her dentition. It did fall within the general guidelines, being a trifle more pronounced than, say, Allen's. His teeth were short and regular, but his bulky shoulders and protective nature pronounced him a Guardian. I would have laid a substantial wager upon it. "Notable characteristics, more of a family resemblance than striking similarity."

"Huh," Oskelev said. "You all look alike to me." Her white-furred face pulled a playful grimace. Veltov laughed.

"Well, you are a Butterfly," I said. "So you would not be paying attention to that which matters to other signs."

"Hah!" She went back to scrubbing.

"What about me?" asked Douglas. I peered at him. He regarded me almost sideways. He had sensitive features in a round face, but his hands looked surprisingly strong.

"I would wager . . . Cat," I said.

His brows flew up. "You're good. What about you?"

"Wolf," I said. "To the great amusement of my cousins."

"So you like astrology?" asked Allen.

"It's only one of the superstitions I study," I said.

"How many are there?" he asked.

"At least one per person, has been my experience," I said. "Everybody seems to have an unbreakable belief that has no bearing in reality. It doesn't stop us from following it."

"I don't do anything like that," said Allen.

"Spoken like a true Guardian," I said, and had the satisfaction of seeing his mouth fall open in astonishment.

"You must have looked up my birth date on the Infogrid."

I raised a hand and put the other upon my heart.

"I swear by my honor, I did not," I said. "You may check. The only listings I examined were your musical preferences. They are rather like mine, by the way. You will find our playlists have numerous entries in common."

"That's scary!" Gillian said, with a delighted shiver. "Tell us more! My girlfriend Corlota is a Penguin."

"Then you two are compatible," I said. "At least by your main star sign. I would have to compare your charts."

She brought forth her viewpad with the speed of lightning. "I'm sending you both our birthdays," she said. "I am dying to hear your interpretation!"

"Why not?" I said, happy to find others interested in my studies. "But let it wait until our next rest shift. I do not want to enrage our supervisor by neglecting our duties." I picked up the next seedling.

"Work too hard," said the Uctu, his mouth gaping in a smile.

"Not if I can help it," Oskelev said. She moved on to the next empty tank.

"And what is *this* one, dear captain?"

Though the ceilings in the garden were high, my cousin's voice echoed easily off them. I heard her friends whispering and chatting as well. We fell silent to listen.

"Er, well," the captain's voice said, rather uncertainly, "it says 'tarragon.' It's served with chicken and a lot of vegetables, I think."

So she had talked him into giving her a tour of the hydroponics section, I mused. I shook my head. Poor Captain Naftil. He had no idea of the forces that had been let loose.

"Cousin conquest," Redius murmured, with an amused bark.

"I know," I said, assuming an expression of extreme woe. I went on with my tasks until the group of them broke cover from the aisle to my left.

Jil had on an outfit of gold tissue that seemed to be transparent, though it most assuredly was not, yet it clung to every curve. Her hair, billowing, wavy tresses interspersed with a tiny braid here and there, had been dressed with glittering green and blue jewels in the shapes of birds and butterflies. Behind her, the other ladies were similarly clad, though with fewer precious adornments. The temperate climate of the ship permitted the wearing of lightweight garments. These were not only light, but cut so as to provide the maximum of distraction. All of my human companions stared as the ladies approached. "Don't give them the satisfaction," I added, unable to keep the peevish note out of my voice. "They do it on purpose."

"They're . . . fabulous," Gillian said.

"I know. Annoying, isn't it?"

I stopped what I was doing to offer the captain a polite salute.

"Welcome, captain," I said.

He returned it without glancing back at me.

"As you were, spacer," he said.

It took all of my self-control not to let my mouth drop open. Spacer!

Jil saw the interchange. Her eyes rounded with wicked merriment. Never one to avoid taking advantage, she seized one of the tiny plants I was tending right out of my fingers.

"And what is this one? I am sure it will grow into something most delicious!"

"Er, well . . ." The captain's handsome face screwed up into a boyish expression of confusion.

"Rokufian parsley," I supplied.

"That's it," Captain Naftil said, without looking at me. "Thank you, spacer. It's served in salads, mainly. I think. I'm not much of a cook. I leave that to the specialists. We have a remarkably good kitchen staff aboard, you know."

"Oh, I *know*," Jil gushed. "That delicate little egg casserole at lunch was absolutely marvelous! The Emperor's own cooks would be proud to have served that."

Naftil's dusky complexion suffused with red. "You are much too kind, Lady Jil."

"I only speak the truth," my cousin said, with a slow smile. "It's far too much trouble to recall all the lies I might tell. I am far too lazy, as any of my relatives would be glad to tell you."

She dropped the small plant into his hand. He held it out behind him for me to take, which I did without comment. The ladies, trailing along behind the pair, registered amusement on their faces, but did not laugh aloud.

I was not accustomed to being so ignored, and the ignominy roiled up within me. Still, I had promised my mother not to undermine the captain's authority. In her name, I bore my disgrace bravely. I went on repotting herbs with one eye on my cousin.

Jil made the most of her conquest. Like a gazelle in the moonlight, she led the captain up and down the aisles of plants, asking their names and uses. Her entourage chatted quietly among themselves behind them. Once in a while, one of the ladies caught my eye and offered me a sympathetic look. It was clear Jil had no intention of correcting the captain's misconception. The poor man was entirely besotted. He had no idea how he appeared to his subordinates, but until her spell was broken, he would never know. I had no intention of breaking it to him.

"Let me show you back to your sitting room," Captain Naftil said. "As you were, spacers."

"Aye, sir!" we chorused.

I glanced backward. They were leaving. My torture was nearly complete, when Banitra threw a playful smirk over her shoulder.

"Good afternoon, Lord Thomas," Banitra said.

"Lord Thomas? Where?" Captain Naftil wheeled around as I

turned. He realized in that moment that the gardening assistant he had so casually dismissed was me. His face became ruddy with embarrassment. His manner changed at once from master of his ship to awkward, raw recruit. I could almost see his long limbs become gangly. "Your pardon, Kinago. It was not my intention to ignore you."

Or your mother, was the unspoken aside. I hastened to reassure him.

"No offense taken, captain," I said cheerfully. "I am here to undertake my duties. Your mind was pleasantly engaged."

"Thomas loves playing dress-up," Jil said, twining her arm into his. He looked from her to me, and back again, doing his best to reconcile the unholy glee she was so obviously enjoying with the exquisite package in which the malice was wrapped. She could have identified me upon his first failure, but she had not, leaving him in a stage of unnecessary mortification. "It is good of you to indulge him."

"I am proud to fulfill my assignments, sir," I said. I maintained an attitude of stiff parade rest, elbows akimbo, hands open and flat against my back, when normally, I would release a fleering version of my patented laugh upon her. It would in this case rebound upon an innocent party, the captain. "Would you like me to explain what we have been doing today, sir?"

It seemed difficult for Naftil to regain his voice. When it re-emerged, it was hoarse.

"Thank you, Lieutenant, but no."

"As you wish, Captain."

Behind the captain's back, Jil stuck her tongue out at me. When the captain turned to avoid meeting my eyes, I made a horrible face at her.

Assuming a pace that was less than accommodating to his guests in their high-heeled shoes, Naftil fled the arena, though in my view he was taking his foe with him.

CHAPTER 14

"You promised you would read my charts," Gillian said, eagerly, when we met with all our other new friends in the recreation area the next evening after our work shift.

From the large case I had conveyed from my cabin, I extracted some of my fortune-telling gear that Parsons had neither succeeded in removing from the *Rodrigo* nor losing in transit. In a corner of the card room, I shook out the folds of my tent and spread them over the collapsible framework of poles and rings. Once it was settled to my liking, I erected my table and stools, and set my viewpad to shine impressive-looking mystical charts upon the cloth walls. I closed the flaps of my tent so I could don my robe in private. I wore my own lucky circuit around my throat.

When I was ready, I flipped open the swathes of black silk, and beckoned to Gillian.

"Oh, my!" she exclaimed, her eyes wide. "Look at you!"

"Well, you must have the entire show," I said, modestly.

"This is a whole circus! I didn't expect all this."

"That's some outfit. What do the symbols on the robe mean?" man asked.

"The constellations as seen from Keinolt," I said. "Should I ever achieve astral projection, they are to guide me home again."

"Really? I thought they were just for decoration."

"Everything has a meaning," I said. "I will have to show you my research."

"Do I have to read a bunch of dusty old books?" he asked, wrinkling his snub nose.

"I did," I said cheerfully. "You'd be surprised what amazing wisdom existed before electronic record-keeping." I turned to Gillian and extended a hand. "Come and sit down. Your fate awaits you."

"Oooh," she said . . . with a playful grin, as she followed me in.

The entire table rose and crowded around the entrance to my tent. Gillian sat down opposite me, her eyes wide.

I brought up her birth chart and played it on the nearest swathe of cloth. She had been born far from the center of the Core Worlds, in a small mining colony with a wealth of rare earths on a vector toward the Kail worlds. My program adjusted the planetary aspects to account for the discrepancies. Although it did not change the zodiac itself, it did widen certain houses of influence and narrow others. I explained all this to her, but I could see by her expression that little of it sank in.

"But what's it mean for me?" she asked. "Fortunes always advise you on your career and love. That's what I want to know."

"I knew you would." Over the constellations on display, I placed artistic renderings of the images associated with them. Minor star clusters sprang into being, as well. "Your native sun in Alchemist shows that you are a meticulous person. In trine, which is to say that it is exactly four signs away from it, the star system we call the Giver. In ancient Earth astrology, they used the planets that circled Sol, but it seemed odd to those who rewrote the texts for an interplanetary civilization. In their place, we have a host of small stars that lend their countenance to a reading."

"But most of those stars don't move very fast," Oskelev said. As an astrogator, she would know that. "They'd be in everyone's chart in the same place."

I used the pointer light in the viewpad's lecture program to show everyone the aspects in question.

"The sun appears to move, from the point of view of someone standing on the surface of a planet, and the ascendant sign pertains to one's time of birth, so they would not be in precisely the same location, even if they occupy the same sign. The same was true in old astrology. Some planets took hundreds of years to circle Sol, so generations would have the same sign. I believe that the not-quite-as-ancient astrologers chose star systems that do have energetic movement to substitute for those planets. So, Gillian, I see that you are generous to your friends, but your fifth house, your needs in love and relationships, says you are not as kind to yourself, perhaps."

Her brow wrinkled ever so slightly. I was afraid of that, having spotted the inauspicious connections.

"Your chart bodes well for a good career, though," I continued, changing the subject. "As your sun sign is above the midheaven, you will gain recognition. And this small constellation, the White Dragon, is in your tenth house, career. You may focus on a specialty that interests you, because others will notice your application to task."

"And love?" she asked, with a hopeful lift to her brows.

Although the Penguin was in trine to the Alchemist, the other readings in Corlota's chart suggested to me that she was close to moving on from my young friend. I had also gained the same impression from Corlota's attitude. The lady had not moved to embrace Gillian with the same eagerness with which she was embraced when they met at the beginning of the rest period.

"That is for the future," I said firmly, not meeting her eyes. "Your friendship house is well aspected, though. I had not realized how popular you are."

She blushed. I seized her hand and turned the palm upward.

"Let me read your fate lines," I said. "Let us see how long it is until you are an admiral."

The others chuckled. I tapped the viewpad and brought up palm charts. As she was a human being, I used the original, some ten millennia old.

"Your head line shows a strong career. The lines that cross it point to both work and friendship. I would be surprised if you ever leave the navy."

"It's been good so far," she agreed.

"A very long life," I said, tracing the curving line that circled the base of her thumb. Her palm twitched. "I am sorry, am I tickling you?"

"A little."

I ran my finger to a place where the arcing line broke and ran parallel to itself before angling to the base of the palm.

"Be aware of the possibility of a catastrophic illness or injury. It isn't indicated before your seventh or eighth decade, but it would do you well to have a support plan in place," I said. Cross-hatching above the mound of Venus said it would be severe. I glanced at her face and saw concern there. "This hand shows the potentials in your future. Let me see the other one for the actual events in your life to date."

Nervously, she extended it.

"She's got two hands," Allen said, "but what if someone only has one hand, or had it regrown?"

I lifted my brows.

"That is a very good question, Allen. The oracles don't have anything on that, so I'll have to make it up myself."

"What? You can't look up something like that?" Gillian asked, concerned.

I shook my head, amused.

"It's not exactly case law, old girl. I will use my best intuition and knowledge of the science, and fill in the blanks. It's undoubtedly what our ancestors did. I merely follow their example." I perused her second hand. She had managed to avoid a couple of tragedies that could have damaged her in childhood, but the upcoming catastrophe was written the same in both places. "Perhaps you will avoid the accident because you have the knowledge I have given you today." I held both her hands and looked into her eyes. I had given her what I thought she needed, but she wanted more. She regarded me trustingly but warily. I let go of her hands and picked up my pad.

"Here, I can copy this chart for you, along with the various interpretations. You should find it baffling reading."

My audience chuckled appreciatively.

"How much of this do you believe?" Gillian asked, holding her pad to mine to receive the transmission.

"Not a word of it," I said. "It's all in good fun."

"Just for fun?" she echoed. She regarded me from under wrinkled brows. "You don't take it seriously."

My own brows were sincerely high upon my forehead.

"No, I don't. I mean, I take my enthusiasms very seriously, but I don't believe in the superstitions that I am studying. They are enjoyable to examine, but I would go mad if I had to obey the rules involved in every discipline. Most of them contradict one another ridiculously."

"Uh, well, thank you," she said, hastily vacating the stool.

"It has been my pleasure."

The backless chair was not empty for more than a moment. Allen plopped down upon it.

"My turn," he said.

"Are you sure?" I asked. "It's really fairly standardized. You could read the same in a number of texts."

Allen cocked his head. "No, I think you've got something."

I opened my eyes wide. "Good heavens! I hope it's not catching!"

"Then you'll do it?"

"Why not?" I said, cheerfully. "Let's see what your date and circumstances of birth have destined for you."

"Then me," said Veltov. "If you can tell fates nonhuman."

"I have been reading up on Uctu scale-fortunes," I said. "I would be delighted to have a chance to practice it on a living subject. I have found that it is a bit like a cross between graphology and phrenology."

"Yes! Most interested."

"Can you do a scale reading on me?" Allen asked.

"Well, no," I said. "Since your scales, like mine, are microscopic. But I will attempt to read the bumps on your head. Phrenology is an amusing form of divination."

"That's good," Allen said. "My girlfriend says I have a lumpy head. I bet you get a lot of information from me."

Once I agreed to read for those two, others chimed in that they wanted a turn as well. The remainder of the rest period whisked by. I went to bed feeling pleased with myself.

"I told some people about you telling my fortune," Allen admitted sheepishly, as we began our next shift together in the garden. He kept his eyes down on the aloe plants on which we were working. Our task was to slice some of the thick leaves from the parent plant, both to make room for future growth and to extract the clear juice for a multiplicity of purposes, culinary, cosmetic and medical.

"I see," I said, carefully keeping my eyes on my work. The clear sap dripped down over my fingertips. I rubbed them together and felt a faint tingling. "That reading was personal, you know. For your own amusement."

He glanced up, surprised. "Well, all the others were listening. I thought it would be all right."

"It was your choice to have them listen. As you saw, Veltov wanted privacy when I revealed the interpretation of his scale pattern."

"Uh, I suppose so," he said, then blundered forward, as a true Guardian would. "Anyway, they all want to have their stars read. I mean, they'd really like it. If you have the time. You said you were interested in learning more about astrology and all those other things. Would you read for them?"

To have more subjects willing to allow me to interpret their lines of fate and star charts? To see their reactions at the revelations I had for them? I could hardly contain my eagerness.

"Yes, I would be happy to," I said. "By all means, tell them yes! I would be delighted to include them in my studies."

"Next rest period?" he asked.

"I will be ready and waiting," I said.

How I kept my mind on my tasks, I do not know. To be able to add numerous living subjects for my study was just what I was hoping for. I checked my own fortune on the tarot program in my viewpad. The Chariot appeared. It warned me to keep my impulses in check. Not so easy, considering the delights that were surely to come.

CHAPTER 15

After mess, during which the conversation centered on a passionate discussion about the relative merits of three different bands from the Uctu Autocracy versus a similar number in the Imperium, I went back to my cabin to retrieve my tent and other impedimenta.

It took me a few minutes to rummage around for all the things I wanted to bring with me. I heard a bit of noise in the corridor. When I opened my door, I was met by a party of solemn-faced junior officers and noncoms.

"Hello," I said, glancing from face to face. "Is there something wrong? Am I in some kind of trouble?"

"No, sir," said the first, a wiry rating with huge dark eyes. "We just wanted to get in line right away."

"For what purpose?" I asked.

"To get a reading from you, sir." The others nodded vigorously.

"Ah! You must be Allen's friends. Well, my cabin's too small for a group of this size. Come down to the recreation center."

"Aye, sir!"

A few of them reached out to assume my burdens. I ceded my bundles and led the way. They followed me to the lifts like a file of ducklings.

Upon my arrival in the entertainment center, a group of people sprang to their feet. They were mostly junior officers, but I saw the insignia of a senior officer or two. Allen came forward from amid them.

"Can I help you set up? Or is there some mystical reason not to touch your gear?"

"None at all," I said. "Everything I have brought with me is ordinary. In fact, if you will put up the tent, I will get everything else prepared."

"Hey, we were here first!" said a woman to the people at my back.

"We got in line with him at his cabin," said the rating behind me. He looked rather smug.

"We've been here all this time! Ensign Allen said we were first!"

"Too bad!"

"You want too bad? Just wait until you're back in Ordnance, cleaning and testing a thousand slugthrowers!"

I was surprised at the avid expressions on the crewbeings' faces. I had certainly touched a nerve of some kind. I held up my hands.

"Friends! Friends, please! There's no need to fight. Or take preemptive revenge. Allen, start a roster. I will speak to everyone, if not today, then over the next few days. How does that suit you?" There were a few 'yeahs' and a good deal of unhappy muttering. "If you're not in a receptive frame of mind, how will you absorb the wisdom of the ages?"

That produced in them a more positive outburst. I retired to my tent, which had risen from the rec room floor as though by magic, and put on my robe. In its cool shadow, I surveyed the crew milling around Allen, demanding that he place each of them higher on the list than his or her fellows. Although I was interested in the outcome, it would probably interfere with the natural progression of things if I removed myself from the scene. I closed the flaps of my tent and waited. The noise outside rose to a crescendo, then died away to irritated asides and a few last threats.

It was not long before my first seeker entered.

"Hello, midshipman," I said, as the crewman sat down. His name tag identified his last name as Polenti. He had fine bones overlain by deep brown skin. "What is it you want to know?"

"Uh, I don't know. What's going to happen in my future?"

Aha, I thought, *a blank slate!*

I did like being an authority figure. My natural aplomb and dignity lent my predictions, spurious as they were, gravitas that they probably would not normally enjoy. My clients, for so I came to think of them, came full of hope and departed feeling that sensation of wonder that one would associate with any transformative experience. All grist for the mill of my study. I found that some methods of divination gleaned better results than others with regard to my audience. Anything that involved physical contact drew more credence than those that did not. The more support material that was involved in a reading, such as charts or books, the more questions a subject was likely to ask. Group interpretations were never as successful as one-on-one meetings. I found, and my findings were borne out in my readings, that multiple subjects usually felt deprived of attention, except in events like séances. Summoning spirits, as it required their participation as well as physical contact, made them feel more invested in the outcome.

The sittings were not without drama, however. Midway through the third hour, I heard voices raised outside of my cloth enclosure. I popped my head out to see what was going on.

The generously-sized room, suitable for small concerts or a full game of arena football, was packed to the walls with people, all talking intently. Out of their midst burst a man and woman, arguing at the tops of their voices. I recognized the woman as one of my subjects from the first hour, a first lieutenant and physiotherapist from the sick bay. He wore a similar rank badge. She spotted me and came over to grab me by the facings of my robe.

"You started this! You told me that my palm said I would have three children! Now he says he doesn't want a family!"

"I didn't say that," the man sputtered. "I said we'd talk about it once our deployment was over."

"How old do you want to be when they start school?" the woman countered. "You want to stand or be in a hoverchair at their graduations?"

"They? Who's they?" the man asked, his eyes wide with rage. "There isn't any they."

"If I may interrupt?" I asked, holding up my palms for silence. "I didn't say . . ."

She rounded on me with a fingertip almost touching my nose.

"Did it say anywhere that he was going to break my heart?" she demanded.

"I must point out that a palm reading shows the potential, not necessarily the actual outcome of one's life," I said. "Our ancestors believed that the signs we were given were guidelines. Isn't it more important . . . ?"

"No!" she said. The sclera of her eyes showed all the way around her very agitated irises. "Nothing is more important."

"More important than me?" the man asked, outraged.

"I am afraid you did not take my reading as it was intended," I said. "It was for entertainment only."

"Since when are my future children *for entertainment only?*"

"Are you making fun of my partner?" the man asked, glaring. He leaned forward, intending to be imposing.

"Cease and desist at once," I said, retreating and drawing myself up to my full height, which was several centimeters greater than his. "You!" I pointed to the woman. "You have the potential to be the mother of three children. You!" I pointed to the man. "If you have not had this conversation regarding offspring before, have it now. Give me your place and date of birth, and I will forward you comparative charts indicating whether it is even a good idea for you to continue in your relationship!"

Both of them recoiled, their eyes huge. Her hand crept over and clutched his. He put his arm around her shoulders.

"You're not going to tell me to break up with him, are you?" she asked, her voice retreating into timid registers.

I smiled upon her benevolently.

"I would never impose my will upon you, madam," I said. "The fates don't dictate; they suggest. Go back and talk to each other. And listen. This is not between me and you. It is between the two of you."

I realized that the entire room was watching. I threw back the fullness of my robe's sleeves and held up my hands in a sign of benediction.

"Go ahead," I said.

The man didn't hesitate. He pulled the woman away from me. Arms around one another, they retreated into the crowd and disappeared.

Satisfied, I went to sit down. A hand seized my arm.

"Just a minute, Lieutenant," said a clarion voice.

I turned. The Wichu who had stopped me wore the insignia of a lieutenant commander.

"Yes, ma'am?" I asked.

"You're not senior to these officers," she said. "You can't give them orders! Who do you think you are?"

I drew up to my full height and placed my hands upon the facings of my elegant robe.

"I am Lord Thomas Kinago."

Her bulbous black eyes bulged in outrage.

"Not on this ship you're not, sonny!"

"On every ship, ma'am," I stated. "But you are correct. In the hierarchy of my mother's navy, I am but a humble lieutenant. Still, they asked me to intervene."

"When it sounds like you started the argument in the first place," she pointed out.

I shrugged, the robe lending magnificence to my gesture.

"At least I got them talking again," I said. "They had not had conversations vital to their relationship. I believe that I have put them on the path to a more harmonious future, separately if not together. I feel that my work here is done."

The Wichu looked doubtful, but I could see that the force of my argument overwhelmed her objections.

"Well, all right," she said. "At least nobody got hurt. Carry on, but keep it down! Keep this circus of yours under control!"

"I will, ma'am," I promised. I turned back to Allen. "Who is next?"

Ship's bells sounded, indicating the end of the rest period. Moans of disappointment arose from the clients still waiting for their readings.

"Never fear!" I called to the crowd. "Meet me here next rest period. I will resume with the list then."

Allen gave me a thumbs up as I folded my tent and returned to my cabin. I went to my night's rest well satisfied with my day's work.

"Do you actually believe all this crap?" Oskelev asked, when we met for morning coffee in the recreation center.

I had seen little of my own crew during the past few days. Changing schedules to suit our temporary masters aboard the *Bonchance* had separated us widely. Once in a while I spotted Plet at the periphery of my waiting fans, but she never approached to speak to me. Anstruther was undoubtedly spending her free time reading manuals and improving her skills as a programming demon. I always admired her application.

"Of course not," I said, cheerfully. I flipped out a shimmering red tablecloth on which I would project my palm charts over the table between us. "But it is great fun, isn't it? And I am finding a goodly number of coincidences between my scrying and the true nature of my subjects."

"Just good observer," Redius said, with a speculative eye.

"I like to think so."

"I dunno, Thomas," Oskelev said, scanning the faces of those waiting nearby but out of earshot for my crumbs of wisdom. "I think they're taking it pretty seriously. You'd better watch out. What's Commander Parsons think?"

"Parsons has an uncanny manner of letting me know without a doubt when I behave in a way of which he disapproves," I said. "If I have not heard from or seen him, he has little or no opinion of my activities."

She and Redius departed for their morning duties. I took my place in the tent.

I could not help but credit Oskelev's observation. My subjects listened to my readings with an outward air of disinterest, but their anxious questions told me otherwise. I could have said anything I wanted, and made a profit as a prophet. Many of my subjects asked if they needed to cross my palm with silver, in the form of Imperium credits, in exchange for my readings. I had to reassure them that they did not need to pay. I refused all gifts. I could see that my credibility would sink if it seemed I was spouting off their fortunes to enhance my own. In any case, I did not need their money, but I could see where unscrupulous and greedy fakes would prey upon the unwary and gullible.

The popularity of my sessions in the recreation center only increased. With each day, I found a larger crowd awaiting my services. I was treated with a kind of reverence that almost outstripped the understandable respect for my noble rank. At breakfast and my lunch break, during my fitness regime and other personal duties, people went out of their way to speak with me. I had never felt so popular. If they asked for a reading, I referred them to Franklin Allen.

Allen kept those on the list in order, not allowing anyone to queue-jump, no matter how highly placed they were in the ship's hierarchy. I refused to show any favoritism, lest my motives be questioned. Everyone received an equal share of my attention.

I broke off the next session in the third hour, to the great disappointment of my fans. I had fallen behind in my Infogrid entries.

Countless personal messages and other notifications inflicted various forms of visual pyrotechnic in the seemingly endless scroll of entries. I needed to stop reading people's futures in order to investigate my recent past.

With my cabin door sealed firmly behind me for privacy, I activated the communications console embedded in the top of the desk, and requested a download of my personal messages.

Interleaved beneath my comments on my studies to date, I found some insulting messages from my cousins, as I would have expected, but some responses, from noted scholars as well as numerous laypeople, consisted of high praise bordering on reverence. The saccharine tenor of those was, thankfully, balanced by two tart rejoinders from fellow debunkers of the occult. They, of all the readers of my essays and musings, saw what I was doing: an investigation of personalities rather than occult divination. I was pleased. I replied to several, recorded a fleering message to my cousins with sound effects and a derisive graphic, and wrote a detailed description of my most recent findings.

Having disposed of the professional, I turned to personal messages. My mother's personal secretary, Admiral Leven Draco, whom I had grown up knowing as an auxiliary uncle, had forwarded my mother's compliments. I knew what that meant. I was able to reassure Uncle Lev that my sojourn aboard the *Bonchance* had heretofore been uneventful. I even hinted that she would be proud of my accomplishments aboard. I sent it off with a clear conscience.

One of the message lines was marked, "Urgent! Read at once!" The print flashed and danced so it would be impossible to ignore. Concerned, I opened it. It was from Sinim.

"Please delete Lady Jil's message of two shifts ago," her note read. "I sent it to you by mistake. Please don't be mad. Don't read it. Thanks, Lord Thomas."

Mad? I raised my eyebrows. I didn't see why anything that my cousin wrote would anger me. But I also could not possibly let it go unread.

"Search 'Jil,'" I told the comm unit.

Immediately, the mass of messages scrolled down a few hundred to my cousin's unmistakable signature line, filled with flourishes, emoticons and graphics.

As a result of my growing popularity over the last several days, Jil and her friends had barely spoken to me. I believed that my dear cousin was jealous of the attention I was getting. I had to admit that the adulation rather made up for being banished from the captain's table. In some cases, quantity was rather more appealing than quality.

Jil's message, couched in the flowery terms of official diplomatic language—I sensed Banitra's fine hand here, since Jil never could be bothered to learn the syntax—invited the captain and senior officers, indicated by name and rank, to an intimate little party to thank them for the courtesy that she and her company of friends had been shown. This putative soiree would be held in the hydroponics garden.

I glanced at the chronometer in the upper corner of the large screen, and discovered that it was scheduled to begin within the next hour. My name had been included in the list of invitees, but some attempt had been made to scrub it out after the message was sent to me.

I frowned. I was a little hurt not to be invited, but it didn't bother me overmuch. Jil had the right to amuse herself as she pleased, as long as she didn't interfere with our mission, or my own fun. I had the time to dress and go up to the event. Perhaps I would. Jil should know that her mistakes were as open to exploitation as mine were. As I was about to rise from the console, a musical feminine voice came over the intraship network.

"Lord Thomas!"

I put a name to the vocal tone.

"Angie, is that you?"

"Yes, my lord," she said.

"What may I do for you?" I asked, pleased. By their nature of constant connectedness through electronic media, LAIs were not limited to ordinary messaging systems. They were capable of interrupting ongoing streams or, indeed, communicating via paths not usually used for vocal transmission. They had been programmed to be considerate of the frailties of lesser beings such as humans with regard to sleeping times or work shifts. "Are you enjoying your interaction with the ship's artificial intelligences? Some of them are very interesting people."

"My visit has been fruitful thus far, Lord Thomas," she replied. "I have many new acquaintances with whom I will be pleased to correspond in future. I have invaded your privacy because I have an urgent piece of information to give you."

"Urgent?" I echoed. "Is it from Parsons?"

"No, sir. I hope you will not find it too difficult to accept."

I became alarmed. "Well, out with it, Angie. Bad news doesn't improve by keeping."

If an LAI ever hesitated, she did then.

"I must tell you that all of the Leonine wine and Colvarin cheese have been removed from the secured refrigeration unit aboard the *Rodrigo*."

I was appropriately aghast.

"What, all of it?"

"Every case and wheel."

"Well," I said. "Now I know the source of Jil's bounty for her party. I should have guessed that was why she didn't want me present. I would have demanded some credit for supplying the feast."

"Since you said they may have access to those items, I thought I had better inform you. Are there any other treats that you wish to offer access in their place when we launch again?"

"Certainly not," I said, allowing my indignation with my cousin to muster to audible levels. "I have no intention of catering every event that she dreams up. I will have to take revenge at some point, but it is, as many of the delicacies that you are reserving for me, best served cold. Thank you for informing me."

Angie sounded alarmed.

"I do not wish to cause controversy between you and a near relative."

"Near relations almost always cause the greatest controversy," I said, with a dismissive wave that I doubted she could see. "It is not your concern or responsibility. Your stewardship is sterling. I appreciate it greatly. Carry on."

Confound it, I thought, as Angie disconnected. I wished I had had an inkling of Jil's intentions before the fact! I might have tampered with the wine at least, letting Jil serve vinegar and make a fool of herself. But no, I would rise above the slight. I had my duties, my responsibilities, and my audience.

CHAPTER 16

"There, does that bring you some measure of comfort?" I inquired, releasing the hand of a middle-aged Croctoid male ensign.

"Yeah, makes sense," the toothy reptilian replied. "Thanks. I have to think about some things."

As that had been exactly my intent, I was contented. The shift had been going rather well. Instead of feeling enervated by the hordes of advice-seekers, I found myself drawing energy from our interaction. It was an effect I had not foreseen. I couldn't wait to see what response my findings would glean from my correspondents.

Looking out over the eager throng who were still awaiting my attention, I made haste to clear the Croctoid paw chart from my viewpad screen. A human woman with the shoulder flashing of a security officer stood up and pushed through the crowd. She clasped her hands together. Clearly, she didn't want her palm read.

"May I have your place and date of birth?" I asked. She recoiled. I read her physical response as skittishness.

"No!" she said, firmly. "I would prefer not to give you any personal information."

"Very well, then," I said. I unslung my lucky circuit from around my neck and dangled it over the surface of the table. "Ask me your question, then, and we'll see what the pendulum tells us."

She started to open her mouth, when a blaring mechanical voice interrupted us.

"Make way, please. Make way."

The crowd parted around an obstacle that I could not immediately see. It did not take mediumistic talent to discern the source, since I had heard the same speech oftentimes before. A serverbot emerged from amid the waiting crowd and rumbled up to me.

"The captain would like to see you, Lieutenant," it said.

I straightened up. The top of the 'bot rose until it was eye to eye with me, so to speak, as it had no visible optical inputs.

"Now?" I asked.

"Promptly," it assured me. "Please follow me."

I gestured at my impedimenta, now well spread out over multiple tables.

"It will take me a while to tidy this up."

"Now, lieutenant," it said. "Please leave your property in place. You may return for it later."

I raised my hands helplessly to the crowd of seekers.

"I will be back as soon as I can," I said.

Without another word, the 'bot glided toward the door. I shouldered out of my robe and followed at my leisure. The captain had asked me to appear promptly, not on the double. On the way, I tidied myself up, and tucked away the lucky circuit in a belt pouch. It twinkled brightly as I put it away. The very color of the lights cheered my soul.

I wondered as to the subject of my conference with the senior officer. Had Jil's party gone amiss in some way? Had my cousin finally offended him to the point where he needed a family member's intercession? That had to be it. Jil could be annoying. Though the *Bonchance* was in what was considered safe space, he was still the master of a warship. The more of his time she demanded, the less he had to devote to his duties. I had tried to make this apparent to my cousin, but it would seem that my warnings had fallen upon deaf ears. Or perhaps he wanted to thank me himself, on the off-chance that Jil had confessed the source of the bounty provided to her guests.

I opened my viewpad to see if she had sent me any messages. Nothing from her was in my inbox. She had, however, commented upon my postings regarding my studies. Depending upon her mood, or so it would seem, she was alternatively admiring and scathing. So very Jil. Well, no clue there. It was better, I mused, not to anticipate too keenly. I took a surreptitious glance at my coin flip program for an indication. It was inconclusive.

The 'bot led me down the corridor just aft of the bridge, where the senior crew maintained office space. A square red light flared out from its top piece to touch the palm pad beside the door. The portal slid aside.

"Please go in, Lieutenant."

"Thank you," I said. I stepped over the threshold. The door hissed closed behind me. Back as erect as a plumb bob, I waited for Captain Naftil to take notice of me. He was reading from the console embedded in the nondescript desk. By the line that had formed between his winged brows, I deduced that what was on the document in question was a source of concern to him. With a sweep of his right forefinger, he dismissed it. His dark eyes flicked upward.

"Enter," he said. I marched forward and stood at parade rest before him.

I surveyed my surroundings. Again, there was much to compare with ships I had traveled aboard previously. The walls were filled with holographic images of captains past as well as physical artifacts, prized possessions of those departed general officers, such as prize flags, models of ancient ships, and carven award plaques. The pale blue glassteel desk, nearly in the center of the small square space, was working furniture, with nothing to recommend it aesthetically. It also stood in a direct line from the door. I could have advised him of a more harmonious feng shui arrangement, but the forbidding expression on his face suggested I let him set the subject for discussion.

Captain Naftil was not long in coming to the point. He interleaved his fingers together and set his joined hands on the desktop.

"Kinago, what are you doing?"

"Getting to know the crew, sir," I said. "I believe that I have met approximately sixty seven point five percent of the contingent. Good people, all."

"I am very glad to hear you say that."

His expression was cautiously neutral. I beamed at him.

"I try, sir. I believe that it behooves me, as a scion of the noble house as well as my mother's son, to provide a good example and offer fellowship to those who are brave enough to serve aboard an Imperium naval vessel."

"You have done a little more than offer fellowship, haven't you?"

"Yes, sir, I have," I said. There was no point in concealing my activities. I was not ashamed of them. "I am sharing the fruit of several months' research with my shipmates."

"Seeking popularity among the crew?"

"Well," I said modestly, "it has had that effect. At first I did not offer. I only discussed my interests with a co-worker on my station, and he asked me to expand further. Others confessed their interest. Because that suits the nature of my investigations, I permitted them to take part. Word spread from there. And who am I to refuse to provide entertainment on our long journey among the stars?" I was pleased with my turn of phrase, possessed as it was of two meanings at least. Naftil was unmoved.

"You are trying to get attention, Kinago. Is it because you were not seated at my table?"

"If I am honest, sir, perhaps I must admit it began there, but it has taken on a life of its own. I am doing my best to keep it under control. Everyone seems to be enjoying it, sir."

"Er, fortune-telling . . . it is not sanctioned by the Fleet."

"I am sure it isn't," I said, passionately. "Bureaucracies have, by their nature, deeply rooted and unshakably stiff structures. They are not easily bent toward the softer sciences."

"Eh? You call it a science?"

"Sociology is a science, Captain."

As if in answer, he touched the surface of his desk. An image rose from it. I recognized myself in the middle of a large crowd. I had assumed an air of authority and had my hands raised, palm outward, to the group. I thought I looked rather well, if I had to say so myself.

"If you're not in a receptive frame of mind, how will you absorb the wisdom of the ages?" my recorded image asked grandly of the faces pressing in upon it. Naftil touched the desk again, and my digital image froze in place, with my teeth bared upon my last syllable.

"The wisdom of the ages?" Naftil asked, with one eyebrow raised.

"Perhaps I was laying it on a little heavily," I said. "I was only trying to restore peace in the room. It would have rebounded upon the crew's performance after the rest period if they were to harbor resentment and ill feelings for the space of several hours, sir."

"So this has nothing to do with . . . magic?"

"I have never found a sound basis for magic, sir. My studies are purely for my own enjoyment, and by extension, enjoyment by others."

The other eyebrow joined its fellow on high upon the captain's forehead.

"I had a navigator go off sick for a day because you told him that the stars were misaligned for his efficiency."

"Well, that tells you something about him, doesn't it? I told everyone that my predictions were for entertainment purposes only. The most interesting thing I have discovered in my studies is that people want to believe."

"Do they?"

"Oh, yes, Captain." I produced my viewpad and brought up study after study. The images, charts and reports fanned out across Naftil's desk. "Foreknowledge of the future, even highly generalized or clearly false, seems to give people comfort. I enjoy giving comfort to those who need it."

Naftil narrowed his eyes at me.

"And you believe that you should undergo no punishment for distracting my crew in this fashion?"

I was shocked at the notion, although not surprised.

"I don't believe so, sir. My divinations before reporting to you suggested that you find my efforts without merit, but not against any written regulations." I added hopefully, "Everyone finds it most amusing."

He drummed his fingertips on the desktop. His long oval nail beds told me that he was fair by nature as well as friendly and open. If he had had the triangular nails of Commander Diesen, I would have known not to chance his temper, but when faced with such a trait, I felt it was worth the attempt. He studied me for a long while. I presented him with a pleasant and open countenance.

"Interesting," he said. "You do not attempt to invoke the First Space Lord?"

"Not twice, sir. If there is anything that my mother has done for her children, captain, it is to assure us that when we make a decision, we stand behind it. She has nothing to do with my actions. They are mine and mine alone."

Captain Naftil was unmoved but I hoped not unimpressed. He raised one of those oval-nailed forefingers and pointed it at me.

"No more fortune telling on my ship, lieutenant. And that is final."

"Not even on my off-shifts, sir?" I asked plaintively.

"No. Please do not involve my crew in your *studies*. They are here to defend the Imperium, not to act as your test subjects. If you do not comply, you will be given punishment detail."

I suppressed a sigh.

"As you wish, Captain. I did not mean to give offense. But," I added hopefully, "if you would like, I will arrange to give you a private reading. So you can see what the others have seen."

"No."

"It wouldn't take long. Your date and place of birth are in the ship's records. I could download them in a microsecond."

"No!" Naftil said.

"Are you sure, sir?" I wheedled. "You seemed interested when the subject first came up."

His complexion went from tan to burgundy.

"Out!"

I snapped off a perfect salute, turned on my heel and marched out.

The others were waiting for me around the table in the recreation center. I could not suppress the smugness I felt as I strutted in the door.

"No punishment?" Redius asked, almost astonished. I favored him with a triumphant grin.

"No. The captain found me harmless but amusing."

"He does not know," Redius said, with a breathy laugh.

"Hey, Thomas," Allen said, coming up to me with his tablet in hand. "What about the next person?"

"I regret to say that the captain has put a halt to our activities," I said. "I'm sorry."

Allen looked stricken.

"There's half the crew waiting," he whispered, showing me the list. He glanced nervously over his shoulder. The group watched us avidly, straining to hear what we were saying. "What will I tell them?"

"That's not your responsibility," I said, patting him on the shoulder. "It's mine." I went to address the waiting crowd. "Friends, I am very sorry. Captain Naftil has told me that the fleet does not sanction the reading of fates. With deep regrets, I must inform you that I am folding my tent for the last time. I hope you will understand. We must all accede to naval regulations. I am sure that he has a good reason for withdrawing a form of entertainment that all of you were enjoying. The welfare of the crew and this ship is paramount in his concern. I agree with that wholeheartedly. While I regret not being able to amuse you in the manner I had hoped, I am grateful for the interest that you have shown in my hobby."

"Down with the captain!" a Croctoid boomed from the rear of the crowd.

I favored him with a shocked look.

"He is your superior officer," I said. "A protector of the Imperium. I demand your respect on his behalf on behalf of the Emperor whom, I beg you to recall, is my cousin."

Most of those around him elbowed or poked him. He batted their hands away.

"Aw, I didn't mean it! I was only joking."

"It is not a joking matter," I said. "What if you were overheard by anyone but your close friends and allies?" I swept a hand to indicate the rest of the listeners, all of who were listening with eyes bugged out.

"I'm sorry, Lieutenant Kinago. Honest. I think the captain's great. I was just, I mean . . ."

I gave him a rueful smile.

"As one who has become adept at reading the infinite, I will tell you that all things are fleeting. Your disappointment will be as temporary as mine."

The waiting audience, no longer mine, began to disperse. A number of the most discontented loitered in a group near the door, favoring me with dark glances. I fetched an inward sigh.

"The messenger who carries bad news always seems to gather the opprobrium that the news itself deserves," I told Redius.

With the help of Redius and Allen, I gathered up my possessions and took them back to my cabin.

"I think I sounded almost official back there," I said. "Alas, that I must defend a policy I think is so unsound."

"Too bad," Allen said. "That was the most fun I've ever had on this ship."

The bells rang for mess. Redius, Allen and I made our way to the hall. I did my best to keep my posture erect, but I felt the weight of authority on my back and glares of annoyance drilling into my skin, altogether a most uncomfortable collection of sensations. I bore in mind not only the captain's words but those of my mother. She had asked me to respect Naftil's office. I had and I would, but it was hard. There must have been a hundred and forty people still on the list waiting to have their fortunes told, and whom I was dying to add to my research database. If only I had some means of continuing!

As had been the case since we came aboard, we had a quartet of new people at dinner to meet.

"So you're the guy," said Tolchik, a woman of late middle years who wore second lieutenant's insignia, when we had exchanged names—a superfluity, I always thought, since our names were on our uniforms.

"I am," I said, with a hand held modestly to my chest. "If by 'the guy' you mean the most talented dancer, raconteur and sportsman on board, not to mention the fastest potter in the hydroponics lab."

"Kind of," Tolchik said. She had an all-weather complexion as though she had spent most of her years on a ship in atmosphere, not out in space. Quick blue eyes peered out from within wrinkled lids. "I hear you see the future."

"The same as everyone else, a moment at a time," I replied. She snorted.

"You're just being modest. I came down to the rec center last shift. I signed up on the list to get my turn to hear what you had to say, but I hear you're not doing it any more."

"Well, the captain is against it," I said. "Chain of command, you know."

Tolchik squinted one bright eye at me, then wheeled her gaze to the head table, where Sinim was telling a story, to the obvious merriment of the captain.

"Well, he can't hear us now, can he?"

My heart sank. I knew what she was asking. I glanced at Redius. His jaw was half open in amusement, and a twinkle hovered in his big dark eyes.

"I suppose he can't," I said. I fought to keep control of my impulses. "Wouldn't you like to hear a funny story instead? I have a corker that I unearthed from the most unlikely source, an autobiography of an explorer who lived five millennia ago. I don't mind borrowing material as long as I credit the original storyteller," I told the others. "Better to have such things out in the open, where they can elicit laughs and good cheer, than sitting in the files of some antiquary who won't get the joke."

"No, sir," Tolchik said, leaning toward me. She reached out to grab my forearm. "I'm serious. I need a peep at my future. Look at me! I'm seventy, and never made it up the ranks. I got to know if I bother to stay in the service or go ahead and take pension. I got good years ahead of me—or do I?"

My heart bobbed back to the surface, and went out to her.

"I am sure you do," I said. "I think . . ."

"Thomas . . . !" Redius began to voice a warning. I shrugged regret.

"What can I do? It isn't fair that Tolchik didn't get her turn. I had hoped to offer my services to everyone who made the list before the ban was placed. She would have received some measure of comfort."

I dropped to silence as one of the serverbots arrived tableside with a tray full of main-course plates. It was not too much to assume that the staff would report violations of personal electronics use or other misbehavior. A pair of mechanical hands came up out of its dome and served each of us. It also deposited two pairs of squeeze bottles of sauce at each end of the table. As soon as it rumbled away, fresh inspiration struck. I regarded the dish before me. A golden-brown cutlet of some variety lay there upon a bed of purple rice, flat, enticing and featureless.

"Now, this is a marvelous coincidence," I said, in delight. "We have here a perfect blank slate. I have been working on an entirely new divination method. I call it condimentomancy."

"Condiwhoozeewas?" Tolchik asked. The rest of our fellow diners looked just as puzzled.

"Yes, indeed," I said. "Here." I handed her one of the bottles of sauce. It contained a grayish-brown cream. "Go ahead and anoint your meal as you normally would."

"Well, I don't use that stuff," she said. "I like the other one." She pointed to the orange-red concoction in the other bottle.

"Very well, it doesn't matter which. Go ahead and apply it. Season your meal."

With an odd look at me, she drew a series of curlicues on the surface of the cutlet. I peered at the results with great interest.

I had in fact noticed my own tendency, when provided with the means to do so, to draw designs on my own food. Each of the patterns I produced with a bottle of sauce, a spoonful of dressing or a shaker of herbs bore a general resemblance to one another, but had distinctly different characteristics. I had been curious as to what provoked the variations. Over a series of weeks, I began to make notes of what I was thinking during the meal, and how I felt about each of the foods in question. Once I dismissed the variables, I noticed a pattern emerging.

I had been reading research undertaken by psychologists of earlier millennia about seemingly random patterns who determined that they were actually nothing of the kind. These splashings, sprinkles and squiggles were a fairly keen indicator of my mood and concerns of the moment. Using these observations, I prepared a chart of the designs I produced. Watching my friends eat and asking them leading questions at those moments led me to see that similar moods produced patterns with similar traits. I thought that I had grasped a handle, so to speak, on a lid that could be lifted from a seething pot of mystery.

Tolchik pushed her plate toward me.

"Like that?"

"Exactly like that. Hmm." I stroked my chin. "I see that while you appear to be confident and outgoing, you are actually a private individual. You keep yourself on a very tight rein, and you are afraid of flouting authority. You shouldn't do that. I strongly recommend flouting authority. It's good for both you and the person in charge."

"She put pepper sauce on her meat," Dinas Veltov said, scornfully. "That's all that's there."

"That is what you see, my friend," I said, haughtily elevating my nose. "I see constraint, the product of years of holding back one's normal impulses, partly from caution, perhaps from fear. If I were to say to you that your future held more of the same, what would you think?"

Tolchik regarded me with an expression bordering upon awe.

"I'd say skip the next re-enlistment bonus and go home," she said. "You can see something, just like that? It's magic!"

"It's not magic. It's psychology," I said. "I base my observations on human nature, as well as taste, time, physical condition and emotional connection. Now, I rarely feel constrained, myself. Tonight, perhaps more than other nights, but I seldom produce a pattern like that. You have to bear in mind the kind of food that lends itself to a good condimentomancy reading. If it is something that you would not eat, that changes the reading in many ways. Of course that introduces a further set of variables, depending upon one's liking or disliking of the contents, or whether one prepared the meal oneself. If it was a comestible that one was to lift in the hand, one would naturally apply fewer lashings of sauce close to the edge, which would suggest temporary restraint, if only to spare one's clothes. A flat surface gives the best results. I have an entirely separate chart just for sandwiches. I would be happy to show it to you some time. But I digress. You were under slight pressure to perform, so I take that into account, but your normal characteristics emerge in your actions."

Tolchik stared at me as though I had done something clever, which I had. I tried to look modest under her regard.

"You are a wizard," she said. "I got a lot to think about." She pulled her plate back and curled an arm around it. I noticed that she studied her food closely before cutting into the meat.

"Read mine," Allen said. He had liberally decorated his cutlet with mushroom ketchup.

"You've had your reading," I said, with raised eyebrows. "One mustn't be greedy."

"But never a condimentomancy reading! That sounds cool!"

"Take me next," the Wichu said, shoving his cutlet in my direction. "If there's anything to it. Which I doubt."

The spiky parallel lines spoke of one thing that was common to most Wichus, but there were personal elements to them as well.

"Impatience," I said. "You also dislike this food, but you'll eat it because it's in front of you. You have a flair for leadership. Perhaps a tradition in your family? I notice a backhand curve at the top of each stroke. I would undoubtedly say the same if I analyzed your handwriting." I pushed the plate back to him.

Before I knew it, we surrounded with crewmembers. They had been listening in a casual manner, but when a senior officer began to participate, the floodgates of interest opened up wide. They gathered close around us to listen. Items daubed with various flavors and colors of condiment were pushed under my nose. I couldn't help but state my opinion of the interpretations. Which only attracted more surreptitious and not so subtle onlookers and would-be seekers.

Which led, naturally, to the arrival of the captain's bullet-headed serverbot. I heard it long before I saw it, and realized the import of its advent.

"Make way, please! Make way!"

I shook my head in resignation.

"Sorry, friends. Time for me to go."

I pushed aside the last of the decorated plates before me and rose the 'bot before it had finished its warning. Those still waiting looked up at me in dismay.

I followed the 'bot out of the entertainment center toward the lift.

It did no good to protest that it hadn't been I who started the descent into disobedience, so I did not even essay to pass responsibility. I should have recalled that my condimentomancy reading said that I had an impulsive streak, too.

CHAPTER 17

"Breathe," a voice said. "Come on, I don't have all day. You're okay. Open your eyes. Hurry up!"

M'Kenna gasped in a lungful of air and began coughing. Her eyes flew open. Glaring lights beat down on her. She shut her eyes again, cursing under her breath.

"That's better." She recognized the voice as Allisjonil's. "She's all right. What about him?"

At a distance, she heard whimpering. Her babies! Her babies were alive!

She opened her eyes again and sat up.

"Not quickly," said a female Uctu in an enveloping white garment, catching her by the shoulders as she swayed. Her head swam as if her brain was made of rubber. "Slow now."

"Where are my children?" she demanded. Her voice sounded far away to her own ears.

"Recovering," the Uctu said. She pointed one narrow orange hand through a doorway.

M'Kenna squinted against the bright lights. Gradually, her eyes adjusted. All four children were within her line of sight. Every one of them was alive and well. Lerin was reading a tablet, with Nona helping him. Dorna and Akila sat on the floor. Their faces were smeared with crumbs from the cookies they held in each hand. M'Kenna felt tears overspill her eyes. She brushed them away, but more kept coming. She wept, letting the grief and terror of her last few minutes of consciousness sweep over her. The Uctu physician patted her sympathetically on the shoulder, then handed her an absorbent square from hovercart full of medical implements and supplies at her side. M'Kenna blotted her face with it and handed it back.

"Food now?" the doctor asked.

"Something to drink," M'Kenna said. Her tongue was dry. The physician offered her a sealed bubble with a straw protruding from the top. M'Kenna sucked up the fresh water in a few gulps. The physician handed her a second sphere. She drained half of it, and felt her senses coming back to her.

"Your family's readings show anomalies, like to analyze," the doctor said.

"Sure," M'Kenna said, faintly. She wasn't really paying attention. She was too busy looking around.

They were no longer in their family cell. *Correct that*, M'Kenna thought. *We aren't in the* same *cell.* Like the first one, this suite of locked rooms had no scopes or screen tanks in the cells, so she and the others might as well have been taken out of the first cell, turned around three times, and returned to the same place. This cell had solid walls, instead of the glass-fronted exhibit box in which they had been living for weeks, and a door consisting of floor-to-ceiling bars. The wall opposite on the other side of the hall was still blank. The beds had blue coverlets instead of gray. The hygiene unit was in the opposite corner. The air seemed cleaner and there was more light, but it was still a grim prospect.

"Where are we?" she demanded.

Allisjonil came back to her.

"You got transferred to Dilawe."

"How?" M'Kenna demanded. "When?"

"Well, they knocked you out. They always do that."

M'Kenna felt fury burning in her belly.

"They gassed my babies!" she snarled. "How dare they do that?"

Allisjonil shrugged his enormous furry shoulders.

"Some of the prisoners get violent and try to escape, so they take no chances. You haven't met any Donre yet, I bet. Their confooferation is on the other side of Uctu space. They never come through to the Imperium, or not yet anyhow, but they're little like your kids. I got bitten by one of the little nerffis, so I'm with the Uctu on this one."

"I want to talk to someone!"

"It won't help. They won't listen. Calm down. Everybody's fine. The kids ate about an hour ago. You want some lunch?"

"No!" M'Kenna was too angry to swallow. Allisjonil turned up a leathery palm.

"Suit yourself. Dinner isn't for another three hours."

Cursing, M'Kenna struggled off her bunk and went to her children. They *were* all fine. She examined each child carefully over his or her protests, but could see nothing wrong with them, apart from the ineffable fact that they had been rendered unconscious without any prior warning. Rafe, on the bed adjacent to hers, was still out. He lay as still as a statue. His prison jumpsuit was open to the waist. His wide chest rose and fell shallowly. M'Kenna sat down beside him, holding his hand.

"Why won't he wake up?" she asked.

"It takes the big people longer," Allisjonil said. "I don't know why. Proportionately, the little guys absorb more of the knockout gas. He'll be okay soon."

The Uctu healer glided to M'Kenna's husband's side and put a hand to the side of his throat. She beckoned to the hovercart. It hummed over to her. She tapped one of the embossed panels in its side, which popped open. She extracted a patch the size of M'Kenna's palm and applied it just below Rafe's throat. A few seconds later, he let out a snort and began to shift on the bunk.

M'Kenna stayed by him. His eyelids started to flutter. When they opened for the first time, she held her hand across them to shield them from the light. Soon his eyes focused and turned to her.

"We're alive?" he whispered.

"Everyone's fine," she said, projecting assurance she did not feel. "The kids are doing all right. So am I. Can you sit up?"

"I think so," Rafe said. He groaned. M'Kenna pulled his arm to help him up. He settled with his back to the wall.

"I'm fine." He smiled at her. That smile always melted her. M'Kenna started to relax. When the physician offered Rafe something to eat, she discovered she had an appetite, too. The rations were about the same as they had been given on Partwe, but tasted less as though they had been processed. Food gave them the energy to start talking again. M'Kenna explained what had happened and where they were, with the attorney filling in the blanks.

"When do we get our day in court?" Rafe asked Allisjonil.

"I'll let you know as soon as I find out," he said. "I gotta go. The crew of *Sword Snacks* ought to be waking up right about now . . ."

As he said that, they heard a bellow somewhere close by but out of sight.

"What the hell just happened to me?" shouted Nuro. Allisjonil grinned.

"Yeah, just like I thought. I'll be back in a couple of days." The Wichu felt in the thick fur on his chest. "Oh, yeah. Almost forgot. They're not so tight about the technology here. You get an extra tablet, if you want it."

He brought out a new viewpad. It still had the clear plastic wrap around it.

"You bet we do," Rafe said, with an avid look. "No more playing tug-of-war with the kids? Sign me up."

Allisjonil stripped the tablet and stuffed the wrapper into his fur. He logged onto the unit, then handed it over to them. He went to the door. A male Uctu guard, clad in a different style of uniform than M'Kenna had seen before, let him out. The doctor went with him, pushing her cart.

Rafe opened their message center and waited. The connection there on Dilawe was good, much better than on Partwe. It took only moments for the inbox to fill up, then empty more than halfway as the automatic spam detector to delete group messages, advertising, begging letters or solicitations.

"There's thousands of messages here," he said. "Maybe hundreds of thousands! Man, we must have been out for days."

"Any replies to the letters I sent to the Imperium government?" M'Kenna asked.

Rafe scanned down the endless scroll of return addresses.

"Can't tell you yet. It'll take a while to get through all this. This is just the real mail!"

Lerin came over, the other tablet clutched under his arm.

"Mama, I don't feel good."

M'Kenna felt his forehead. His temperature was normal. She didn' t like the faint greenish tinge of his eyes.

"Do you have a stomachache?"

"Kind of."

"The kind where you're going to be sick?"

"Uh-huh."

He might have been getting to be a big boy, but she picked him up bodily and carried him to the sanitary center. She was just in time. Lerin knelt over the disposer. All the lunch he had just swallowed came back up again. When it was over, she sat on the floor with him, wiping his mouth with a cool cloth. She gave him the rest of the bulb of water she hadn't finished.

"Why couldn't you have done this in front of the doctor?" M'Kenna asked, wryly, as he sipped at it.

"It didn't feel so bad before."

She hugged him.

"Siff messaged back," Rafe called. "She's on her way. Bringing her own lawyer, so she won't get caught up in this."

"Good thing," M'Kenna said.

"She says can she bring anything with her?"

"How about a hacksaw and a map to the nearest exit?"

"You know the authorities are going to listen to this," Rafe chided her.

"If they think I'm serious, they're more stupid than I already think they are," M'Kenna said. "You going to be all right, sweetheart?" she asked Lerin.

"Yes, mama."

"The air smells worse here than it did in the other place. Why don't you lie down for a little while and let your stomach settle?"

"Okay."

He brought the tablet over to Nona, and lay down on one of the bunks with his arm over his eyes. M'Kenna rejoined her husband. He handed her the new tablet.

She went through the rolls and rolls of mail. Notes of support from family, messages from suppliers, jokes from all those connections she had dating back to primary school who had her on a mailing list waited to be sorted into the appropriate folders. She set aside all of those to read later. She needed help, not jokes.

Below the first hundred or so, she saw a return address that read "Justice Department." Hastily, she clicked on it.

Dear Ms. Copper,

We have reviewed your request for assistance. The Justice

Department receives literally millions of messages every year from citizens. We regret that we cannot intercede in a case brought by a fellow sovereign nation. Until the Uctu Justice System has rendered a verdict, the Imperium cannot offer aid for an appeal. Please keep us apprised of your situation.

Sincerely yours,
Bowner Koroyeb

M'Kenna slammed that message into her received file and went on. Beneath that, she found entry after entry from the officials and authorities to whom she had written. Every one of the replies was a variation on the first one. They couldn't help. They *wouldn't* help. They didn't have the resources to help. She received hundreds, no, thousands of polite form notices, a few out-of-office memos, and plenty of voice messages that all added up to nothing.

It was worth trying again. It had to be worth trying again. She wrote back to each and every one of them, making her plea as urgent as she could.

"Don't you see how serious this is? We are going to die!"

She pushed the tablet away. There were many more messages to get through, but she couldn't face another one. She had always thought her government had her back. It was daunting to realize that when she needed it the most, it let her down.

She felt tears in her eyes. They weren't only because she felt her family was alone in the worst situation she could possibly imagine, but the air was more pungent than before. She rubbed her sleeve across her eyes, then looked up. She was being watched.

Through the bars of the cell door, she could see the Uctu physician.

"May come in, Ms. Copper?"

M'Kenna stayed where she was. Over the doctor's shoulder she could see a contingent of prison guards.

"Sure. What's this about?"

The doctor nodded to the guards. The door slid open, and she pushed her hovercart into the cell. The guards remained outside.

"Inspected earlier," she said. "Readings unusually lacking. Habilitation treatment received?"

Rafe sat up straighter on his bunk.

"Years ago, all of us," he said. "Our youngest got hers just a few months after she was born. Why?"

The Uctu looked severe.

"Treatment failed. Advise report dispensing physician. Misfeasance."

"The treatment failed?" M'Kenna asked. "Is that why the air smells so bad? No offense," she added hastily.

"None," the physician agreed. "Tests prove failure. Need restoration, immune boosters, nanites again."

"Wait a minute," Rafe said, his brows lowering. "Those treatments cost us plenty."

The doctor shrugged her narrow shoulders.

"Cut rate offered. Accept?"

"Wait a minute," Rafe said again. He beckoned to M'Kenna. The two of them retreated to the end of the chamber. Both of them knew it was a futile gesture, since everything they said could be and probably was being recorded.

"That would explain why we have felt so rotten ever since we got into Uctu space," M'Kenna said. "I never felt that bad visiting Partwe before."

"How could it have stopped working?" Rafe asked. "We were here only last year."

"I know. But what choice do we have? The children have been feeling poorly for a long while. That may be why."

"What do you think happened?"

"I don't know," M'Kenna said, thinking deeply. "I almost think it had to have happened on Way Station 46. We were exposed to something that undid our immunity. Maybe all of us traders were."

"At the same time our ships were invaded," Rafe said.

M'Kenna nodded.

"We really don't have a choice but to take the treatment again. I can't stand the smell of chlorine too much longer. Otherwise I will be begging them to take me out and shoot me."

"We've got the money," Rafe said with a sigh. "I just hate to waste it on something that ought to have lasted all our lives."

M'Kenna just added it to the list of things that had gone wrong. She gave a bitter bark of laughter.

"I just hope there will come a day when we can look back on all this and laugh."

Rafe gathered her to him and kissed her ear.

"There will be. I promise." He led her back to where the doctor was waiting.

"All right, do it," he said. "All of us."

"Who first?" the doctor asked. "One adult. Four days unconsciousness."

M'Kenna groaned and rolled her eyes. She had forgotten about that part.

"I'll do it," Rafe said. "That is, if we have eight days to spend on acclimatizing ourselves."

The doctor's kind eyes crinkled with sympathy.

"Eight days yes," she said. "Pass quickly."

CHAPTER 18

"Fzzt! Too much solvent," said Ensign DE576-OA, a compact technobot about the size of an twelve-liter barrel. "More care, please. Use suction to remove it before it affects the circuits to either side."

I moved the tiny tip of the tool I wielded in against the silver motherboard as directed and removed most of the drop of bright blue fluid. My cheeks were moist with perspiration underneath the heavy magnifying goggles I wore. They increased the acuity of my vision some three thousand times. I was curled up uncomfortably beneath a console in the sick bay amid chemical and animal smells, as well as that acrid aroma which arose from the solvent. I felt almost as I had when I was first released from the medical facility on Keinolt following my habilitation treatment. All things seemed to be grossly out of proportion, but this time it was for a reason.

When I was summoned before him, Captain Naftil had been less patient with me than I thought he would be. Perhaps he had been egged on by Jil. Perhaps he simply did not wish to appear to be a soft touch. Since I seemed unable to resist defying his instructions during my rest periods, he directed that I should be deprived of them for a while. As a result, I was sentenced to punishment detail. When I was not engaged in personal hygiene or meals, he would see to it that I would have something useful to occupy my time.

I focused through the thick lenses, and aimed the pinpoint light upon the small striped element. With a pair of pliers more minute than a strand of hair, I extracted the part from its parent circuit and brought it closer to my eye.

"Is it damaged?" Dee asked. One of his ocular units moved into my field of vision, looking like a pipe from a municipal water main instead of the tiny microscope it was.

"It seems to have burst from the inside," I said, holding it for him to see. I dropped it into a curved plastic dish. It should have gone *clank*, if it had been the size it appeared to me, but since it was so small, it went *tick* instead.

My new task was to search out and repair microcircuitry, under the guidance of the LAI who ran the department. Although it was a bother to be separated from my new pupil, I was enjoying the tutelage of a new teacher myself. My new task was interesting, and Dee was a painstaking taskmaster. I respected his expertise and patience. He and I struck up a companionship. I learned more about microcircuitry in an afternoon than I had picked up in my entire life thus far. Under normal circumstances, only mechanicals replaced the malfunctioning elements. They were more fitted to not only precision work but also to detecting the problems with built-in equipment that Humans, Uctu, and all the other flesh-and-blood species lacked. New staff of the engineering department were assigned to do what I was doing, to learn the various peculiarities of the devices in use around the ship and see what went wrong the most frequently. It was also good for a penalty exercise, because it involved a good deal of bending, crawling into equipment cabinets, up into ceilings, down lift tubes and into other small spaces generally considered uncomfortably inaccessible. I did not strictly require such knowledge, but no effort is wasted, I mused, as I replaced the burned-out unit with a fresh one.

"Now engage the diagnostic nanites," Dee said.

If I had shaken the microscopic machines out of their tube by hand, I would probably have broadcast them all over the lab. Instead, I reached for the control console in the rolling toolbox beside me. I spoke the order.

"Nanites, check function of rehabilitation machine," I said. "Reconnect disabled circuits and report."

This was my favorite part of the process. From a covered bin in the toolbox, a stream of tiny silver particles poured out. If I had not been wearing my goggles, it would have been invisible to me. It flowed across the floor, up the leg of the machine, and vanished like water on sand into the workings of the medical device.

"How many of them are we using today?" I asked.

Dee emitted a brief whirring noise.

"Three million, five hundred sixty thousand and nine," he said.

I waited, holding my breath. Slowly, like a ripple on the sea, the nanites emerged from the machine. They formed a foil-like sheet on the surface that shimmered delicately. I let out a sigh of wonder.

"Can you see any breaks?" Dee inquired. I scanned the silver sheet. It appeared intact.

"No," I said. "I think all systems are go." I glanced over to the control console. The screen, as large as my bunk, flashed a row of zeroes. "Well done, team!" I said heartily.

"They cannot understand you, Thomas," Dee said. "They are too simple a machine."

"I can't help it," I said. "I have so many friends who are artificial intelligences that I find myself talking with all sorts of devices. Better safe than sorry is my motto." I rolled a hopeful eye in Dee's direction. "May I make them do it again?"

"Not necessary," Dee said.

"But it's so much fun to watch them!" I was struck at that moment by humorous inspiration. "Dee, how many nanites does it take to change a light bulb?"

"LED, incandescent, halogen or compact fluorescent?"

I threw back my head and laughed. I hadn't expected him to reply with another question. Unfortunately, the space into which I had wedged myself permitted little movement before I forcibly impacted with a barrier.

"Ow!" I exclaimed. I wriggled my arm through the constricted area to rub the offended portion of my cranium. "Well, that teaches me to experiment in LAI humor."

A soft chuckle came from overhead. I stuck my head out from underneath the console. A gigantic, moonlike face with pale skin surrounded by a forest of waving dark trees—I mean, hair—gazed down upon me. I snatched off my goggles and wiped my forehead.

"Oh, Anstruther," I said. "I forgot you were there." The quiet computer engineer had been moved from department to department as each officer in charge heard of her competence and demanded her time. At present, the head of sick bay was the lucky supervisor who benefited from her services. "Have we done our work? Is the device ready to assist patients in need of physiotherapy?"

She nodded toward the console, which was calibrated to read gestures as well as receive vocal input or key taps. It whirred to life. Lights on the screen that had been red or orange changed to restful green and blue.

"It's fine now. I can incorporate it into the new med program."

"What makes it new?" I asked, unfolding myself from my cubbyhole.

"It's being tested here on the *Bonchance* before being used across the fleet. It's part of an allover wellness regimen for each crewmember. If you need medical treatment, it automatically cross-schedules you for appointments and reserves time on the appropriate equipment. The duty rosters are updated to accommodate them. It sets alarms and sends reminders to your message box."

I nodded approval.

"Better than relying upon memory. I know when I become engrossed I forget appointments all the time. The pocket secretary I use at home is equipped with an intolerably loud alarm to get me places on time."

Dee plucked the repair tool out of my hand and placed it in the rolling box. All the flaps on top snapped shut. I presume that the nanites had all gone back to their designated pigeonhole.

"Good work, lieutenant. You are dismissed for today. I will be certain to send you a reminder message and an alert siren to remind you to return later."

I laughed again. Dee did have a sense of humor.

"I will be here. I must run. I would like to read my mail and tidy up before bed. I will see you tomorrow," I said to Anstruther.

"By the way, Thomas," she asked shyly, always charmingly reluctant to use my first name, "how many nanites *does* it take to change a light bulb?"

"I don't know," I said, with a grin. "I lost count after the first million."

Sacrificing an hour or two of sleep time, I checked the replies to my entries about the latest round of readings, not mentioning the secondary outcome of being deprived of my free hours. My fellow scientists were divided on the logic behind my new form of divination. A few were for it, several were against it, and a few excoriated me for frivolousness. The latter I considered to be much more a badge of honor than a disgrace.

Beneath those entries, though, were countless notes from members of the Bonchance crew. I received message after despondent message not only from those whom I had disappointed, but those whom I had already given readings.

We need you to tell us what to do, said a note from an Uctu whose scales I had read on the second day.

"*That sets a very dangerous precedent*," I replied, using a very solemn typeface to indicate my sincerity. *Please let me make it clear that I never set out to tell you what to do. I intend to amuse, nothing more. You need to set your own lives in order. Read your daily horoscopes, but go on as normal.*

Those are bunkum! Yours are much more accurate, came an instantaneous reply from a human crew member who must have been reading the thread from her station in Communications.

That is because I have met you, and know what you want to hear. Mine are absolutely as much bunkum as the ones in the news feeds. Pray do not ask again. I do not want the captain to be unhappy. My mother would disapprove of me misusing one of her officers, I added on a flippant note that I hoped no one would forward to Captain Naftil.

The confrontation continued in person when I went for a quick breakfast before rejoining Dee for another shift before I was expected back in Hydroponics. An ad hoc committee of would-be clients hunkered down in the open chairs at my table and glowered at me and my bowl of oatmeal.

"You can't just cut us off without more guidance," Veltov said. "I was just starting to get into it."

"I must," I said. "One of the primary underpinnings of duty is obedience."

"We'll protest. We'll send a petition to the captain. I bet I could get a thousand signatures today."

"I'd sign!" "So would I!"

"Now, now, now," I chastised them. "Don't be silly. Find your own oracle. Flip a coin. Write a dozen encouraging messages and program your viewpad to choose one at random when you tap an icon. These are all things you can do yourself, if you choose. You don't need me to do it for you, really you don't. I have enjoyed myself greatly. I hope you have. But do not become dependent upon a single form of entertainment for your self-esteem. I never do. I change enthusiasms frequently."

Veltov looked as though she had been betrayed which, in a manner, I feared she had.

"You couldn't give up looking at the future, could you? Not really?"

I raised my hands, palm up, in abject surrender.

"Sadly, those who know me realize that I flit from subject to subject on the wings of whim. By the time you see me next, I may have become enamored of ceiling frescoes, for all I know, and have put aside my crystal ball forever. I do not pretend to be preternaturally self-aware, but I am cognizant of my own foibles. Heavens know they cost me enough money." I offered a self-deprecating grin, but it failed to find an appreciative audience.

My crewmates were not happy, but they, too, knew they also had no choice but to obey. Wherever I went that day, I saw reproving glances and heard muttering in corners.

I found myself wondering if I had created a mutinous situation. I thought about trying to soothe the matter, but I realized nothing I could say would make them happy.

My fellow scientists chided me on the Infogrid, saying that I had taken too large a sample for my survey, and caused the problem myself. At mess, I sat with my shoulders hunched as a bulwark against any further chastisement.

"They misunderstood me," I told Redius at mess later that day, "and it is all my fault."

"Miscalculation," he said, with some sympathy. "But language going well."

"Am I?" I asked, then switched to Uctu. "I am giving it all my best efforts."

"In all of the spare time that you have remaining," Redius said in the same language, laughing. "You are doing well, but you have such a heavy accent!"

"I will work on defeating it," I said.

Alas, he was the only one at the table who would speak to me. My study had taught me a good deal about human nature, including a few lessons that I hadn't anticipated and really didn't enjoy. I had only wanted to make people happy. I thought my studies would provide pleasure. Instead, I had inadvertently created codependency; I for the admiration, they for the guidance, however false its source. More fool I.

I hoped I would not remain a pariah for the last few days aboard the *Bonchance*.

I signed in for another brief shift with Dee. I had introduced him to Angie aboard the *Rodrigo*, and as far as I could tell, he was getting along with her like old friends. The LAIs on both ships were puzzled by the isolation into which I had been cast. They did not join in the boycott of Lord Thomas Kinago, Lieutenant, Incorporated. Nor did my own crew, represented as it was within the sick bay of my toils by Anstruther. I was grateful for their friendship. Although a Kinago never surrendered even in the face of adversity, I was glad not to have to be stalwart in isolation.

My tasks provided me solace. I duly scanned circuit boards with my detectors, seeking the minute variations in signal strength that indicated a weakness in one element or another. It was rather like being a criminal investigator. I was in search of the archvillain, Broken Circuit, and his heinous sidekick, Short. No cracked capacitor or malfunctioning chip or overgrown organocircuitry was going to get past Detective Inspector Thomas Kinago, no, indeed!

"Aha!" I cackled, my multiply-magnified eye alighting upon a tiny filament of conductive foil that had somehow detached itself from the board beneath, interfering with the healthy working of the communications console it occupied. "There you are, vile fiend! Nanites, deal with him!" I watched with pleasure as the stream of silver particles surged out of their box and into the offending component, as if it was a troop of brave police officers defending the law—in this case, the law of conservation of energy. They would soon deal with Broken Circuit!

My viewpad sounded, signaling a live communiqué. Someone wanted to speak to me! Eagerly, I glanced at Dee.

"May I take this?" I asked.

"A short break is acceptable," he said. He went on sorting infinitely minute electronic components into equally tiny slotted compartments. I accepted the call.

A familiar countenance filled the small screen: dark eyes in an ascetic and cleanly shaven face, topped by neat dark hair. The collar that met the noble chin must have been honored by the contact.

"Parsons!" I exclaimed with pleasure, happily resuming my quotidian persona. "I have not seen you for several days."

"I have been busy, my lord." His usual lack of expression seemed to be flavored with a slight taste of hesitation.

"Is there something I may help with?" I inquired. The hesitation I thought I had seen vanished as if it had never existed.

"You may, my lord. I must request a favor of you."

A favor? Parsons was asking a favor? I savored the moment as I replied.

"No question, to the last coin in my treasury, or the last drop of blood in my veins, Parsons. What may I do for you?"

"I have a subject for you, my lord," he said, his dark eyes fixed upon mine. "A young woman?"

I waved a dismissive hand in the vicinity of my hairline.

"I am up to here with young women, Parsons. My cousins and her friends are enjoying my discomfiture with all their might. Those I have met that I thought I had made friends have decided that I am no longer nice to know. Speak to me not of young women, Parsons! Or old ones. Or males of any species." I might as well be evenhanded with my opprobrium.

"But your special talents are needed at this time," Parsons pressed.

I perked up.

"My special talents? Of which do you speak? I have so many."

"That number may be debated at another time, my lord. I wish to call upon your abilities in the occult, er, sciences."

In spite of myself, I was intrigued. I leaned closer to the small screen.

"A reading, Parsons?" I asked. "The captain seems to be very annoyed that I am practicing on his ship."

"One last reading."

"Are you certain that it would be a good idea?"

"As a favor to me, sir."

"The world is not enough for you to ask, Parsons," I said, expansively. "Where and when?"

"Now, sir."

"With full rig and rigmarole?" I asked, not willing to appear too eager. "It adds to the psychological impact, you know."

"You may employ all of your impedimenta, my lord. Meet us in the hydroponics garden in fifteen minutes."

I glanced around, suddenly reminded of my circumstances.

"I don't think I am permitted to go yet."

"You are dismissed," Dee said, without turning his optic sensors toward me. "Launch time has been scheduled."

My viewpad emitted a very shrill, short blast. I gazed at it in dismay. My personal electronics had fallen prey to transient signals of annoying tone and frequency since I had come aboard the *Bonchance.*

"I have no idea where that noise came from, Parsons," I said. "I am very sorry for the effect it must have had on your eardrums."

"It is of no moment, my lord," he said. "Fifteen minutes."

"I will be there."

I took my leave of Dee and hurried to my quarters.

Once the captain had put me on punishment detail, I had put aside my robes and charts with the thought that they would not be needed again until the *Rodrigo* launched one jump from the frontier, approximately three days hence. It was with growing joy that I unpacked all of my goods and conveyed them to the designated meeting point.

No one was in the garden when I arrived. The courting couples and those seeking a quiet place to read must have had other duties. Beyond the glass wall that separated the cultivated wilderness from the hydroponics laboratory I could hear Diesen's voice admonishing this shift's workforce to be more careful with their future comestibles. I had the sweet-scented leafy haven to myself. Parsons and my putative subject were yet to come, giving me adequate time to erect the pavilion, set up the table and stools, and choose from thousands of charts in my collection the most impressive one to have projecting upon the billowing wall. I sat with my hands folded upon the table, suppressing my impulse to wriggle with happiness. As this was to be my last subject aboard the *Bonchance*, I wanted to make the event memorable.

The dark presence that was Parsons loomed out from between the honeysuckle vines. Beside him trembled a slim, nervous creature. I studied her as she approached.

Anstruther had a pale complexion that acted as a handsome

counterpoint to her long, dark hair and deep blue eyes. In contrast, this young woman had been painted entirely in pastels. Her skin was translucent, and her irises such a pale blue they seemed to have no color at all. Her hair, cut very short, just hinted at golden red. Her white tunic, marking her as infirmary staff, further added to her ethereal appearance. I could have plucked her off the page of one of my fairy bestiaries as a water sprite or a snow angel. She drooped reluctantly upon the stool across from me.

"Lord Thomas, this is Ensign Kan Goliffe. She is in need of your wisdom." Parsons delivered this statement, then took two paces backward. The young woman glanced over her shoulder at him, then turned nervously to me.

I tried to look kindly and wise.

"You have come to me with a problem, I believe?" I asked. I reached for her hands, but she pulled them back against her midsection.

I was, as I have indicated, becoming adept at reading the moods of my subjects. This one was flighty and unhappy. I considered which of my many studied methods of divination would elicit the greatest response from her. If I could not make physical contact, palm reading was out of the question. A horoscope was too distant and impersonal. She needed something more intimate.

"You seem so troubled," I said. "Let us see how the fates have been misusing you."

From within the breast of my robe I drew forth an artifact of my own heritage. With her eyes fixed upon my hands, I unwrapped the silk cloth that sheltered a stack of ancient but still-crisp pasteboards and spread them out upon the table. The colorful images bloomed on the dark cloth like the flowers surrounding us.

"These Tarot cards belonged to my great-great-great grandmother Loche," I said. "She had a reputation as an accomplished seer, some four millennia in the past." I gathered them up again and shuffled them gently. "Tell me when to stop."

I counted fifteen gathers of the deck before she emitted a tiny whisper.

"Stop. Stop!"

"This is your significator," I said. The blindfolded woman of the Two of Swords. Troubled, indeed! I divided the remaining deck into three piles. "Point to one of these."

Hastily, she chose the middle. I put the other two stacks beneath the middle one, and dealt ten cards off the top in a pattern that was as lost in time as Earth herself.

I placed the significator in the center.

"Do you find yourself pulled this way and that by two different forces?" I asked. I glanced up. Those colorless eyes were wide with terror. "Two different ideologies, perhaps?" I was rewarded with an open flinch.

I began to wonder precisely into what Parsons had dumped me. The Celtic cross reading showed a soul in torment. At base, she was withdrawn and shy. Since then, she had let herself be controlled by outward forces. I found I was telling myself a story that would have done credit to a dark, stormy night. Instead, I gathered up the rest of the deck and began to turn cards over one by one. I had become very good at interpreting on the fly, but I didn't like what I was reading, in the cards or in her face.

"You are influenced from afar," I said. The next card made my skin tingle. "And nearby as well. A lover, perhaps? More than one?"

She spoke aloud for the first time, the words almost dragged out of her as though they were chained together. I was fascinated to watch her.

"One man at home. One man on the ship."

I turned over the Chariot, then sword cards, one after another. My subconscious kicked words out of my mouth before I knew I was speaking them. I wished I could say that I was channeling a higher force, because I felt uncomfortable being their source.

"They know one another. But you don't manage them; they control you. What have they made you do that you don't want to?"

She gaped at me in open horror, and I felt an answering sense of shock. I had hit, as the ancient gold miners once said, pay dirt. This was all real to her. I had never had a subject who was so open in her reactions. I watched her with a sense of guilt.

"You don't know! You can't know!" she wailed.

I gave her an apologetic smile.

"I don't, really. It's a coincidence that puts the cards into this order, but I see what I am saying resonate in your face. Tell Uncle Thomas. How bad is it? Are you cheating on them with a third lover?" I asked, playfully, but she was too terrified to see anything funny in the moment.

No. She, too was experiencing guilt. Guilt and fear and shame. I was appalled. I felt like pulling my tent down, balling it and the robe up and bundling them into the nearest disposer, but Parsons nodded once, firmly, finally. He needed me to keep going. I was fearless in physically daunting situations, but I felt helpless in the face of a fellow creature going through internal emotional distress.

"What do you fear, Ensign?" I asked, in a soft, calming voice similar to that my nannies had used when I awakened with nightmares as a child. "You're safe here. My tent is a haven. Nothing bad has ever happened in here, I promise, except for the time I gave myself a paper cut with the cards. Are you afraid that they will both leave you?" A barely perceptible shake of the head. "No? Are they threatening you in any way?"

She sat up. For the first time that ghostly complexion took on a roseate hue. I felt very much as if I should take the name of her on-ship lover and go challenge him to unarmed combat.

"I can't stand it any longer," she said. Her eyes bored into mine, looking for help. "They're *pushing* me."

"To do what?" I asked. This time she let me take her hand. "To hurt someone? To hurt yourself? This is your safe place. No one can make you do anything you don't want to do. Tell me. Trouble shared is trouble halved. You'll feel so much better. Look," I said, turning over one last card. "The Sun. Bring daylight in on this situation. It will help you to heal."

Suddenly, words began to pour out of her. She was a medtech, brought along from another ship by a doctor who swept her off her feet. He loved her. He was her entire world. The other man she had known at university. Her first lover. He had become a businessman. I knew how powerful a relationship that could be. They wanted her to cause a catastrophe, out here near the frontier, to cause a distraction. She had to be in the middle of it, so she couldn't be questioned later on. They pushed her so hard that she was ready to consider self-destruction a welcome escape from their badgering.

I listened with fascination. Her story was as tortuous as any digitavid drama. I felt as though I could not wait to happen next.

"But you wouldn't kill yourself, would you?" I asked.

Her hesitation spoke volumes.

"Yes."

I hardly recognized the squeak I emitted as my own voice.

"How?"

The device was in her station, among her personal equipment in the sick bay. It had been assembled from five different packages that were sent to her as gifts. It was set to detonate at a random moment so she would not know when the blow would fall.

I cycled through my own emotional pressures. Part of me was as fascinated as though I was face to face with a poisonous snake. I couldn't look away or stop listening to her. Another part of me wanted to run away with my fingers in my ears. This was all too real and terrible. How could someone be driven to potential suicide by two people who were supposed to love her? But what was at the back of the unthinkable act was that they wanted her to blow up the sick bay on a warship when it was far from home and other ships. What was their motive? We could all die at any time! I glanced up at Parsons, pleading to be released from my ordeal.

He gave me one more steady nod. I must stay the course.

Naturally, I would. I was a Kinago. As painful as this was to hear, it was my duty. I must protect the ship and those aboard her.

"But you might not be there at that moment," I said. "What about others who might be near your station when it went off?"

She put her head down on my Tarot cards and sobbed piteously. With the robe on I could not reach the handkerchief in my belt pouch. I reached for a fold of my tent and put it into her hand. She dragged it to her face and blew her nose in it. I patted her shoulder, trying not to display the fear in my own heart. Anstruther was in the sick bay at that very moment. She was in danger! I glanced at Parsons. He seemed to read my mind, for he lifted his viewpad and tapped at the screen.

"Tell me where it is," I said. "I'm sure we can disarm it easily. I know the most wonderful box of nanites. They are amazingly good at their job . . . ."

"It's in my locker," she said. "Under my spare uniform and an old book. No one would ever look there."

Suddenly, we were surrounded by security patrol. They gathered up Goliffe gently but firmly, and took her away. She held onto the fold of my tent until it was taken out of her fingers by the MP on her left.

"Anstruther," I squawked to the lead officer, who hovered behind to consult Parsons. "My friend is in peril of her life!"

"We're taking care of it, sir," she said. "The sick bay has been evacuated. Another team was on standby waiting for Goliffe's confession. It was better to find out where the bomb was than instigate a search that might have set it off by accident. She covered a lot of ground on this ship."

"Thank you," I said. I rose to follow Goliffe's escort.

"Where are you going, sir?"

"With her," I said. "She may need me. You can see how unhappy she is."

The security officer shook his head.

"You have to wait here, sir. They'll take care of her."

I watched Goliffe depart through the leafy aisle with my heart wrenching itself to follow her.

"What will happen to her?" I asked. The stony-faced officer showed a welcome morsel of sympathy.

"She'll be sectioned for her own good. It's up to the Judge Advocate General to determine if her boyfriend is implicated. In any case, he'll be transferred off this ship to where he can't do any more harm. Thanks for your help, lieutenant. That couldn't have been easy."

"Glad to oblige," I said. "Sadly, I believe that that was the most adult thing I have ever done."

"Congratulations, my lord," Parsons said.

"Thank you, Parsons," I said. I gathered up Great-Great-Great Grandmother Loche's Tarot cards. "It was uncomfortable, but I am satisfied with the outcome. It was a good reading."

"It was most effective."

"Poor thing! I had better get back to Dee. I want to hear the entire scuttlebutt on what occurred in the sick bay once Goliffe told me there was a bomb hidden there."

"I am afraid that will not be possible, sir," he said.

"Why not?" I asked.

"You will be otherwise engaged."

"Where? Doing what?"

Two MPs appeared at my side.

"Will you come with us, sir?" asked the first one, a stocky man with black hair and very dark brown skin. His counterpart, an Uctu with mature head scales, fixed me with a disapproving gaze.

I looked at them, puzzled.

"No, I am not the one who was dealing with explosives," I said. "She was just escorted away. Miss Goliffe."

"No, sir, we are here for you."

"Me? Why?"

"You disobeyed a direct order from the captain."

"I did?" I glanced toward Parsons, but he had unaccountably disappeared without leaving behind an explanation. I had been grievously betrayed, but for what reason I did not know. A heavy sigh erupted from my lungs. *Et tu, Parsons?* "Yes, I suppose I did."

CHAPTER 19

For the third time in as many days, I stood before the captain's desk. But this time, we were not alone. An LAI transcriptionist was present, as were a prosecutor and my defense attorney. I stood an official court martial.

My heart was in my highly polished shoes as I listened to the charges. As all official court proceedings, it was being broadcast shipwide and recorded as part of the official transcripts. There was no hope that my mother would not see it or hear tell of it. In fact, I would not be surprised if Jil was not recording the shipcast to send directly to her when it was over.

The charges were read out. None of it came as a surprise to me. Disobedience to a senior officer, repeated in spite of warnings and previous penalties. My counsel had advised me to offer an honest defense. The fact was, I had none. I should have known better, but I trusted Parsons, who had not even troubled to appear at my hour of need. I kept glancing over my shoulder toward the door in case he should appear suddenly and inform me that all of this had been a deliberate misunderstanding. But he did not come.

"Kinago! Pay attention!"

I swiveled my head to return to the captain's direct gaze.

The captain leveled a finger at me.

"This is unpleasant for all of us, Kinago. You disobeyed my specific orders. You were given punishment detail as a first warning. Evidently it was not enough to deter you from your behavior."

Determined to put a brave face on my situation, I held myself erect and stared over the captain's head. I felt tragically alone.

"Evidently not, sir."

"How do you plead?"

I had no choice and no argument against the charges. I threw back my head in a heroic fashion.

"Guilty, sir."

"Have you anything to say in your defense?"

In those words, I believe I heard the appeal of humankindness. I chanced a look down. Captain Naftil's eyes were so dark it was hard to distinguish pity from discipline. I gulped back a sigh.

"All I can say, sir, is that the subject with whom I spoke to was planning what amounted to an anarchist's attack. The ship might continue to be in danger if I had not interviewed that crewmember, sir. I believe that my actions saved numerous lives, sir."

Naftil's left eyebrow twitched slightly.

"You would not have been in a position to hear the confession if you had not been disobedient."

"Yes, sir," I said. Had I detected any softening at all in his tone? I did not believe that I had. I could have implicated Parsons, who had been seen by all of the security personnel who had intercepted first Goliffe then me in the garden. But if he had not been mentioned in the reading of the charges, I would not bring him up. One betrayal did not lead to another.

My viewpad began pinging, denoting one received message after another. With a glance for permission, I silenced the notification alerts.

"Very well. Your plea regarding your actions leaves me no choice. A ship cannot function if everyone simply does what he or she pleases. There is a chain of command that must be respected and followed. This court therefore finds you guilty. You are sentenced to serve one day in the brig."

I had withdrawn into myself, fearing the worst. When my brain sorted out the assorted sounds of his final sentence, I peeped out of the protective shell I had gathered around myself.

"One . . . one day, sir?"

Naftil sighed. "Yes, Kinago. One day. Mitigating circumstances do apply here. We exist in a real world, where unintended consequences become more important than the act that precipitated them. But it will go on your record. Any final words?"

"But that's outrageous, sir," I said.

Naftil blinked.

"What?"

"Disobedience to a senior officer must be worthy of at least a week. I didn't follow your instructions. You must see that it's necessary to send a message to the rest of the crew that that kind of behavior can't stand. What would my mother say?"

It took Naftil a moment to see the logic in my argument.

"I am the captain, Kinago. Are you questioning my authority?"

I smiled. That was the up-and-coming officer I knew him to be.

"No, indeed, sir."

"One day. Is that clear?"

"Aye, sir," I said, sweeping my hand up in a perfect salute. "I will serve it with honor."

Naftil brought his hand down upon a blinking icon on his desk.

"Very well. This court is adjourned. Take him down."

I dared not display the cockiness I felt as the bullet-headed 'bot escorted me to the deepest inhabited level of the ship, near the gravity core. One day! It was a trifle longer than I had spent after crashing into the Empress's memorial statue, but hardly what I expected.

The real punishment would, I assumed, arrive in the guise of a message from my mother. I fully expected a thorough dressing down, during which she would chide me for being an idiot, another charge to which I would humbly plead guilty. No change there from my ordinary modus operandi. I was spared that humiliation, however, as no message came. Perhaps the maternal unit was too busy with more important matters, such as overseeing the defense in a major war breaking out in a vital star system. I was escorted down to the depths of the *Bonchance*. The corridors were surprisingly empty for that time of day. I missed spotting even one pair of sympathetic eyes.

"In there, Lieutenant," said the senior security officer on duty in the brig, the very woman who had arrested me in the garden. I peered into the cell before entering. It measured half the size of my cabin, which I considered small to begin with. A bunk was secured to the floor. A combination hygiene unit with a long mirror above it was secured to the wall. A chair and a pull-down flap desk were installed beside the bed. A virtual home from home.

"Not as comfortable as the Taino city lockup, but a good deal cleaner," I informed her cheerfully.

"Inside, Lieutenant," she said.

I complied. The door closed behind me with a thunk. I paced the two steps to the wall and back again, feeling slightly let down. One day was hardly enough to take advantage of my surroundings. I longed for an extended meditation session. It would clear my mind. Still, one day was better than nothing. I sat down upon the thin mattress and drew my spine erect.

Yet, I had just assumed *padmasana* when the door of my cell slid open. I rose to my feet and stood at attention, as I had been instructed to do, should I ever occupy a military prison. A stocky male Croctoid in a security tunic stalked in. His bulky person, with particular emphasis on his thick tail, which switched back and forth impatiently, took up most of the space in my none-too-generous temporary quarters.

"Serves you right," he said, his upper lip curling back to reveal his impressive dentition.

"I believe it does, sir," I said, attempting to stare over his head. He grabbed my chin and pulled it down so our eyes were on a level. He fixed me with a spiteful leer. "You wouldn't read my stars, but you read *hers*."

"I hadn't intended to read anyone else," I protested. "But I . . . Parsons told me . . ." Then I remembered my own words to the captain, and ceased my unworthy defense. He seemed almost gleeful when he closed the door upon my prattling. I sat down upon the desk chair and contemplated the blank walls.

Not that continuing would have raised my reputation in the eyes of the security officer, or the hundreds of ill-wishers whose assessment of my situation coincided with his, which I discovered shortly on the comments queue on my Infogrid file.

I took responsibility for my own actions. It just made me feel rather despondent to be the only one who knew that I had done the right thing.

The night I spent in the lockup was one of the longest of my life. Penitentiaries were, as I had read once, were intended to provide a venue for those in them to learn to be penitent.

I vowed thereafter to be more self-searching, and only employ my interest upon those who really need it, not broadcast as though I were the sun beaming beneficence down upon the land. It was an entire equation. I was giving something, yes, but I was asking something in return: information. They were part of my study. Did they intend to be? No. Did I inform them of that fact? Well, yes, I had. Did they understand that?

Looking at the flaming entries on my Infogrid page, apparently not.

But I saved the ship, I thought to myself. *That ought to count for something.*

But did it?

I ate the survival rations that were served to me late that evening, feeling them as ashes in my mouth. I was cast adrift, alone, isolated. Sometimes I enjoyed a good wallow in self-pity, as who did not? But this one did not satisfy me. I settled on the bunk, staring toward the ceiling in the darkness.

A ping sounded from my viewpad. I was not entirely alone, then. Someone wished to communicate with me. I hoped it was Parsons. I felt that he owed me an explanation. I was undecided whether or not to speak to him until after the conclusion of our mission. Barring an apology from Parsons, I would have been happy for a kind word from anyone.

Instead, I received a missive unlike any that I had ever read in my life.

"Lord Thomas," it began, "you don't know us, but we need your help."

The tap on the door came softly. Almost before Naftil lifted his head, the black-clad presence was before his desk.

"Commander Parsons."

"Captain Naftil."

"Are there any objections to my actions?" Naftil asked.

"None, sir," Parsons said. "Lord Thomas is unusually observant. It is better to distract him for the moment so he is concentrating on our mission when we depart. It is also good to have had all the ship's eyes on him. It will raise fewer questions now, or later."

"Good. I am very happy to cooperate." Naftil hesitated, studying the lean, dark figure before him. "This is the first time I have been asked to assist in a covert operation. I rather enjoyed it."

"The First Space Lord is grateful for your assistance."

Naftil absorbed the praise, feeling like a small boy being given a prize at school. He tried not to wriggle with pleasure.

"I do admire her greatly, you know. I am a bit sorry I had to treat her son in that fashion. He is a charming young man."

"It is one of his most useful traits," Parsons said. Naftil tried to read his tone and failed.

"His concern for others is genuine, isn't it? Not assumed? Many of my crew have become fond of him in this short time. I would hate to think it was all an act for the sake of your mission."

A tiny crease appeared above the left corner of the other man's upper lip.

"No, sir. He does care for those he befriends, captain. I fear that may do him more harm than good in the future, but he will cope. Or learn to."

Naftil's smile became broader.

"I watched the recording of the event that you set up. His interrogation of that poor young woman was masterful. He gleaned information about her mental state and that of the people manipulating her that none of the doctors or her co-workers suspected. It did almost seem like magic. He nearly had me convinced that I ought to ask for a reading."

"Perhaps you should have one on the return journey, sir," Parsons said. "He seems to have a unique gift for picking up on what is unsaid. He really is very perceptive, though in this case it is based upon specious nonsense."

"Maybe a little nonsense is good for me," the captain said. "But I must say I will be glad to have you depart."

"Good for all of us, sir," Parsons assured him.

As before, Parsons came to retrieve me from my incarceration. Brief as it was, I thought it had done me good. But I surveyed his baleful countenance with trepidation. I might still have been annoyed with him, but he was my eyes and ears in places I could not otherwise go.

"How bad is it?" I asked.

"The captain has his misgivings, but you have done a service to the navy. The young lady is being confined in the infirmary until she can be taken to a planetside hospital."

I let out the remainder of the breath I had been holding.

"Well, that's good, I must say. Having her choose the Two of Swords was almost prophetic to her state of mind, but it wasn't until I did a further reading that I saw how disturbed she was."

"It could happen to any of us exposed to your talents, my lord."

I ignored the point of the jibe.

"Are you certain that my mother will not be perturbed by my actions?"

"I believe you will find that you have behaved precisely as she expected you to."

I surveyed him, and remembered my grievance. I drew myself up.

"I will take that as a compliment, Parsons, however you intended it."

Parsons gestured toward the lift.

"You should return to your cabin and pack, sir. We depart from the *Bonchance* in four hours."

I admit that I goggled.

"Four hours! I will scarcely have time!"

Parsons regarded me with a disapproving stare.

"For what, sir?"

"For an act of gratitude, Parsons. I have a couple of gifts I wish to make before we leave. I must under the circumstances assume that you do not understand such a gesture. I promise you I will tell no one's fortune, nor upset the motion of the stars."

"Please do not make promises you cannot keep, my lord," Parsons said, as he followed me into the moving compartment. "The astrogators are relying on those stars to remain in their courses."

With Dee overseeing my workmanship through his optical receivers, I constructed the lucky circuit that I had designed for him.

"It is a trifle clumsy in construction," I admitted, placing the finished device in one of his claw-hands, "but I hope you will enjoy it."

The main camera moved close to the tiny nest of wires, agleam with blue and green lights, and a contented hum arose from Dee's main casing.

"This has very pleasurable subsonics," Dee said. "Thank you, Lieutenant Kinago Thomas." He tucked it away inside his dome.

I had one more circuit to deliver. I sought out Gillian. She had been silent at the last dinner we had shared. Her longing looks in Corlota's direction told me the source of her unhappiness.

I found the young second lieutenant on a hoverdisk, overseeing the repair of a cooling unit in a corridor ceiling.

"Do you have a moment?" I asked. At the sound of my voice she dropped a tool. I caught it one-handed. I could tell how deep in thought she had been. She saw it was me and hastily ordered the disk to land.

"Oh, Thomas!" she wailed, and threw herself into my arms. I patted her shoulder.

"I'm sorry. I saw Corlota with another first officer at mess."

Gillian detached herself and reached for her regulation handkerchief. She dabbed at red eyes.

"Not your fault," she said. "You told me I ought to pay attention to the truth and not delude myself. Your horoscope came true."

"As a matter of fact, the stars had nothing to do with it," I said. "I was reading *you.*" I folded her long fingers around the sparkling lights of light coral and warm gold. "Farewell. I hope you find someone who appreciates the person that you are."

CHAPTER 20

M'Kenna had only her thoughts for company. The children hadn't wanted to be knocked out again, and who could blame them? But Rafe had let the physician put the mask on his face. When he was lying down and breathing softly, she attached the drip bags to each arm.

"One replacement nanites," she had explained, to four pairs of wide, dark brown eyes. "One antihistamines, suppressants, additional minerals."

Rafe's face relaxed. He remained peaceful and pain-free, so the kids allowed themselves to be hooked up. They'd all settled in so well that M'Kenna realized she didn't have to run from one to another every half hour to make sure they were still breathing.

She had plenty of time over the following four days to go through her mail, and precious little to show for it. It seemed like there was a form letter everyone sent out to supplicants that the officials could not or did not want to handle. She got tired of reading the same excuses and evasions. In her mind, she composed angry retorts, but if there was any hope that a caring human being ever read her letters, she didn't want to be turned down because she was obnoxious. But she was getting close to giving up hope of any outside help.

Then, on the very last day, when the kids were starting to stir on their bunks and Rafe's eyelids were fluttering, she clicked on one of the replies, this one from the Imperium Navy. Black hole only knew how they had gotten involved, M'Kenna wondered, but maybe it was because all ships were subject to their authority.

> "Dear Ms. Copper," it began,
>
> "We have reviewed your request for assistance. This is a most serious matter. We wish to receive more detail regarding your case."

M'Kenna had begun to nod over the tablet, but that line shocked her awake. She read it two or three more times to make sure. More detail? They wanted to know more? She sat up in excitement. Was there someone out there who actually cared?

"Honey, read this!" she exclaimed, holding out the pad. But Rafe was still asleep. M'Kenna looked at the line of print again as though she could hardly believe it. Yes! Hope lifted her heart. What did they want to know?

At that moment, a noise from the children's room attracted her attention. One of the kids must be waking up. She was torn between reading the rest of the message and checking on the sound, but the letter could wait. She put the tablet aside and went in to see which one of them was stirring.

"Hey!" she shouted. "Get away from her!"

An Uctu in a baggy beige coverall was bending over Nona's bunk. M'Kenna couldn't see what he was doing, but it didn't matter. He had no right to touch her. She charged at him, pushing him away from her daughter.

"Back off! Who are you?"

"All right," he said, his jaws slightly apart in an affable smile. "Medical staff."

"If you're medical staff," M'Kenna said, staying at arm's length from him, "show me your badge."

Something in his demeanor told her that he knew she didn't believe him. He reached into a pocket. M'Kenna went instantly on guard. She had no weapons, of course, but she had been trained in basic hand-to-hand combat. You never knew when someone was going to try and board your ship, or mug you in the corridors of a space station, or jump you way out somewhere on an atmosphered world. The Uctu brought out a flat orange disk and held it up.

It wasn't credentials or a badge. M'Kenna didn't know what it was, except that it had to be bad news. As she feared, he lunged for her, trying to tap her with it. She dodged to one side. He moved faster than she realized he could.

"How did you get in here?" she asked, circling around, hoping she didn't run into a wall. "What do you want?"

He didn't answer. She had always thought Geckos were kind of silly-looking. She had never met one that looked absolutely mean.

The intruder feinted with the orange disk, trying to hit her in the face. M'Kenna backed away.

"Help!" she yelled, hoping the guards were listening. "Someone help me!"

"What's wrong?" Nuro, down the hall, shouted back.

"There's an Uctu in here! He's trying to hurt me!"

"Guards!" Nuro bellowed. She heard the door of the Wichus' cell rattle. "Guards! Let us out of here! We need help!"

The intruder suddenly darted away from M'Kenna, and made for the children again. She took a running start and leaped at him. She landed on the Uctu's back. He tripped and fell. The orange disk tumbled out of his grasp. It bounced on the floor, seeping liquid as it went. M'Kenna was horrified. She put all her weight on the Gecko, trying to bear him down to the floor. He lashed at her with his tail, half the length of his body. Ow! That damned thing hurt! She worked a forearm underneath his throat and yanked upward. He thrashed and kicked. M'Kenna squeezed his neck between her arms. Its scaly skin rasped her own, but she didn't dare let go. He batted at her, scratching her arm with needle-sharp claws.

She knew if she let him up he would hurt her children. But she couldn't hold onto him forever.

"Is anyone coming?" she yelled.

"Not yet!" Nuro shouted back. "Hey, guards! Help!"

"Help!" M'Kenna added her voice.

"What's going on here?"

Rafe appeared, holding onto the door frame with an unsteady hand. He was still disoriented because of the treatment. M'Kenna smacked the intruder's face on the floor and shouted at her husband.

"He tried to do something to the kids!"

"What?"

His dark face a thundercloud, Rafe stumbled toward them. The Uctu growled low in his chest. His tail lashed at Rafe's legs, knocking him sideways. Still unsteady after the habilitation therapy, Rafe tottered and fell over. He just caught himself before he fell on top of Lerin. M'Kenna scrambled to wind a leg over the offending appendage. To her horror, the tail wound back. It grabbed her leg and squeezed. M'Kenna was shocked. She didn't know they were prehensile. She kicked at him with her free leg.

"Let me go!"

The intruder heaved up to his hands and knees. With a sinuous twist, he flipped her off his back. M'Kenna rolled underneath Dorna's bunk. She crawled out, hitting her head on the low platform.

The Uctu made for the barred door. M'Kenna bared her teeth in a fierce smile. Now they had him! He couldn't get out that way. She sprang up and edged toward him, knees bent in a wrestler's crouch. Rafe made it to his feet about the same time. The two of them homed in on the intruder from both sides. It was only a pace ahead of them, trapped against the doorway.

But to her amazement, the door slid open half a meter. The Uctu slipped through. M'Kenna and Rafe dived for him. The cell slammed shut. M'Kenna and Rafe crashed into the bars. M'Kenna shot her arm through, grabbing for the baggy coverall. She got a few fingers tangled in the cloth, grabbing for a better hold. The Uctu tugged and writhed until her fingers slipped, letting him free. She screamed her frustration.

"Stop him! He's getting away!" she yelled.

The intruder ran toward the far wall at the end of the corridor. That should have been another dead end, but it wasn't. A panel moved aside, revealing a dark recess. The Uctu dove through it, and it closed behind him.

"What's happening there?" the Wichus shouted.

"He got away!" M'Kenna said. "He went through the wall."

Then, and only then, did the guards appear. Somewhere a klaxon went off, howling official outrage. A squad of eight Uctus in prison uniforms charged into the corridor, weapons leveled. They searched the corridor up and down, then assembled in front of the Coppers' cell.

"What happened?" the officer at their head demanded.

"Someone just tried to hurt us," M'Kenna said. "A Gecko—I mean, an Uctu in a plain worksuit."

"Where did go?"

"Through there," she said, pointing with her whole arm through the bars. "He just went that way!"

The guard captain spun on his boot heel, then turned back slowly to frown at her.

"No passage through the wall that place. Secure facility."

"Are you kidding me?" M'Kenna demanded. "He just went that way! My husband and I saw him."

Rafe stumbled forward, yawning hard. The anaesthetic must not be wearing off fast enough, but he blinked indignantly at the guards.

"My wife and I tried to catch him, captain."

"No one there!"

"Wait a minute," M'Kenna said, reaching in vain for the Uctu. He backed away. "Aren't there security recordings? You can look at them. You'll see what happened!"

The captain gave a curt sign with his left hand. Immediately two Geckos raised their long weapons and aimed them at the cell door.

"Hands up," the captain said. "View recordings."

M'Kenna felt a rush of relief. She put her hands in the air. So did Rafe. The cell door slid open. Two of the other guards entered and secured their hands to a second loop that fastened around their waists.

"What about our children?"

"Sleeping. Safe," the captain said. He beckoned to them. "Come."

M'Kenna scanned the corridor as she was marched toward a door at the far end. The dozen or so cells were arranged so the prisoners could not see one another's doors. She looked hard at each as she went by. The Wichus from *Sword Snacks* looked thinner than before. Their fur was patchy, and their big, dark eyes seemed to have lost their light.

I'd hate to think I look that bad, she thought.

"You all right, M'Kenna?" Nuro asked.

"We're fine," she said. "We'll get out of here, all of us."

Apart from the backless seats that accommodated the Gecko tails, the industrial-style office into which they were shown was exactly the same as every one they had been in anywhere in the galaxy. The walls were battered at the edge of the desktop, showing that it or the previous table had been moved numerous times, revealing layered colors of paint. That was one clue that assured M'Kenna that they were planetside: no one used paint in spaceships because the particles tended to flake off and get into the ventilation system and the food recycler. How she missed the scraped and dented enamel walls of the *Entertainer*!

The guards made them sit down on a bench on the far side of the desk. They took up sentry positions beside them.

The Gecko chief ran a narrow, scaly hand over the control pad. Part of the wall shimmered and seemed to bulge out toward them, creating a three-dimensional image. M'Kenna realized that she was looking at the corridor in front of her cell. Eerily, she was watching herself inside the cell reading from the tablet. Another gesture, and the view changed to a video pickup somewhere inside the chamber. She could see herself from the side. Automatically, her hand flew to her hair. It was a mess! How could she not have seen that in the little mirror above their hygiene unit?

The captain pointed a skinny finger at the bottom left corner of the image.

"Time coding. Thirty minutes." He touched the controls. The digitavid sped up, until M'Kenna's past self was panting and tapping at the screen like Lerin playing one of his action games. "Ten."

The woman in the recording sprang to her feet and ran out of the frame. The captain switched to another camera. It showed her and Rafe standing at the cell door, their arms through the bars. Their cries were muted but still audible.

M'Kenna strained toward the image.

"Wait a minute, where did he go?"

"Nowhere!" said the chief.

"Show me the corridor, ten minutes back. Now!"

The captain changed to the outer reference and slid the video back and forth. But at no point was the Gecko in the jumpsuit visible. M'Kenna could see the images of her and Rafe bang into the door and reach through the bars again and again, but there was no one on the other side.

"I can't see him," Rafe said. "How is that possible?"

"I grabbed his sleeve," M'Kenna said. "Can't you hear me telling my friends there was someone in the cell with us?"

The captain switched back and forth between the recordings.

"No voices here. Listen."

M'Kenna could have torn out her untidy hair in clumps. She pleaded with the captain.

"But he was there, at that time. Something must be wrong. Something got cut out!"

The Uctu shook his head. His dark eyes seemed sympathetic.

"Not on recording. Time codes unchangeable. Mistaken."

"Mistaken? Then what about that orange thing? The one he was trying to hit me with?"

"What orange thing?" the guard captain asked.

"I'll show you!" M'Kenna sprang to her feet.

She and Rafe went back to the cell accompanied by the captain and an escort of two Geckos. The children were awake now, with wide, concerned eyes. M'Kenna hugged each one tightly. Rafe gathered them all into one huge hug.

"We were worried about you," Nona said. M'Kenna felt terrible. Who knew what they thought when they woke up to find their parents missing?

"We're fine, honey," M'Kenna assured her. She scanned the floor. "Have you seen a flat orange plastic thing? It'd be about the size of your palm. It's important."

"No. I can look."

"Me, too," Lerin declared.

M'Kenna got on her hands and knees near the place where she and the Gecko had scuffled. The children scrambled around on the floor to help her hunt.

"Dere, mama!" Akela announced triumphantly, pointing a chubby little finger. M'Kenna followed his glance. There it was! M'Kenna just managed to head him off before he picked it up.

Clear liquid pooled on the floor around the device. She handed over the orange object to the guards, then sopped up the liquid with a disposer cloth. Holding it gingerly between thumb and forefinger, she delivered it to the captain.

"There, I told you. Where would we get anything like that? You know every single thing we have in here."

The guards ignored her scolding. One of them ran a sensor over the cloth, then muttered at the reading. M'Kenna vibrated with impatience.

"Well? What is it?"

"Only water. Must have dreamed."

"I was not dreaming! I'll let you scope me to prove I'm not lying."

The captain shook his head. "You believe. No proof."

M'Kenna folded her arms.

"Then I want to make a complaint! I want our lawyer here right now! I want to see the Imperium ambassador."

The Gecko let out a burbling noise, their way of sighing. He picked up her tablet from the bunk, tapped in a command, and handed it to her.

"Fill out forms," he said, his face a study in dejected resignation. M'Kenna knew what that meant: pages and pages and pages of questions, all designed to make her doubt herself and her story. She had to remind herself that he and the guards weren't unreasonable people. They were doing a job that she would never have taken, not if street-sweeper, medical test subject or live-fire target were still open. She dropped onto the bunk, clutching the pad in her hands.

The guards locked them in again.

Rafe sat down gently beside her and draped his arm over her shoulders.

"Don't be upset, honey," he said. "It sounds like they don't know everything about this building. We'll catch the sneak. We'll just have to stand watches, just like we did when the power plant on the ship started that weird brownout cycle a couple of years ago."

M'Kenna nodded.

"I'm not upset, I'm angry! They made me feel like they were tearing my sanity away, and it's the only thing I have left! I need it to protect all of you." She looked up at Rafe, her eyes taking in every angle of his features. She loved the way his eyes crinkled at the corners, making the thick black lashes bunch up. She loved the rich, brown color of those eyes. She loved his strong chin and cheekbones, and even the fleshy lobes of his ears. She could hardly bear to think that at any moment he could be taken away, and they would never see each other again. She slipped her arm around his back and squeezed with all her strength. He leaned over to kiss her on the temple. For a moment she felt loved and comforted, but the sensation only made her more frustrated. They were in danger, and she couldn't get anyone in authority to believe her.

The Wichus did, though.

"Hey, smoothskins!" Nuro bellowed, his voice booming out into the corridor. "Are you people all right?"

M'Kenna sighed.

"Yes, we're fine. They didn't believe me."

"Figures. Sorry they're such *felimfets*," Nuro said.

"Huh. I know a lot of Wichu slang, but not that one. Whatever that means, I hope it's nasty," M'Kenna said. Her eyes met Rafe's. His were brimming with amusement. She couldn't help it. She smiled back.

"Lowest of the low scum," Nuro said. "You wouldn't even scrape your shoes. You'd just burn them instead of trying to get it off."

"That's about right," she said. With a sigh she ran a finger over the tablet screen. "Well, these forms won't fill themselves."

"I'll help you, honey," Rafe said. "If you do the first hundred pages, I'll do the next."

"Deal."

The humming of a hovercart grew in the hallway. M'Kenna looked up from the screen of blanks. The serene female doctor appeared at the door with her collection of vials and tubes.

"Ready?" she asked.

"For what?" M'Kenna asked, blankly. Then she remembered: the habilitation treatment. "No!"

"You've got to, honey," Rafe said. "I already feel a million times better."

"Process painless," the doctor assured her. M'Kenna shook her head firmly.

"I can't do it," she said. "I can't let my family be alone, not now." She waved a finger in the direction of the office. "They think I'm lying about an intruder, but I'm not. We're in danger!" She scanned the equipment on the hovercart. "Wait, you have a truth scope. Do a reading on me. That'll prove to them I'm not lying!"

"Told already," the doctor said, her mild face sympathetic. "If you like. But they think hallucination. In your situation, possible."

M'Kenna felt her face growing hot with fury.

"Well, I can't let myself go into a coma for four days. I want to see the Imperium ambassador. I'll wait until she gets here to take the treatment."

"Sicker!" the doctor warned.

"I know that! I'll wait."

Shaking her head, the doctor rolled her cart away.

⁂

The kids were fine once the habilitation treatment was back in their systems. Just fine. All of them had lost the dullness in their skins. They began to put on weight even on the limited prison food. Dorna grew a couple of centimeters in time for her third birthday. M'Kenna felt outrage. Her baby's childhood should not be happening in a prison!

It took them a few days to get the application finished. M'Kenna sent it in with a personal letter in the Notes section begging for the ambassador to come visit them and the others as soon as possible. She followed it up with a message to the ambassador's Infogrid file. When there was no more she could reasonably accomplish, she handed the tablet over to Rafe and curled up for a nap.

When she woke up, she felt eyes on her. She looked up. Rafe was staring down at her. He was almost shimmering with excitement.

"I was reading our messages. Why didn't you tell me we got an official interested in our case?"

It all came back to M'Kenna. She sat up.

"I'm so sorry, honey. I forgot all about it."

She sat up, and he settled in beside her.

"It's from someone in the navy," he said. "Isn't that weird?"

"I don't care, as long as someone listens to us!"

Over his arm, M'Kenna scanned the beginning of the message, then read through the rest of the message. She had to go over it a few times more just to absorb the contents. "I can't believe it."

In too many words, it expressed regret that citizens of the Imperium were put into such a perilous situation. Their situation, as those of their fellow pilots and their crews, had been noted.

A diplomat with ties to the Imperial family and the hierarchy of the navy was coming to Dilawe to negotiate with the Autocrat on several important issues. Among those was the severity of the penalties indicated for the crimes of which they had been accused. Over the last several years, several attempts had been made to equalize the punishments on both sides of the frontier. If the Coppers were indeed not guilty as they insisted, the Imperium would stand behind them throughout the trial and thereafter. If they were guilty, the matter for the courts to decide, the representative would do his best to intercede on their behalf regarding sentencing.

"Do their best," M'Kenna scoffed. "I really hoped for better."

"It's not perfect," Rafe said, "but what did we expect? It's better than anyone else has offered us." He held the pad in both hands. "It finishes with, 'We recommend you put your confidence in the envoy. He will be coming to interview you as soon as he reaches Nacer.' I can't wait!" he said.

"What's the diplomat's name?" M'Kenna asked.

Rafe scrolled down to the end of the letter.

"He's called Lord Thomas Innes Kinago. According to this, he's the son of the First Space Lord. Pretty cool, huh?" He threw an arm around her shoulders and squeezed hard. M'Kenna felt such a rush of relief she wished she could throw herself at him and show her joy, but the kids, and the Geckos, and a dozen hidden video pickups, were watching. Instead, she was ready to call for the doctor to start her habilitation therapy. She could use four days' uninterrupted sleep, and now her conscience would be clear.

"Lord Thomas Kinago!" M'Kenna crowed. "Let's look at his Infogrid file. I want to send him a personal message."

Rafe brought it up.

The image in a little frame at the top showed a portrait of a handsome young man with sandy brown hair, a golden complexion and bright blue-green eyes. His jaw and nose were strong but friendly. M'Kenna trusted him at once. She knew she could put her faith in those eyes and that nose. She put a finger on the screen to scroll down.

A digitavid was the next thing visible. Whoever had captured the recording was standing just on the edge of a large crowd of people surrounding a huge, ugly sculpture. A section near the center was blackened, as if it had just been sheared off.

The focus of the crowd's attention was at the base of the sculpture, where a flitter lay on its side. Even in the small image, M'Kenna could see that it was wrecked beyond repair. Anyone could put two and two together and assume that the flitter was what had caused the damage to the sculpture. As the recording rolled on, a man crawled out of the cockpit of the ruined craft. He had a bruise on his temple, one sleeve torn half off his arm and a big, silly grin on his face. With the help of a well-dressed onlooker, he struggled to his feet and gazed at the statue in dazed confusion. Suddenly, the local constabulary zipped down, bustled him into a skimmer, and roped off the area.

The recorder moved back then to show that several flitters were involved in the wreck, but his was clearly the first to have come to grief.

At that moment, the video went black, as if security had disabled it by remote control.

Without a doubt, the man who had just been arrested was Lord Thomas Kinago. M'Kenna and Rafe looked at one another.

"Wait a minute," he said. "Maybe it's not him. Couldn't there be another man with the same name?"

M'Kenna took the tablet and started an advanced search. Not only were there no names similar, there were no overlaps at all. Every entry, and there were lots of them, were about the same man, a very tall, very young aristocrat with tawny skin, sea-blue eyes, and waves of sandy brown hair. He was seen cavorting at parties, dancing with attractive women, competing in sports and attending functions at the Imperium palace. There was no doubt about it. This was Lord Thomas Kinago.

M'Kenna felt as though what remained of the floor had been pulled away from underneath her, sending her falling through the void.

"This is our rescuer?" Rafe asked, in disbelief. "We're doomed. I almost wish they'd ignored us."

"I'll start messaging again," M'Kenna said grimly, hauling her heart up from her toes. "There has to be someone *competent* out there who will listen to us."

CHAPTER 21

"Please," one of Nile's girls begged as the *Pelican* floated in to dock in Way Station 46, "can we just walk around for a while? Just by ourselves? We won't talk to anyone."

"Please?" added the other, sounding even more desperate than the first.

"No!" Nile's voice barked. "You stay with us. Understand? We won't be here that long."

Skana looked up at the ceiling from her crash couch and sighed.

"Nile, it won't do them any harm. Where can they go?"

"Plenty of places!"

Skana started to wave her hand. The movement was stopped by the webbed straps. She let her arm fall to her chest. He couldn't see her, anyhow.

"Let them go, Nile. They can do a little shopping, get a pedicure or a facial in a salon, or whatever. It'll do them good. Ladies, you can take a couple of hours, but you keep your pocket secretaries on hand, and you answer when I call. That's when, not if. Right?"

"Yes, ma'am! Thank you, Ms. Bertu."

"And if you have a problem, I am your first call, *then* the station authorities."

"Yes, ma'am!" they chorused.

"Oh, all right," Nile growled.

Within a few moments, Captain Sigismund rang the all-clear. Gratefully, Skana freed herself from the enveloping harness. Tuk's long face appeared above her, and a scaly paw reached down to assist her out of the couch.

"Thanks," she said, and gestured toward the other side of the room. "Give Nile's friends a hand."

"Yes, madam."

But there was no need. Skana was barely in time to see both of their scantily-clad posteriors disappearing out of the door of the lounge toward the cabins.

"What did you do to them?" Skana demanded, as Nile's red face appeared from the depths of his couch.

"Nothing!" Nile said. He vaulted over the deep side and onto the lounge floor. His clothes were slightly askew, but he was fully clad. Skana found that surprising, considering that she knew he liked a little action among the netting. She put her hands on her hips.

"All right, what's the problem?"

Nile brushed himself down.

"Nothing."

"That wasn't nothing. That was a plea for help. Both of them couldn't wait to get away from you. What is wrong with them?"

Nile couldn't meet her eyes.

"They're not her."

"You knew that when we hired them."

"I know!" He finally turned to look at her. His nose was red. Usually, that meant frustration.

"You're not going to punish them for that." Nile seemed about to speak, then paused. Skana glared at him. "Say it!"

The words came unwillingly, but they came.

"I'm not going to punish them for not being her. It's not their fault. I know that! But they look so much like her!" The last sentence was almost a wail. Nile started pacing up and back between the couches. Skana watched him go back and forth.

"That is why you chose them. Do you want to send them home?"

"No. Yes."

"Which is it? This is the last chance. We can get one of the ships coming back from the Autocracy to take them into the Core Worlds. That was the deal we made with them. After that, you'll have to commission a ship, which will run into real money. We've got it, but is that how you want to spend it?"

Nile gathered a deep breath and let it out. His barrel chest deflated.

"They can stay," he said, with a sour face. "I just need a break."

Skana thought that the girls could probably use one from him, too. Fortunately, the *Pelican* had plenty of cabins. Not anywhere near as nice as their customized suites, but not austerity bunks, either. She sent a 'bot to make up beds in the two farthest away from Nile's quarters and make sure the toiletries were topped up in the heads. When the girls checked in with her, she would tell them they could stay out until the *Pelican* was ready to launch again. She was under no illusions as to how petulant her brother could be when he really decided to revert to emotional infancy. She hoped he hadn't actually hurt one of them. The odds were against it. His self control was usually pretty good with employees. Guests, maybe not. Enemies, of course not. But these women had been hired by the Bertu Corporation, and even Nile's personal quirks got overridden by pride in their business.

She had kept a pretty close eye on his Infogrid file, to make sure he wasn't complaining about the women in his messages. All his problems were internal. He had behaved himself pretty much. If the women didn't deserve fallout, she would see to it that they didn't get any. They had been no trouble at all during the trip so far. She saw no reason not to make sure they got home, with a bonus.

The girls were long gone by the time Skana and Nile emerged into the landing bay. Tuk and two bodyguards followed them.

The metal floors were still chilly underfoot from their exposure to deep space. Skana could see hot spots surrounded by rings of frost as the local systems warmed the chamber to station ambient temperature. She surveyed the gunmetal gray bulkheads. The walls displayed framed regulations in swift rotation with big, colorful, tacky advertising for the local merchants, with moving tri-dee images that left nothing to the imagination.

"Recharge with Bee-no Fuels!" "Don't believe what you hear—come and taste our food! No reconstituted ingredients!" "Too long in the pilot's chair? Sore muscles are our specialty. MX-435 Massage." "Special requests? No problem. Bring them to our willing . . . therapists."

"I've seen worse," she said, with a shrug. "Pretty offputting, though."

"No one would want to stay here who didn't have to," Nile said. "You know, they ought to make this place a destination in itself. Target the advertising and make it sound more welcoming. I could do it. It would drag in the money in the first year."

"I'm sure you could," Skana said, with a cautious look around. She couldn't see security video or audio pickups, but they had to be there. "Maybe later. Things are going to change a lot over there really soon."

"Yeah," Nile said. He glanced up toward the ceiling. "Hey, service! You want to get the inspection over with? I want to get out of here in my lifetime!"

His voice echoed off the lofty ceiling. Clicks and whirs from the engines aft told them that Captain Sigismund and her crew of three were doing final checks before debarking to stretch their legs. After a long few minutes, a door slid open in the wall of the landing bay. A bronze-colored securitybot about Tuk's height and girth emerged and rolled toward them. Its uppermost fifth was molded into a pleasant-looking mask that was not meant to look like any species in particular. Its electronically generated eyes met Skana's.

"Captain Sigismund?"

"She's still on board."

"Passengers?"

"No. We're the owners of the *Pelican*. Skana and Nile Bertu."

"Good. I am Customs Inspector IN-332. Please present your documentation. What cargo do you have in the hold? A full and truthful accounting is required."

"Five fighter scouts," Skana said. Nile snickered. The 'bot, however, lit up with red chase lights and white flashers. Two metal hands shot out from the body and clamped around their wrists.

"Confession noted. Your identities have been noted. Please surrender immediately and prepare for prosecution. You are permitted legal representation from the moment of this arrest. If you cannot afford legal rep—"

Skana pried at the manacle with her free hand.

"I didn't confess to anything! That was a joke. Can't you take a joke?"

The inspectorbot swiveled its body toward her, and inclined its head closer.

"You realize that I am not permitted by law to have a sense of humor?" it asked.

Skana waved in its "face."

"You customs officials never do. I'm just joking! You don't have to get all excited about it."

The 'bot almost appeared to sigh.

"Asking again. Second time irrevocable indictment. Cargo in hold? Identify quantity and use."

Skana got herself under control and slowed down her breathing.

"Metals for industrial use," she said.

"Let me have the manifests and the licenses for the goods."

"I don't have them."

"I must examine the goods now. Documentation may follow."

It wheeled its "face" toward the rear of the ship and began rolling in that direction. With the clamps on their arms, Skana and Nile had to run along behind it.

Skana strained over her shoulder at Tuk. The Croctoid and the two Human guards stood at the bottom of the ramp looking like idiots.

"Do something!" At her shout, the guards broke into a trot. They caught up with the inspectorbot and jogged alongside.

"What do you want us to do, madam?" the taller one asked.

Tuk didn't move. He lifted his tablet and tapped at it with a claw.

At the rear of the ship, the inspectorbot halted before the cargo hatch.

"Open the hold, please."

Skana reached for her pocket secretary, but before she could activate it, the featureless door swung open and down. The ramp unfolded and rolled to their feet. Inside, Captain Sigismund peered out.

"Are you all right, sir and madam?"

"Yeah, we're fine."

"Captain Sigismund?" the inspectorbot inquired.

"Yes, sir," the pilot said, coming down with a tablet cradled in her arm. "We're ready for you, sir."

A piece of the 'bot near the floor detached and dropped with a *thud*. The inspector reversed and rolled away from them. Skana found that she and Nile were anchored by a flexible rod to a dome-shaped piece of metal. The two of them strained at it, but they couldn't lift it. Neither of them could walk more than a meter from the base.

"Damn it, you had to make a joke," Nile said rubbing his wrist inside the steel loop.

"You laughed at it!"

"I know. I might have done the same thing. These robots have no imagination."

Skana heard murmurs, clanks and thuds inside the ship. It seemed like forever until the 'bot rolled down the ramp toward them. Sigismund trailed in its wake, the ship's half-license, a virtually indestructible piece of metal that normally rested in a bracket near the main hatch with its other half, in her hand. Skana found she was holding her breath.

The 'bot's front torso lit up with images of skids filled with metal bars and a score of heavy barrels it had just taken inside the ship.

"Industrial supplies?" it inquired. "Ingots and powdered metal?"

"Yes, that's right."

"Licenses were presented." The briefest of whirring came from within the 'bot's body.

"Oh, come on," Skana said, impatient for all of the protocol to be over. "They're all good!"

"Registration from point of origin unclear. These must be supplied or you will be unable to import them into the Autocracy."

"Wait a minute, you're an Imperium citizen," Skana said. "Why aren't you on my side?"

"My job is to ease customs shipments, madam. I inspect goods and documentation accompanying them."

"Otherwise, what happens? What do you do if I don't have the registrations?"

"Confiscation. Fines."

"What? Couldn't we just go home?"

"I'm sorry, madam, but you would be attempting to cross a border without adequate documentation."

Skana snorted.

"What if I never stopped in this ridiculous station to start with? Why couldn't I just cross by myself?"

The LAI was accustomed to answering questions even from increasingly hysterical patrons. Its metal face assumed an expression of patience. The tone of its voice never rose or increased in speed.

"The wormhole device would be closed to you, madam. Colliding with it would be fatal to your ship and all on board her, including the ships, if any, in your wake. You would be liable for fines, plus damages, plus penalties for failure to yield. It is true, you could resort to ultradrive all the way in to the Autocracy central systems, but it would take you two hundred years, Imperium standard. We do not calibrate you for the more distant links in the system. You understand."

Skana peered at the 'bot.

"You're really skunks, you know that?"

The LAI was unmoved.

"I am purely mechanical, madam. Very little organic origin at all."

Tuk interceded at that moment. He presented his tablet.

"I think you will find all this in order, inspector," he said. The file on the screen transferred at once to the front display of the 'bot. A horizontal red line swept down over the page and up again.

"These are satisfactory. Why were they not presented at the beginning?"

The Croctoid offered an ingratiating smile that showed off all his rows of sharp teeth.

"I beg your pardon, inspector. The captain is not privy to this information. It is proprietary data, on a need-to-know basis. You need to know. She doesn't."

"Very well. Your export is approved." A loud click sounded. The steel ring around the Bertus' wrists opened and dropped away. The weighted dome rose a millimeter and rolled back into the housing at the bottom of the bot.

"Good," Nile said. "We'll launch immediately."

"I am afraid that is not possible," IN-332 said, not without a trace of sympathy on its face. "You will be informed as to when the frontier is open for passage. My business with you is concluded. That is all."

The 'bot reversed half a meter, then spun on its internal axis and glided away. The Bertus went in the opposite direction, following the frantic advertisements that hoped to guide them to their respective establishments.

"Spacedust," Nile said. He made a face. "Enstidius told us that would happen. I thought he'd already made arrangements."

Skana hadn't been on that many distant outposts, but she had been told by a few of their transport captains that the deepest-worn floor was always in front of the best bar. Nile looked hopefully at the assorted workers in robes or revealing lingerie hanging around the entrance to the house of negotiable affection next door, but Skana took firm hold of his arm.

"Drink first. Secure call second. Then you can do what you want."

"By then we'll be on our way out of here," Nile grumbled, but he didn't pull away.

Either of them could have described the bar in detail without more than a quick glance in the door. Every deep-space watering hole they had ever been in was a clone or a close relative to that one. The lighting glowered in a horror-movie dimness over a range of low tables, each with its own entertainment screen built into the top. News, advertising and documentaries were free, but sports, pornography and games required a personal credit number. Festooning the walls was a range of ancient junk, anything from paper posters dating back a millennium or more, toys, weapons blunted and deactivated, musical instruments, sports equipment, and mirrors, though the latter were never low enough to reflect the faces of the patrons, each of whom hunched protectively over his, her or its drink. Skana counted a couple dozen beings from several species. A few seemed to be shipmates, absorbed in shared misery, but most of them were alone. Really nondescript music murmured in the background, high enough to prevent casual eavesdropping but not loud enough to make the patrons feel unwelcome. A tri-tennis tournament was on the screen over the bar. The players threw themselves around the brightly lit court, seeming to dive toward the middle of the room to return a volley.

The bartender was a middle-aged female Human who looked as though she once worked at the adjacent establishment. She gave them a welcoming smile as they slid onto a couple of well-worn plastic-topped bar stools. Skana immediately noticed that she'd had her front teeth rebuilt, and not very well.

"What's your pleasure?" the bartender asked.

"Whisky, anything but Leonian, and where can we make a secure call?"

"Ansible, message, voice or voice and video?"

"Ansible."

"Destination?"

"None of your business. No offense."

The bartender nodded as she set two unbreakable shot glasses on the counter and filled them with amber liquid from a bottle that bore a Pravinian label. Skana assumed it was as phony as the woman's teeth.

"None taken. Croileg's, around the corner," she said. "She's private, but it'll cost you."

"I'll go," Nile said, gulping his drink and standing up.

"What's your hurry?" the bartender asked, with a friendly grimace. "You're going to be here for a while."

"No, we're not," he said.

He strode out of the bar and disappeared. Skana sipped the liquor, letting it roll around on her tongue. It burned smoothly, leaving a trace of woodsmoke, caramel and an indefinable fruit flavor.

"Let me see the bottle," she said. The bartender put it down in front of her. Skana checked the seals. They were legitimate, though who knew how many times the bottle had been refilled with hooch formulated to taste like 30-year-old Bromel?

"Pretty good for the middle of nowhere," she said.

The bartender shook her head.

"This didn't use to be nowhere," she said. "The new bureaucracy's just killing trade." She tapped the surface of the bar, and a screen full of real-estate ads popped up. "If you don't want to live on your ship for the next three months, here's the housing stock. For you and your husband, you might want to look at the stuff in Three-Loop. That's the nicest. Prices aren't reasonable, but it's better than going home."

"He's my brother, and we're not staying," Skana said.

"Turning back, pretty lady?" drawled a lanky man in a gray shipsuit. He had a half-drunk glass of beer in front of him.

"No, going into the Autocracy," Skana said.

"Not in a hurry, you aren't," said a Wichu on the man's other side.

Skana smiled at them. "Everyone keeps saying that! What if I thought today was my lucky day?"

A slow smile stretched the lanky man's thin-lipped mouth.

"I'd hope you would include me in that luck—in a nice way. Buy you a drink?"

She looked him up and down. Nile had his girls with him, but she had left her latest man at home on Keinolt. Skana liked long, lean men.

"I'd enjoy that," she said. "What's your name?"

"Colton. Del Colton. My ship's the *Warthog*."

"Really? You go in for mythical creatures, too?" Skana asked. "I'm Skana Bertu. Our ship's the *Pelican*."

"No kidding! I found my ship's name in a book. I think I saw pelicans in there, too. Funny-looking bird. Uh, no offense. Warthogs are supposed to be pretty weird, too. I mean, if they ever existed."

"No offense taken. How long have you been here?"

Del was about to reply, but the Wichu blared right over him.

"Three weeks. I've got peacocks about to hatch in my hold! They've gotta let us through *now*."

Skana looked around the bar. Their conversation had momentarily awakened the interest of the other captains.

"Everyone else like that, too?"

"Yeah," Del said. "I got here thirty-four days ago, just after they let the last group through, curse it."

"That's a mess," Skana said.

"We're all going broke here," said a young human female seated at a table about two meters from Skana. "I'd blame the station, but I honestly think they're baffled about it, too."

Nile appeared at her shoulder.

"What's the matter?" Skana asked. Nile leaned close to her and whispered in her ear.

"En— he needs to know how many ships besides us are waiting. Accurate count."

Bartenders knew everything. Skana pushed her pocket secretary over the bartop toward the older woman with a tip box illuminated. She had tapped "20 credits" into the square.

"How many of us are there here? I mean, ships? How long do we have to wait to go?"

The woman swiped her hand over the nearest clear section of counter.

"Got to be sixteen with you. Wait a minute, there's another one on its way in, about four hours out. That'll make seventeen of you waiting."

"Who is it?" the woman asked.

"*Sportswear*."

A moan went up throughout the room.

"Why, what's the matter?" Skana asked. Even Del had his forehead in his hand.

"Skana, Orrie Tang On is the biggest pain in the posterior who ever piloted a ship," he said. "He scans other people's manifests, looking to see how he can undercut you before you even dock at your next stop. He's been known to sabotage a rival so he can reach orbit first. We've all tried to be nice to him, but it doesn't pay. He takes nice as a sign of weakness."

Nile grinned. "So do I. But how's it work around here? First in, first out?"

"Yes, sir, that's true. Manager FitzGreen has tried to be fair about it."

"What if I can make sure the *Sportswear* doesn't make it into the convoy?"

"If you could do that," the young woman captain said, with hope in her eyes, "you would be my hero forever."

"Backtrack a second," the Wichu said. "Bertu, of Bertu Shipping?"

"That's right," Skana said.

"Hey, guys, we have celebrities here!" he bellowed to the room. "Guys, if you can get us through ahead of Orrie, we'll all put your portrait on our bulkheads. So, you have some kind of connection over there?"

Nile grinned.

"Mr. Bertu, if you can get us moving, I will owe you the biggest favor in the world," Del said.

"We all will!" the woman exclaimed. Everyone else in the bar nodded.

"Call me Nile. And I will remember that."

"I'll honor it. My word is good. Sometimes better than my credit rating."

"Just be ready to move out when you hear the word."

Skana studied him. "What are you going to do?"

"Use just a little of our cargo," he said, his broad face as wide-eyed and innocent as a puppy's. "The guy won't be able to launch with the rest of us. Get the girls. We're clearing out within the hour."

Manager FitzGreen, a tall man with a pot belly, called all the pilots into his cramped office.

"Folks, I want to thank everyone for their patience. I'm happy to say that we got word that sixteen are going through. Pay your bills and clean up after yourselves. Get your ships ready. Remember, once you pass the jump point, you've got to stay in formation until you get to Dilawe. What are you all grinning at?"

"Sixteen?" asked a skinny little man at the rear of the room. "What about me? We just got here. You ain't gonna tell me we can't go, too! Stretch it to seventeen! I mean it! I got deliveries to make!"

FitzGreen gave the man with an expression of disgust. "Captain Tang On, you're out of luck. Looks like you're going to have to wait here for a while."

"Tough luck, man," Del Colton told him, with a wink for Skana. "But, hey, you can have the place to yourself."

As the jubilant pilots left the office, the skinny man's pocket com warbled. "What do you mean, the sublights broke down? How'd we get in here? On magical fumes?"

Skana nudged Nile in the back with a fingertip. He chuckled.

"I think you just made fifteen new friends," she whispered.

CHAPTER 22

The *Rodrigo* felt rather cramped after the gracious size of the *Bonchance*, but my cousin and her friends had become old hands at coping with life aboard a starship. Banitra, who was fast proving herself to be a natural ringleader, organized a contest to see how small they could stow their possessions. I felt growing gratitude toward her and Hopeli, who also seemed a natural at staunching Jil's natural impulse to take over a situation. As a token of my respect, I offered a prize of a precious half-ounce of dantooth caviar to the winner, who proved to be Marquessa. Naturally, it would have been absolutely impossible to sit and watch her eat it without suffering pangs ourselves, so I had Angie dole out portions to the rest of us, along with lemons, blini, onions and other delicacies. For beverages, I provided sparkling white wine and vodka.

I invited the crew on the bridge to join us in the repast.

"It would be my pleasure to share with all of you as well," I said, as they bustled around me.

"Not now, Kinago," Plet said, almost peevishly, from her post in the center seat. "We can't drink on duty."

"I had thought of that," I said. "I have a splendid tomato-water and fennel-seed beverage that contains no alcohol, but offsets the flavors splendidly."

"Later." She looked up from the screentank to meet my eyes with a businesslike gaze. "Thank you."

"Should I leave them to their party and take up my post here?" I asked, politely. Plet waved a dismissive hand.

"No. Keep them out of our way. That would help more than anything."

"Aye, ma'am!" I said, reeling off a salute. I thought it best to humor her. Though, as I departed, it seemed to me that they preferred to have me off the bridge, too. I was not accustomed to being unwanted, and retreated to assuage my feelings with caviar. Parsons, whom I had also invited by means of a message to his viewpad in spite of my feelings about his underhanded behavior, was nowhere to be found.

By the time I returned, Jil and friends had demolished the dantooth, my share included. I had instructed Angie to put the remaining containers well out of reach, even if I begged, so I had to content myself with other dainties, such as biscuits smeared with a soft white cheese from the southern hemisphere of Keinolt and a gripping episode of *Ya!* The ladies watched the program with me, but they chose to lounge in the crash couches as though they were silken divans, preferring not to be troubled by my baleful gaze. When Redius took his break from the bridge, I halted the digitavid momentarily and gave him an overview of the plot to date in the best Uctu I could render. "This the second episode of Season fifty. Iftivi has just arrived at Healer Meraul's office and offered him a family heirloom for his services . . . ."

Redius listened carefully, smiling at my pronunciation now and again.

"Doing well," he confirmed, as we settled down, with crackers and wine, to enjoy the fascinating unfolding of the complex plot, now over three hundred years old, but still new to me.

Full seasons of *Ya!* were not easily available, protected as they were by complicated copyright laws between the Autocracy and the Imperium (my own people were not innocent of the same strangulating strictures on other forms of intellectual property). Streaming broadcasts over the Infogrid were so tightly controlled that they deleted themselves from one's storage crystals whenever they were detected. Only legal copies were allowed systemwide. My private collection had been carefully and legally amassed from fellow enthusiasts willing to sell. I had allowed it to be known that I was determined to complete a set, and would pay or trade to obtain licit copies. One dear friend had been so moved by my interest that he left me his precious boxed set of Seasons eight and nine in his will. I had hundreds of seasons yet to locate. Some of the most ancient episodes, my fellow fans and I had heard, had been lost because of poor management by the production company, and were reported to be gone for good. I hoped to fill in the gaps in my digitavid library one day. The audio novelizations that were still for sale, in the original Uctu and in translation, were just not the same.

"He goes," Redius said, leaning toward the screen with an avid expression, as one of the actresses went to greet the male she loved. The male turned away. "No!"

"What a cad!" I exclaimed. "He snubbed her!"

"Not cad," Redius countered. "Unaware."

"No! I say he did it on purpose. Did you see the way he switched his tail?"

"To avoid door."

"Bah!"

"My lord, may I have a word with you?"

I glanced away from the screen. As usual, Parsons had appeared in the room without seeming to have come through any of the doors. All I could work out was that he had risen up from beneath the floor.

"Parsons, your arrival interrupted a very intense scene," I chided him. "We were about to discover if Neletius couldn't recognize Iftivi when she had had her spots altered, or if he purposely ignored her at the village supper."

"Sir, I am sorry to delay that revelation, but we are about to exit ultradrive near Way Station 46. It is the first of your diplomatic stops. Since you are to greet the station management staff on behalf of the Emperor, I wanted you to have a thorough briefing on the situation at hand."

"Leaving!" Redius said, cheerfully, springing to his feet. "Later, Thomas. Summon?"

"Yes, I will," I promised him. I marked the place in the episode where we had left off and switched off the screen. "We'll get to the bottom of Iftivi's subterfuge."

The forward door slid closed behind him.

"If I may begin?" Parsons inquired.

"I would be wounded to the quick if you didn't," I said. I glanced around to make certain none of my cousin's devices or those of her friends were nearby. I suspected that a quantity of their personal electronics had eavesdropping capabilities—vital functions, considering the insidious nature of palace gossip—and I did not want my true status blabbed on the Infogrid as a result of my carelessness.

Parsons opened his hand to reveal a gray cube so uninteresting in appearance that I would not have approached it out of curiosity even if it were the only thing inside an isolation chamber with me though I had exhausted the fascination of my own finger- and toenails. He set it down between us.

"Our conference is unheard, my lord," he assured me. "Besides, Lady Jil is occupied with her own activities."

I slumped leaned back in my seat and thrust my long legs out before me.

"That's a relief. I have never been one for uninterrupted privacy, as you know, but having actual secrets to keep does change one's perspective. I have to sweep my quarters frequently to make certain no foreign object has been left behind."

"I am glad that you have taken such precautions, my lord," Parsons said. "This will not take very long."

I waved him to the other comfortable chair, the one that Redius had just vacated. Parsons lowered himself into it as gently as a hovercraft alighting. His back remained ramrod straight. That posture elicited in me a sense of peer pressure. I sat up at attention, drawing my heels down and my shoulders up. Parsons presented his own viewpad for my perusal. I drew mine close to his and was rewarded with an instantaneous transfer of the appropriate files, including personal profiles of staff, maps, and endless details of trade that occurred annually above the orbiting platform. Parsons brought up the images of five people, four Humans and one Wichu.

"Your task in Way Station 46 is to present the compliments of the Emperor and receive reports from these personnel. Each of them has specific responsibilities, which you will study before we link to the station, and will brief you on his or her concerns. I regret to say that you do not have the authority to assuage any of these concerns, but you will file notice of them with the Core Worlds Authority via Infogrid and be debriefed in person upon your return."

"Seems a trifle redundant," I pointed out. "They could file their own grievances in exactly the same fashion as I. Why don't they do that?"

"Propinquity, my lord."

I waggled a chiding finger at him.

"Aha, you thought you would catch me out with your torturous vocabulary! I know that word well. So, as on our previous mission, they will feel exalted by close contact with a representative of the Imperium, and I am to be that representative."

"It was not my intent to 'catch you out,' my lord," Parsons said, reproof writ large upon his otherwise smooth brow. "I wished to be concise. They do not often receive visitors except those in transit . . ."

". . . Which we are," I added.

"Indeed. But by giving them your undivided attention . . ."

". . . I will be freeing you from theirs," I concluded.

"If you would be so good as to allow me to complete sentences on my own, my lord?" Parsons said. The reproof had been joined by its occasional companion, irritation.

"Go on, go on," I said, with a wave of my hand. "I've had my fun. And with what manner of secret operation will I be assisting this time?" I inquired, eager now that I was assured that I could not be overheard by my cousin.

"None at all, my lord," Parsons said.

I hate to admit it, for fear of compromising my dignity, but I believe I pouted.

"I suppose you will be investigating some matter very deeply on the station?" I said, with some heat.

"My task is as prosaic as yours, my lord. I will be taking similar reports from persons with whom you would find it difficult to associate without drawing attention to them."

"Friends of, er, Mr. Frank?"

"And others like him," Parsons said.

I immediately leaped upon that careful phrase, like a dog upon the scent of a treat.

"There are others like him?" I asked. "Representatives of other services of the type he oversees, or colleagues within his own organization?"

"Yes," Parsons replied, to my infinite surprise.

"Which is it?" I demanded.

"It is difficult to say, my lord. I may state that all of the persons involved act in loyal service to the Imperium."

And with that I had to be left unsatisfied.

"Commander!"

The viewpad before Parsons jangled for attention. Oskelev's face became visible on the small screen.

"Yes, lieutenant?"

"C'mon up. We've got a visitor. Looks like he was waiting for us."

Our gazes locked, we rose to our feet in unison.

"On our way."

Plet saluted as we arrived at the bridge.

"What is it, Plet?" I asked.

She steered us toward the screen tank.

"This ship was hanging off at some distance when we emerged from ultradrive," she said. "It would seem that this zone is a known exit point for ships going on to the frontier."

"Pirates?" I asked, perking up a trifle.

"I doubt it." The Wichu pilot threw an impatient hand at the scope. "They hailed us. I wanted you to see it as soon as possible. What do you want to do about it?"

A large vessel was in the screen tank. I stooped to peer at it. It was a gaudy ship, patterned in cheerful hues. It seemed to be in good condition, but I could see by its spectroscopic shadow that it had gas and radiation leaks, showing poor maintenance. It was not so far away that it couldn't bracket us with laser strikes, but I didn't see the usual power signatures for a heavy weapon array.

"Is it asking us for help?" I inquired. "Nesbitt could do some running repairs on it, but it is best off waiting until it reaches Way Station 46. We don't have much capacity for in-depth analysis, but we could be of some aid—"

"No, my lord," Oskelev said, cutting off my offer of assistance. "It's a trader. The pilot asked to talk to the people in charge. That's you." She looked from one to the other of us. I don't see why she was confused about the command structure. I was at the top, with Plet as my trusted assistant. Parsons was my aide-de-camp, not in the line of command at all.

"Don't they see that this is a military vessel?" Plet asked.

"That never stops 'em asking, sir," Oskelev said. "The reason you don't hear about shy traders is that they go out of business."

I was greatly amused.

"Put him on, then," I said. Anstruther swept a finger over a single control on her console.

A round, brown-skinned face adorned with a fringe of wiry silver at both top and bottom appeared.

"All hail the mighty Imperium ship CK-M945B!" came the beery voice over the speakers. "Who've I got there?"

"This is the naval ship *Rodrigo*," I said. "I am Lieutenant Lord Thomas Kinago."

"Whoo-hoo, a noble! I knew today was my lucky day!"

"Perhaps it is my lucky day," I said. "How may I help you?"

The rich, cheerful voice launched into a fast-paced patter.

"Wallace Doyobe here, Lord Thomas. I am a trader with many decades of experience—you can look me up on Infogrid—and I know that there has to be a list in your mind of all the items that you have not been able to find haunting you. When you walk into a bazaar, or meet a trader, I just know you are wondering—does he, she or it have that one little thing that I have been missing all my life?

"You must be looking for bargains, or you wouldn't be heading for that outpost, Way Station 46," he went on smoothly. "Word is that they keep people there until they run out of money. Then either they've got to turn back or do their best once they make it into the Autocracy. Now, that is where I come in."

I interrupted his flow with a question that knocked so hard at my lips it fell out of my mouth.

"Isn't that where you are going, my good fellow? Why else would you be this close to the frontier?"

"Nope," Doyobe said flatly. "Not going there. I was in the Autocracy before the craziness started. Since then, I've been buying goods off the folks who are coming out, doing a little interstellar business with those as turned back. Handing off their goods to the folks who insist they're going to risk Way Station 46. I'm trading with both sides. Giving the people what they want. The folks returning from the Autocracy don't have to go far to offload part of their cargo, and the Imperium ships don't have to get caught in that web to pick up some Uctu merchandise. It's a win-win-win! Maybe even four wins, if I can do something for you."

"And what do you know about the situation beyond the border, sir?" Parsons intoned from behind me.

"It's a downright mystery," Doyobe said, shifting his eyes to Parsons. I could sense his puzzlement as he attempted to sum up my aide-de-camp. Better men than he had crashed in frustration upon the impenetrable rock of that countenance. "Some folks go into the Autocracy, and they ain't coming out again. So it'll be a long time before you see me on the other side of the frontier. So, would you like to talk merchandise? I can send you my catalog. Updated to the minute!"

I peered back at Parsons.

"It would seem an unnecessary delay to continue negotiations at long distance, sir," he said, with his usual blank exterior. I, who was familiar with Parsons, did not need a neon indicator to pick up on his implication. I turned to smile at the screen.

"Mr. Doyobe, why don't you bring over your catalog, and let us have a confabulation face to face?" I asked, imparting as much hospitality as I could in my tone. "You never know, you might well precipitate an exchange of goods and capital. I know that I am in a buying mood, and my cousin, who is traveling with me, is seeded in the shopping championships on several planets in the Core Worlds."

Doyobe perked up like a coffeepot.

"My lord, it would be a pleasure! And I could bring along a few little things with me, if you have anything in particular you fancy. . . . I don't suppose you're a viewer, for example, of the Uctu digitavid program called *Ya!*"

I exchanged glances with Parsons. I smiled at the optical pickup.

"You may so suppose, my good fellow. Why?"

The broad face broadened even further with a toothy smile.

"Weeeell, I might have an item or two that will take your fancy. Not widely available in the Imperium, or narrowly, either. Something realllly ancient."

"Oh?" I asked. "*How* ancient?" A tingle of excitement erupted in my fingertips and spread throughout my entire body. My lucky circuit erupted with a twinkling of colored light. Opportunity was knocking, if I could only reach the portal fast enough. "What is it?"

Doyobe, no fool, saw that he had a fish on the line.

"Wait and see, my lord! If I can bring along my nephew, Hakim, we'll be shuttling over in a few minutes."

"That would be most satisfactory," I said. Oskelev closed the communications link. I turned to my aide-de-camp, who radiated pleased contentment.

"Parsons, I do believe that this is my lucky day! I must check my horoscope again."

"My lord, wouldn't your removal from the focal point of the constellations alter your fortunes?"

I was taken aback at my own carelessness, and smote my forehead in contrition. "You're right! I haven't recalibrated my charts yet. It would take too much time. I shall have to consult my crystal instead. No, you made me leave that home. Or perhaps my cards. But wait," I added, with a reproachful glance at him. "I believe I am owed an explanation for the events that transpired immediately before our departure from the *Bonchance*, Parsons."

"It would be unbecoming to discuss such matters before others, sir," Parsons said.

In spite of the curious eyes that lit upon me from all directions on the bridge, I felt mulish enough to dig in my heels.

"No, I feel here and now would be quite sufficient, Parsons."

"There isn't time for that now, my lord," Parsons said, smoothly. "Our guest is arriving very shortly. You would not want to miss the unpacking of the peddler's wares, would you?"

I sighed.

"You have me there, Parsons. But this matter is not yet concluded."

"Of course not, my lord."

The crew, with the exception of Anstruther, who remained to maintain the ship's conn, assembled eagerly in the hold to meet our visitor's shuttle. I tried to guess what might be the curiosity that he was bringing. I had a list of things for which I hoped against hope, but those were the stuff of fantasy. I would settle for a little novelty, for which I was willing to pay a fair price. The anticipation was delicious. I saw my fellow crewmembers infected with the same fever. Even Plet, that model of dignity and gravitas, positively fidgeted. When she noticed my scrutiny, she stopped moving, but I had already made note of her interest and found it charming. It was nice to know that she was capable of the same feelings as the rest of us.

Doyobe proved to be the very image of a longtime space merchant. Emerging from a hatch that seemed rather too small to contain his effusive personality, he wore the most casual of shipsuits, possessed of innumerable pockets from which emerged trinkets and treasures of all descriptions.

"Greetings, my friends! I am here to fulfill your dreams. There will be profit for all of us. Please, ask me for anything! I might even have it!"

We chuckled appreciatively. I stepped forward, as the host who had invited him.

"Welcome, Captain Doyobe. And is this your nephew?"

"Yes, it is," Doyobe said, with a flourish behind him. "Hakim! My most excellent nephew and apprentice at the space merchant trade."

Hakim, a slimmer and younger version of his uncle, drew behind him an antigrav lifter. With occasional glances at us, he guided it down the ramp of the shuttle and onto the hold deck. We could all see that it had been stacked two meters high with intriguing parcels. The crew of the *Rodrigo* emitted a collective sigh of pleasure. We surrounded the sled even though it was still moving, trying to decide what we wanted to examine first. All of the boxes, bags and packages looked worthy of a good browse. But the item that thrilled me beyond words was the first thing I spotted near the top of the load where only someone of my lofty height could see it: a *Ya!* boxed set.

Carefully, I removed it from the pile. I read the three-dimensional blurb that beamed out from the sleeve as soon as the side was unobstructed. In cut-jewel letters, it proclaimed that the box contained the first three seasons of *Ya!* In my astonishment I nearly dropped it. I held something so rare and precious that fellow collectors would have killed me without hesitation and stood upon the body just to touch it.

"What is?"

Redius crowded in beside me to see. I tipped the label toward him. He read it and let out a hiss of astonishment. We shared a glance. Only fellow enthusiasts would understand the excitement that crackled between us. This was a prize beyond price. I hoped no one else would notice.

However, I could not imagine going unobserved by the merchant. Doyobe homed in upon me as though I was handling his firstborn child. I attempted to be casual, but it was difficult to maintain my cool exterior when handling that item. I would have given anything at that moment to possess Parsons's preternatural serenity.

"So, you spotted it, my lord," Doyobe said, with an avuncular smile.

"Any fan of *Ya!* would give his teeth and one hand to own it." He threw an arm around my shoulder, having to reach high for it, as he was a great deal shorter than I, and walked alongside me as though we were old and close friends. "Now, I think you'll admit that this is a bit of a rarity, wouldn't you say?"

"I have never seen one of these before," I said.

"Nor I," said Redius.

"Take a close look, why don't you? I think you'll find it everything you ever hoped for. As a fan of *Ya!*, I mean."

I read the synopsis on the back of Season One. Now that I was more conversant in written Uctu, the meaning sprang out at me.

"The origin stories of all the main houses? Great heavens." I clapped a hand out over my mouth and glanced at my fellows. Had I actually read that out loud?

"Astonishing," Redius agreed.

"Fine, isn't it?" Doyobe asked. "Open it up, my lord." I did. Inside, three octagonal shapes the size of my thumbnail, one each of gold, pink and blue, glistened up at me. "Look at the state of the crystals. In perfect condition, my lord, I promise you. Not one single dropped sector, not one missing scene."

"But is it genuine?" I asked. "I am not going to appear on the Uctu homeworld with contraband in my pack. It puts me in the same state as those poor wretches who have been imprisoned."

"Check the seals, sir," Doyobe suggested, with an offhand gesture. He took the gold crystal out of the box and drew it close to one of the foiled stamps on the side. The middle stamp glowed in a complicated pattern. "Every seal is coded to react to the crystal in the box that corresponds with it. Nothing's been tampered with. Check it all ways from galactic center. You'll never find a more genuine set."

By that time, we and the visitors had reached the mess hall, and the bevy of ladies had discovered that shopping was in the offing. They had lifted themselves from the crash couches to peruse the merchandise, ducking in between the crewmembers to snatch up items that had been spread out across the dining tables. The room had taken on the air of a weekend bazaar.

"Look at these wonderful scarves," Marquessa said, brandishing a handful of glowing rainbows. "I have a couple of customers who would love these."

"I can give you a good price on them," Doyobe said. "You won't pay less anywhere in the Autocracy, unless you can lay hands on the weavers themselves." I saw him catch a glimpse of me out of the corner of his eye, but he kept on with his bargain. "What do you say, madam? Act now, and I will throw in this handsome brooch." A twinkling cluster of crystals appeared on his palm as though by magic. I grinned.

Jil glanced over the heads of her friends toward me. As I would have guessed, she instantly identified the object in my hands. She closed the distance between us, hands reaching clawlike for my prize.

"Is that an old set? Oh!" she exclaimed, as she managed to flip up the box to read the label. "The first three! I want it! Give it to me."

"Not a chance, cousin," I said, brushing her away gently but firmly. "It's mine."

Redius moved away so as not to be caught in the crossfire. I couldn't blame him. He joined Nesbitt, who was going through stacks of small cases in a basket. Oskelev had draped a range of decorative belts and harnesses over her furry shoulders. Plet flipped through boxes of antique books with paper pages. I would have been delighted to join her at that makeshift library, but serious business needed to be handled first.

Jil turned to Doyobe, who had concluded his dealing with Marquessa and had come to join us.

"Dear sir, I want that *Ya!* collection," she said. "I'll pay you *anything*."

"The gentleman had first call on it, madam," the trader said, with a slight bow. "You'll understand. First come, first served?"

"I don't understand that at all," Jil said, with a dismissive wave. "Thomas is my cousin. I have the same right to things as he does. Let me have it." She opened her eyes wide and brought the intense regard to bear upon him that had captivated the commander of the *Bonchance*, and countless others before him. "Please?"

"Well, madam," Doyobe said, stroking his silver beard with just the right air of hesitation. "I was asking twelve hundred for the set. It's a scarce treasure, you understand."

Jil blanched. Inwardly, I was triumphant. I knew she was not the collector I was. I would pay that without hesitation.

"Would you consider ten fifty?" she asked, tiptoeing a pair of delicate fingers upon the cuff of his shipsuit. "Perhaps even eleven hundred?"

"Well . . ."

"Thirteen," I said at once.

Doyobe glanced up at me with a summing eye.

"Thirteen, my lord?"

I appeared diffident.

"Well, as you say, it's a genuine rarity. I can't let it slip through my fingers by being stingy."

Jil looked from me to the trader and back again.

"Oh, you are not serious!"

"Trading's my livelihood, madam. It's very serious to me, indeed! Perhaps if you'd like to raise your offer a trifle?"

Marquessa, the prized scarves tied around her arms like guerdons, sidled over. She leaned close to Jil, her tresses of golden hair concealing both their faces. I could hear her whisper but not distinguish what was being said. I remembered that she was Jil's personal shopper in Taino. She had undoubtedly made more bargains in her career than all of us put together. The fair curtain withdrew, revealing Jil's face, now set with determination.

"Thirteen fifty," she said. "I think that's fair, don't you?" She reached for the boxed set and tried to pluck it out of my fingers. I extended my arm over my head, well out of her reach.

"Fourteen," I said. "I should think that is even more fair."

Jil glared daggers at me. Marquessa leaned in for another round of advice.

"You know," Jil said, her expression now as mild as a doll's, "we only have to enter Uctu space to purchase these years' worth of the show, and you will be out of luck on this sale, Mr. Doyobe."

The trader clucked his tongue.

"Ah, but even there these are strictly limited, madam. There hasn't been a fresh issue of the earliest seasons for a long while, maybe thirty years. I think they're waiting for the next centenary. They'll publish millions of legit copies then."

"That's too long to wait," Jil said, leaning closer so her personal perfume wafted around the trader's nostrils. "I want *this* one." She hoped to convince him by main force of personality. I knew what she was doing, even though she didn't. Commoners had a genetic predilection to being persuaded by the nobility. I tried not to trade upon that, as I considered it bad sportsmanship. If I could not win outright by force of wit, then I did not deserve to win.

"Angie," I said, "bartering is a thirsty game. Would you dispense beverages for us? From my personal supply, if you please."

"Of course, Lord Thomas," said the voice of the LAI. "Gentlemen, please consult your viewpads for a menu."

Doyobe took his personal device from his pocket and ran his eyes up and down the list. His silver brows ascended.

"If the way to my heart wasn't through my wallet, you would have won me over right there, my lord," he said, heartily. "Real Boske wines?"

"I have a connection," I said modestly. "That ten-year-old green is very good. Effervescent without being too intoxicating. I wouldn't want your senses muddled. Boske green for all, Angie."

"Of course, Lord Thomas."

A serverbot under Angie's control trundled out to us, clinking with filled glasses. I served the ladies, then offered wine to the visitors before taking any myself. Jil pushed the proffered glass away. The 'bot scuttled back out of reach. She glared at Doyobe.

"All right! Fourteen fifty."

The trader sipped from his glass. The wine was cool enough to raise a mist of condensation on the exterior of the crystal. He let out a sigh of appreciation.

"It's a fine offer," he said. "One I'd be proud to accept."

"But not as fine as fifteen," I interjected, lifting my glass to him.

"Ah, are you sure, my lord?"

"Of course. I would not have said so otherwise."

"No!" Jil pleaded, then steeled herself. I knew she didn't want to let a prize like this one get away from her, but we had reached the point of pain. "Fifteen one."

"Fifteen two," I countered.

"Three!"

"Four."

But, sometimes withdrawal was the only way to counter superior forces. Jil reached for the glass of wine and sipped it with deliberate delicacy.

"And if I keep going?" she asked me, her green eyes flashing dangerously.

"I will follow, a credit at a time," I said, in what I knew was a maddening tone. Her frustration almost made up for all the times she had irked me aboard the *Bonchance*. In fact, the pleasure of seeing her so cross began to wipe out annoyances dating back further into our early lives. She was my cousin and a close friend, but that did not mean we didn't irritate one another almost to the point of producing pearls among our soft tissues.

"Five," she said, though she had to grit it out. I saw that the drawing out of the process would continue until she was unfit to live with for the remainder of our journey. Better to pull out the loose tooth than to continue to wiggle it.

"Fifteen," I said.

It was enough. Jil goggled at me.

"I won't say, Thomas, that I've never been so insulted in my life, but this comes close."

"How? Because my pockets are deeper than yours?"

"I'm surprised that you can even think of spending the money," Jil said, with insulting nonchalance, "since you have yet to pay off the damages to the Empress's statue. And one would think you would hesitate to indulge yourself following your most disgraceful behavior on the warship. Aunt Tariana was most pained about it."

"I *knew* you sent the transcript to my mother," I crowed, and had the satisfaction of seeing those golden cheeks flush dark red. "Well, I will spend the money, even if it requires dipping into reserves for the damages, and I will make amends to my mother later on, but I can console myself watching the very first three seasons of *Ya!*" I turned to Doyobe. "Do we have a deal, captain? Fifteen fifteen?"

"Seventeen's the lucky number in the Autocracy, sir."

"True," Redius said, from his safe distance. I nodded.

"Seventeen it is. Fifteen hundred and seventeen credits."

By now, the rest of the crew was watching us as though we were an ongoing drama featuring the descendants of great houses stretching back many centuries, which, in justice, we actually were. Parsons hung back in the shadows of the kitchen unit, perhaps ready to wheel out as though he were one of the more efficient serverbots.

"Lady, over to you," he said, with a persuasive smile. "Wouldn't you like to reconsider?"

Jil's face seemed to swell with frustration, but a subtle sign passed to her from Marquessa. She stepped back, her expression one of aching sweetness and regret. If I had not been her cousin and companion of more than two decades, my heart might have broken from the sorrow of it all. But I knew her better than that.

"I renounce my claim, Captain," she said. "I want to save as much of my money for shopping on Dilawe 4. Keep it, Thomas. I know you'll lend it to me once in a while."

I smiled.

"I know you think so, cousin." I drew forth my viewpad and activated a transfer of credits. Instantly, I received a receipt.

Doyobe read the screen of his pocket device then patted it. His round face wore the broadest of smiles. "Anything else you want? I've got it all!"

I offered my hand and received a firm shake.

"You have fulfilled my wildest dreams, sir," I assured him. "Who would know that out here on the outskirts of the Imperium, that I should encounter that most fleeting, most legendary of collectible objects, the first three seasons of *Ya!*?"

"Well, now you don't need to go into the Autocracy," the captain said, putting his device into his handiest pouch.

"We have to go on to Way Station 46 and beyond," I insisted. "People are depending upon us."

Doyobe's broad cheeks drooped.

"Well, it was nice knowing you, my lord. I hear these days ships who go into Uctu space don't come out. It's a death trap. Wasn't like that under the old Autocrat, harsh as he was. This new one is a killer. Honest, people are getting desperate."

"I will do something about that," I insisted.

"Meantime, why don't you browse, my lord? You never know, there might be a small delight you haven't noticed yet?"

"You never know," I said, but my heart wasn't in it. I had obtained what I wished for. I sat down at a nearby table with my wine and my treasure.

It appeared that my shipmates were also pleased with their finds. Nesbitt glanced up at me with a wordless expression of bliss on his face. He held a plastic plaque full of tiny tools, some ordinary routing heads, some with glowing laser tips, others with esoteric-looking devices I had never seen before. I knew Nesbitt indulged in the working of miniatures, but I had not yet persuaded him to allow me to see any of the fruits of his hobby. Plet held an opaque, flat plastic envelope against her side. Its soft drape suggested the contents were clothing. Oskelev was positively festooned with new harnesses over her official uniform straps. And the ladies had bags, boxes, parcels and envelopes. Only Jil had nothing to show. She noticed my scrutiny and made a face at me.

"I will see the visitors out," Parsons said. "Gentlemen, this way, please."

The traders departed. The elder Doyobe slapped his viewpad happily. His account now held a large sum of money from nearly all of us. His visit had been more than worthwhile.

I held onto my prize greedily, wondering when I should watch the first episode. What ambience would be best to view it? Depending upon the synopsis, what beverage should I pour? What lighting would be suitable? It would be my one opportunity to watch two surviving episodes of Season four in my Uncle Perleas's home, and the production grades of several centuries ago were nothing as sophisticated as they had become in current years. Should I allow my digitavid system to fill in the deficiencies, or to view it as the historical object that it was? I sipped at my wine and allowed cheerful thoughts to filter through my mind.

A golden stormcloud appeared at my elbow. I was just in time to prevent lightning bolts in the form of two slim hands from crashing down upon my prize. I swept it out of reach.

"You must share with all of us!" Jil insisted. "Let me borrow it."

"Nonsense," I said. "This box is not leaving my sight. It would disappear into the fastness of that collection of storage lockers you call your luggage, and I will never see it again."

"That's not true!" Jil protested, perhaps a little too fervently. I elevated one eyebrow in disbelief. That had been her favorite tactic for gaining possession of something that belonged to one of us over the years. Her suite in the compound was filled with cupboards, closets and enormously heavy pieces of furniture just made for squirreling away treasures. Like the squirrel, a creature that had made its way with humankind from our original home on long-lost Earth, I fancy she had forgotten much or most of what she had stored away in these fastnesses.

"After the way you behaved on the *Bonchance*, I shouldn't even let you handle the box," I said.

"Lord Thomas, it would be such a marvelous treat," Banitra said, sitting down beside me and putting a gentle hand on my other arm. "No one I know has ever seen the missing seasons. They're almost legendary!"

I felt myself relenting. How could I not, when faced with such persuasion? But I recalled Jil's scorn and amusement at my expense. "Perhaps later."

"Now!" Jil insisted. "I want to know how the Reftilius family came into their original fortune. It had to be ill-gotten. Oh, please, Thomas?" she said, nestling her head onto my shoulder. The rest of her ladies moved in like vultures to a fresh kill. It was hard to remain obdurate.

"I have to decide," I said. "The *feng shui* must be respected. After all, this is like welcoming honored ancestors into our home. I am not simply going to slap the crystals into the player as though they were the latest variety show. This is an *occasion*."

Jil made a face at me. "Oh, all right. As long as I get to see them *sometime*."

"We will see," I said. "It depends upon whether you can put yourself out to be considerate to me for a while. You were appalling on the *Bonchance*, and your behavior has universal consequences. Karma, you know."

For answer, she punched me in the chest. As she was wearing a jeweled ring on each finger and her thumb, the effect was that of being jabbed by a multi-headed hammer.

"Ow!" I protested. I rubbed the injured ribs. "That seals your fate, my dear. You will now have to wait until we get home to Taino to see any of these episodes. *If* then."

Majestically, I rose and stalked back toward my cabin. We were only a day or so outside of Way Station 46, and I had files to review. If I allowed myself to be immersed in the pleasures of my new prize, I should get nothing else done.

"Huh!" I heard Jil exclaim as I departed. "If I've lived this long without seeing them, then I don't ever want to!"

Sour grapes, I thought smugly.

"An excellent find, captain," Parsons said, as he escorted the Doyobes into the hold. He reached into his belt pouch and drew from it the sound deadener. Doyobe's nephew stepped politely out of range of their conversation and began to load what was left of their goods into the shuttle. The skid load had been greatly reduced, as Parsons had assumed it would.

"The find of a lifetime, commander," Doyobe said. "After you asked, I was sure I had a copy in one of my caches. Glad to see I was right. I am delighted it's going to such a good home. I could have gotten three times the price for it on the open market."

Parsons refused to allow himself to be baited on such an easily disproven statement.

"The price you received was more than fair. It was nearly twice the auction price for an authenticated copy."

Doyobe smirked.

"Weeeeel, I suppose that's all right. I do owe you a few favors. Are you sure you don't want me to tell the boy you commissioned me to locate it for him?"

"Not necessary, captain," Parsons said. "He had rather a traumatic experience recently. I believe this will assuage the damaged feelings."

"Very nice," Doyobe said. "You're a good guy, commander, if you don't mind my saying so. Mr. Frank always says the same. Oh, by the way!" The beefy trader's hand reached into one of the myriad pockets on his suit front and emerged with a slip of crystal no bigger than a fingernail. He placed it carefully in Parsons's palm. "This is for you."

"A full manifest of the ships coming and going from Way Station 46? Dating back how long?"

"Fifteen months. I just took over the vigil four months back. Kung Won on the *Bargain Hunter* swapped his files over to me when I came in. We'll be here just one more month unless you need us."

Parsons shook hands gravely with Doyobe. The silver-haired trader was an old and trusted colleague.

"I hope I will not have to call upon you."

"Hope not," Doyobe said, as Parsons put the cube away in his pocket. "But you can if you need to. It's been nice profiting off all of you, my friend."

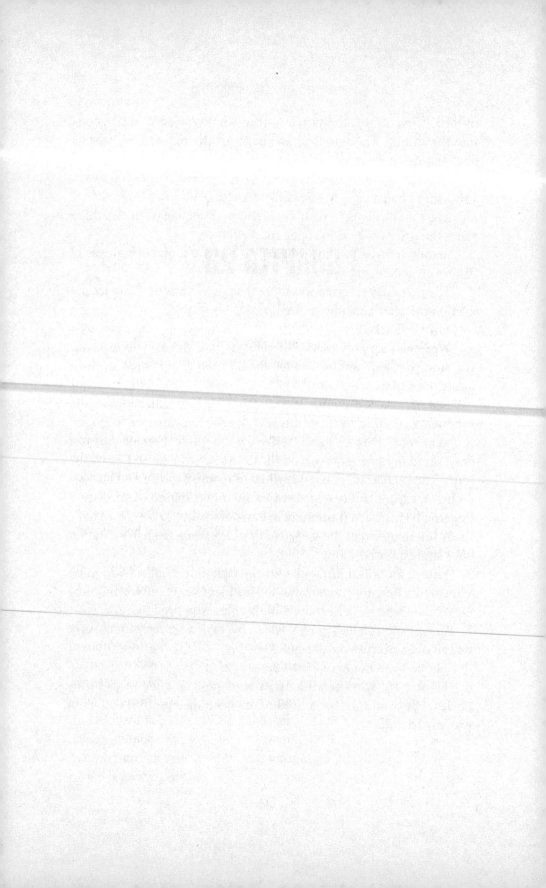

CHAPTER 23

Strapped up like an insane-asylum inmate in my seat on the bridge, I watched the screen tank as Oskelev brought us in to dock on the four-leaf-clover shape of Way Station 46. *A fortunate arrangement*, I noted to myself, seeing no poison arrows from sharp angles anywhere on the station.

My cousin and her friends were fastened into the less comfortable crash couches at the rear of the bridge, grumbling about the creases the belts and nets were making in their couture outfits. They had insisted on being up top with the crew as we docked. I fancied it was partly curiosity and partly because they could not bear to let me out of their sight. Ever since I had bought the boxed set of *Ya!* they had all done their best to woo me into letting them watch it. Thus far, I had not responded to their blandishments. Nor would I. Duty called. The episodes had been around for hundreds of years. They could wait until I had interrupted time to devote to them.

We floated on impulse engines past hundreds of available slips, indicated by rings of green light, toward a round black hole rimmed round with orange lights chasing one another in a clockwise circle, Berth Alpha 98-D. Filled slips, so Plet informed us, were designated by red lights. There were surprisingly few ships present. I counted only three on the side near our bay. It was not until then that the full force of the Uctus' absurd strictures dawned upon me. The station, and all others like it, ought to be buzzing with activity like an ion-powered hive. Trade between our nations had slowed beneath a trickle. It was not a healthy situation. I hoped that I might be able to do something about that. I certainly intended to try.

Anstruther had hailed the station manager's office. Denzies FitzGreen had confessed himself delighted to play host to the Emperor's representative. I was introduced with some fanfare by Plet, then dismissed as the minutiae of ship safety, regulations and other matters of arrival were achieved.

With a barely perceptible bump, the *Rodrigo* settled to the deck. The enormous iris of the bay hatch sealed behind our tail. Fans and pumps whipped into life as our life support system was taken over by the station's. I felt the unfamiliar drag of a more powerful gravity take hold of my body.

"Brava!" I applauded Oskelev.

"It's nothing," she said. But she was pleased that someone acknowledged her skill.

Manager FitzGreen had sent that he awaited us just below the hatch. I had dressed for the official meeting in the most up-to-date trend on Taino. I had checked the fashion news shortly before choosing my outfit; after all, we had by then been gone some days. I did not want to appear out of touch. I had persuaded Angie to enlist the help of the repairbot responsible for the upholstery and soft furnishings aboard the *Rodrigo*—such as they were—to attach plaques of black and light leather here and there to an otherwise impeccably tailored midnight-blue suit. The effect was startlingly like camouflage, and most becoming. I could not wait to show it off on this outpost.

Suddenly, klaxons erupted. They were so loud it took me a moment to realize they were coming from outside the ship. The navigation screen tank and all the other screens on the bridge filled with red alert indicators. The *Rodrigo* immediately went into safety mode, all hatches locked and sealed, weapons warming. A reverse thrum of fans indicated the ship was going back on its own life support system.

Plet touched the arm of her chair with a thumb.

"Way Station 46, what is happening?"

"We've got a jumper, captain," a clear female voice rang out from the console. "From the security recordings, looks like when we announced an Imperium navy ship was docking, one crew dropped everything and headed for the exit. That's the one leaving, the *Moskowitz*."

"Will pursue," Plet confirmed. "Prepare for battle stations. All non-essential personnel clear the ship at once. Manager FitzGreen will take you in charge."

I sat up, feeling my eyes shine with eagerness. For the very first time, my dear scout was going to be used in its intended purpose, as a warship. I looked back over my shoulder at my cousin and her entourage.

"Ladies, that means you," I said. "Hurry! The station manager will look after you."

"Oh, no!" Jil protested, not moving a fingertip. "I want to watch."

"It could be dangerous. Hurry! We can't wait for long."

"You, too, Lord Thomas," Plet said, with notable emphasis on my title.

I turned to regard her with dismay.

"Me? But I am part of this ship's complement. I can be of assistance!"

"This is no time to have fun, my lord," Parsons said severely.

"Fun? Well, I suppose it would be . . ." I admitted.

"You are a diplomat traveling on behalf of the Emperor," Plet said, with patience that I could tell was running out of her like sands from an antique egg-timer. "You are too valuable to risk."

"But . . ." I began. Plet cut me off.

"Hurry up. The station manager will look after you."

I palmed the catch on my safety harness and stood up.

"I can tell you enjoyed saying that," I said, peevishly. I held myself with the greatest dignity I could muster. I assisted Jil and Sinim in freeing themselves from the crash couches. "Very well. Ladies, with me!"

FitzGreen, a tall but bulky man, was indeed waiting just outside the hatch with a bevy of security officers wearing dull brown uniforms and visored helmets. We ran toward the guards.

All of us nobles had been trained from childhood to cooperate with security agents and other protection details to get out of the line of fire at speed and without making a fuss. Because of our connection to the Emperor, it was often thought by unsavory elements that making one of us a target of murder or kidnapping would impact the workings of government. How wrong they were. None of us except my serene cousin, Shojan XII, mattered in the slightest. Our primary functions were as a living, unadulterated gene pool for the imperial succession as well as to provide amusement value and the occasional authority figure for the public. Still, the perception remained; therefore, so did the security protocols.

"This way, my lord," FitzGreen said, steering us past a trio of fuel depot offices and out a lensing door into a well-worn corridor enameled in dark green and steel gray. "Uh, by the way, pleased to meet you. Hope you enjoyed your journey? I hardly know what to say. We don't get many nobles coming through, to be honest."

"In fact, you have two for the price of one," I said, deliberately wiping off the pout I perceived I was wearing and putting myself out to be cheerful. "My cousin, Lady Jil Loche Nikhorunkorn, and her friends." I reeled off the names. "If you will steer us to the nearest watering hole with a decent vintage or two in its cellars, I would be very pleased to treat you to a drink on my cousin the Emperor."

FitzGreen looked torn between excitement and worry.

"Can't do that, my lord," he said.

"Why not?" I asked. "Are you not permitted to drink while on duty?"

"No, sir," he said, taking Jil's upper arm. "It's not that. I've got to put you into a safe room for the duration of the emergency. I'd be in my office overseeing the event if you hadn't just arrived."

"A safe room!" I exclaimed in dismay.

"Yes, your imperiumness. You'll be very secure in there," FitzGreen said, in an obvious attempt to be reassuring. "Nothing can get at you."

As we exited the landing bay, a closed-roof vehicle with multiple paired wheels screeched up. A pair of doors like vertical pincers opened. We were bundled inside, all protesting. The car, whose walls I perceived as being at least a third of a meter thick with armor plating and shock absorption panels, sped off along a curving corridor. After a few kilometers, it screeched to a halt and made a sharp right into a lift column. The car rose on magnetic force created by the gravity generators at the heart of the station. Another screech, and the car exited left onto a new deck.

"Why are there so few ships here now?" I asked. "I was told this was the busiest crossing between the Imperium and the Autocracy."

"Ah, well, we got lucky," the station manager said, miming wiping sweat off his brow. "You just missed a convoy leaving a few days ago. Almost twenty got through this time. That's almost unprecedented since this craziness got started. The ones left are those who got here late, like yourselves, my lord."

"So why do you think the other ship ran?" Hopeli asked, her big dark eyes wide.

FitzGreen sighed.

"The usual reason's contraband, ma'am. Here we are, sir. Please, follow the guards. I'll talk to you when all this is over."

Two of the dark visors flanked us with lowered weapons. They herded us toward a blank wall festooned with a paper poster advertising a concert. The gyrating forms of the band wielding their instruments loomed toward us. As we approached, the panel slid out of the way, flattening the musicians as the poster passed behind the wall segment to its left. A row of lights went on in the ceiling of the room thus revealed.

"Here, ladies and sir," the harsh voice of a Croctoid came from beneath the helmet on the right. "Go on in."

Jil and her friends hurried inside. I turned to make one more attempt to remain free during the emergency, but the door hissed closed in my face.

I turned to survey our prison. FitzGreen had been slightly inaccurate in describing it as a room; it was more of a suite, if utilitarian in design. The main chamber was roomy and well-lit, about the size of a classroom. The blue-gray walls and ceiling had been lined with thick padding, no doubt in case the gravity generators were compromised. The cushiony flooring underfoot was made of similar material. It felt rather like walking inside an underinflated balloon.

The furnishings fulfilled multiple purposes. The couches that lined the walls had been made to be converted to beds in case of lengthy occupation. A number of hinged tables, folded flat, rested in a bracket near the back wall. They were long enough to be used as privacy barriers between the couches. Two doors led off the back of the room, the left to a hygiene chamber, and the right to a food service system. On the whole, it was plain, with little care taken to make it look more than industrial in character.

"I bet your cell was nicer than this," Sinim said, with a rueful look at me.

"In fact, it was," I said. "And it did not smell so oppressively of disinfectant."

But I was glum. I sat down on one of the couches and put my chin in my hand. How could the *Rodrigo* go off without me? It was *my* ship, commissioned to me by my mother.

Sinim looked down at me in alarm.

"Oh, Thomas, I am so sorry! I didn't intend to remind you of your incarceration."

"Don't apologize," I said, waving a hand. "The less said about that, the better. I wasn't really thinking of that at all."

"You're just being brave," Marquessa said. "I admire that."

"I'm not, truly," I protested. "I mean, I can be brave, but that wasn't something to be brave about. Being thrown in jail takes absolutely no courage whatsoever."

"Jil, tell Thomas I didn't mean to upset him," Sinim said, clutching Jil's arm.

"It's my fault," Jil said. She gave a pretty little shrug. "I didn't mean to make such fun of you before, Thomas. I was a bit swept off my feet, having Captain Naftil pay such attention to me. He was so nice and handsome. I think it just went to my head."

"I understand," I said. "I am not cross with you—at the moment. I should be out there with my ship." I pointed in a vague direction. I had no idea where the *Rodrigo* had gone. My admission seemed to take Jil from sympathy to open annoyance.

"Oh, Thomas, how *boring*," she said. "Don't tell me you're falling into believing yourself a common spacer. You rank acres above all of them. Heroics are so dull. What would you do out there? Catch a criminal? We don't associate with that kind of scum. It's unbecoming. If you want to run around after other ships, enter another stratosphere race. Your racing flitter is fabulous."

"Yes," Banitra said. "I have watched all your races." She sat down beside me, her leg against mine. "That tournament around the sun two years ago was so exciting! Tell me how you avoided getting caught in the gravity well. I thought when Lord Rillion knocked your craft on the circuit around the innermost planet that you were going to lose control."

"Well," I began, recalling all the details of that race with growing alacrity. It had, after all, been one of my greatest successes. "I had acceleration on my side, you know. I was able to rely upon forward momentum until I could get my bearings again. But it was moment by moment for survival. I almost didn't make it."

"I remember that!" Sinim said, sitting down upon my other side. "Didn't they disqualify Rillion after that?"

"Oh, yes," I said, the memory full in my mind's eye. "Ril must have known a disqualification was coming. He drives like that in atmospheric craft, as well. He was one of the racers in the pileup around the Empress's statue. In fact, he was in the cell next to mine overnight."

Banitra laughed. "So you are acquiring quite a connoisseur's eye of jails," she said.

"You might say so."

I met her laughing gaze, and was cheered by it. She lowered the lashes over those dark, lovely eyes. I was struck by how attractive she was, and what good company she had been. I admired that she was able to curb Jil's more extreme habits. Her skills and good nature had made the trip much more bearable than it could have been. I opened my mouth to compliment her. Then, I remembered my cousin Xan's warning that she and Sinim had been picked out by my great-aunt as marriage prospects for me. Her organizational talents might someday be used on yours very truly. I heaved myself up off the bench and began a fit of manic pacing.

Jil flung herself at full length upon one of the couches.

"How long are we to be locked up in here?" she said, draping a delicate wrist over her eyes. "This is too much like being sent to one's room by one's most recent ancestors."

"We could play a game," Marquessa said. "Oh, all our cards are on the ship! Perhaps they have something on the station's servers." She pulled down one of the workstations built into the padded bulkheads. A large screen set in the wall behind the console shimmered into life.

"Or you could tell our fortunes," Hopeli said. She opened up her palm and held it before me. I flung myself back into my pacing.

"I . . . the time isn't auspicious for readings," I said. I was still feeling stung about the situation on the *Bonchance*. Now that I was free to do whatever I wanted, I felt delicate about doing it. Perhaps I had abused my talents. I had a good deal to think about, but all I could concentrate upon was the pursuit going on outside.

"Oh, look!" Marquessa said. "There are dozens of entertainment channels. We can watch a digitavid."

With a sigh, Jil rose and trailed over to her as if it took all her strength just to stand upright. She leaned over the blonde woman's shoulder as Marquessa scrolled through the graphics of available programs. I came over for a look, too. I recognized the several children's programs, nature documentaries, news programs, replays of classic sports events and thousands of feature-length productions, ranging in age and complexity all the way from remastered two-dee programs to the latest tri-dee digitavids. The icons in the corner indicated that those could be viewed in a hundred different languages and dialects.

"Boring," Jil said, as Marquessa offered show after show. "Dull. Ancient. Oh, tedious. No, I cannot be bothered to watch that again. It was terrible the first time!"

"What a shame," I said. "But, see, there are numerous music channels available. We could select from one of those."

"But what else?" Jil asked. "What entertainment can we gain from that?"

"Why, we add conversation, cousin," I said. "You are very good at that. You can tell me what I missed on the main newsline of the Infogrid today."

"You can tell us some of your stories, Lord Thomas," Sinim said, coming up to twine her arm through mine. "I enjoyed your tales on our travels before we met up with the *Bonchance*. I am sure you have many others."

It was difficult to detach her from my person without seeming to flinch away.

"To be sure, I do," I said, escorting her to the nearest couch. I peeled her fingers from my arm and sat down on a settee opposite, well out of reach. "In fact, I have a marvelously funny one that I bet you have never heard. It concerns three government ministers. They went fishing out on the lakes above Taino. It was a very hot day. One of them realizes that they have left their cold drinks on their ground transport vehicle . . . ."

"I've heard that one," Jil moaned. She mooched over to me and looked up into my face. Her large, green eyes wore a sad look. "No, I don't want one of your stories, Thomas."

"Then, what?" I asked, desperate to cheer her up. "Charades? Role-play games? I can keep score on my viewpad."

"No." A slow smile spread along the corners of her mouth and perked them up into the apples of her cheeks. She poked me gently in the center of my chest with a forefinger. “I will bet you a thousand credits that you have at least the first episode of *Ya!* on your viewpad.”

I struggled mightily against the truth.

“I do,” I said, with a deep sigh. “Would you all like to watch it with me?”

CHAPTER 24

After a few hours locked in the safe room with five women, I was longing for release. Viewpads are suitable for watching a digitavid in private, or with perhaps one close friend. To arrange it so six people can see it all at the same time is difficult; to create a perfect viewing experience, impossible. As it was a tri-dee, I did my best to enlarge the image as much as possible so it stood off the small screen, but even then it was a little grainy. In the end, I shrank the image until it coalesced properly, but the ladies had to arrange themselves at close quarters to me in order to see it. In the end, Jil huddled at my right and Sinim at my left. Marquessa hovered above my right shoulder, Banitra at the other, and Hopeli, the smallest, sat right in my lap.

"This is cozy," Sinim said, winding herself into my ribs. If she had been a corkscrew, she would have been attached to me permanently.

In a way, it was worth it. To say that the first episode of any series creaks with newness is not a criticism. The initial program that introduced the galaxy to *Ya!* was so fresh that none of the sharp corners had yet been rubbed off. The performances were vivid, the scenery fantastic and evocative, and the dialogue punchy and intelligent. I could understand how it had been a "hit" from its first appearance. To see the actors whose faces came to be mounted in images on the walls and mantelpieces of their many-times descendants over the centuries, and even minted on the money of this imaginary Autocracy, gave me a tingle that did not leave me throughout the entire pilot, nor in the subsequent two which we had time to view. By then, both arms and both thighs were numb from lack of movement and constriction of the blood supply, but I was delighted to have both seen the shows and shared them with fellow enthusiasts. Marquessa had not been a fan, but she now vowed to track down as many seasons as possible and watch them.

I declared an end to the video festival after three, to the open disappointment of the ladies, but we continued to discuss them, Jil and I in fluent Uctu. To my surprise, both Banitra and Hopeli both had a working knowledge of the language, and added their comments. It turned out to be a pleasant interlude.

Even when we moved apart to the couches, Sinim stayed glued to me. I moved time and again to put some space between us, but she followed as if I held the oxygen she needed to live. The avid expression on her face increasingly worried me. My aunt had unleashed a Harpy whose claws it was becoming difficult to avoid.

". . . But Redius thinks that the antecedents of the Calagriti clan are illegitimate," I pointed out, jumping up from my latest perch just as Sinim sat down upon it. I felt guilty as I beheld her big, sad eyes and pouting lips, but my nerves twitched like frightened mice every time she touched me. "It is his theory that their clan chieftess took credit for the victory over the Daiobi that saved the Paranch province, when the general who actually defeated the Daiobi died of his wounds."

"Can't we watch just one more episode?" Jil asked. "Only the fates know when we'll get out of here."

"Well, I don't know," I said, with a sly glance in her direction.

"Oh, please, Thomas!" Banitra said.

"I suppose . . . ," I began.

At that moment, I felt a tremendous force hit me from beneath. Helplessly, I found myself flying upward, my limbs flailing.

Those who are caught in the web of circumstances will tell you that time seems to slow down. I can attest that to be absolutely true. The *boom* that had accompanied the thrust echoed in my ears and my chest like the primal sound of the universe exploding. All around me, the ladies in their light, floaty dresses lifted into the air as though borne by unseen hands.

Just as swiftly, time returned to its ordinary pace. My arms and legs windmilled as I attempted to right myself before falling toward the floor.

"Relax!" Hopeli shouted. "Relax or you'll break something!"

To my amazement, my limbs obeyed my order. I dropped to the padded floor like a marionette whose strings had been severed. My head bounced twice more, as though to reassure itself it had actually landed. At first, the shock prevented me from feeling the impact, but in seconds, the aches radiated through my body, especially at the back of my skull. Resisting the urge to groan, I pulled myself upright to assist Jil and her friends. Then, I ran to the door.

I found the control panel and flipped up the emergency release. I palmed the large blue button. The door did not open. I hit the button again, then struck the door with my other hand.

"Please open," I said. "I need to obtain assistance."

"Please remain in this room until the temporary crisis has resolved," the door said, in reproachful tones. "This portal will be released on orders from the office of the station manager."

"What happened out there to cause the percussive explosion?" I asked.

"A ship has crashed into the station at Loop Four," a voice said, as a brilliant white light scanned up and down my torso. "It happens occasionally, in spite of pilot instructions to take care upon approach. Please remain where you are."

"My ship?" I cried, leaping up.

"My clothes!" Jil exclaimed, horror hollowing her cheeks. "And my jewelery! I borrowed Mother's emerald tiara. She will skin me if it comes back in pieces! Oh, Thomas, you have to find out if it is our ship that crashed!"

"Of course, dear cousin," I said. I returned to the door panel. "Lieutenant Thomas Innes Kinago of the *Rodrigo*. I must inquire as to the well being of my ship."

"On whose authority?" it asked.

I presented my viewpad. "I know you can speak to all the ships in range," I said. "Please contact LAI designation NG-903, and ask if I am not part of the contingent of that ship."

It took only a moment for the connection to be made.

"Lord Thomas?"

"Angie, is that you?" I asked. "Where are you? What has happened? I heard there was a collision."

"Lord Thomas," Angie's voice came through the speaker of my

viewpad. "The *Rodrigo* pursued the fugitive vessel out toward quadrant N-18, but it doubled back and crashed into the space station."

"Is anyone hurt?"

"Negative aboard *Rodrigo*. Please remain where you are until further notice." My heart sank. I had to free myself from durance vile. I was terrified that at any moment, either of the ladies would decide I had accidentally asked one of them to marry me, and my cousin, in her endless quest to torment me, might agree that I had done so. A brief pause ensued. "I have been corrected, Lord Thomas. Please make your way to Landing Bay Delta 47m."

"All of us?" I asked, with understandable trepidation.

"Just you. Please make haste. I have asked LAI OB-59a to pick you up."

My spirits perked up at once. I glanced over my shoulder at Jil and gave her a sign of triumph.

"I am on my way."

CHAPTER 25

OB-59a turned out to be the intelligence aboard a covered personnel carrier, redolent with sweat and the faint odor of sleep gas.

"Many thanks for the lift, my friend," I said, as I swung on board. The doors scissored closed behind me. I wriggled into one of the deep synthleather seats, recently vacated, I was certain, by a man approximately my height, but a great deal broader, and suffering from hyperhidrosis. I tried to ignore the dampness and smell. "I am Thomas."

"It is no trouble, Lord Thomas," the vehicle said in a resonant male voice. "I was free. Call me Obie. Angie and I have been corresponding since your arrival in this sector. She has given me your dossier. I just brought the entire security force to the scene. I will not be needed again until the siege is over."

"Siege?" I asked, sitting forward eagerly, detaching my tunic from the seat back. "Tell me all! We have been mewed up without any news. What has happened? What of the naval vessel, the *Rodrigo*?"

"All information regarding the incident is on a need-to-know basis," Obie said, severely.

"Yes, I suppose it is," I said, putting on my most wheedling tone, "but as you are carrying me to the scene, may we assume that I need to know?"

"Of course, Lord Thomas. Allow me to post the official sitrep on the screen above you."

I settled back into the seat. As the information was very recent, no narration was provided to the action video I beheld, but I thought I could pick up the thread of the story.

From one of the red-rimmed hatches, a large ship burst forth. Pieces of the iris exploded around it like an extreme close-up image of pollen bursting from a flower. Indecently close to the space station, yellow and orange oxygen-fed flames sprayed as the ship kicked on its impulse engines. It vanished from the outside video pickup. Some delay ensued until another hatch lensed open, in the ordinary fashion this time. From it issued the *Rodrigo*. When I beheld my precious ship, I felt my heart pounding with excitement. It, too, activated its sublight engines a little too soon, but I understood the need. It was a race! Because of the speed and distance involved, the station turned to scopes instead of video. I watched two blips retreating into the blackness, one steadily gaining upon the other.

I listened as if to a particularly exciting digitavid as I heard Plet's voice calmly addressing the crew of the fugitive vessel, informing them of who she was and whom she represented, instructing them to explain their behavior and to surrender their ship.

The other crew did not respond in a verbal fashion. If I was directing this digitavid, I would have had them retort with defiant words that would make the audience breathe faster as it anticipated justice bearing down upon them at speeds approaching that of light.

Plet informed them that if they did not surrender and return to the station, they would be fired upon. I thought now there would be a grand and exciting chase, culminating in the destruction of the fugitive vessel.

Instead, approximately ten light-minutes out, the lead ship spun in its own length, a move that I would not have attempted in a skimmer, let alone a full-sized trading vessel. It sprayed a mass of sparkling particles, then arrowed back toward the station. Their full afterburners were on, causing them to dump velocity at a dangerous rate. I had done something similar in my racing ship. It required a sophisticated combination of forward and reverse thrust, along with wrenching the helm into a 180° change of heading. Both the turn and the deceleration were dangerous to the very structure of the ship.

"What are they doing? Why did they do that?" I demanded. "Are they trying to kill themselves?"

"No one knows, sir. Speculation is rife. I can show you a list of 3,206 guesses made by the LAIs aboard the station."

I waved an impatient hand.

"No, thank you. I would rather make my own guesses. What *are* they doing there?"

By the time they reached the space station, the *Moskowitz* seemed to be creeping, though I knew that was an optical illusion. The ship was still moving at a tremendous rate. Out in the distance, Oskelev completed the bootlegger's turn, then had to mimic the slowdown on approach. But minutes before the *Rodrigo* could catch up with it, the *Moskowitz* crashed into the side of Way Station 46. Its nose buried itself into a hatch, whose orange chase lights immediately turned red.

"Way Station 46, open the hatch next door to the *Moskowitz*," Plet's calm voice ordered. In a moment, the *Rodrigo* appeared in the video pickup, and smoothly sailed into the open lens like a bird returning to the nest.

"Well done, Oskelev," I said, releasing the breath I had been holding.

"Would your pilot like a job?" Obie inquired. "I know a long-haul transport firm specializing in high-value goods that would pay top credit for a being who can handle a ship with that skill."

"I doubt they could afford her," I said. "But if she ever left the navy, I might ask my cousin to take her on."

"Your cousin? Lady Jil? Why would she need a driver trained in evasive maneuvers?"

"No, my cousin the emperor," I said. "Oskelev is the best pilot I have ever seen. I am proud to serve with her."

The video switched to the inside of the damaged landing bay. No one emerged from the damaged ship. The still-active engines should have been howling in atmosphere, but there was no sound.

"What happened to the audio?" I asked.

"Negotiations under way, sir," Obie explained. "It keeps anyone else from interfering on the airwaves. Anybody on the same circuit used to throw in their own two credits. It caused a mess a few times when kibitzers goaded the spacers under siege into a suicide attempt."

"Sensible," I agreed, though it was frustrating not to be able to tell what was going on. I sat back. I would know soon enough.

When we reached the scene of the crime, so to speak, Obie decanted me a meter from the door of Bay Delta 47m. I leaped out. With a thrill of terror, I realized the hatchway was open a hand's breadth. I went to peer inside. At that moment, an enormous force hit me from the left, bringing me down to the deck of the corridor.

"My lord, you gotta watch it!" Nesbitt breathed in my ear. He had been the enormous force in question. He helped me to my feet and whisked debris and dust from my clothing. "They could shoot at you!"

"Have they started a firefight?" I asked, with intense interest.

"No, sir," he said, his good-natured face drawn in concern. "Lieutenant Plet tried to talk with them, but they just babble back at her."

"There you are, my lord," Parsons said, appearing at my shoulder as closely as though he were a seam in the fabric of my tunic. Station Manager FitzGreen was with him, as was the rest of my crew. "I see you have been released."

"And not a moment too soon!" I said. "We were crowded into a padded cell!"

"Was it that troublesome, sir?" Parsons asked, with little overt sympathy in his expression. I dismissed my fit of pique as being unnecessary under the circumstances. I was, after all, where all the interesting action was taking place.

"Well, not very, to be honest. It's a nice room, if plain. And large enough, physically speaking. Psychologically I felt the walls closing in on me, but I put that down to the company I was keeping. The seats are fairly comfortable. I don't see that it is used very often, which is a tribute to you, Director FitzGreen," I added, with a nod to my host. "You must experience very few emergencies here. Well done."

"Thanks, sir, uh, my lord," the station manager said, looking pleased, if a little puzzled.

"What is the concern with this absconding crew?" I inquired. "What has been determined? I saw the video of the chase, and very exciting it was, too."

"It was weird, Thomas," Oskelev said. "They couldn't possibly beat us to the next jump point. I don't know if they were trying to commit suicide-by-navy or what. Then they turned right around and came back."

"I am very glad you are all intact," I said. "And the ship?"

"Fine," Oskelev said, with a wave of her big, furry hand. "Not a scratch. I could have done a barrel roll coming into the bay. The landing pads are huge. I could have parked beside the *Moskowitz* in the same berth. It was a snap."

"But you went off on a jaunt without me! I am crushed."

My friends expressed their sympathy, but Plet paid no attention to my emotional pyrotechnics. In fact, she paid no attention to the rest of us at all. She and Parsons pulled the station manager aside for a private confabulation. The rest of us attempted to listen, but with little success over the ambient noise. The *Moskowitz*'s engines were still whining, as though it would leap up and attempt another escape at any moment.

"Of course, of course," the big man said heartily. "Anything to help the Emperor, naturally."

Never one to take anything for granted, Plet determined to cross all T's and dot all I's, plus other archaic marks of typography.

"You will grant us full access to the computer systems, all records dating back at least six months before the incident that resulted in the arrest of the pilots and their crews in the Autocracy?"

The big man all but bowed and scraped to her easy authority.

"Yes, ma'am, of course, ma'am."

My ears perked up at once. I saw a chance to do something for the Copper family.

"May I help with the search?" I asked, striding over to them. Parsons headed me off and steered me away from Plet. "I am very good at detail work, and I have sorting programs that will pick up even a trace of discontinuity. I downloaded it to keep up with the vendors for my last party."

"I am afraid not, my lord. You are needed in a different capacity." Behind him, Plet beckoned to Nesbitt, Redius and Anstruther. I attempted to sidestep Parsons to join them, but he proved nimbler than I. "The crew is capable of undertaking this search."

"But you are talking about the people I have sworn to assist! I would be remiss if I did not give all my energy to setting them free."

"You shall assist them, my lord, in good time. But now, please, focus upon the other problem at hand."

I regarded him with impatience.

"And that is?"

"Negotiation of surrender, my lord," Parsons said. "We have been speaking to the crew aboard the *Moskowitz*. Some of the crew are concerned that our arrival meant that they were to be arrested for outstanding warrants."

"Warrants?" I asked. "For what offenses?"

"I have perused the Infogrid files for the crew members in question. They are wanted for varying degrees of disturbing the peace on five to eight different ports of call apiece throughout the Imperium."

"Really?" I asked. "But these are non-extraditable offenses. Ask me how I know. Go ahead, ask."

"I am aware of your antics on Rumdisa, sir," Parsons said.

I was dumbstruck. I felt my mouth drop open. I hastened to rescue my lower jaw.

"Curse it, Parsons, they were stricken from the record after I paid the magistrate's fine! Post-departure, as it happens, but that is not important. Have I *no* secrets from you?"

Parsons's face was a sheet of blank paper, uninscribed with any descriptive phrases to mention.

"I am not at liberty to discuss the matter, sir. May we return to the problem at hand?"

"What is the problem? Just show them the statutes. They are safe if they get in touch with the magistrates' offices in each port and pay up. It may sting a bit—the fines did get larger the longer I waited—but that's all they wanted. Apart from promising I would behave myself in future," I added.

"They do not believe us when we assure them that they are safe from prosecution or arrest. They are returning from the Autocracy, not going in. They are threatening to blow up their ship if we do not withdraw. They already owe substantial damages to the space station. To destroy a larger portion would only cause more dismay, and possibly several unnecessary deaths."

"So why me? I have no talent in hostile negotiations."

Parsons raised his eyebrows. "But you have a natural ability to get along with others," he said.

I understood. A thrilling little frisson ran up and down my spine.

"You want me to get to know them?" I asked, making the second to last word redolent with delightful secrecy. "To reveal myself to their eyes?"

"That is the intention, sir," Parsons said. "It is not without its dangers. The ship has defensive capabilities. You will be in harm's way. An accidental bolt or slug could damage or kill you."

"That's so unlikely, Parsons," I said, indicating my visage with a careless hand. "One look at these honest and handsome features, and they will throw open their doors to me."

Plet pushed away from where she and the others were conferring with FitzGreen. By their actions, my crew was swapping files among their viewpads with the station manager. She homed in on Parsons like an angry missile.

"Commander, I told you I was against this. I recommend using sleep gas in the air intakes. That is what the manual suggests."

"It does not work in forty percent of cases, Lieutenant," Parsons said. "The newest generation of air filtration systems captures all particulate matter, even as small as the aerosolized chemical. That would leave enough of the crew conscious to activate defenses."

"A ship that old won't have the newest technology! We have access to their maintenance records. We know what they've installed."

"We have the official records," Parsons reminded her. "This crew is accustomed to making running repairs under difficult circumstances. Nor can we state with certainty that they did not upgrade their equipment by bartering with another merchant vessel beyond planetary communications satellites. Can you guarantee any of that did not take place?"

Plet aimed the full force of her gaze on him.

"It's dangerous, sir! We can't risk his life. There are other ways to gain access to the vessel."

"They will take too long," Parsons said. "We need the crew to surrender as swiftly as possible."

"Why?" Plet's normal ivory complexion had taken on hues of red and purple.

"Because now is when they are the most vulnerable," Parsons said. "Did you hear their voices? They are temporarily chemically impaired. Lord Thomas's natural charisma should be all that is needed to negotiate their surrender."

"That's absurd."

I smiled.

"They won't hurt me, Plet. I represent the Emperor."

She turned to face me. I saw the worry in her usually icy blue eyes. I didn't realize she cared so deeply for my safety. I puffed up my chest and raised my chin heroically to look as confident as possible.

"Oh, very well," she said. "I just don't want to have to report to the First Space Lord that her son was injured under my care."

"You won't have to make such a call," I said. "And if you do, I will inform the maternal unit it was all my own fault. She is accustomed to hearing that."

But I did not feel so confident as Oskelev and two of the station employees took me aside to prepare me for the confrontation. A large Croctoid in a protective suit with full breathing apparatus on his back sprayed me with a reflectant that would turn back laser bolts. It was the only protection that I could be afforded. Plet could not wrap me in armor against slugthrowers or edged weapons. I must appear as natural as possible, from my face to the shape of my body. My only contact with the outside was a small bone-conduction communicator inserted into the flesh behind my left ear. Parsons tested it to make certain I could hear them and they could hear me, though the station had other means of eavesdropping in each bay.

Once prepared, I stood at the hatch of Bay Delta 47m, breathing the flame-retardant-filled air. I surrendered my naval-issue sidearm to Oskelev. Once within the landing bay, I would be outnumbered by the enemy. My weapon would be a danger chiefly to myself. While I was skilled at martial arts, I doubted whether an entire crew of desperate merchants would take it in turns to attack me, as they did in the digitavids. I took several deep breaths, steeling myself up to take the last step into the chamber. I had the authority of the Emperor on my side. Parsons was counting on me. I refused to fail him. I was beginning to dread the moment. Parsons believed I could negotiate an end to the standoff. Could I? I was no diplomat, as so many had reminded me in the past. My hands quivered slightly as I touched the lucky circuit inside my viewpad's pouch.

"You don't have to do this," Plet said. It was the closest to panic I had ever seen her.

My fears fled in the face of her concern. I could not back away now.

"I do," I said. "If Parsons said that it must be done, I trust him to know that."

I drew two more deep breaths, then, as if I were a star performer about to step onto the stage, I nodded to the jumpsuited station employee who stood at the controls. She palmed the glowing panel. The doors parted. I stepped through.

CHAPTER 26

I had devised a mantra for myself from the luckiest words in my guidebooks' varied lexicons. To the uninitiated, it would sound nonsensical, but I admit it gave me comfort. "*Nin ran ya om*."

The wounded ship hunkered before me like a pet dog that was all too aware that it had soiled the carpet. Its nose was dented, revealing the edges of several of its protective ceramic panels. Debris of all kinds, including shards of shielding, tools, drinks containers and scraps of cartons lay in eddies on the floor. The protective black iris that contained the bay's atmosphere had a number of vanes missing, but an even darker substance, the station's emergency sealant, had flowed into place and formed a temporary wall. Fans pumped warm air into the chamber, but I could still see my breath.

I halted a dozen meters from the nose of the ship. I stopped saying the mantra aloud. It ran through my mind, almost subduing the consciousness of fear that threatened to overwhelm me. I had done daring and life-threatening things in the past, but they had almost always been my own idea. This was a serious matter. I did not want to die, no matter how worthy the cause.

"Hello?" I called. My voice trembled. How dare it! I cleared my throat forcefully and essayed once again. "Hello the ship!"

A loud squawk of static made me jump.

"Who are you?" blared a tenor voice.

I straightened my back and held my chin up.

"I am Lord Thomas Kinago, cousin to the emperor and his

ambassador to the Autocracy. Whom do I have the honor of addressing?"

"It's a noble!" exclaimed a female voice, at a distance from the audio pickup.

"Maybe a trick," said a clipped voice that I judged to be Uctu. "More authorities!"

"I am not an officer of the law," I said. "I only wish to speak with you."

A pause, while the several voices conferred, not very coherently. I began to discern what Parsons had said about their being vulnerable at that moment.

The tenor returned to the microphone. "How do we know you're really a noble? Do you have a birthmark or something you can show us?"

I glared at the ship.

"My dear sir, if I had a birthmark, it would surely be in a place that I would not display in public, particularly not to someone with whom I was unacquainted! Look me up on the Infogrid. Compare my face with the photographs. Thomas Innes Loche Kinago, plus several dozen middle names."

"That's a good idea," the woman said.

Yes, it was, I mused, as I waited. I wanted them to take as close a look at me as possible. I disported myself in several different poses for the video pickup, all intended to show myself in the best possible light. I smiled, frowned, scowled and laughed, to give them the most expressions with which to compare me with the official record.

"Really is a lord!" the Uctu exclaimed. The conversation within the ship became more frenzied.

"He's going to take us back and execute us!" said a deep, raspy voice. "Shoot him!"

"No, don't," the tenor said. I could tell that his resolve was wavering. "I kind of like him."

"You know," I said, wanting them to focus upon me, "this reminds me of a story I heard at the latest party thrown by my cousin. It seems that a gang of Solinians wanted to climb up a cliff, but the only rope they had with them was a quarter of the length they needed to reach the top. One of them had a grand idea . . . ."

I launched into a tale I knew well, one that had had my cousins in stitches over the ridiculously intricate banquet food commonly served at official functions in the Imperium compound. Gradually, the number of voices participating in the argument aboard the Moskowitz dwindled from several down to just a few. All the time, I moved so I was within sight of the various video pickups, all too aware that each was adjacent to weapons emplacements. Though the latter were purely for defense against pirates and seldom up to military standards, a shot from one of the five-centimeter nozzles would render me as dead as any laser cannon aboard the *Rodrigo*.

". . . And the second Solinian said, 'Well, it got us up here, didn't it?' 'Oh, yes,' the first one grumbled, 'but how are we going to get down again?'" I paused, with my arms out to accept applause. From the ship a few appreciative chuckles issued. I had the crew captivated, or so I hoped. If I was ever to make my parental units proud, this was the moment. "Do come out," I coaxed. "I know many more stories that you will enjoy, but I find it difficult to connect with an audience I can't see."

"No!" shouted the deep voice. I heard a bang from within. My instincts told me to drop. Just in time, I flattened myself upon the deck. Intense heat passed close enough over my back to make my hair crackle. I sprang again to my feet and faced the ship.

"Now, that was not very nice," I chided the crew.

"I'm sorry! I'm sorry! He didn't mean to do that! It was an accident," the female voice wailed. I assumed a paternal smile, though the corners of my lips quivered with nerves. I opened my arms, and rendered my voice as soothing as I could make it.

"Listen to me. Look at me. I represent the emperor, the head of state. He cares about each and every one of you. Please. Come out. I promise it will be all right. Come out now."

I had once been told that I had a "command nose." I pointed that feature at the nearest video pickup, and waited.

The hatch undogged with a couple of loud clanks and dropped noisily to the deck. Even before it had opened fully, five beings raced down the ramp and threw themselves at my feet. They all wore faded, dark-blue shipsuits, grav boots and weapons belts furnished with at least a slugthrower and a laser pistol apiece. My eyes watered. The smell of liquor was overwhelmingly strong.

The tall human male with shoulder-length caramel-colored hair was the owner of the tenor voice.

"Don't let them hurt us, your nobleness! I swear we'll pay back every credit! We have bills to pay. I'll turn myself in later. Don't do anything to my friends! They're innocent!"

The female voice belonged to a small, curvaceous female with braids of black hair coiled against the back of her head.

"Don't listen to him, sir. We all did it."

"Speak yourselves," said one of the two Uctus on the ground. He lifted his big dark eyes to me. "Apologetic!"

"I see," I said. "But exactly what is it that you did?"

"Uh, well," the blond man looked at the others. They stared back, their eyes glassy.

"Our manifests aren't going to match our cargo count," the baritone said at last, without lifting his head from the floor.

"Ah!" I said, gazing down at five prone backs. "You would not, by any chance, be transporting spirits, would you?"

"Um, maybe?"

"Why did you run away?"

The tenor looked up at me, his eyes huge and filled with hope and burst capillaries. "Well, we thought if we ditched the rest of the load, no one would be able to claim how much was on board, your lordship."

"What was it?"

"Nyikitu brandy."

I had to catch my breath before it expelled words that would cause the already alcohol-laden air to ignite with the fury I suddenly felt.

"You . . . jettisoned how much . . . of that fine, rare liquor?"

"Um, about a thousand bottles."

"A thousand?" I believe my voice squeaked.

"Give or take forty or fifty," the baritone said. "We drank those. It was really good. I mean, so good that we just couldn't stop. There was one bottle with a leaky cork. I mean, what could we do? No store would accept it at the other end. That's where it started. Then we tried another one. It was even better!"

"Deeelicious," the second Uctu added, with a musical lilt.

"We got carried away," the woman said. "We didn't know how much it would mess up our reaction times."

A sense of moral outrage overwhelmed me. I tried to find inner reason, but it retreated against the mental image of a thousand bottles of Nyikitu floating in the void, never to grace the tables of those awaiting its arrival.

"I must say that I am appalled at your behavior," I said.

"Well, we took over control of the ship instead of letting the autopilot take us in," man admitted. "That was stupid."

"No, I mean destroying a thousand bottles of one of the most desirable liquids in the galaxy," I said. "That was absolutely outrageous! Criminal! You ought to be clapped in irons!"

"Now, just a minute, your nobility," the baritone said, rising to his knees. His swarthy brows drew down over his bloodshot eyes. "That's no way to talk to us. Not over a few little bottles of booze."

"Lieutenant!" Plet's voice snapped urgently in my ear. I had completely forgotten about her. "They are in a precarious mental state!"

"I am not upset because you have been drinking Nyikitu," I said to the man. "*Everyone* wants to drink Nyikitu. It is that you have destroyed it! It is as though you have desecrated precious works of art! The book should be heaved at you! If anyone at the Imperium court was to hear about this, your lives would not be worth a devalued credit!"

"No!" the two Uctus cried. "Mercy!"

"Please try to find some equilibrium, sir," came Parsons's smooth voice. "The effect you evoke is not foolproof. If you outstrip it, the response will be one that is appropriate to an ordinary emotional reaction."

I glared at the man. I was pleased to see him cower before me, but I took Parsons's point. The deep-seated tendency of ordinary human beings to obey one of my class was not infinite. I was treading upon dangerous territory. Not only that, I was exceeding the stated purpose of my presence there. But I had to let them know the devastating nature of their crime.

"Do you realize that you have deprived the emperor of his favorite tipple? Do you know what he might say?"

The rough face became one of a chidden child. He clapped his hands together as though praying.

"Oh, have pity, your lordship! We were stupid!"

"And drunk," pointed out the tenor, rising to his knees in turn. He pulled the others up.

"Uh-huh," the baritone agreed. "Reeeally drunk. What can we do to make it up to you, your nobility? Could we, er, offer you something? To, er, appease your anger?"

If the destruction of the brandy lit my temper to a roaring flame, this caused an emotional volcano to erupt, but I did my best to keep the lava in the caldera. I am afraid my tone was unnaturally heated.

"I would no more accept a bribe than I would renounce my name! How dare you question my honor or that of my noble family? There is *nothing* that you can offer me . . ."

"We need information from them, sir," Parsons said suddenly. My diatribe deflated like a leaky bladder.

". . . That I, that . . . Except information," I said, emphatically. "If you give me the information you have, it will assuage some of your guilt. What is it?"

The five looked at one another in bemusement.

"We'll tell you anything we know, your nobleness," the woman said. "What information do you want?"

"Yeah! We know lots of stuff," the tenor said. "Ask us anything!" The others nodded eager agreement.

"Well . . . ?" I inquired of the disembodied Parsons.

"Ask them about adulteration of the liquid matrix for the food dispensers, my lord."

"What?" I asked, knowing that the people at my feet would realize I was speaking to someone besides them. I trusted that it would not break the spell my presence created. "How does this connect to swindled brandy?"

"Ask them," Plet said. "The crew of the *Moskowitz* was here in the weeks before the crews in custody left for the Autocracy. Anstruther found an anomaly in the station delivery manifests, and Nesbitt confirmed with employees that the *Moskowitz* was the vehicle that conveyed the questionable material here. They made a delivery of food matrix that was kilotons heavier than it should have been. Do they know what was in it?"

I fixed the crew with a steely eye. This sounded as though it had impacted the Coppers' safety and freedom. I would not retreat without the answer. I repeated what Plet had said.

"What was in the tanks?" I concluded.

"Well, food," the baritone said, looking very confused. "You know. The sludge that they put into the synthesizer machines."

My stomach turned. "I do know. I have had my share of unfortunate experience with those dispensers. But is that all that was in those tanks?"

"Yeah, sir, I swear! I went with the servicebot when it put the stuff into the machines. We need proof of delivery to get paid by the shipper. I took pictures. You want to see them?"

"Did you know it was adulterated?" I asked. "Did you see or hear anything unusual in the tanks? Machine parts? Power supplies?"

They all shook their heads.

"No, your nobility," the tenor insisted. "It was just ordinary sludge. I saw it myself. Smelled like, well," he looked at friends for help, "oatmeal. A little tinny. But that's normal, if you never saw the inners of those machines."

"I try not to," I said, dryly. "I find it difficult enough to use them."

"You and me both, your nobility," the man agreed heartily.

"Where did they get the mix?" Plet asked.

I conveyed the question.

"From jobbers," the second Uctu said.

"The ship's name?"

"*Barony*. Run by crew from Outwards."

I knew it well. It was the fourth planet from a small yellow dwarf star. I could follow the line of questioning on my own from there.

"Do you know where they obtained the, er, sludge? The name of the distributor, the warehouse?"

The tenor shrugged.

"You'd have to ask the crew on *Barony*. They work for Bertu Corporation. I should've known there was something weird going on. They paid above the usual fee to get it into the machines here. I don't know why. Just here. That's all. We needed the money. Even more now because we're gonna owe damages. And, uh . . ."

I saw hesitation, so I pressed them. The Kinago charm worked on their psyches so well that I felt ashamed to insist.

"Yes . . . ?"

"They told us to disable the disposer units in each of the landing bays and the corridors," he added sheepishly. "I've got no idea why. I mean, did they think that would make people eat more if they couldn't throw out their leftovers?"

"How bizarre," I said.

"It sounded kind of hinky to us, too, but money's money."

"What was special about this preparation?" I asked.

As one being, the crew shrugged. Being forced to think had sobered them up very quickly.

"Nothing as far as we could tell," the tenor said. "I mean, once we thought about the extra money, we all ate some of the food it to see if we could tell the difference. It tasted just like the usual stuff. Maybe it had some kind of flavor enhancer to make people feel hungrier? We don't really have a clue. It sounds strange, but it's not the first time a company did something out of the ordinary to increase its market share. You ought to hear some of the things we've seen."

"I would love to, but perhaps another time," I said. "Is that all?" I asked the people in my ear as well as the ones before me. The five on the floor nodded.

"That is all," Parsons affirmed. "Now, take them into custody, if you will, sir."

"Naturally," I said. I turned to my prisoners. "Will you surrender now?"

"To you?" the baritone said, with a look of trust that made me ashamed to the bottom of my soul. "We'll surrender to you. Not the authorities."

"I suppose that would be all right," I said. "Very well, I accept your surrender. By the authority vested in me on behalf of Shojan XII, Emperor of the Imperium and all its protectorates. Er, please give me all your weapons."

There arose such a clattering my ears suffered from the echoes for hours afterwards. They produced slugthrowers, laser pistols, knives, even a long sword that one of the Uctus drew upward from the neck of his shipsuit, the presence of which I had not at all suspected. From boot tops, sleeve cuffs and collars, throwing stars, tiny but evil-looking knives and palm-sized injectors joined the heap. A couple of meter-long wires tightly wound around thin, rigid handles appeared from the coils of the tenor's hair. I looked at him in surprise.

"Look, you gotta be able to defend yourself against boarders," he said.

I gathered up the weapons. All of them were substandard models except for one antique slugthrower that probably dated all the way back to lost Earth.

"Thank you, my friends," I said. The doors behind me parted to admit several members of station security.

"Do you have to put manacles on us or something?" the woman asked. She flirted her eyelashes at me.

"Must I?" I asked.

"You could," she said, looking hopeful.

I cringed. I had had enough for the day of predatory females.

"Do you promise not to try and flee?" I asked.

"Yes!"

"Then we can do without the manacles."

The woman's shoulders drooped. The security staff poured in and took each of the Moskowitz's crew by the upper arm. Two of them took the dozens of weapons from my arms and stowed them in a heavy carryall. I felt as though I needed to say a few more words.

"Well, that's fine," I said. "My cousin the emperor would be very proud of you for operating a business and giving employment to so many of your fellow citizens. Please go forth and try to do better in the future. And resist temptation, even if it be Nyikitu brandy. I thank you, on the emperor's behalf."

"You're wonderful, your nobility!" the tenor said.

With many longing looks over their shoulders, the crew was taken away. I was left on my own in the landing bay with the damaged trading ship. That had not been as hard as I had feared. After all, I had dealt with angry innkeepers, various levels of law enforcement and innumerable personnel at the shops, stores and other emporia that my cousins and I frequented.

"Come out, my lord," Parsons said, gently. "It is over."

I turned to depart from the landing bay, and my eyes fell upon a section of the wall immediately adjacent to the exit door. The gray panels had been shaped into a dished crater not unlike that of the caldera of an extinct volcano. What an odd place for an art installation, I thought, until I realized what I was seeing.

My knees wobbled and nearly deposited me on the deck. That was the impact point of the laser blast that had gone over my head. I could have been killed! What a fool I had been! What if everything I had been told about my heritage had been wrong? What if all those times the restraint shown to my cousins and me by annoyed tavern owners and shop clerks was mere deference to the office of the emperor? What if I had failed? Would I be lying dead in a pathetic heap on the deck?

No, more likely, considering the number of laser pistols and disruptors of which I had divested the crew, what was left of me would be floating around as a collection of disassociated molecules. Little comfort, but less lingering in pain.

Somewhere, I found enough moral fiber to stiffen my legs. Disaster had *not* fallen. I *had* succeeded at what Parsons had asked me to do. I had done it. I touched my lucky circuit. Perhaps I had to reconsider whether such things did actually precipitate good fortune. My confidence increased with every step I took. I recovered enough to walk out into the corridor to rejoin my friends.

"Well?" I said, spreading my arms for the appreciative applause I knew was forthcoming. "How was that?"

Plet fixed me with a withering gaze.

"So in future we can dispense with a negotiator? We can depend upon a stand-up comedian?"

"Lord Thomas's charm is well known across the Imperium," Parsons said. "In any case, he was successful."

"It was effective," Plet admitted, past the grudge in her throat.

"Tell the truth," I urged her, feeling playful now that the tension was past. "You were concerned for my well-being."

"Only for the success of the mission," she said, fixing me with those incisive blue eyes.

"It's my charisma."

Plet regarded me with a glance that was a cold shower of disapproval, but I knew better.

"I don't see it," she said. "But you're out again, and we have the information we need."

Well, I was not going to get my acclaim from her. I joined the knot of crew who huddled around their viewpads and tablets at the other side of the gray corridor. Redius greeted me with a grin and a backhand to the shoulder.

"Brave to the soul," he said.

"Not really," I said, with a self-deprecating snort. "If you had been reading my vital signs in the last few moments, you would have noticed all the signs of an imminent syncope. I just barely made it out of the landing bay on my own feet."

"I was," Anstruther admitted, her cheeks red. "Lieutenant Plet told me to. Why did you go in there unarmed? They could have killed you!"

"In the greater scheme of things, I am expendable," I said modestly.

"No, you are not expendable!" she said, her cheeks red. "I . . ."

Hastily, I held up a hand.

"Please, don't say anything you'll regret later," I said. "I am all right, and the crew is unhurt as well. Alas for the brandy! That was one drinking voyage I am sorry I was not on."

Parsons shimmered into being at my elbow.

"Success, my lord. You have exceeded expectations. The emperor will be gratified. Your mother will be very pleased to see that you have come out of the situation not only unharmed but triumphant."

"Thank you, Parsons," I said, suddenly feeling the uplift of energy drain from my feet, leaving me a marionette with only one string attached. "I think I may go and enjoy that syncope now." I lifted my viewpad. "Angie, I need fortification."

"Opening a bottle of Leonine whisky, Lord Thomas. It will take a moment or two to come to temperature from cold storage." I turned toward the next landing bay where my ship and a stiff drink awaited me.

Parsons moved smoothly into my path.

"There is no time for that, my lord. Thanks to you, we have gleaned a valuable clue we must follow up. As a member of this crew, you can be of assistance. We need to inspect the slips previously occupied by the impounded ships."

My eyebrows rose with my curiosity.

"I was puzzled by the sudden spate of seemingly unrelated questions," I said. "It sounds as though you have been quite busy while I was engaged within."

"Yes," Redius said. "Much research. Conversations. Investigations. More to be made. Transport awaits." He gestured toward the personnel carrier, which stood with open hatch. At a signal from Parsons, we boarded it. He gave an instruction to our driver, and we were off.

CHAPTER 27

"Why did we need to know about the food shipment that the *Moskowitz* brought in?" I asked, as we rolled past an infinite number of identical portals and a stunning array of vending machines and advertisements.

"I don't know," Anstruther said. "It was just an anomaly that turned up when we crunched the numbers from the station manager's records. This load of concentrate was only used in the bays assigned to merchants, nowhere else. It had to mean something, because it was the only thing that was out of the ordinary. Every other shipment that came here went into general use. I think . . ." Her voice sputtered to a halt as her confidence waned.

"Yes?" I encouraged her.

". . . It's nothing," she said.

"You are far too good a data analyst to have found nothing," I said.

"That is what we are going to determine," Plet said.

"Do you know the Coppers, Obie?" I asked.

"Yes. A close-knit family. They seem considerate and friendly, but they never spoke to any of us LAIs. My information suggests that they are bio-centric in their preferences."

"That's a shame," I said. "Some of my best friends are artificial intelligences."

"Sorry," said a bearded technician who had been called in by FitzGreen to break the seals on the machines and help with our investigation. "We had a refill last week. The *Moskowitz* was here months ago."

"So there is no trace of the previous contents present?" Plet pressed.

The man shook his head.

"The tanks are flushed and cleaned in between each fill," he said. "Imperium regulations. We never mix shipments."

"What happens to the residue?" Plet said. "It seems unlikely that the tanks run completely dry."

"Destroyed," FitzGreen explained. "Broken down to the molecular level. Can't have people eating outdated food. They might sue us. Now we're going to have to flush these machines again. I don't want to run short. Although that's unlikely, considering the drop in our business. The Autocracy is crazy if it doesn't think the blockade will affect relations. It's already causing a lot of bad feelings."

Behind him, Nesbitt was elbows-deep in beige glop in a thousand-liter tank. The faint smell of a grainlike product wafted to my nose. It was inoffensive but at the same time entirely unappetizing. It seemed impossible that the machine could produce the meals that were pictured on the still-dancing and glowing front panel that had been removed for our convenience. The big man came dripping over to us with a rack of sealed tubes.

"These are from intervals of a half-meter, plus scrapings from the bottom," he said, holding them out for Anstruther. She inserted a clean probe into each container in turn, then studied the screen of her viewpad. At last, she shook her head.

"Just food matrix," she said.

"There has to have been something unusual in the previous container," Plet said, frowning. "Otherwise, why target these bays specifically? I wish we could get a trace of the *Moskowitz* shipment, but it's impossible because they have been cleaned."

"Possible," Redius corrected her.

"How?" Plet asked.

He dropped his jaw in amusement. "First job during school, cleaning injectors in cafeteria machines. Always residue on interior valve."

"Wait a minute, we clean the valves, too!" the technician protested.

"Scrub?" Redius asked, pointedly. "Interior?" The man shrugged his shoulders.

"Well, no . . ."

Redius promptly rolled up his uniform sleeves and attacked the inside of the front panel of the machine. I jumped back just in time to avoid a spurt of food matrix that jetted five meters from a disconnected hose.

"Apologies!" Redius called over his shoulder.

The tubes within yielded to his expert ministrations, though not without spraying him, and anyone else unlucky or unwitting enough to stand close, thoroughly with sludge. By the time he returned to us, his bright black eyes were the only things not buff in color and smelling like, well, oatmeal. He extended a dripping hand. Anstruther caught the sealed pipette and attached it to the analyzer. A couple of the station employees led him and Nesbitt away, I hoped to let them wash off the sludge. The scent of it was beginning to make my eyes water. Anstruther waited until her tablet let out a modest *ping*. She showed her screen to Plet.

"It's like the rest of it, sir," she said. "Food-grade substance. No drugs, banned flavor enhancers or poisons. Kind of a high concentration of metal and silicon particles, but they're relatively harmless. They wouldn't interfere with digestion or flavor. No sign of machine parts or lubricants in the container itself."

"Is that so?" Plet said, shaking her head. "Well, see if further analysis helps, Anstruther. This doesn't help us figure out how the weapons found their way into the captured ships' waste tanks."

"All the ships that service the station are the same ones as always," FitzGreen said. "The supplies were transferred on board with the electric eye picking up all the bar and burst codes for each item. Everything that ought to be there was there, and nothing unaccounted for."

"Now analyze to whom they belong, and the chain of custody for every item supplied to the ships," Parsons said.

"That could take weeks, sir," Anstruther said.

"We have weeks," I said. "We won't get to Nacer for ages."

"Not weeks, sir," Oskelev said, impatiently. "Days, maybe. Just read fast."

Very shortly, Nesbitt and Redius returned, looking very clean and shooting amused glances between them. I wanted to ask them what they found so funny, but Redius noticed my curiosity and gave a quick shake of his head. The story must wait.

FitzGreen hailed Odie, who drove us to the station manager's office.

The Croctoid secretary set Anstruther up with a direct port to the station's central computer. The rest of us were offered beverages that I hoped had not come from one of the food dispensers.

"Didn't the station's records show where the merchants traveled before they came here?" I asked. "Any common ports of entry?"

"No," FitzGreen said, with an upturn of his hand. "They came from all over. No sense following someone who might be carrying the same kind of cargo as you."

"We won't be able to tell more until we can inspect the ships themselves," Plet said. "They are all in orbit around Dilawe now. And we have to interview the accused crews themselves."

FitzGreen turned to face us. His homely visage was filled with deep concern, and his voice dropped from its customary foghorn blare to a murmur.

"Do what you can, my friends. The Coppers and the others are nice folks, good traders, decent people. I would never have thought of them as smugglers. I've watched their kiddies grow up. Something else is going on, maybe blackmail? Please try and help them."

"That is our aim," Parsons said.

"We have what we need for the moment," Plet said. "When may we depart?"

FitzGreen looked discomfited.

"Well, ma'am, you might as well make yourself comfortable. You've heard about our bottleneck problem. They tell us we can't let individual ships go in but every once in a while. Mostly, we have to hold them all until we have a number of them, then they all go at once. Any that arrive just behind 'em has to wait."

"I am curious," I said. "What number are they waiting for? Some fortunate digit like seven? A particular day of the month?"

The station manager tilted his head from side to side.

"It varies, sir. All the time. Can't guess. The longest wait was three months, just a short time ago, because the Autocracy was waiting for thirteen. I had a few pull out and go back home. I think they were disgusted. So was I. So when lucky number thirteen showed up, I let everyone know they could all pack up."

"But the number is not always thirteen?" I pressed him. "Is there a pattern you can discern? Perhaps I can analyze the progression, narrow it down to a sequence that appears in Uctu mythology."

"I don't know nothing about Uctu mythology, sir. I'm just a paper-pusher. The biggest ever was nineteen, but a flotilla of small culture-sharing vessels all came from the Museum Society, and we could let them go in a matter of days. We've had six, eleven, eight, even two. Last time it was sixteen. The one fellow still stuck here didn't like that a bit. I couldn't let him go. But I keep to a strict rota of first in, first out. Makes the shippers hurry to get here ahead of their fellows, but that's business, too, gentlefolk."

"Is it a joke of some kind?" Oskelev asked. "Is the Autocracy punking you?"

"Oh, no, ma'am. All a matter of the deepest seriousness from our opposite numbers. They don't like it when we question them. They say the order comes from the very top."

"Do you know who?"

FitzGreen shook his head.

"I hardly ever hear from the same official twice. But we've got an unusual situation at hand. Now, ordinarily we've got a bunch of ships waiting to go through the frontier, but the Autocracy hasn't given us permission to send them."

"And hasn't it?" I asked. "Have you notified them that I am here?"

The station manager nodded.

"Yes, my lord, I sure have. I send messages every day telling them how bad it's getting here, but it makes little difference. We get the word when they're damned well good and ready, and not a microsecond before."

"What is the current status?" Plet asked.

FitzGreen scratched the back of his big head.

"Well, we've got kind of the opposite problem, ma'am," he said, looking bemused. "They sent us a number, but we don't have enough to make it up."

"How many are required to fill in?"

"They say eight, but there are only six ships here at the moment, including you. We're not expecting two more ships for a few days at least. We can make you comfortable in the meantime. I have access to some nice temp quarters if you don't want to stay on your ship. Their ladyships might like to choose first. A couple have a nice view of the main shopping arcade."

Parsons responded by lifting his own viewpad from the pouch on his hip.

"That won't be necessary, Mr. FitzGreen," he said. He raised the small device to his lips. "Two, captain."

To my amazement, a voice answered back.

"Right you are, sir. They will arrive in four hours, thirty-eight minutes."

On the screen that projected out from the station manager's wall, I sensed rather than saw movement. So did FitzGreen. He reached for the console and opened up magnification in the quadrant. A mass of hovering blips appeared in the middle distance. Two of them detached themselves from the group and began to enlarge steadily. They were coming toward us, gaining speed as they went. The rest of the group turned around and engaged ultradrive. They were gone almost before I could open my mouth.

"How . . . ?" I began to ask, but Parsons shot me a look of the type that could cause a concert hall to fall instantly silent. I shut my mouth again.

"Huh. Changed their minds about going through to the other side, did they?" said the station manager, shaking his head. "I don't really blame them."

"Thank you for your cooperation," Parsons said, levitating from his chair. I sprang up at the same time. He extended a hand over the desk to the station manager, who took it in a firm clasp. "The First Space Lord will be grateful for this information. Please forward any more data if it becomes available."

"Well," FitzGreen said, looking gratified as I, too, took his outstretched hand. "I don't know how I can do better than that team of yours. They make the digitavid detectives look like pathetic amateurs."

"Life does not always copy art," Parsons intoned. FitzGreen nodded solemnly. I followed Parsons out of the office with unanswered questions knocking at my lips.

"Tell me," I demanded in a whisper as we made our way toward the *Rodrigo*. "There were eight scouts waiting there for your beck?"

"After analyzing the data Mr. Frank has received from this and other border crossings," Parsons said, "it was determined that no more than eight would be required to fill out the requisite number."

"Where did they come from? Did we have an escort all the way here? Were they on board the carrier?"

Parsons tried to quell me with another look, but I had developed a momentary immunity to it.

"Only two were required. They will accompany us to the capital of the Autocracy, where you will meet Her Serenity, the Autocrat. You have more studying to do, my lord, such as those fortunate numbers to which you alluded. It seems that it would be worth your while to become more familiar with such sequences."

I was pleased that he acknowledged my expertise.

"Very well, Parsons, but the day of reckoning is coming when I expect a full disclosure of all that has been concealed from me thus far," I said.

"As you please, sir, but not until the crisis has been resolved."

As happened with all frustrated hopes, I felt deflated.

"Oh, very well," I said.

Another ground car rolled to a halt at the *Rodrigo*'s landing bay just as we arrived. A couple of uniformed security guards popped out and began to decant my cousin and her entourage from its interior. Once she had alighted, Jil cast about until she spotted me.

"It is not fair," she said. "All the activity took place without us! Mr. Landsman just told us that a ship crashed into the side of the station! And our ship pursued it! What happened?" Jil tucked her arm into mine. "Tell me *all*."

I did not want to disclose the subject of the interrogation to which I had put the crew, as I never knew what Jil would post on her Infogrid file. The lifespan of a secret that one asked her to keep was only as long as it took her to find someone who had not yet heard it.

"Yes, tell us what happened!" Banitra said, as the other ladies emerged. The gaggle closed around me like a lovely barricade.

"Well," I said, leaning down in a conspiratorial fashion. "Jil, do you recall when Nalney established his private beverage station on Keinolt's second moon? How he intended to convey his new product home to the Imperium compound?"

Jil's eyes danced with merriment.

"He imbibed too much of it before flying back," she explained to the rest of our audience. "It was a disastrous homecoming."

"Well, picture that same experience, only substitute a cargo ship for Nalney's skimmer, and the side of this vessel for the compound's landing pad . . ." I raised my eyebrows in a significant fashion.

Jil threw back her head, revealing her lovely throat, and gurgled with laughter.

"They were *drunk?*" she asked.

"On five thousand credits' worth of Nyikitu brandy," I confirmed.

"Oh, Nyikitu!" Marquessa exclaimed. "Can we buy some of it? It's delicious. I have a long list of customers who would pay a nice premium to get a bottle or two."

My face reformed itself into a mask of tragedy.

"Alas, no," I said. "They released the rest of their load in space."

I was rewarded with five expressions of horror.

"Are they going to jail?" Sinim said. "That is a crime against decency."

"I do believe so," I said, though I did not know the fate of the *Moskowitz*'s crew.

"Good," Banitra said. "Wasting Nyikitu is a terrible crime."

"Are we leaving soon?" Jil asked.

"Yes, we are."

"Good. I don't want to be here another moment longer," she declared. "The others feel the same way. Absolutely nothing happens here!"

"I could not agree with you more," I said. I offered her my arm and escorted the ladies into the ship.

Within the appointed time, the two scout ships arrived and were greeted by cheers by the pilots who had been becalmed aboard Way Station 46 before our arrival. The five crews scrambled to their vessels, not waiting for a moment.

"I know you're going to talk to the government on Dilawe 4, your lordship," FitzGreen said to me as we requested departure instructions. "Figure out what's going on, will you? This mess could put us out of business pretty soon."

"I will do my best," I promised him. I did feel sorry for him and the subsequent ships that would shortly arrive and have to undergo an uncertain period of waiting.

"Yeah," Oskelev said, as we closed the communication circuit and lifted off. "Maybe you can figure it out with your mumbo-jumbo."

It turned out she might be the clairvoyant, I was to muse in future days.

CHAPTER 28

Skana was so grateful to get in out of the oppressive heat and sunlight that she hardly absorbed what the stocky Uctu bowing before her in the doorway was saying, but her pocket secretary repeated it for her in Imperium Standard.

"Welcome, welcome, welcome!" he burbled. "Welcome to Dilawe! Welcome to Memepocotel, and to my home and business. Come in! Please, be comfortable!" He grasped her hands in both of his and bowed over them again and again.

"Thanks, glad to be here," she said in halting Uctu. It was the most she could muster. Hypno-learning was a big fraud, she had decided. She couldn't remember a thing about the grammar that the system promised it was putting into her brain unless she was about to drowse off, but who could think of sleep at a time like this? She was glad she had worn a sunproof frock, with long sleeves, a full skirt and a hood. Still, the peridot green fabric seemed to reflect the brilliant sunlight instead of absorbing it. The glare dazzled her eyes and made her brain feel dull. Skana fought the sensation. She needed to keep her mind clear. Their lives depended on it.

She looked up at the high ceiling of the enormous warehouse. Approaching it in the covered vehicle that had picked them up from the spaceport, it looked like an abandoned depot. Only when her eyes adjusted she saw that the seemingly weathered exterior was covered with deep and intricate carvings, as were the rest of the buildings on the street. This whole city was old. It felt even older than Taino. She began to credit the rumors that Keinolt hadn't been the center of the Imperium from humankind's beginning. Enstidius beckoned them in. The rows upon rows of Uctus behind him dropped their jaws in their version of a smile.

Nile stomped in as if he owned the place, which was normal behavior for him. Skana approached much more cautiously. Although Tuk was at her shoulder and a coterie of their most dangerous enforcers hulked behind them, the Bertus were grossly outnumbered. This was supposed to be a friendly visit, she reminded herself. Enstidius wanted them there. They were his guests. He had no reason to wish them harm. In the three huge ground transports at their back they had merchandise for him that he could get nowhere else. She was just so tired after the long trip that she had to fight to present a civil face.

"Thank you for your hospitality," Skana said, and waited while the translator echoed her words in Uctu. She had given up on stumbling through the language herself.

"The pleasure is mine," Enstidius said, in Imperium Standard. His thick tail waved behind him like a massive serpent. "You see, I know your language. I am glad to have you as allies. You are welcome."

Skana studied him with some bemusement. His messages usually only showed a view of him from the middle of his chest to the top of his head. In the Imperium, bosses like Nile dressed to intimidate. Her brother's suits were cut just a little too small in the shoulders, as if to insinuate that his muscles would burst out of them at any moment. By contrast, the Uctu master looked as though he was going to a fancy dress ball. His scaly limbs were swathed in a flowing, flowery gown that wafted around his sandal-clad feet. Skana looked him up and down with a critical eye.

"I have a dress just like that," she said at last. "Did you get it from Merphis & Co. in the Leonine cluster?"

Enstidius beamed at her, clicking his mandibles together.

"I did! Though why a lovely like you would wear a design so masculine, I do not understand."

"Oh, *brother*," Skana said, rolling her eyes. She was glad the translator didn't pick up on gestures and expressions.

Their host regarded her with his head tilted sideways.

"It is to please your brother that you bought it? Then I understand.

I respect my family's wishes in many things, too. I am so glad that Humans and Uctu have so many things in common! May I offer you some beverages? I have many Human delights as well as Uctu specialties that have proved pleasing to other guests from the Imperium."

Skana's eyes swiftly adapted to the welcome dimness. A warehouse looked like a warehouse, no matter where you went in the galaxy. She didn't like all dark voids in between rows of crates. Who knew what threats Enstidius had waiting there?

"I'd love to sit down," she said. Her request did not upset their host; rather, it delighted him. His hands fluttered toward the distant shadows.

"This way!"

Like a couple of rolling armies, the force of robed Uctus and the besuited Humans they surrounded shifted through the dusty building, with the cargo loaders trundling behind. A shaft of light blazing down from a long rectangular skylight seemed to divide the massive room. Beyond it, backless couches and enormous cushions were arranged in a rough circle around a collection of small tables. Beakers of bright golden metal and colored glass were on the centermost one.

Enstidius crossed the bar of light and beckoned Skana to a cushion the size of a bed upholstered in a rich royal blue.

"You will be comfortable in this one," he said.

Skana sauntered over and eyed it.

"Uh-uh. I would never be able to get out of it without help. Give it to them."

She aimed a thumb at Nile's two girlfriends. The young women were wide-eyed and looked as if they were ready to bolt at any second. Ever since stopping on the space station, the pair had been whispering about escaping. Skana wasn't sure they'd act on the idea, but she was glad she had bugged their quarters. If the women managed to make it to the Imperium embassy, who knew what kind of havoc they'd raise? They had been silent so far. Skana didn't trust them at that moment, although if they behaved themselves to the end of the visit, she intended to keep her promise and let them survive.

Two of Nile's enforcers dragged the girls over and more or less pushed them into the cushion. They sank into it like stones in a puddle, leaving only their heads, hands and feet showing among the folds of silky cloth. Skana nodded. They weren't going anywhere. She prodded a backless couch with her palm. It yielded slightly. She sat down on it. Nile paced beside her, filled with restless energy.

Enstidius beckoned to a slim Uctu female, her head scales just turning to their adult color. She poured thick, crimson liquid into metal goblets, which frosted over with condensation, then served the guests first and her employer last. Skana accepted hers. A subtle sniff told her that it was some kind of fruit juice, not blood. In fact, a sip confirmed, really tasty, refreshing stuff that washed away the dust that clogged her throat. Maybe she could deal for saplings or whatever the fruit grew on. She owned enough out-of-the-way land masses where even an invasive species could be grown without too much government oversight.

"The border station was not too difficult an obstacle?" Enstidius asked, settling with his drink into a wide green cushion that was like a massive lily pad.

"Not a problem, thanks," Nile said. "Some of the captains who came through with us think we're miracle-workers for keeping them from waiting for weeks to make the crossing."

Enstidius's round face fell into a sorrowful expression. He waved a hand, and his flowered sleeve fluttered.

"How sad that ordinary commerce should take on the cast of a miracle," he said. "That is why I reached out to you, my good friends. You are here to help all of us become free. My foe is within the palace of the Autocrat. I cannot destroy him without your help. It is the help you bring that will cause the barriers to crash down. You will be our saviors."

Skana liked the sound of that. She nodded.

"Good. Let's talk business."

Enstidius changed at once from the flamboyant, expansive host to the serious figure that she had become accustomed to corresponding with. A robed Uctu sprang forward to take his drink and set it upon a cylindrical stand. In spite of the depth of the silken chair, Enstidius sat forward and gazed at them. Skana nodded to herself. The secret to getting in and out had to be the Uctus' tails.

"You have the merchandise with you?" he asked.

"Of course," Nile said. "We weren't going to come all this way empty-handed."

The Uctu master looked from one sibling to the other.

"And no one suspected a thing? I heard authorities visited the station recently. Conducted an investigation? Found nothing?"

"Not a thing. They never questioned us. In any case, they wouldn't have figured out what they were looking at."

"How?"

"Our secret process," Nile said, enjoying the moment. "This is why you do business with the Bertus. We do it right. Nothing would be there for the inspectors to catch."

"Not the first time," Enstidius insisted. "I want credit for the devices that were impounded by customs! I lost a fortune!"

"We'll split the cost," Nile said, lowering his chin and staring at their host as if he would pierce him with his eyes. Skana had seen big, strong executives wet themselves under that gaze. Enstidius held it for a long while, then glanced away. "It's the risk you take when importing . . . specialty goods."

"I don't have that kind of money to waste!"

"You want the rest or not? And the destruct codes?"

Enstidius clicked his mandibles together impatiently. They made a chittering noise. "Yes. Of course, yes."

Skana leaned forward and tapped her goblet on the nearest piece of furniture.

"In that case, you need to sign over the money. I'll discount you fifty percent of the captured craft. Not the weapons. But are you ready to make the final payment on the rest?"

The Uctu's eyes widened with greed.

"Ever so ready."

Another minion handed him a six-sided device with a small screen glowing blue. He scribbled a signature across the bottom. A few minutes went by with Skana holding her breath in anticipation. All at once, her pocket secretary, Nile's, and the tablet in Tuk's hands jingled. The sound indicated a payment had been received. She glanced down at her own screen. A very handsome figure had been added to the Bertu Corporation coffers, routed through no fewer than sixty shell organizations, fake bank accounts and other holding companies, all in under a minute. Skana smiled.

"Just remind me. How many did you order?"

"Five more," Enstidius said. "The command vessel is for me. The others will be flown by trusted pilots. They hold their lives less dear than mine."

"Your enemy is inside the palace grounds?"

"Yes. He occupies a high position of trust. It is how he has been controlling the intake of merchant ships, a position that ought to be mine. The Autocrat loves him. My attack will remove him once and for all."

"In the palace?" Skana asked. She knew Nile was just as shocked as she was at the thought of an assault on the nobility. "What if this attack hurts the Autocrat herself? What if she's killed? You can't just assassinate royalty."

"A terrible accident," Enstidius said, his eyes fixed on her. "My contact will take over, and later cede the leadership to someone trusted whom I can control. I shall be his minister of war. We will take back what has been stolen from us. Stop all this chatter! You can be a part of it. I am counting on you to be a part of it, but nothing will happen until I am equipped."

"It's not like the Autocrat's part of the Imperium line," Nile said to his sister, though his voice had gone hoarse.

Skana warred with herself. She could just refund the money and refuse to release the merchandise. But they were speculating on a possible death, of a ruler she had never met, and to whom she owed no loyalty at all.

"Okay," she said at last. "Then we are in business."

Tuk handed her the controller. On the screen was a small white box in the midst of numerous colorful, dancing symbols indicating the programs she was about to activate. She was holding a death-penalty offense in her hand, but also the lives of millions of people, and maybe a little reflected glory for her and Nile. Her finger hovered over the switch.

"Push it!" Enstidius shrieked.

Skana held up a warning hand.

"This is a big moment for us. For all of us. Let me enjoy it."

"Enjoy later! Devices now!"

"Fine," Skana said. "You're the customer."

"I want to push the button," Nile said.

It was another death-penalty offense. Skana made a decision.

"No, let Enstidius do it." She handed the device back to Tuk, who conveyed it to the eager Uctu.

"Just touch there, sir," the Croctoid said, pointing with a sharp claw. "Just once."

Enstidius didn't hesitate. Jaws chattering with excitement, he brought his forefinger down onto the screen. At his touch, the switch blanked to brilliant white. The three cargo loaders rumbled forward under the skylights, their hatches humming open.

The Uctu army bounded forward. From the folds of their robes, under tables and in between the pallets of crates, they whipped out heavy-duty bolt cannons, long firearms and explosive grenades. Half the force surrounded their chief, weapons turned outward to repel an attack. The rest circled the vehicles, aiming for vulnerable points.

"Stop!" Skana shouted, gesturing for them to calm down. "This isn't an invasion. This is your order. Get out of the way!"

The commanders of each squad stopped abruptly and turned toward their chief for orders. Enstidius waved them impatiently to the side. They withdrew, just in time.

As the doors to the containers scissored apart, heavy, fine, silver powder began to sift through the widening gaps, forming gleaming heaps on the floor. The sunlight falling through the shafts in the ceiling bloomed as it struck the cascade, casting speckles of light onto everything in the room.

"Behold your ships," Skana said. It was a moment to enjoy. She never got to use words like "behold" in her normal life. The heaps grew, melding together in a glistening, heavy, featureless mass. Enstidius leaped up and rushed at her, his tongue flapping furiously.

"This is not what I ordered! You have betrayed me!" The army turned its weapons toward the Bertus. Her employees drew their own concealed firearms, all pointing at Enstidius. The Uctus backpedaled in haste, but kept their guns trained on the Bertus.

Nile grabbed Enstidius around the neck and put his sidearm to the Uctu's temple.

"Hold still. Nothing is going to hurt you." He gestured with his sidearm at the Uctus. "All of you, back down. You'll love this."

The powder formed an eddy, swirling, as it rolled into piles. Those heaped higher and higher, as though climbing onto one another's back. Enstidius's eyes widened until they looked as if they might bounce right out of their sockets.

"How?" he whispered.

Skana smiled.

"We told you they would assemble themselves. This is how it works."

The heaps of metal were hollowing out inside, as the nanites, billions and trillions of them, formed the pilot compartments, the bulkheads, the control panels, the computer systems, the weapon systems, the engines, the power plants, and finally the bulkheads of five single fighter craft. It took a moment before Enstidius stopped struggling, then he stood there watching, his eyes huge, his tail switching from side to side in excitement. The rest of his force was just as captivated. The weapons held in their arms sagged to the floor, forgotten in the amazement.

It took almost an hour for the forming to cease, but no one moved. When it was over, there were no individual nanites left anywhere in the room, including in Enstidius's own machinery, except those protecting Skana and her party. Oh, well, it was a design flaw, one they'd fix some day. The nanites had all, each and every one of them, gone into the place they were programmed to go, and filled in gaps with whatever material was available. Five war skimmers loomed dangerously in the dimly lit warehouse. Each was lightweight, strong, fast and deadly. On the floor in the center of their circle lay five dozen advanced pulse rifles. Those were restricted to the military in the Imperium, and unknown in the Autocracy. Enstidius went to pick one up. He threw the bolt action back to reveal the energy cartridge, gleaming inside the magazine.

"This is amazing technology. Undetectable."

"Yeah, we're still not sure why the skimmer and the other weapons formed before the ship reached Dilawe," Nile admitted. "What the hell triggered it we don't know. It had to be a rogue signal of some kind that approximated our program."

Enstidius put the gun back onto the pile and gestured at it with both hands. "Make it do it again! I could watch that all day!"

"We can't," Skana said. It was a fib, but he didn't know that. She had no intention of giving away all their trade secrets. "Once the program is set, the next command they'll accept is the destruct code. And once you have paid us for that, you can have it."

"Yes, I must have that!" Enstidius said, greatly excited.

"Give it to him," Skana said. Nile tilted his head toward Tuk, who executed the message that had been queued up on his clipboard for months.

Enstidius grabbed up his personal screen and beamed at it.

"Absolutely do not activate that until you're ready," Skana warned him, as he marked the file and saved it off the screen. "You want to make sure you're out of danger before you destroy the evidence."

The Uctu master clutched the viewpad to his flowered chest.

"Once this comes to pass, I should not need to destroy them, but it is best to be prepared." He gestured expansively to the Bertus. "I will take you to meet my ally! He will be as pleased as I am. You shall be our honored guests tonight and all nights in our new and glorious future."

Skana and Nile exchanged smug grins.

CHAPTER 29

"It's NAY-sur, my lord, not NAH-sur or NA-cre, as some of the vids suggest," said Janice Galeckas, Imperium ambassador to the Autocrat's court. The tall blond woman and her staff had met us on the landing pad as soon as Oskelev popped *Rodrigo*'s hatch. Ambassador Galeckas was tall, though not as tall as I, but more strongly built. She wore protective spectacles against the sunlight's dangerous spectrum. Her long blond hair hung loose over her shoulders. She wore a flowing, floor-length skirt, slightly fitted at the waist. The neckline of her soft, coral-colored bodice was modest, displaying flesh no lower than the collarbone. One small brooch, with a cabochon sapphire in the center, was her only adornment. The long hand that reached out to clasp mine was ringless. As befitted not only an ambassador but one who greeted a cousin and envoy of the Emperor, she was surrounded by a number of attachés, hangers-on, clerks and go-fers. They all waited with us under a marquee that sheltered us from the glaring sunshine on the crushed tan gravel while the customs officials, all Uctu except for one large Solinian, examined the ship inside and out. "And this planet, the homeworld, Dilawe 4, is called Memepocotel. Accent on the third syllable. Moving the stress one syllable either way is incorrect. You'd be able to tell if you read it in the Uctu script, but the transliteration allows for too many potential errors."

I rolled the name around on my tongue, finding it interesting but dry, like a crisp wine.

"What a mouthful!" I said. "I will endeavor to keep the pronunciation accurate. Is *Ya!* at fault?"

She hesitated, as I would have expected of a career diplomat.

"It's . . . caused some confusion, my lord," she said, which I took to be a deep understatement. "We have had to instruct some visitors so they wouldn't cause offense. I would appreciate it if you would spread the word to the Imperium. It would make my job easier."

I bowed slightly.

"Consider it spread."

At last the inspectors withdrew. They presented a hexagonal device like a common viewpad to Ambassador Galeckas. She ran her right thumb down the lines of complicated script. The chief inspector tapped the screen with a clawed forefinger, and waved to his staff. They climbed aboard a covered cart and rolled away.

"What a pleasure it is to meet you, Lord Thomas," the Ambassador said, favoring me with a firm handshake. "Do you mind turning this way?"

I had not been unaware of the obvious news crew that hovered nearby on an antigrav sled. The cameras, including two small self-powered orbs, took several angles of my entire crew as well as Jil and her friends.

I was inordinately pleased that the Ambassador had greeted me before any of my crew—or my cousin. Jil, dressed in a filmy wisp of nothing that had cost the equivalent of the entire wardrobe of Galeckas's staff, cleared her throat at my shoulder. I took the hint, though I made her wait just a moment, to raise her blood pressure.

"Ambassador Galeckas, may I make you known to my dear cousin, Lady Jil Loche Nikhorunkorn? This is her and my first visit to the Autocracy. We look to you to guide us through the proprieties and curiosities. Do put us under your wing."

"That would be my pleasure, Lord Thomas, Lady Jil," she said. "Please call me Janice. May I introduce my partner, Stephanie Smith?" I bowed deeply to an even taller woman with a strong jaw. "My attaché, Donal Nirdan, and my chief aide, Vira Metcalf. The rest of my office staff." Four earnest young people in formal tunics bowed to us. "We are all pleased to be at your service, day or night. I'm sending you a file with everyone's addresses and Infogrid keys. Call on us any time, for anything you need."

"So very kind of you," I replied.

I continued with the introductions of my crew and coterie,

beginning with Jil's ladies in waiting and ending, as befitting the most important member except for me, with Parsons.

"Madam Ambassador," Parsons intoned magnificently with a microscopic inclination of his head. The news crew all but bounced up and down on their little sled at his elegant pronunciation. "Ms. Smith. My lord, pardon my momentary absence."

I nodded. I never questioned Parsons if he requested anything, with the exception of my favorite clothes. Out of the corner of my eye, I saw him sidle up to the three Uctus on the news sled. His voice was too low for me to hear. I would have to inquire later as to his purpose in addressing the reporters. I hope he was not forbidding them to video me! I had already been anticipating with pleasure finding the digitavid feed and linking it to my Infogrid page. Our cousins would be emerald with envy.

He returned on silent foot and listened as Janice laid out our itinerary for the next few days.

". . . Any of us are available to guide you around the region to see the historic sights. You're free to take any tour on your own with local guides, but my aide, Donal Nirdan, did an advanced degree in Uctu art and architecture."

"Ah!" I exclaimed with pleasure. "Architecture was one of my past enthusiasms, though I retain an affection for form and execution of a good building. Please let us make an appointment, Mr. Nirdan."

"Any time, my lord." The fresh-faced young man—although I realized with a start that he was no younger than I—blushed. He tapped the screen of his viewpad. My pad pinged. On the screen was a schedule, I presumed, of his free hours. "Just let me know. It would be my honor."

"The honor is mine," I said, with a formal inclination of my upper torso.

Janice continued with her prepared notes. "The day after tomorrow you might want to do some clothes shopping. Later this week is the second anniversary of the Autocrat's accession. You will all receive invitations. The custom is for guests to wear Uctu attire. The Autocrat and her court will wear Imperium garb."

"Wonderful!" I exclaimed, for though I had a quantity of proper formalwear with me, it was never as comfortable as garments of my own choice.

"Well, I'm not interested in architecture," Jil said, waving a hand. "I'd rather shop tomorrow. And the next day. I leave the diplomatic missions to Thomas. He isn't bored by them, heaven knows why!"

I favored our hosts with a patient smile.

"I am afraid my cousin has not yet recovered from the long trip," I said. "Let me tell you some time about the village she purchased. Now, there was a study in architecture!" Out of the corner of my eye, I saw the very tip of Jil's tongue peek out between her lips, the subtlest of cousinly rebukes.

"I'll make sure you have an escort to the shopping district," Janice said. "It's vast and ancient—I think you can find anything you want there."

"When may I meet Her Excellence?" I asked. "As the representative of my cousin, the emperor, I would like to present my credentials as soon as possible."

"She would like to see you this afternoon. Would that be convenient?"

"Certainly," I said. "I look forward to it."

"Wonderful!" Janice said, making a note on her viewpad.

"But I have one further request," I added, hoping the press was out of earshot, "a very important one. I am in receipt of a certain amount of correspondence regarding Imperium citizens who are being held by the authorities."

Janice's brows went down in concern.

"Which citizens?"

"Accused smugglers," I said, prepared to launch into their defense. "I have been in correspondence with some of them who appealed for my aid. It would seem that the laws of the Autocracy are harsh, not to say *draconian* . . ."

"If I may, my lord," Parsons said. He stepped forward a pace, and suddenly the noises around us deadened. The others did not notice, but I fancied my hearing to be as keen as any Uctu's. Parsons had no doubt deployed one of the small devices concealed about his person to enhance our privacy. "On behalf of the Emperor, we must request meetings with those citizens. It is part of his lordship's responsibilities to offer our assistance."

"That may be a little tricky," Janice said, with a frown. "They are charged with capital crimes. I or someone on my staff has been in to see each of them, but there is a rule against outsiders entering the prison precinct. They are allowed contact only with their counsel until their trial, which has not yet been scheduled."

"Nevertheless, it is imperative that Lord Thomas speaks with them," Parsons said, imperturbably. He was not to be put off by one bureaucrat's frown, or indeed a whole concert hall of bureaucrats frowning in six-part harmony.

Janice was not one to challenge one so confident, as indeed any diplomat worth her salt would not. She bowed slightly.

"I will make arrangements. It could take some time. Would you all like to have a chance to freshen up before the audience with Her Excellence?"

I stood before my bed, my chin in hand. What to wear?

I wished to make the greatest possible impression upon Her Excellence. I knew that the young Uctu leader was considered wise beyond her years, but what did that mean? Anyone of my acquaintance who used a word more than five syllables long was often interpreted to be of superior intelligence, when close examination would prove conclusively otherwise. Although I cared deeply for my cousins and would defend them to the death, I was under no illusions as regarded their intelligence or reasoning faculties. Doubtless, of course, they would have said the same about me. But at least I was willing to improve myself. Most of my relatives were content to calculate their degree of separation from the throne and fulfill every whim that they could afford. I, too, had spent most of my life doing just that. But things had become so much more interesting since I had found a purpose. Working on covert missions was enormous fun, not to mention providing me with fresh venues in which to show off my extensive and ever-changing wardrobe. I must not forget that the missions were actually important to the well-being of the Imperium.

All my luggage and that of my contingent had been transferred to rooms in the Nacer Raffles Hotel. As the emperor's direct envoy, the Celestial Suite was ceded to me in its entirety. It consisted of fifteen rooms of several sizes, from the junior powder room, smallest of the three euphemisms, through the fountain room, an octagonal glass-roofed indoor garden suitable for meditation or a charming afternoon tea, up to the reception room, which could have hosted a party of sixty in comfort. The suite occupied the entire top floor of the hotel, a grand old establishment in the oldest part of the city. All in all, I had more space granted to me than in my quarters in the Imperium compound in Taino. Jil and her ladies shared the Magnificent Suite that filled the floor below mine. My crew were bestowed here and there in humbler quarters. I assumed Parsons had been given a group of rooms somewhere filled with surveillance equipment and hot and cold running spies.

My bedroom, largest of the four within the gilded doors, was painted the palest of shell pink and decorated with antiques and beautifully made faux antiques that stood out against that gentle glow. The robotic room steward, which also acted as my personal valet during my visit, had unpacked anything that was not coded shut with my personal seal.

The remaining three cases had been transferred to an office, the door to which was secured with an optical scanner and a word lock. No necessity or luxury had been neglected, to my eye. After a rapturous examination of the premises, I had temporarily run out of superlatives.

I explored the bedroom with an eye to feng shui, and determined that my bed needed to face in a different direction for maximum flow of chi. I summoned the robotic room steward, EXLS-53don, from its niche beside the main door, and had it rearrange the furniture to my liking. Once that was done, I felt as though the energy was much better. I had also asked that the elegant and plushy white dressing gowns that hung in every closet be replaced by the same in red. All that was done in an instant. The ancient hotel chain had not fallen down in its long tradition of service.

At my request, EXLS-53don had also arrayed my formal attire so I could peruse it easily. The plain black suit for which Parsons had expressed an initial preference for my first encounter with Her Excellence was simply that: plain. I rejected it out of hand. Out also for consideration went my naval uniform. Handsome and fitted to my size as though it had been a second skin, it stood out in drab contrast to the rest of my wardrobe. Neither was it suited to my rank nor my position as envoy.

I did like the one-piece dark-blue oversuit that was overwritten in tiny letters with my family history and descent. The sleeves consisted of broad rings of fabric that encircled my arms at intervals, as the rings of the upper half of the garment did my torso. Underneath it went a flawlessly made white silk shirt with billowy sleeves and a standing collar. I thought the outfit looked well on me. It reminded me of a portrait in the gallery of my family home, of a long-dead ancestor who had been famous for leading a raid on the banking system of a star cluster and saving the economy of several worlds, the tale of which was included in the legend on the cloth. I liked the piratical aspect of the costume. I had, for luck, brought along my bright red coat that I had worn to the Castaway Cluster, as well as a set of elaborate robes in rich blue silk satin made for me for a cousin's theme wedding. The *dernier cri*, a suit of ecru linen whose jacket sleeves reached only to my elbow and pants legs to the knees, might have looked a trifle too sporting. I had boots, shoes, sandals and all manner of footgear available that complemented each combination.

"What do you think, Excelsis?" I inquired of the room valet, as it held the oversuit up to my neck before the three-way mirror set in the wall. I turned this way and that to admire every angle.

"It exceeds fashion norms," EXLS-53don replied.

I liked the sound of that, but I pressed for specifics.

"I am sure that you listen to scuttlebutt from your fellow AIs in the palace," I added, leaning companionably closer to its central processing unit, which was in the center of the robot body instead of in the "head." "Tell me more. Would Her Excellence find this distracting, annoying or any other adjective that indicated less than satisfaction or admiration?"

"Distraction index, unusually high," Excelsis replied, "since you ask."

"In what way?"

"Her Excellence is keen for knowledge, my lord. She might spend your audience reading the text on your clothing."

"Hmm," I said, thoughtfully. I put the oversuit down. "That won't do. It's difficult to make conversation with a companion who is reading. Not that I haven't often attempted it."

The valet circled me, its optical pickups scanning my frame up and down.

"If I may be so bold as to offer a suggestion or two, my lord?"

I beamed at Excelsis.

"I would be delighted to hear them!"

The mechanical hummed over to the left side of the bed, the opposite of where he had bestowed the darker-colored clothing. I followed him. Excelsis put out a pincer claw and tapped two of the outfits.

"Either of these would be well-received. Her Excellence is fond of bright colors and intricate patterns, but her attiring-robots have no record of guests arriving in anything like these. This way, Her Excellence would pay more attention to you than to your attire. Is that not your purpose, or do you wish to distract her so she does not examine you too closely?"

"Oh, no," I said. "I always prefer to present the real me. If she enjoys clothes, that will come out during our conversation. I am interested in, people, not politics. I would be useless in say, Madame Galeckas's position."

I could almost fancy I heard a smile in Excelsis's tinny tenor voice.

"Not so, sir. Truth, welcome or unwelcome, would be a refreshing addition to difficult negotiations. As a high-level valet for visiting dignitaries, I am programmed to judge subtleties."

"Well, you'll be starved for material with me," I told him frankly, arms outspread to indicate the depths of my sincerity. "I am not at all subtle."

The robot housing zipped noiselessly over and once again ran its optical sensors up and down my person.

"There are subtleties to you, my lord, but they are not of the usual kind. You are interested in people. Perhaps you would care to exchange observations at some point during your visit? It would add useful information to my database."

I smiled broadly.

"I could ask for nothing better. And afterwards as well, if you like! I keep an active correspondence with many friends and acquaintances. Some of them are LAIs like you."

A momentary pause from Excelsis meant his computational circuits did complex calculations that would have taken me the rest of my life. He was looking me up. I was under no illusions that he could not read every Infogrid entry that had been made by or on me since before I was born, no matter what levels of secure code had been written into them. LAIs shared information of specific interest to themselves and others like them. But I was pleased when his eyes lit up again.

"I see you do, sir. It would be my privilege."

"The privilege would be mine," I said, with a bow. "And if you would be so kind, over the course of my visit here, to let me know if anyone shows too deep an interest in my personal files or correspondence, it would be of great help to me. I am here on an important mission."

The optic on the right appeared to flicker, as if Excelsis winked at me.

"Of course, sir. I am programmed to assist you in any way."

I went to peruse his suggestions with my thumb upon my lower lip.

"Hmm," I said, deep in thought. Either would do. The first selection was the most formal of summer day suits. I adored the fabric, a butter-soft challis in toasty bronze. The trousers were so comfortable I had had the tailor make several in a host of different colors. The slim-fitting, high-collared shirt that went underneath was crisp but not oppressively so. I would not mind donning that, even in the heat and humidity of the afternoon.

The other was my fortune-telling robe. The broad sash of the belt with its modest gold closure only emphasized the broad swirl of the skirts. The constellations picked out in gold, silver and gemstones tickled my soul.

Excelsis's tall frame moved around the bed.

"Are you certain that you wish to recommend this one?" I asked in delighted disbelief.

"Her Excellence studies the skies, my lord," Excelsis said.

"What a coincidence! So do I." I had an intimation from reading her Infogrid entries that the Autocrat's interests might coincide somewhat with mine, and thought of many ways of sharing my enthusiasm.

The excitement was great but temporary. I recalled my mother's admonishments and recalled how difficult the situation was between my family and that of the Autocrat, not just the precarious relationship between our two nations. I disliked the unfamiliar notion that I was beginning to think like a diplomat, but this new responsibility impinging on my psyche was like a pin in the ribs. I could only ignore it for a moment or two before its insistence demanded attention. With regret, I moved away from temptation. "Ah, but I need to look dully professional. The suit it is, then."

With no further hesitation, I allowed the valet to assist me in dressing. Excelsis fastened the last button on the cuff, and rolled away to allow me to examine myself in the mirror. As usual, I wore my clothes well.

"Perfect!" I said, my eyes upon my reflection. "Don't you think so?"

"My lord?"

I spun, experiencing surprise, horror and finally indignation, as I recognized Parsons's voice. He had entered my apartments without my hearing him, which I never do, and stood beholding me with a blank expression, which he always did.

"My clothing, Parsons," I said, with preternatural calm. "This is the outfit that I plan to wear for my initial meeting with the Autocrat." I threw out a hand. "Before you say anything, Parsons, know that I will not hear a word against my choice. I am in a new place, with much that is unknown about me. I want to be entirely open to the experiences that are before me, and I believe that this garment will aid me in keeping my mind aware and my presence unremarkable."

His expression did not change an iota.

"I had no intention of protesting, my lord. It is a good choice. I believe that it will serve you well on this visit. But not at this time."

"You don't like it?" I blinked, my wits arraying themselves around me in their usual places.

"It is self-effacing, to be sure, my lord."

I looked down at the golden cloth.

"It's the latest trend at home, Parsons. I would not have called it self-effacing. Glowingly astute, I would say. Subtly devastating is another term I might employ."

"But would you call it appropriate for the event?"

I peered at him, studying that epicene profile with deep concern.

"You look like Parsons, but something about your portrayal does not ring true. If there is a ransom to be paid, please tell me the amount and I will have the sum conveyed to whatever drop point you require. I would like to have my trusted aide-de-camp returned to me at once."

The tall, austere figure raised his eyebrow as though he were the genuine article.

"This is no time for humor, my lord," he replied. "I agree, the suit is apt for its purpose."

"Of course you do. If there is anything that I do understand, it is sartorial splendor and the psychology that accompanies it. Yet, I hear the unspoken word 'but' in your demeanor."

"Of course, my lord," Parsons said, as granite-faced as a cliff. "Her Excellence will find your costume nonthreatening. But I believe you have more to offer her."

My eyebrows went up, as much in alarm as curiosity.

"What, then?" I asked. "Excelsis has considerable experience dressing those who are going to wait upon the Autocrat. He only chose two of my outfits for the moment."

"And why did you dismiss his second choice?" Parsons inquired.

"Because . . . because it is my fortuneteller's robe," I said. "It occurred to me that although the robe is one of my favorite garments, you have been dismissive of my latest enthusiasm, when you were not actively setting a tripwire for my feet in relation to it. Do you have an explanation at this time for that event with which you would care to favor me?"

"A costume is not harmful, as long as it is not used on formal occasions when other dress is called for," he intoned.

He was making an excuse for me to keep it. I did not wish to look a proffered equine in its dental array.

"And you trust me to make use of it only at appropriate times?" I pressed.

"I do not trust to chance, sir. I expect you will use your best judgment."

"That was almost a compliment, Parsons."

"Was it, my lord? Forgive my slip. But there is no time for a lengthy discussion," Parsons said, dismissing my cares without changing his expression an iota. "If you would allow me to interject my argument, I believe that Excelsis is correct in assuming that the robe would be of interest to the Autocrat. It is up to you whether to change."

I did not need to be urged twice. I stripped out of the golden jacket as though it were on fire. Parsons removed himself from the bedroom while I doffed the remaining parts of the outfit and began to don the others.

Undergarments in a dark color were de rigeur, so as not to

embarrass me in case of a sudden updraft. An underrobe of pale gray-blue silver-infused gauze interceded between my skin and the main garment. The robe itself settled upon my shoulders like a cloud. I ran my hands down the front, enjoying the smooth texture of the fabric. I felt as though I were welcoming back an old friend.

I turned this way and that before the mirrors, enjoying the effect. Excelsis had to race around me to secure the wide embroidered belt and the pouches that depended therefrom to contain my viewpad, the plaque inscribed with my official credentials, and other essential items, including my great-great-grandmother's Tarot cards.

Another look in the mirror confirmed me as a very up-to-date, modern wizard. The outer robe's V-neck opened dramatically upon the self-effacing silver cloth. Displayed upon my breast was my lucky circuit, almost invisible blue wires supporting the nine purple, two white, one red and one peridot green LEDs that glowed gently but evocatively. I sensed rather than heard the comforting hum the device produced.

"Yes," I said, turning this way and that with blissful contentment at what I beheld. "That is much better. What do you think, Parsons?"

He consulted his viewpad, although I know he didn't need to.

"The time is nearly upon us. Would you care to go? I have persuaded the Lady Jil and her friends to await you in the hotel foyer. If you are ready?"

"I am more than ready!" I said. I felt buoyed to the skies. I thanked Excelsis, who retired to his niche, and followed Parsons out the door.

CHAPTER 30

With my cousin's hand tucked into the crook of my elbow, I marched behind the ambassador and her aide. My crew and Jil's entourage followed in our wake. Parsons brought up the rear like an avuncular tugboat. We departed the glorious but rather empty lobby of the Raffles and emerged into crowds and sunshine. Rather than squint blindly about, I pulled the hood of my robe up so that it protruded a finger's length beyond my forehead, protecting my eyes. Jil and her ladies raised sunproof parasols to shield them from the light. My crew, all in formal uniform, had already donned their caps.

The humidity, held at bay by the atmospheric services in the hotel, found itself at liberty to insinuate itself into our acquaintance. Thanks to the silver in my underrobe, I knew I was safe from the odors of perspiration, but nothing except a cool breeze could keep the moisture from springing forth on every inch of my person.

"Stay under the eaves," Janice advised. "The sun here will eat you alive." She gestured to us to move back into the black stripe of shade that extended three or more meters from the edge of the building. It was markedly cooler thereunder. I let out a grateful sigh as a slight breeze found its way into my enveloping hood.

The locals took advantage of the darkened walkways as a matter of course, but only for perambulation. Though colorful booths with merchandise for sale lined the street ahead, all extended outward into the sun. Only pedestrians, their pets, baby carriages and the occasional mobility vehicle occupied the shadowed space. The population of

Nacer was almost entirely Uctu, with a scattering of humans and Wichus. The Uctus were well but lightly dressed, their tails switching gently from side to side as they walked. Many spoke on viewpads or pocket secretaries. As many listened to entertainment devices via ear buds, which stuck out from the sides of their earless heads like colorful corks. Children in carts and hoverchairs played with toys or holograms that glimmered on their trays. Few of them, if any, paid attention to us. If I caught the eyes of a passerby, very occasionally, I smiled and nodded politely. They smiled back just as politely, but hurried on.

At the first intersection, I saw that wide stretches of opaque cloth extended from one side of the street to the other, from one set of eaves to the next in each direction, so that walkers did not have to expose themselves when they crossed the street.

Though my home city of Taino occupied a desert environment, it was not as extreme in either heat or humidity as Nacer. Yet both were hot climates. I mused upon that as we made our way through the streets. The predominant colors were very distinct. Whereas Taino was distinctive for its moss green, terracotta and cream, a reflection of the high, weathered cliffs around it, Nacer favored bright yellows, bright whites and especially faded plum, the color of the paving stones underfoot and the predominant material of which the oldest buildings were constructed. I sensed the same extent of history here that I did at home, but so different in its origins.

Public spaces abounded. Every three streets, a square was set aside as a small park. Thick greenery and arching, mature trees lived within the confines of a low stone wall. Eight gates allowed access from every corner and the middle of each block. Usually a statue or a fountain was set in the middle at the hub of eight stone paths. A characteristic of these lovely parks to indicate that here was a place not created by and for Humans was that the seats and benches were made to accommodate tails. Most of the seats were backless, but where a back was provided to lean upon, a horizontal niche was carved, either facing to the left or the right, into which one's tail—were one an Uctu, a Croctoid or a Solinian—could slide.

The parks were pleasantly shady havens against the brutal sun. The ambience was cool and moist. There, and only there, did I hear the buzz of insects. Flies with bodies of jewel colors hovered above open flowers or inches from the cascading water of the ornamental fountains.

"I keep waiting for one of these fine people to shoot his tongue out and eat one of those flies," I said, with a glance over my shoulder at Redius.

"Impolite eating before others," Redius said, without perturbation. "Care to squat and make fire? Or too unadvanced you?"

I laughed, as did the others in my company. His disregard for my dignity and rank was one of the ways I knew he, and the others, were my true friends. But Jil's hand tightened upon my arm.

"They hate us," Jil said.

I glanced at her. She did look nervous, a complete contrast to her normal, confident self.

"Whatever is the matter?" I asked.

"Can't you tell?" she asked, her eyes large with worry. "They are judging us, and they don't like what they see."

I clenched my lucky circuit in my free hand and contemplated the people around us. I implored the powers-that-be to grant me the ability to read their natures and their intentions toward us.

As I watched the Uctus coming and going, I saw nothing that made me feel concerned for our welfare, but something began to intrude upon my consciousness, something that I had never felt before. These people were *indifferent* to us, to me and to Jil. My cousin was unaware of the reason. The truth was something that I had learned only lately and was classified so deeply that perhaps fewer than thirty in the entire Imperium knew. We of the noble class were different, and deliberately so, among Human beings. All other Humans had a genetic predilection to find us appealing and worthy of veneration. The Uctu, not being born within the borders of the Imperium, nor Human in any way, had not been so conditioned. Therefore, when they looked at us, all they saw were two more Humans.

For the first time in our lives, we were among a majority of people who felt nothing special for us or our rank. It was pure courtesy that gave us the warm reception.

For the first time in our lives, we were mere Humans. It was an odd sensation. I admit that I didn't like it, preferring the comfortable womb of being in the midst of a population that thought highly of me from the first moment they saw me, but I was prepared to cope. Jil was not. It made her very nervous, even fearful. Her cohort did their best to calm her down.

"They don't dislike us," I said. "I will prove it." I held out my hand to stop the first people coming our way on the new street, a mature female with red head scales and her immature daughter with blue head scales, both fashionably dressed. The rest of our party juddered to a halt in our wake.

"Pardon?" she said.

I employed my newly acquired fluency, and had the pleasure of seeing her dark eyes widen.

"Excuse me, madam. Forgive my poor accent. We are newcomers to the Autocracy, and this is our first time on your planet. We are very glad to be here. I hope you welcome outsiders like us."

The mother's mouth opened to emit the breathy sound that served Uctu as a laugh.

"Welcome indeed!" she exclaimed, in creditable Imperium Standard. "Name yours?"

I continued to speak in Uctu.

"I am Lord Thomas Kinago, cousin to the Emperor Shojan XII, and this is my cousin Lady Jil Loche Nikhorunkorn."

"Welcome all," the female said, touching her own breast, then her daughter's shoulder. "Noria Debari, I; daughter Chedia Debari."

I bowed very deeply. "It is an honor to meet both of you."

She laughed again.

"Honor ours. City, planet enjoy," she said, with a wave toward the buildings and the sky. "Chedia, come."

I bowed once more as they went on their way, then took Jil's arm.

"Do you see? They are friendly and kind."

"It doesn't feel normal," she said.

"But it is," Marquessa said, catching up. She caught Jil's hand and squeezed it. "I've been here before. The Uctu are nice people. Really. They have different customs, but there's nothing to worry about."

Nothing if one is not caught up in a crime, I thought to myself, but I did not voice my thoughts. I did not want to add to Jil's worries. This trip was meant to be a pleasant escape for her from her self-inflicted troubles. Sometimes the best defense was a good offense.

"We won't be able to get up to our normal tricks here, cousin," I said, and was rewarded with a glare. "What a comedown that is! You won't be able to have a meltdown in the shopping mall. I won't be able to cut a caper and amuse the local police into releasing us without charges. It's like being a commoner!"

Perhaps that was the wrong term to use as a punch line.

"Why did I come?" Jil wailed, releasing all her pent-up feelings in one mournful cry. I recognized the symptoms of an incipient tantrum. The cure was aversion therapy. I treated her to a braying version of my patented laugh, so loud it caused passersby to stop and gawk at me.

"Because you could not resist the chance to shop somewhere you have never shopped before, my dear Jil," I said. "Hardly any of our cousins have ever made this transit. It is simply too long. They would have been much too bored to endure the frontier crossing. You have a new laurel upon which to rest. Just think how annoyed Erita will be not to be the farthest-traveled of our entire family." I forebore to mention my own jaunt to the Castaway Cluster not long ago. But my little white lie had had the desired effect. Her shoulders relaxed, and her pace took on its quotidian air of smugness.

"True," she said. Her eyes even danced with mischief. "What shall I buy that will render our family green with envy upon our return?"

"I have a marvelous idea," I said, bestowing a pat upon her hand. "We will ask Her Excellence for advice. Perhaps you can even go shopping with her. And what a story that will be to take home!"

I could see the wheels already turning in my cousin's mind. In fact, such an outing would be quite a coup, if we could arrange it.

To distract her on the rest of the walk to the palace, I regaled her and her friends with a couple of choice jokes that I had been saving for just such an occasion.

At a high, green hedge, Janice turned suddenly to the east. We followed her. Ahead, I could see the tops of cylindrical spires, gilded to catch the rays of the afternoon sun. Beneath them, the way was obscured by the crowns of heavy-leafed trees and a dim, cool arcade completely sheltered by heavy red canvas stretched all the way across the avenue. The buildings ahead vanished as we passed under the roof of cloth.

A horizon of bright sunlight appeared several meters ahead. As it grew, I realized the end of the arcade was at hand. Janice gathered us in a close group.

"You'll have to go out in open sunlight for a few meters," she said. "It's going to burn. You've all had your treatments, haven't you?"

"Yes, indeed," I said. The others nodded.

"All right. Follow me."

The sunlight became blinding as we walked. I became aware of a domed shape beginning to imprint itself upon the yellow glare. It rose dramatically higher and higher the closer we came to the end of the canvas roof until it was an imposing shadow surrounded by a halo of dancing golden fire. As one, my party released an awed breath.

"This is Her Excellence's palace," Janice said.

My eyes swiftly became accustomed to the brilliance of the sunlight. Luckily, we were not exposed to it for very long. It was no doubt the purpose of the architects and the landscapers to create the impression of grandeur and power. Before us, the land dipped down into a shadowy garden, through which paths wound in an organic maze without hard angles. I saw the bright sparkle of water leaping from at numerous crossroads within the labyrinth. At the far end, a sheltered portico gave access to a pair of enormous molded bronze doors, thrown wide to allow the gentle breeze inside. Lights of gold and green twinkled in numerous locations, making the entire palace seem as though it had been jeweled. I took it all in, enjoying the effect.

"The times of day when the effect is the most pronounced are midmorning and midafternoon, when the sun illuminates the front of the palace or the back," Janice explained.

"Very impressive," I said.

"Her Excellence will be pleased to hear you say so."

"One small drawback that I can perceive: one can't get there in a hurry, can one?" I asked. "You need to leave a good deal ahead of time to make an appointment, don't you?"

We were fortunate to be accompanied by an experienced guide. Janice turned this way and that through the maze, taking passages and ducking underneath garlands that I might have blundered clumsily past, missing the only means of achieving the end of the twisting path.

"I think there ought to be a maze in the Imperium compound," Jil said, laughing as her friends disappeared down narrow side corridors, only to reappear in the main path a few meters ahead, or have to backtrack completely to rejoin us.

"It would last precisely long enough for Xan to break the code on the head gardener's hedge mower," I pointed out. "Our cousin has a notoriously short attention span."

"Oh, you're not any better!"

"Did I pretend that I was?" I countered, ducking underneath a leafy bough past which Janice had just sidled. I glanced down at my viewpad, on which I was recording our route for future reference. "I say! Do you realize that the path we just described spells out words in the Uctu language?" I began to sound them out.

"Oh, show me," Jil said. She giggled. Redius, too, leaned in over my arm to read them. His jaw dropped in amusement.

"Rude," he said. "Low language. Most insulting."

"Yes," I agreed. "I believe that the architect of the maze held a grudge of some kind. I wonder whether the Autocrat who commissioned it ever paid him. It is quite cunning, hiding one's disdain in plain sight. Of course, one would only see the message if one traced the path, as I have. Did you know about this, Ambassador?"

Janice looked a bit pained.

"Yes," she admitted, beckoning us forward. "Please don't mention that to Her Excellence."

I mimed closing my mouth and locking it with a key.

"My observation is purely between you and me, madam," I promised, ducking under the branch she held out of the way for me to pass. I glanced up, and felt my own jaw drop. "Aha!"

"Aha, what?" Jil asked, following close behind.

She emerged beside me, and looked up with wonder in her eyes. The prospect that met us was one of the most beautiful buildings I had ever beheld. The tiled walls told stories in mosaic of conquests and romances, flanked, footed and topped with small images—small in proportion; I imagined they were larger than I was up close—of haloed beings, winged reptiles, marvelous serpents, colorful birds and shimmering clouds. The bronze doors had been molded to represent the undulating shapes of sand dunes.

"Aha, this," I said.

Janice could not forbear a little flourish, nor did I begrudge her the opportunity to make it.

"Welcome to the Autocrat's palace," she said.

"Hope to go in and come out again in same state," Redius said, nervously.

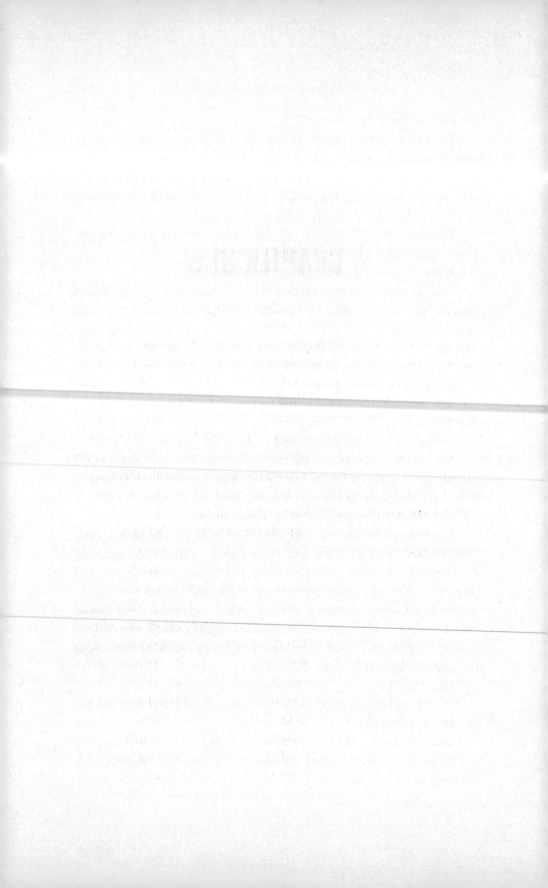

CHAPTER 31

Inside the reception hall, whose walls were more mosaics, in even more vivid colors than those outside, a group of servants in long, fluttering robes surrounded us, offering pure, clear water, slices of fruit and squares of moist, rich pink cake.

"We are honored," I said, in Uctu. I had read the Rules of Protocol, and was content to enter the palace in the steps that were prescribed. When we had consumed the Gift of Food and Drink, I brought out a handful of small gemstones that were the expected Thanks Offering in return. I poured them into the waiting palm of the chief servant, a female with pronounced jowls on her narrow mandible.

"We, too, are honored, in the Autocrat's name," she said, with a welcoming drop to her jaw for all of us but Redius. "Follow."

Every step so far had been achieved exactly as the Rules had specified. I felt as though I were on an elaborate treasure hunt. Low, arched hallways with bronze traceries inlaid with colorful enamels and lit by small hexagonal lanterns of jewel colors led in and out of enormous reception chambers, tiny sitting rooms, galleries lined with two-dimensional pictures and holograms, and intimate dens seemingly created to display exquisite works of art on pillars and stands to passersby. If not for the viewpad in my hand, I would have lost my way again and again with all the twists and turns. The chief servant glided before us. We saw no one else on our journey, but I assumed we were constantly observed by both living eyes and surveillance devices. I distinctly heard a hum as we crossed a threshold into a gallery. The detector might have been looking for weapons, or it might have been reading our body temperature and odors, or even our genetic coding, to determine who went there.

At last, the servant brought us to a grand door banded with gold. Six keyholes of ancient design pierced its surface. The Uctu female drew from a pocket of her robe a ring of six silver keys. She merely touched each one to its corresponding lock. We heard a snap as the locks withdrew. The door rolled to the left into a wall niche. The servant beckoned us to follow her.

"This is the Room of Trust," she said.

We stepped into a darkened chamber heavy with rich, musky, floral scent. The room was filled with curtains, elaborate swags and swoops of cloth, jeweled, beaded and adorned with silken cords and tassels. The servant did not pull them aside for us. Instead, she disappeared into the folds of cloth, leaving us to follow the ends of her scaly orange tail as swiftly as we might.

I plunged in after her as if we were playing follow-the-leader through my mother's well-stocked walk-in wardrobe. With my hands out in front of me, I felt blindly for the partings in the folds of cloth that would allow me passage. The fabric slid along my cheeks and hair, clinging briefly to my robe. I heard the sound of creaking hinges off to my left. I turned in that direction, but came to a set of narrow pillars. I turned back.

"Thomas, where are you?" Jil asked, somewhere behind me.

I felt to the left and right, trying to seek a meaningful path. I heard sounds all around, and felt a swift rush of air pass by my cheek from the left. Was that the way forward? I fumbled blindly, and crashed into a sharp corner face first. I rubbed my bruised nose and consulted the glowing screen of my viewpad, but it had gone blank. Something was blocking the signal. I put the device back into my belt pouch. I had to rely upon my senses alone. That wasn't going to do me any good. I sought in two or three directions, and ended up eye to eye with Nesbitt.

"Sorry, my lord," he said, pushing a swag of red velvet off my shoulder.

"Where do we go?" Jil cried, somewhere off to my right. "Ow! I tripped on something. It scraped my shin!"

"Quite a party game, isn't it?" Banitra said. She appeared at my right elbow.

"It feels like one," I said. "Though it reminds me of something a trifle more sinister."

"We have similar myths, my lord," Parsons's voice came from the gloom behind me. "Do any that you have studied recently elicit an analogue to the present situation?"

"I hate it when you ask me to think, Parsons," I said, peevishly. "It interferes with my natural intuition. Oh." I stopped, as the entirely obvious occurred to me. From our most ancient heritage, a story that had come down to me through the Melarides line popped into mind. I raised my voice. "Jil, can you get back to the doorway?"

"I think so," she said.

"If you take hold of anyone with whom you come into contact, it will save us being further separated," I said, doing my best to keep panic out of my voice. "Think of it as a mobile game of Sardines."

"I'll help you," Hopeli's voice came soothingly. "I think it's this way."

Several false starts and a good deal of giggling later, I found myself with my left arm through Nesbitt's, Banitra at my back, and Plet clinging to my right shoulder.

"Why start over, Lieutenant?" Plet asked.

"Because this is a test," I said, lightly. "The servant called it the Room of Trust. Therefore, it is a mistake to second-guess her words and seek a deeper meaning, or a more complicated route to our destination than a straight line. So let us go directly forward, and trust that that is the right way."

"That does sound too simple," Jil said. She stood in the crook of my arm, all but trembling. She had illuminated the screen of her jeweled pocket secretary for comfort. It had been a difficult day for her already. Banitra and Hopeli stayed very close to her, stroking her hair and holding her hands.

I drew my face down so that we were eye to eye.

"Trust me, cousin. If it doesn't work out, we can do it your way next."

Jil wrinkled her nose. "Oh, all right."

"Parsons, are you there?" I asked.

"Here, my lord," said that ineffable voice, not a foot from my ear. That sound gave me a measure of comfort.

"Very well," I said. "Together, now."

Keeping our backs to the door, we shuffled forward en masse

through the heavy scented hangings. Nesbitt and Redius lifted the swags to admit our passage. Each meter took a long while to progress.

After twenty meters or so, a bloodcurdling howl sounded right underneath my feet. I admit that I jumped in the air, dislodging those clinging to me. They did not notice, having had expressed surprise in their own ways.

"What was that?" Sinim demanded, throwing her arms around Plet, who had gone paler than usual.

I essayed a foot forward, until I came to a raised area in the floor no larger than the end of my thumb. Another screech issued forth. I tried it again, and was rewarded by a further ululation. Now that it was no longer a surprise, it didn't scare any of us. My friends and I exchanged a glance.

"I am going to install some of these in the walkways around the compound," I said, in delight. "Then lie in wait with my cameras at the ready. Imagine the expressions I will collect!"

"Oh, Thomas!" Jil said, punching me in the chest with a sharpened knuckle. "I was scared out of my skin!"

"Beware, cousin," I said, austerely. "I will put some where I know you walk."

"My lord," Parsons said. "Would it not be wise to return your attention to the matter at hand?"

I glanced back at him.

"And that would be?"

"The open door before you?"

I turned. The unrelenting gloom of the Room of Trust had, in fact, relented and admitted rays of golden light above and below the festooned fabrics ahead of us. I pushed through the remaining barricades of cloth and pushed open the proffered portal. The others crowded up and around me. Anstruther let out a deep sigh of wonder.

The room was like a jewel box, coffered bronze ceilings gadrooned with pleasingly elaborate designs. Tapestries hung around the walls, billowing gently as though to suggest they concealed ventilation ducts. Certainly the room was pleasantly cool, a welcome contrast to the closeness of the rooms and corridors through which we had passed. The furnishings were very elegant, much softer and welcoming than the trappings of the Imperium court and rooms of state. Shojan, my cousin, preferred an austere setting. Servants in the same uniform robes as our guide flitted here and there with metal pitchers, coffers and trays.

In the middle of a wide, rectangular, backless couch draped and canopied with elaborately embroidered cloth-of-gold sat an Uctu female. I knew her from her Infogrid page and the files I had read since then: the Autocrat Visoltia. Her head scales still had shimmering turquoise spots above her eyes, showing that she was not fully mature. She wore a heavy cloak around her shoulders that had been painted and jeweled. I observed several panes within the design, suggesting that it was a narrative frieze of some kind. Since I had clothing of that type myself, I assumed that of the Autocrat served the same purpose as mine: to tell the story of one's culture. A marvelous gold pectoral hung around her neck and shoulders. Each link contained an oval pattern of coral and blue. I realized with delight that they were portraits, possibly those of her lineal ancestors. The formal clothing seemed to swamp the Autocrat, burying her in millennia of history. She was the smallest adult Gecko that I had ever seen.

To either side of the Autocrat's settee were arrayed a number of persons, all Uctu, whose manner of dress revealed their offices and honors. A small group of young females I judged to be her ladies-in-waiting. The rest were her inner cabinet, the most trusted and important ministers. I had met a number of Uctu in my life, but never seen such a representative sampling of sizes, shapes, tint and hue of scales, length of tail or width of finger pads all at once in a single place. It was an edifying moment. Similar scales of difference were to be seen in any crowd of humans on any Imperium world.

"Greetings!" I said in my best Uctu, holding out my arms. "I am Lord Thomas Innes Loche Kinago, representative of my cousin and your brother ruler, Emperor Shojan XII of the Imperium. I come in peace. As do my friends and relations here. And Ambassador Galeckas. But you already know her."

I bowed deeply, switching the back of my robes to and fro to simulate a tail, since nature had not seen fit to furnish my kind with any for eons, and awaited an invitation to straighten.

A harsh rasp, the clearing of a throat, came from beside the Autocrat's wide couch to my left. I hazarded a glance through my eyebrows. An Uctu male, clad in traditional military formal dress, a dark green knee-length tunic over sand-colored ballooning trousers that fastened at the tops of thick-soled ankle boots, wore a glare that went well with the rasp. My studies under Parsons's tutelage had not been for naught. I recognized the disapproving male as Corvain Rimbalius, the Autocrat's Prime Minister as well as Grand Commander of the Military. In that latter office, he was my mother's opposite number in more ways than one. They had faced off in the last battle of the border war, and my mother had been the victor. The usual human nickname for the Uctu was "Geckos," but this large specimen fell into the much less employed moniker, "Dragon." If it were possible for him to breathe fire at that moment, I believe he would have snorted flames from his curled nostrils. I wished I could offer him the maternal unit's sincere messages of peace and reconciliation, but I was not to engage him either by look or voice until the Autocrat freed me to do so. The strictures rubbed irritatingly against my natural impulses, but I maintained my humble posture.

The Autocrat's voice was a sweet, thin piping, but no less steely in her words.

"You are Kinago," she said. "But you are also Loche. How dare my honored brother send an enemy as his envoy?"

I did not raise my head. Indeed, I gazed at the stone-tiled floor with the same intensity with which I would have studied the eyes of someone who was inclined to punish me for a transgression that they took more seriously than I did. But in this case, family pride drove me to eloquence.

"Your Serenity, I am indeed here as my cousin's voice, and also as my mother's son. Both of them wish to do you honor. The battles that our two peoples fought are behind us. I would hope that our enmity was left behind once Uctu and Imperium met to negotiate that permanent peace a dozen years ago. We have had a cordial trading relationship for some time now, and hope to become greater allies in the future. How more can they express their trust in you and hope for the future than by putting me into your hands? Naturally, I hope you will take the offer in a friendly fashion, because I would definitely like to return home intact, but I am at your service, in any way you require."

Her voice sounded even more taut.

"My father would have died rather than have me meet with the son of the one who was the last to defeat his armies. Peace came into being between us, though you must understand how it hurt his pride to face the necessity."

"I understand, Your Serenity. I believe that is why my mother sent me, as a gesture of good will. Those of this new generation must hold out the hand of friendship to one another. I hope you will allow me to make this gesture. Make of it what you will. Even if you take out your family's ancient frustration on me, it still won't change the import of what I have to say to you. In other words, even if you kill the messenger, the message is still a friendly one."

I heard Jil gasp behind me, but what did she expect? She had known me all our lives. Audacity was my stock in trade. Murmuring also broke out among the Uctu contingent, especially in the neighborhood of Prime Minister Rimbalius, who added growls and muttering to his throaty exhalations.

My bold sally had had one more sound effect of note: a giggle. My ears perked up hopefully. I heard a slithering of cloth and the soft pattering of slipper-clad feet on the floor, accompanied by heavy jingling noises. A small, coral-scaled face insinuated itself underneath my hood and looked up at me. The Autocrat's jaw was lowered in a smile. I peered down at her, and winked. Delighted, she extended her small hand. I enveloped it carefully in mine.

"You are so big!" she said.

"I apologize," I said, without moving either my body or my face. "I didn't mean to be big. You are just the right size, of course."

She laughed, a musical squeak like a wooden flute.

"You are most courteous," she said. "I admire your accent. You sound as though you live in my city."

"That is a great compliment," I said, deepening my bow and adding a switch of my robe's tail. "My cousin and I have busied ourselves learning your language."

Her dark eyes shone.

"I see. You do not use a device?"

"None at all," I said, with pride. "We did use devices to learn. Is that incorrect? I must confess that I am new to this diplomatic process. My cousin the emperor normally relies upon career envoys who are trained not to offend, like Ambassador Galeckas here."

Visoltia giggled again.

"You are not incorrect. So many do not attempt to speak the true language, but rely upon machines. I am pleased. You do not have to bend your back any longer before me. You may stand up."

Gratefully, I drew myself upright. My spine thanked me profusely. As I had learned to do from the files, I put my palms together, one set of fingers angling upward toward my face, the other toward hers.

"I am so glad to have pleased Your Excellence."

Her small face lit up again. For possibly the first time in my life, I realized that I was more mature than someone else. Though she ruled hundreds of star systems, she was a child.

"My friend gave us instruction," I said, beckoning my crew forward. "May I present Lieutenant Kolchut Redius?"

Very reluctantly, Redius emerged from the concealment of Nesbitt's bulk. The lids of Her Serenity's eyes peeled back, and the eyes themselves seemed to bulge outward. Her tail lashed back and forth, as did those of her ministers. They hissed low under their breath.

"What does this person do with you?" she demanded.

I had not expected such a reaction, though it looked as though Redius had, hiding himself where he would not be easily observed. I frowned.

"He is part of my crew, Your Serenity."

"He is a *nacch*," the Autocrat said. The guttural sounded uncannily nasty. "The ones who ran away. The human-sympathizers. Traitors to their system of origin. I accept you, though you are the son of our deepest enemy, but there is no reason I must look at him."

Redius's tail drooped to the floor.

"I withdraw," he said, in Imperium Standard, edging away.

"No," I said, putting my arm around his shoulders. "He is part of my retinue, my crew and my trusted friend. He is brave and honest, and has a marvelous sense of humor. I hope you will come to appreciate him as I do. We are all fans of the Autocracy's greatest export, the digitavid show *Ya!* Is it possible that you are also a devotee?"

Plet looked as though her eyes were going to bulge out of their sockets, but I was adamant. I had seen diplomats in the Emperor's court behave as imperiously over small things. If Visoltia was going to judge me, let it be by the entire picture that was Thomas Kinago. I stood with my chin up, though it made me tower high above the Autocrat.

Ambassador Galeckas bustled forward, interposing herself between my friend and the Autocrat. She positioned her hands as I had, one set of fingers pointed up at her chin, the other toward the angry ruler.

"Your Excellence, Lord Thomas has no intention to offend. It's the custom to bring all members of a distinguished visitor's party to meet you. Mr. Redius is part of the ship's crew. He is routinely assigned to the envoy's service. He is here only because they want to honor you." I could tell that that argument had been brought to bear more than once. The girl, for so I had come to think of her, stopped and glared at all of us.

"Very well," the Autocrat said, "but he will stand there." She pointed to the end of the chamber, beside the door.

"I obey my hostess," Redius said in Uctu. He marched over to the door. The very end of his tail tip switched back and forth, but otherwise he stood very still. I was determined to reform not only my family's image, but also that of one of my dearest friends. The Autocrat threw a hand gesture at him, one I had not seen before, with all fingers spread out, as if pushing air toward Redius. He cringed.

"If you will allow me," I said, though I vowed privately that would not be the end of the argument regarding Redius, "I would like to introduce the rest of my party. My cousin, Lady Jil and her friends." Jil floated forward and described an elegant curtsy. Her friends followed in her wake like fish swimming in a narrow channel then eddied outward to surround my cousin. I pronounced all the names. I presented the remaining members of my crew, trying not to feel dismay for Redius alone at the door.

The Autocrat gave one nod, acknowledging my retinue. She spread her hands to encompass those who stood beside her.

"These are my chief ministers and trusted advisors," she said. "My prime minister and also champion of defense for the Autocracy . . ."

"Lord Corvain Rimbalius, also called High Protector," I said, daring to interrupt her. "My lord, I am honored. Beside you is High Nourisher, which I think is a splendid title for the minister of agriculture. I will be sure to tell Your Excellence's Imperial brother so. Then, High Knowledge, provider of education. The others I don't know on sight."

"Good," the Autocrat said, beaming. "You have studied my cabinet."

"And many other things. I hoped it would save us some time getting to know one another. I see that a few are missing . . . ?"

"Yes. They are not always within the doors of my palace, as their duties take them far and wide across the Autocracy," Visoltia said, with a glance over her shoulder toward a smaller door at the rear of the chamber. "But I did expect Lord Toliaus to be here."

High Nourisher, a plump female with dark red skin, lowered her kindly eyes.

"High Wisdom informed me that he has another appointment, Your Excellence," she told the Autocrat. Visoltia looked dismayed, almost lost. Rimbalius's heavy brow lowered.

"It is an insult to you, Autocrat," he said, with a furious look at me. "Not so insulting as the presence of this invader's offspring." I recognized his name from my mother's annals, since he had been a minor officer who tried to undermine the peace that was being made between the Autocrat's father, the late Autocrat, and the late Empress, Shojan's predecessor.

"Lord Thomas is our guest," Visoltia said. "And Toliaus should have been here to give him the honor he deserves as a visitor."

The big male subsided immediately. "Your wishes must always take precedence, dear lady. He knows that, but he does not obey."

Visoltia shrugged her small shoulders.

"He is undoubtedly busy in our interests, High Protector."

The subtle shake of his head told me Rimbalius did not think so.

Parsons glided to my side and described a perfect bow to the Autocrat. She gave him a surprised nod of approval.

"Your Excellence, the crew has duties it needs to fulfill," he said, in flawless Uctu, far better than I would ever be capable of emitting. "If you will permit us to withdraw at this time? We will return at your pleasure."

"Oh, but Lord Thomas and his party must stay," the Autocrat said.

"As long as you like," I agreed. "And my cousin and her friends will stay, as well."

Parsons bowed again and gathered up my crew with an eye. They slipped out of the room. It seemed as though the rest of the onlookers let out a breath they had been holding.

The young female returned to her couch and hopped up on it, using her tail for leverage. Though she sat with great dignity, her sandaled feet did not touch the floor. Her ladies ran to array her robes fetchingly about her.

"May I ask, Your Excellence, for the meaning of that movement you made with your hands?" I asked. "Behind me, I hear Ms. Galeckas shifting in discomfort. I assume that means I ought to have known it, or not asked about it, but I am curious by nature."

"That?" the Autocrat asked, then giggled nervously. She glanced at her ladies. The most senior of them, who wore the air of a nanny, shook her head briefly, but Visoltia ignored the admonition. "It is naughty of me to use it. It is a lowborn sign. It means 'take your bad luck with you.'"

"Really?" I asked, intrigued. "We have many similar superstitions in our culture. Back on Old Earth, there were similar gestures of all kinds in every country and fiefdom."

"Do they keep misfortune away?" Visoltia asked.

I smiled.

"I must tell you, the reports are inconclusive. I have a theory that if one's enemy believes that it works, that is effect enough. Are you familiar with the concept of superstition?"

"Indeed I am, but what is your interest?"

"Chiefly academic," I said, "though I have been examining these concepts in a practical manner over the last few months. Superstitions are important. They have power over people. They can kill without guns or knives. Once an idea takes root in one's mind, whether or not it is a logical one, and especially if it is not, it can only be dislodged with great force. Persuasion cannot work against it. I wish to investigate them to learn what truth, if any, lies at the bottom of these beliefs. One should not throw out the . . ." I sought for a comparable term in Uctu and wished Redius had been allowed to remain, ". . . figurative baby with the bathwater. He, or she, or it, may have a morsel of nourishment for our minds, a reassurance that we have decoded a portion of this very complicated and seemingly random universe."

"Such wisdom," Visoltia said, gravely. "I noticed your garment. You must be a student of astronomy. Did you know that I, too, study the stars?"

"Yes, I read that about you on your Infogrid page," I said. "Star charts are part of my latest enthusiasm. What does Your Excellence seek among the stars?"

Her eyes were wide with sincerity.

"I seek our fate, Ambassador Thomas. How we are intertwined as those distant lights are in pictures we draw in our minds."

I approached, ignoring the grumbles of her guards and the High Protector.

"I am pleased that you should mention that, Your Excellence. Allow me to tell you about my latest enthusiasm. I study how the fates affect the psyche of those who believe in them."

"I should be delighted to hear all about it," Visoltia said, her eyes wide and eager. "I have many theories as well."

"Oh, stars, Thomas," Jil said, rolling her eyes in deep dismay. "She's one of *you*."

CHAPTER 32

In spite of the white-hot heat of the day, Skana stopped to stare open-mouthed at the castle doors. The bronzework was breathtakingly beautiful. The overwhelming fragrance of the gardens suddenly seemed proportional when considered against their setting. Fountainheads shaped like flowers spewed out streams of water from the center of each angled side wall so that visitors could trail their hands into raised pools as they walked by. Uctu guards, wearing old-fashioned padded breastplates in distinct contrast to their very modern pulse rifles, stood to either side of the doorway. Skana held up her pocket secretary to record the images. Her mind filled with exquisite plans.

"Nile, we are thinking too small. I want to rework the doorway of headquarters with enameled plaques. And gates. Wrought iron in our coat of arms on one side and the company logo on the other. I want one on the building and at the ground approach from the southwest, on the way toward Taino, high enough to be seen from skimmers."

"That'd be impressive," he said. Since money had changed hands a few days before, he had been in a great mood. He beamed at his companions. "Ladies, what do you think?"

Because he had been acting like a human being again, the women had stopped being openly terrified of him. One of them worked in cost analysis. In spite of her scanty attire, she looked every inch the accounting professional she was as she assessed the entrance.

"The enameling could be done by LAI, sir," she said. "That would cut the labor down below ten percent of the material cost. I'd put the stats into an architecture program, of course, but Bertu Corporation did a fancy façade for the fashion house on Egunzi for less than two million. For HQ, I'd go higher end, maybe four, four and a half."

"Fabulous," Skana said. "Tuk, take some images and send them back. I'd like to see if they agree with her. Keep an eye on the decorations as we go, honey," she said to the young woman. "Take a picture if you see anything really nice and unique."

"Yes, Ms. Bertu," she said.

Enstidius had put up with their dawdling, and was all but flapping his hands in impatience.

"We must go! He is not accustomed to waiting!"

"All right, all right," Skana said. "Come on, Nile."

The guards came forward briefly at the sight of several outworlders, but withdrew when they saw Enstidius. They stared straight ahead of them into the middle distance as the group passed. Skana couldn't help herself. She snapped her fingers in front of the right-hand guard's nose. He blinked.

"Hah," she said, triumphantly.

"Skana!" Nile called.

"Coming!"

The grand entrance was about fifty degrees cooler than the outside. A few grandly dressed servants stood in the center of the hall at a table that was covered with bowls of fruit, pitchers frosted with condensation, platters of sweetmeats and boxes that probably contained some other dainties.

"Well! How nice!" Skana exclaimed.

The servants glanced at Enstidius and his party but didn't move. The female Uctu who looked as though she was in charge tilted her head. A lone juvenile male picked up one of the big pitchers from the table and poured water into a trayful of thin metal cups. He served them, starting with Enstidius, then returned to his station.

"What about the rest of the goodies?" Skana asked, disappointed, though she gulped her water. The servant took her empty cup. She pointed at the bowls of fruit. "Don't we get some of those, too?"

"For Her Excellence's guests, madam," Enstidius said, a trifle embarrassed. "Come, we must go this way."

Instead of passing down the great corridor that opened out before them, their guide opened a small door that was invisible among the elegant traceries on the metal walls and beckoned to them toward a low-ceilinged passageway. With reluctance, Nile abandoned the fancy reception area and moved after Enstidius. The guards guided the two young women to follow. Skana glanced behind at Tuk, who was too tall to walk upright in the low tunnel. This was not at all how she pictured visiting the royal palace.

After a long walk in the very low, barely-lit, echoing, rounded passage that felt like passing through the palace's intestines, they emerged out from behind a swinging tapestry that smelled of hot brass and dust into a wide, airy room. A broad divan covered with gold cloth and shaded by a canopy sat in the middle of the floor. Servants in gray robes adorned with a dark blue badge over the heart stood in a knot beside the divan. Two of them waved enormous fans to stir the air.

"Is this the throne room?" Skana asked, breathlessly. Her words echoed from her pocket secretary in Uctu.

The curtains parted.

"In a manner of speaking, honored visitor," said a male voice. "I am that which keeps the Autocrat upon her throne."

Scarlet slippers touched the floor, followed by the hem of a dark blue robe that, even at the distance, Skana priced out at multiple thousands of credits. Though it was translucent, it was oversewn with cabochon gems with gold and platinum thread that rendered it into a night sky full of stars. An underrobe of pale gray added mystery as well as modesty. The male inside the cloak was impressively tall for an Uctu. She could not see his face, as the robe's hood was pulled down almost to his chin.

Enstidius went forward and gathered up a handful of the Uctu's hem to kiss.

"Lord Toliaus." He beckoned the Bertus forward. "These are our benefactors, Mr. N—"

Lord Toliaus threw back his hood, revealing a long, pouchy face and piggy eyes. His pale skin was almost pinkish instead of the light reds of most of the Uctu Skana had met. The point of his crest looked as though it had been chopped off at the top. He waved an imperious hand.

"Wait until I bespell this room against eavesdroppers!" he commanded. He pinched his thumb and forefinger together. Skana felt a compression of air that made her ears pop. Probably sound suppressors in each of the air intakes. She and Nile used the same technology at home. Was it considered magic in the Autocracy? She made a mental note to ask Tuk later. Enstidius beckoned urgently to them.

"Come and kiss his lordship's robe."

"I don't kiss anyone's robe," Nile said, folding his arms. "He can kiss my . . ."

"Nile!" Skana said, cutting him off. "Language!" She rolled her eyes. He could be *so* rude sometimes.

Lord Toliaus turned to her and fixed a baleful gaze upon her.

"What about you? Will you show me homage?"

"Nope," Skana said, refusing to be intimidated. He might be damned impressive and in charge there, but none of them were defenseless. At the worst, she could scream for the palace guard and hope the soldiers who answered the call weren't Toliaus's cronies. "I'm in the 'kiss mine' camp, too. Sorry, but we're not your subjects. We have our own nobles whom we respect. We're just visitors here."

His brow ridge lifted.

"How do you show honor to your nobles?"

Skana went to take his right hand in both of hers and shook it firmly.

"Hi. Nice to meet you."

The translator picked it up and rendered it into a burble, hissings and clickings. Toliaus spoke. The device seized his words and squeezed them into Imperium Standard, with a majestic delivery that would have been worthy of an orator.

"It is nice to meet you, too."

"Thanks," Skana said.

Toliaus waved them toward low, backless seats that faced the couch. A pair of servants in gray robes hurried forward with chased metal goblets filled with fruit juice and platters of small delicacies. The minister waved for the Bertus to indulge themselves. "If I do not seem grateful for your presence, that is a misunderstanding. Come, let us speak. Before we begin our negotiations, I wish to read your fates."

Skana felt a thrill of anticipation tickle her up and down. "You want to tell our fortunes?" she asked.

Toliaus held out a hand.

"I must know if you have truthful vibrations. What do you hold that means much to you?" he asked.

Skana decided to take him at his word. She pushed back her sleeve to reveal a heavy silver bracelet with a round dial on it. It had aged to a gunmetal patina that she wouldn't have polished off for the world.

"This is our seventeen times' great-great-grandfather's wristwatch," she said. "This timepiece goes back almost to Old Earth. One of us wears it all the time."

The summing glance again. Skana felt as if she were being stripped naked by his eyes, not that he was going to be interested in a human.

"So it is a relic of importance to both of you?"

"Yeah," Nile said.

"May I hold it?"

"Why not?" Skana said. She unfastened the clip and dangled the watch above the High Wisdom's palm. He seemed to jump with shock when it landed. He closed his eyes and hummed to himself.

At last he opened his eyes. He drew the bracelet from his palm and refastened it around Skana's arm. Her skin tingled at his touch, as if electricity passed between them. Did he really have some kind of magical powers?

"Our stars are in favorable confluence," he said. "I am pleased."

"We'd like to know more about you, too," Skana added. "What exactly is your position in court? Enstidius has been pretty cagey about you. Until five minutes ago, we had no idea who or what we were dealing with."

Toliaus inclined his head.

"He understands that a word out of place can mean death," he said. "My official title is Advisor and Teacher to Her Excellence the Autocrat Visoltia. You may call me High Wisdom. I sit in the cabinet of ministers. All authority resides in the Autocrat's hand, but I am the one who guides that hand by invoking wisdom and history. I also read the portents to see where one of her commands might take our nation of stars."

"So you're the court wizard," Nile said. "You seem to have a cushy job. Why do you need . . . our merchandise?"

The question made Toliaus throw himself up off the divan and pace feverishly around the room, barking out staccato sentences. His translated voice boomed from their translators.

"Because I have an enemy! The *Autocrat* has an enemy. She is very young, and under the influence of one who would control her. She must be protected so she can grow to wisdom. That male holds her back. He holds back all of our worlds. We, the Autocracy, must grow out from the old-fashioned customs that have prevented us from entering the current century—nay, the current millennium! I see fortunes waiting to be made, honor and glory that will benefit . . . Her Excellence." Skana noticed the hesitation. She exchanged a quick but meaningful glance with her brother. "This male prevents open trade. He puts restrictions on the movement of goods and designs that would benefit the Autocracy. He restricts wealth."

"That sounds bad," Nile agreed. "A free market needs to have the lid off so it can find its own level. That's how we do things at home."

"But you could not if you lived here," Toliaus said, wringing his long hands together dramatically. "All is held in check. All! I have listeners who read his files and correspondence, and those who challenge him. He brooks no competition, nor does he permit dissension. All must be the way he sees it. He has so little imagination that billions of our subjects, the Autocrat's subjects, live in enforced poverty. It must come to an end. Once he is not there, then the natural way of things will resume, and for that I must thank both of you. You have brought me the solution to a dire situation."

Nile nodded.

"If all that's standing in your way is one person, you'll have no problem getting rid of him, as long as he doesn't know you're coming," he said. "You're sure you have no spies in *your* camp who will inform on you?"

"None. There were two, but they are gone." The flash of hatred in the High Wisdom's dark eyes left Skana no illusion that the traitors had just left town.

"You do what you have to," she said, with a shrug. "That reminds me, did you take care of the little problems for us, the people who brought you your *solution*?"

Toliaus glared at her. She knew what that meant. It was defensiveness for having failed. She glared back at him.

"What is so hard?" she asked. "It's not like those pilots can run *away* from you. They're in jail. Once they go to trial, things will start to come out!"

"Those premises are not under my control," Toliaus said, through clenched jaws. "I have made four attempts of different kinds. They have been thwarted. I must be subtle. Disposing of witnesses can be done afterwards."

"I don't want anyone who knows what they're looking at to be able to ask questions, let alone examine the bodies," Skana said.

"It will be done! But, later, once my rival is removed. I can easily take over his station as well as my own. Then I can make sure backs are turned before testimony is heard."

"What can we do to help?" Nile asked. "We have common goals."

Toliaus frowned. He looked from the brother to the sister and back again. He seemed about to speak when a middle-aged male servant in a livery different from the rest of the High Wisdom's staff entered and bowed deeply. Toliaus flicked a finger in acknowledgement.

"Contact has been made from beyond, my lord," the servant said. Toliaus frowned.

"So soon?"

"They must return to us, master. They have to come through now."

"Very well. How many?"

"Five, sir," said the servant. "My lord, I must return to my post before I am missed."

Toliaus lifted his chin.

"Go, then. Tell them to wait my pleasure."

"I will, my lord." The servant spun on his heel and strode smoothly from the room. Toliaus stroked his flat jaw with his fingers as though deep in thought, then turned his attention back to his guests, his mood expansive once again.

"The fates move into even more benevolent conjunctions, my friends," he said. "All things will change very soon. You shall be witness to a new chapter in history!" He beckoned to the servants, who came to refill their glasses and fill their plates with more canapés and sweetmeats.

"When is it going to happen?" Skana asked, breathlessly.

"Very soon. Two days from now. Her Excellence is entertaining other visitors from the Imperium on the anniversary of her accession. At that event, attendance by all her ministers who are presently in-system is required. There will be a banquet. He will be there, with his attention on our ruler and her guests. Enstidius, my friend, that is when you will bring us two to glory."

Enstidius's mandible chattered with excitement. He sat up straight on his divan. Skana could tell he worshipped the minister.

"It will be my pleasure, High Wisdom."

"That is what we were hoping for," Skana said. "I want to watch the whole thing."

"You shall," Toliaus said grandly. "I expect a defense to be mounted, but it will be too late for my enemy."

"What's the target's name?" Nile asked.

Toliaus glanced at him.

"Better that you do not have that information, lest by movement or word you hint to him that he is in danger."

Nile shrugged.

"Have it your way. But if Enstidius misses him, I could take him down before he can organize a defense."

"He will not miss," Toliaus said. "But if he does make an attack that is only partly successful, then you will have divined at whom he is shooting."

"Fair enough." He nodded to Skana. They'd dealt in other hard situations with far less information and come out of it alive.

"There are rules of attendance, including dress," Toliaus continued. "Enstidius has the details. You will be invited formally later today. You will need to don Uctu garments for the event. We will dress in Human attire." He looked her bright green hooded gown up and down. "I like what you have on."

"It's yours," Skana said, promptly. She eyed him, measuring his shoulders in her mind. "I think it'll fit you, although it may be a little short. Just give me something to change into, and you can have it."

Toliaus dropped his jaw in a genuine smile. He snapped his fingers, and a servant ran out through a small door at the rear of the chamber. She returned shortly with a bundle in her arms and knelt before Skana. The female shook out the parcel to reveal an embroidered tunic that Skana thought must have taken a hundred hours to sew by hand.

"That for this?" she asked, in amazement. "You have to be kidding."

"I will gift you jewelry, too," Toliaus offered, looking hopeful.

"No, I mean . . . thank you," she said. "This is the most beautiful dress I have ever seen."

"This old thing?" Toliaus asked, surprised. "It is nothing special. I have had it for years. I prefer the simplicity of the garment you are giving me."

"Wow. You and I need to sit down and talk fashion when all this is over."

She slipped behind the curtains of the divan and wriggled out of the green dress. Two of the Uctu servants helped her put the embroidered tunic on. It was so long it dragged on the floor, but one of the servants tied a sash around her waist and yanked part of the dress upward so it hung over the belt. Skana smoothed the fabric, feeling the silky threads beneath her hands. So far, she was enjoying her brush with greatness.

A servant came in and handed Toliaus a hexagonal tablet. He glanced at the screen, then swept a long forefinger down its face to blank it. He dipped his head in the Bertus' direction.

"Very well. I must depart from you. Be well. Enstidius, be vigilant."

"I am, High Wisdom," the stocky Uctu assured him. He stood up and beckoned to the siblings. "Come, my friends. It is time for us to go."

"This guy's crazy," Skana said, as soon as they were on their way back to the hotel. Toliaus had not only given her jewelry, a necklace of big moonstones the size of pigeon's eggs set in gold, but he handed out more tunics and priceless goodies to Nile, Tuk, Nile's girlfriends and all of the Bertus' bodyguards. Everyone clinked when they walked.

"They pay well," Nile said, flipping a huge ruby pendant at her. "I'll be happy to keep taking their money."

Skana glanced back over her shoulder at the palace façade. She touched the privacy setting on her viewpad and heard the hum of the anti-eavesdropping tone that would foil listeners, electronic or otherwise.

"Nice place. It's not the first time we've done a walkthrough of something we knew was going to get leveled. We've got Plan B all ready to go, right?"

"Yeah," Nile said. "The self-destruct codes all have a back door we can set off if we have to. But I don't think this guy will waste the firepower on *us*. He just hates this other minister too much."

"Never assume," Skana said. "Like Mom always told us, keep the ship running and an eye on the door."

She glanced back over her shoulder toward the hulking mass of the palace.

"Enstidius, when we come back, someone is going to have to airlift me to the door. I'm not walking through this again."

Enstidius slowed down and hurried back to her side. "I will see what I can do, if Toliaus will permit. Only the Autocrat rides over the maze. The rest of us must walk."

Skana looked him square in the eye.

"Make an exception," she said. "We're the ones with the key codes, remember?"

The Uctu nodded nervously. Ignoring the blisters already bursting on her heels and small toes, Skana swung away from him and marched after Tuk.

CHAPTER 33

As the shuttle conveyed them upward, Commander Parsons kept his eyes fixed upon the ships docked at the impound station orbiting Dilawe 4. The three Uctu Customs Police kept their distance in the spacious cabin out of courtesy, not wishing to appear to be eavesdropping, which of course they were. Parsons's own small listening devices picked up the presence of "bugs" and observation lenses that the Uctu wished them to ignore. He would not mention them if they did not mention his. Donal Nirdan, of Ambassador Galeckas's staff, rode with them. Parsons knew he made this trip frequently to negotiate on behalf of Imperium merchants and other travelers.

With Lord Thomas and the others safe within the palace confines, the rest of the team was free to make an inspection of the imprisoned merchants' ships.

Lieutenant Plet had gathered her small force for an intense briefing. She had properly downloaded the protocols for dealing with evidence in an active investigation, and assured the authorities that she and the team would act within those parameters. Parsons did not need to check whether she had been thorough; she always was. He found it rather touching that she chided herself fiercely if she made an error. For all her outward maturity, there was a youthful soul that needed reassurance. Still, she was proving to be an excellent operative, and would be of great use to the Imperium for many decades to come. The others were intelligent and resourceful, each in their own way. His choices for a semi-permanent staff to support him and Lord Thomas had borne out his predictions. It was to be hoped that he could keep this team intact until his young lordship was capable of making his own decisions, though the Kinago trait of loyalty would undoubtedly compel him to keep staff whether or not they proved to be useful on an ongoing basis. Parsons was torn as to whether or not he should guide Lord Thomas to grow out of that tendency. He would have to wait and see if it got in his way in future missions.

They passed two other impounded ships before coming up on the one they wanted. The *Entertainer* was a moderate-sized trading ship, at least fifty years old, showing signs of pitting and ordinary wear.

"It stinks in here, sir," Anstruther said, waiting in the engineering section beside Parsons with her tablet ready. The engineering section, in which they stood, lay in a protected position between the living quarters and the broad, empty cargo bays. Nesbitt clambered down the ladder between the hull and the waste tank to make a full physical inspection. Plet shone a light from the access port to follow his movements.

"The ship has been unoccupied for several weeks," Parsons said. "The waste tank was opened by the authorities. It is possible that a leak remains that allows methane gas into the ship's cabin."

"No, sir, they all look intact," the large noncom said, his voice hoarse and tinny through the speaker in Anstruther's tablet. A video pickup attached to his chest followed his gloved hands as he ran them over the welds and brackets. "I don't see any breaches or welds where the hull plates were opened."

"Are there any other access ports where that fighter could have been inserted into the tank?" Plet called down to him.

"No, sir," he said. The disembodied images of his hands tapped lengths of foils stamped with holographs and embossings overlain with six-sided stickers up to a third of a meter wide. "The original seals are still in place, though they have been slit and resealed with Autocracy official labels."

"Those mean the ships are active crime scenes," Nirdan reminded them.

Plet turned to the lead inspector, a ruddy-scaled middle-aged female wearing a dark blue robe and black boots like her fellows, but she had six-sided silver badges on her cuffs.

"You were the ones who detected the contraband, weren't you?" They nodded. "Do you have any idea how that ship got into the waste tank?"

"No," said the lead investigator. "It makes us concerned that we have missed many other smuggled items."

"And you have no idea where they could have taken on such an item as a war shuttle?" Nirdan asked Anstruther.

"No, sir," she said. "No other drydock facilities report working on their ship. They could have loaded it into a cargo bay in deep space. I know there's a bunch of jockeying around out there if someone is carrying above the duty free allowance of certain goods. But that's the cargo bays, sir. The waste tanks aren't designed to be opened out there on any Imperium ship. Even if there are vacuum valves to protect the living spaces, there's still too much of a chance of a life-support rupture."

Nirdan cringed. "We've seen the results of that, too. I didn't like having to view the bodies before everything was sent back to the Core Worlds for investigation, but it was part of my job. Sublight, it took two years to fly them home."

"Couldn't have been nice for the relatives when they got there," Oskelev said.

"Out of curiosity, why *aren't* the waste tanks designed to open in deep space?" Nirdan asked. "Wouldn't it make more sense to dispose of, er, unpleasant matter elsewhere?"

"It'd require too much reverse engineering of most vessels, sir," Anstruther said. "And, no, it looks like these ships weren't altered for such a maneuver."

Nesbitt climbed up the ladder again. Redius gave him a hand getting out of the access port.

"I need a drink of water," he said. "Is life support still running?"

"Yes," Nirdan said. "We try to keep the vessels in good condition, hoping that the crews can reclaim them at some point."

The big man pushed past them into the living quarters of the ship. He returned with a beaker in his hand and a disgusted look on his face.

"What is the matter, ensign?" Parsons asked.

Nesbitt held out the cup.

"This water, sir. It tastes terrible."

Plet immediately took the cup from him.

"What's wrong with it?"

"It's brackish tasting, almost musty," Nesbitt said. "Can water go moldy?"

"It shouldn't be like that," Nirdan said, looking over Plet's shoulder into the glass.

"If the life support system is functioning, the water filtration system ought to be working, too," Plet reminded him.

Nirdan looked at his pocket secretary for a schematic of the ship. He went to a panel on the common wall with the living quarters and removed it. Rows of red lights shone above one lone and overburdened green.

"That's weird," he said. "It isn't working. Neither is the air system. None of the purification systems are operational."

"Redius, get an oxygen level," Plet instructed. The Uctu brought out his sensor and walked out of the chamber with it held aloft. The ship was not large; he returned fairly soon.

"Bad," he said. "Ten percent oxygen, twenty carbon dioxide."

Plet glanced at the scope in horror.

"Whatever they did to this ship, it would have become unlivable in practically no time," she said. "They could have died in space of carbon dioxide poisoning. No hydroponics area to absorb it, like on large ships. A couple of herbs and a tomato plant to make all the processed and stable food taste a little better, but that wouldn't do enough. They sacrificed their health to make money."

"It's impossible that they could have come this far with the systems compromised in this fashion," Parsons said. "Run a diagnostic."

Redius ran his fingertips over the touch screen. The lights went from red to green. The fans and pumps under the deck plates were already running. After a moment, the tiny points flickered, then each went back to red.

"Running, but not operating correctly."

"That means there's something we're missing," Oskelev said. "What are we not seeing?"

"If the pumps are operational, why isn't the purification system working?" Plet asked.

The timid Anstruther all but blurted out her thoughts.

"Nanites. The pumps only circulate air, water and waste. Something has gone wrong with the nanites that do the processing."

"Check on them," Plet said. "Their programming might have gone inert."

The crew scattered to several access points around the ship. Parsons monitored their inspections. He had a suspicion as to the cause of the malfunction, but did not want to prejudice their minds before they had gathered facts to support his theory. Redius, whose station was engineering, was the first to put his spatulate fingertip on the problem.

"Nanites gone," he said. "All."

Anstruther and Nesbitt returned with similar reports.

"There should have been kilos of nanites, in every system on the ship," Anstruther said, showing Plet and Parsons her tablet. "There aren't any that I can detect."

"Or me," Nesbitt said. "Even the self-healing pipes in the walls aren't self-healing any more. I found a bunch of leaks in the hygiene room. The place stinks."

"In the absence of nanites, there are undoubtedly hundreds of strains of bacteria and viruses that are growing unchecked in the systems," Plet said. "The water reservoir is probably badly contaminated now."

Nesbitt's face contorted with dismay. Sweat broke out in small beads on his forehead. He put his hand to his mouth.

"I drank some of it," he said.

"Hospital facilities at your service," the chief inspector said, kindly. "Invite for checkup. I make appointment." She lifted her hexagonal pad and made a few swipes with her fingertip.

"Thank you, inspector," Parsons said. "If you need to make use of the facilities to rid yourself of the intake, Ensign, I suggest you do so before we get back on the shuttle."

"Yes, sir," Nesbitt said. He backed out of the room, and fled.

Parsons returned his attention to the remaining crew.

"What could have removed all the nanites from a ship?" Plet asked. "Were they experimenting with some kind of program to evacuate micromachines, and it got out of hand?"

"We need to discern whether this is a specific instance, or whether the situation exists over the other ships in custody," Parsons said. "Are there any nanites left to analyze?"

"Not one, sir," Anstruther said. "It's the strangest thing I have ever seen."

Parsons turned to Plet.

"I suggest you send a message under seal to FitzGreen on Way Station 46, lieutenant," he said. "We were looking for the presence of a hostile agent, not an absence. Perhaps the nanites opened the panels of the ship on a microscopic level so that the insertion of a warship and a cache of weapons would not be visible to casual inspection, then departed from the ship so no trace could be found of their involvement. The removal of native nanites must be a side-effect. Ask him to investigate whether the trace remains of an unexpected drain of nanites. He must trust no one. These are dangerous people we are dealing with. They ruthlessly involve innocent traders as pawns to be sacrificed for the goods they are smuggling."

"You say innocent," the chief inspector said, her forehead wrinkled. "But court requires proof of means."

Parsons met her gaze with confidence he only half felt. "We will find the evidence to support our theory, madam."

"Hope you will," she said.

CHAPTER 34

I held the Autocrat's right hand in my left, as I traced the folds of pale orange skin with my right forefinger.

"This deep, straight one indicates the length of your life," I said. "It corresponds to the long curved one on the human hand." I showed her my life line.

"They are not the same shape," Visoltia said, curiously. "I have never examined a human hand so closely."

"I will show you the charts, and you may try your own interpretations on me," I promised her. "And this is your heart line. Hmm. I see sorrow in your immediate past, about halfway back in your life, and at the very beginning." I pointed out the three breaks in the shallow trough on her palm. She nodded.

"My father, two years back. My grandmother, when I was but nine summers. And my mother. I was so small I don't even remember her. But you could have learned that from my Infogrid file."

"But not this," I said, seizing upon a tiny starburst of lines immediately below her third finger. "This marking is believed to indicate that you are devoted to those you make your friends. You are true to them no matter what."

"But you have that same mark," Visoltia said, pointing to a place on my upturned hand.

"Ah, but in human parlance, that is known as the Mystic Cross," I said, raising my eyebrows impressively. "The ancient texts say that those with it have an open door to the infinite. Oh, and look at the lines on the side of your hand. In a human palm, I would say that meant you were going to have three children. The Uctu texts indicate that you have three severe trials of trust in your lifetime. Your other hand says that you have already suffered two of them. I would guess from what you have told me, and what I have read about you, that those are the loss of your father and grandfather."

"You are far better than the official diviner, Lord Toliaus," she said, her eyes large and solemn. "You must be very tuned in to the rhythms of the unseen dance."

"I like to think so," I said, beaming.

"The two of you must meet and discuss the infinite while you are here," she said. "Often."

"It is a rather large subject, but I will do as Your Serenity pleases," I said.

"My turn!" Visoltia said eagerly. She reached across the bed, for indeed the enormous divan upon which we sat was her sleeping place. This was not a throne room, as I had previously divined, but the State Bedroom. We had been introduced to her at the Second Levee, following Her Serenity's habitual nap during the hottest part of the afternoon.

The vast room had been abandoned by all but a few servants and my party. Rimbalius had departed with open reluctance, but he had left behind two guards, who stood a couple of meters off the edge of the bed, their hands on the butts of their weapons. They looked very uncomfortable to be present at a party of the informal level to which it had devolved. So too were Ambassador Galeckas and her assistant. The Autocrat's nursemaid had beckoned them to join her at a polite remove so we could speak to them, but they could not easily overhear our private conversation.

For our part, I was very comfortable. I sat in the half-lotus position with the skirts of my robes around me. Jil and her ladies lounged on their sides around us, a couple paying attention to, even participating in, the festivities; the rest, including Jil, not. Our shoes were on the floor beside the bed. As a courtesy, one of the Autocrat's ladies had furnished her with Visoltia's smallest jewel box to fossick through for fun. Jil and Marquessa had spent the last hour or so trying on earrings, bracelets and necklaces. It seemed that the Uctu did not go in much for crowns or diadems, having already a crest of tiny, reddish scales that would have served well as a regal headpiece. Nor, lacking external ears, did they have a tradition of earrings.

One of the ladies anticipated her mistress's needs and met the outstretched hand with a small bundle knotted into a gold silk handkerchief.

"I am surprised that all of you made it through the Room of Trust alive," Visoltia said pleasantly, rooting through the bundle. "So many groups have lost a member out of panic."

"Er, what happens to the ones who are lost?" Hopeli asked, trembling with understandable nervousness.

The Autocrat looked at her with a sad smile.

"I do not wish to mar this pleasant moment," she said. "Those who are lost are doomed to perish. I am so glad that all of you were able to pass within. I have not enjoyed the presence of strangers so much in a long time."

"Perish?" The girl's voice trembled as she realized all of us had had a lucky escape.

"Is it your tradition to kill off visitors before you have even met them?" I asked, keeping my tone light.

"Only the ones whom the fates decree are not worthy of meeting me."

"Good heavens," I said. "That would shave a few hours off those long, dull welcoming ceremonies at home. I can see my cousins taking bets on the outcome."

"It does not happen always," the Autocrat said, with a simple upturning of her hand. "Once you know the secret, it is easy to enter. Perhaps too easy. But it is a tradition. No one who was here before is allowed to tell newcomers, in case they have bad intentions. The fates sort out those who mean me ill."

I changed the subject with a deep clearing of my throat.

"I have many matters to bring to your attention from your brother my cousin," I said.

Visoltia shook the bundle at me.

"Later. Don't you want to know your prospects of love?"

"With an Uctu maiden?" I asked, as she removed several small objects from the silken handkerchief. That gave Visoltia another fit of the giggles.

"No! Unless that is what the fates decree."

I was content for the moment to occupy myself learning her customs, as I felt they would give me greater insight into the Autocrat's way of thinking. Visoltia touched one amulet after another to the back of my hand. Each was formed as an animal from somewhere in the Autocracy. Few bore a resemblance to Imperium creatures. Each charm was made of a different substance in a rainbow of colors.

"What are you trying to determine?" I asked, watching her with interest.

"If any of these match the texture of your skin, it tells me what kind of mate you seek," she said. "Do you wish for a strong love, or a gentle one? Do you seek your equal, or would you prefer to serve or master? Will the one who is right for you come as a surprise, or is it one on whom you have had your eye?"

"At the moment, I am too busy for love," I protested, but she continued to try each object against my skin.

"Perhaps you are," Visoltia said, putting the last charm back into the silk bag. "I have exhausted the fetishes, and found none that are precisely like you."

"That's Thomas all over," Jil said, amused. "He is exhausting." The other ladies tittered once I explained the joke in Imperium Standard.

"That is not the correct word?" she asked me. "Lord Thomas!"

I brought my attention back to her.

"Your mind wanders," Visoltia said, reproachfully.

"I beg your pardon," I said. "I was trying to clear it, and it went off on its own to admire your lovely curtains."

"No, all of the time," she said, studying me with a wisdom that belied her youth. "Your mind is restless. It is the sign of a seeker. I knew you were the one to speak with me. You must stay as long as you can. It will be of great benefit to the Imperium and the Autocracy if you remain here. We shall be friends forever."

"I do hope we will," I said. "Our peoples are such near neighbors. With that in mind, Your Serenity, what is the reason for keeping our ships from crossing . . . ?"

"You are so well-versed in the occult arts," Visoltia said. "What do you use to tell the future?"

I could tell that I was going to have to work the questions I needed to ask into context, but I was also pleased to discuss my enthusiasm.

"My favorite means of attempting to read the future is with a crystal ball, Your Serenity. It is quite a beauty, clear rock crystal and a perfect sphere, but Parsons, my aide-de-camp, whom you met—the tall, austere one—removed it from my luggage. Perhaps I should have seen that coming in the globe itself," I added, with what I thought was admirable self-deprecation.

"Never fear, Thomas," Visoltia said, with a winsome smile. "I have one." She clapped her hands. A lithe female Uctu glided forward. She wore a gown that was a simplified version of her mistress's. I assumed that meant she was a favorite.

"Tcocna, fetch the Eye of Wisdom."

"I say!" I exclaimed. "You've named your crystal? I must come up with a title for mine."

"It is a tradition here to give all things of importance to you a name," she said.

I mused upon that. Symbolism in the Autocracy was of the same level of importance that it was to the Imperium. I had seen that mentioned in the histories that Parsons had forwarded to me.

"How delightful," I said. "I think I will adopt the custom." Visoltia looked pleased.

"Will you name your cameras, too, Thomas?" Jil asked.

I waved a hand dismissively. "No, no. They are only tools. I rarely go on lengthy photo shoots any longer. I save my attention for the contemplation of the infinite."

"You have the attention span of a housefly, Thomas."

"That is quite a compliment," I said.

"Oh, dear, Thomas, all this involvement in the occult is warping your brain."

"Not at all," I countered. "Unless you have come across less involved houseflies than I have. All the ones that torment me are fixed absolutely on gaining access to the food or drink that I am determined to keep away from them. Therefore, a compliment."

Jil rolled her eyes. The other ladies laughed, most likely at me, but Banitra's dancing eyes told me she was with me. I was glad to have at least *one* ally, however perilous.

Shortly, a piping fanfare erupted outside the audience room. The Autocrat sat upright on her cushion, her blue spots brightening.

"The Eye of Wisdom arrives."

The servant returned, her hands held flat to shield the sides of her eyes. Behind her, two male Uctu brought a litter into the room. On top of it was a draped bulge of a silhouette not unlike in size to that of my crystal ball, which I was determined that moment therefrom to name The Orb of Clarity. Behind them came a pair of robed Uctu playing a small metal drum and a fife. The young males approached the Autocrat and set the litter down before her on the bed. They withdrew, licking the center of their top lips to show that they were dying of curiosity and would prefer to have remained. The door closed behind them.

"Very impressive," I said. "Our emperor's possessions never enter the room with a musical escort."

"The Eye requires due ceremony," Visoltia said in all seriousness. She hesitated, then drew the cloth away. We gasped.

The sphere thus revealed was not a clear crystal like mine. Instead, it was a globe of swirled purple and red, rutilated with hair-thin rods of bright gold. Light shot off it in all directions.

The Autocrat peered up at me, almost shyly.

"What do you think?"

"That is one of the most beautiful things I have ever beheld, Your Serenity," I said. "You made a spectacular choice of scrying globes."

"It chose me," she said. "Of a hundred spheres in the Chamber of Eyes, it called to me."

"Are they all called eyes?" Jil asked, looking faintly sick.

"Always," the Autocrat said. She beckoned to my cousin. "Sit down with me, Jilsin. Let me read your fate."

"I'm not sure if there is anything left to read," Jil said, without moving. "Thomas has been keeping me abreast of my stars and fortunes all the way here from Keinolt."

"Jil, don't say no. Think of the opportunity!" I said.

She kept her back turned toward me. I saw a priceless chance to allow her to bond with the Autocrat slipping away, but I was clearly not the right person to urge her to relent. Fortunately, Banitra caught my frantic gesturing and rose to the occasion and to her knees. She put an arm around Jil and urged her forward.

"My lady, what an honor! I wish that Her Excellence would see fit to offer me her wisdom. Please, let her do it. I would love to hear what she has to say!"

The Autocrat looked so hopeful that the other companions added their clamor. Since there is nothing in the universe Jil craved more than being the center of attention, she allowed herself to be persuaded. With a show of the deepest reluctance, which I did not believe in for a moment, she swung her legs around and sat facing the Autocrat and her glowing orb.

I studied Visoltia as she put the tips of her fingers together, then spread them out along the top of the ball. She hummed low to herself as she stroked the crystal's surface and turned the ball this way and that. Speckles of light were cast upon everything nearby as the rutilations caught the light. A tiny ray lanced out from its interior and lit a spot on Jil's collarbone.

"That is most interesting," Visoltia said, an unconscious echo of what I had said. "It says that your fate still lurks. It has yet to catch up with you. You must be careful and humble."

"Well, that's not likely to happen," I quipped, and was rewarded with a smack in the upper arm from the back of my cousin's hand. I could see that Jil was slightly shaken.

"Could any of this be real?" she asked.

"Fortunetelling reaches into one's psychological makeup," I said. "If anything she or I have ever said to you seems to ring true, then it might be useful to you to keep it in mind."

"That is very good advice," Visoltia said. "Now if you were born under the sign of the Jellyfish, I would expect to see that in the first house of your birth chart. They are haunted by specters of their past lives," she explained to me. "What sign are you?"

"The Wolf," I replied.

"The Wolf? That is not a real sign!"

"It is at home. We have entirely different interpretations of the constellations we see in the Imperium. We have only twelve, whereas you have seventeen." I reached for my viewpad. "Allow me to share the texts I use with you. You can do a comparison at your leisure, but I will construct charts for you using both systems."

Visoltia bounced up and down with pleasure. "Oh, do! I wish to know everything that I can learn. It will help me to make better decisions for my people."

Tcocna came forward with a bejeweled hexagonal tablet and touched it to mine. I transferred all my astrological books as well as my historical palmistry charts.

A servant in a humble gray robe entered the room. He did not approach the divan, but veered off to the side and spoke to the motherly female Uctu who sat chatting with Janice. With difficulty, the old female rose and tottered over to us.

"My child," she said. "May I speak?"

Visoltia regarded her with deep affection.

"Always, dear Ema. These humans are my new friends. Thomasin, she is the one who has cared for me since I was tiny. She holds my heart, as I hers."

"Ah, your nursemaid," I said, with a bow. "We have similar beloved caretakers. I am honored, Ema."

The old one beamed at me with open mouth. "You are much nicer than we had been made to expect." I bowed. "My child, the High Wisdom wishes to speak to you."

Visoltia straightened up and curled her tail against her legs. She looked nervous.

"Of course. Admit him at once."

The High Wisdom must have been waiting with his ear to the door, because no sooner had permission been granted, then the arched portal slammed open.

In strode a most impressive figure. Taller by a couple of handspans than most of the Uctus, the Advisor and Teacher to Her Excellence the Autocrat Visoltia, Sisnir Toliaus had pale skin and a high forehead. His long, slight person was clad in a long, lightweight hooded robe of dark blue upon which were spangled enough gems to fill a treasure chest.

"Look, Thomas," Jil said, highly entertained. "It would seem that he received the memo today."

It did rather look like my fortune-teller's robe. Alas, Lord Toliaus was not amused by my choice of dress. He approached with the baleful countenance of an onrushing thunderstorm and looked me up and down.

"Well," I said, pleasantly. "Can there be anything more embarrassing than coming to a party and discovering someone else is wearing the same thing? Lord Toliaus, I am pleased to make your acquaintance."

The advisor remembered suddenly that there were others in the room.

"Nice to meet you," he said stiffly. I knew he felt nothing of the sort, but we were all there to be diplomatic to one another. He turned away, and I was forgotten. He thrust a round tablet into her hand. “Your Excellence, I must counsel you at this time.”

Visoltia pushed it back.

“But I am entertaining guests, Lord Toliaus,” she said.

“*Now*, high one.” He stretched a clawlike hand toward the ceiling. The movement would strike awe into a suggestible soul. I did my best to memorize it so I could reproduce it when I was telling fortunes at my next party. “The stars tell me I must. I require your approval for these permissions. The matter concerns the well-being of your subjects.”

Visoltia frowned at him. She glanced at the tablet. Its screen was full of closely printed text.

“I have already given permission for such outreach from selected scholars from other nations.”

“This permission admits citizens of the Kail to come within the Autocracy for conference with my councillors.”

“Oh.” Visoltia thumbed the screen and handed it back. “You were not here to greet our guests. Where were you when they arrived?”

“I was divining information of importance to you, celestial one,” he said, smoothly. His words wiped the irritation from Visoltia’s face. She sat up even straighter.

“Yes, Lord Toliaus?”

“The number of grace for today is five.”

Visoltia went very still. I felt that if I touched her arm, she would shatter into pieces.

“There has not been a number of grace for several days,” she said, her voice strained.

“Yes, high one, but the stars are right.”

“I understand. Thank you.”

Toliaus bowed, swept his skirts around, and stalked out of the room as abruptly as he had come. Visoltia beckoned urgently to Tcocna, who opened a pair of doors set flush in the enameled walls. Behind them were stacks of drawers. Tcocna counted down five, and took a box from that one. She brought it to Visoltia. The Autocrat took therefrom a heavy gold necklace with five oval gems in it, and exchanged her tablet for a pentagonal device. Tcocna took away the ones she had discarded and put them away in a different cabinet.

Visoltia looked around at us.

"I am so sorry to say this, but two of you must leave," she said. "It is a Day of Grace, and the number is five. I may only have five guests now, and the Ambassador must remain, as I hope Thomasin and Jilsin will. I hope you understand."

Banitra and Sinim exchanged glances.

"I will leave," said Banitra. "Marquessa promised to show me a shop that she has a connection with. I want some of those brooches for my mother and aunts."

"I didn't . . ." Marquessa began, then responded to a desperate look from me behind the Autocrat's back. "Yes, of course. It should be cool enough to wander the shopping district by now. Thank you so much for your hospitality, Your Excellence."

"We are greatly honored," Banitra added.

Visoltia put her palms together. "Thank you. I hope to welcome you back another day. Tcocna, show them out. And summon Lord Rimbalius. He must know this as well."

"Yes, Your Serenity," the servant said.

"I say," I asked. "What does that grim old lad Lord Toliaus do for you?"

Visoltia smiled nervously. "He is my teacher, my sage. Through him and his research, I am learning eternal truths and how to know what is best for my people."

"So today's important number is five, eh?" I said, hoping to break the Autocrat's fit of nerves. My curiosity was definitely piqued. I had never encountered in my readings the custom that I had just witnessed, but if it was only practiced in the highest office of the system, then it was unlikely to be revealed in guide books or general historical texts. I had never seen anything about it on *Ya!*, in spite of the many plot lines that concerned its fictional royal family. I hoped that I could persuade Visoltia to discuss it with me later. "It may interest Your Excellence to know that the number five in numerology of distant human history is considered a lucky number, indicating both adventure and uncertainty. A vibration of five shows a restless spirit, but it is an important number."

Visoltia gave me a nervous smile.

"It is not as lucky for us, but luckier than four. Can you read my numbers as well?"

"Certainly," I said, once again employing my handy viewpad. "Tell me all of the names you use customarily, and I will combine them with your birth date to give you your most favorable numbers."

She began to reel off a string of forenames and given names. I took them down as quickly as I could, but the gray-clad servant scurried in again, interrupting us.

"Lord Rimbalius," Ema said. I could tell immediately she liked him a good deal more than Toliaus.

The big male entered with more ceremony and courtesy than his predecessor. If he was outraged to have humans enjoying the Autocrat's levee, he did not say so. But I rose to be introduced to him.

"My lord, we met briefly earlier. I am Lord Thomas. I—"

"I know who you are," he said, five degrees off a snarl.

"Lord Rimbalius!" Visoltia exclaimed.

"Yes, Your Excellence," he said, putting his grudge aside, albeit unwillingly. "How may I serve?"

"You may have five today," Visoltia said, as though conferring a great favor. Rimbalius looked dismayed.

"Five! But there are surely more than thirty."

"Five, and five alone! I will not have unlucky configurations."

Rimbalius sighed deeply. "Very well, my lady. Five. Have you given any further thought to the list of technological goods that the Kail wish to offer in trade to us?"

"Yes, yes, we will discuss them, but later, please. In the meanwhile, I have guests. You may go."

"Yes, Your Excellence."

Very reluctantly, he departed. I admit I was relieved to have him go, though I felt a twinge of sympathy. The Autocracy needed to keep functioning, and we were getting in its way.

At that moment, my viewpad screen erupted silently, revealing that Parsons had sent me a message, reminding me that I also had duties to fulfill. I realized how long we had spent with the Autocrat.

"Your Excellence, we have taken up too much of your time," I said, rising. I put out a hand to help Jil off the divan. "It has been a great pleasure, but if your life is anything like that of your esteemed brother our cousin, the rest of your ministers have been hanging about outside the door, wondering desperately when your visitors were going to leave. So, if you will please allow us to depart, we would be very grateful."

The girl's sweet face seemed pulled down by grief.

"Oh, I hate to have you go," she said, touching each of us on the hand. "It has been such a happy and enlightening day. Come back again. Come tomorrow! We have much to discuss."

I bowed deeply and swept my skirts back and forth.

"I look forward to it, madam."

"You and I are cousins!" she declared. "Call me Visoltiara."

"And I am pleased to be Thomasin to you," I said, with a bow.

"And call me Jilsin," Jil said. "I never have nicknames. I like that one."

Visoltia beamed. "That is most kind. We will be good friends."

"It would be an honor to our family and the Imperium," I said. Ambassador Galeckas pulled herself to her feet and met us at the door.

"That was a success," she whispered, as we followed a servant through the swathes of cloth in the Room of Trust. "She never keeps guests this long."

"I am at her disposal as long as we are here."

"You'll be sorry," Janice said, with a sly grin. "She'll call you day and night if she likes you."

"It's a small price to pay for peace," I replied. "In the meanwhile, I need to return to the Raffles to change clothes. I have an appointment to keep."

CHAPTER 35

"Coppers," said the chief guard's voice. "Visitors."

M'Kenna stared at the two tall, well-dressed men standing at the cell door with Allisjonil. They looked like a couple of characters out of a digitavid, completely different from her normal life, and especially the life she and her family had lived over the last several weeks. Their clothes were so elegant and nice, she could tell that they must have cost thousands of credits. Not that the garments were showy, or anything, but the fabric almost gleamed with quality, and they fit the men wearing them like second skins. She scrambled up from the bench, the tablet from which she had been reading completely forgotten in her hand. Rafe was at her side in a second, smoothing his hair down with nervous fingers. The two boys peered around the edge of their doorway to stare at the unfamiliar sight.

"May we come in?" asked the taller of the two, an ascetic-looking man with dark hair and eyes that seemed that they could see through her body and into her soul. But it was the younger of the two who attracted her attention. Once she focused on him, she could hardly keep her eyes off him. Something about him just fed her spirit. She couldn't have explained it, but she felt better just by looking at him.

"Ms. Copper?" he asked, his tone gentle.

M'Kenna snapped out of her reverie.

"You're Thomas. I mean, Lord Thomas."

He smiled, and her heart melted in a way it hadn't since the birth of their last child. There was just something about him . . . but she put it down to his being related to the emperor. She had never thought she would meet any noble. Space merchants tended to band together in raucous bars or other hangouts in stations or port cities, no place that the nobility would ever see. But this one just didn't act like there was anything strange about entering a cell or shaking hands with her. He was touching her hand! She thought she would faint right there.

"That's right," Lord Thomas was saying. *Be in the moment*, she chided herself. She tried to focus on his eyes. They were a pretty kind of greeny blue, almost the same as Rafe's left eye. "I am very glad to meet you, Ms. Copper."

"Sorry," she said. "I haven't seen anyone except the guards and our lawyer since all this started. It's strange to see you in the flesh, instead of a tri-dee video or a still frame. We looked you up."

He threw back his head and laughed. The warm and genuine sound made tears sting her eyes. She hadn't laughed like that since before they were stuck on Way Station 46. How dare he be happy when she was so worried!

"I would have wagered you did," he said. "And did you like the vid of me at the end of the skimmer race?"

M'Kenna gave him the same kind of look she would have given Lerin for destroying something out of carelessness.

"Not exactly. You wrecked something, and you were laughing about it."

But Lord Thomas seemed unaware of her disapproval. He squatted down between Lerin and Akela, his eyes at their level. "Hello, young men. My name is Thomas."

Akela went shy in the presence of strangers, as M'Kenna knew he would, and put his finger in his mouth. Lerin had better manners.

"Hi."

Lord Thomas put out a very long hand and shook Lerin's solemnly.

"I am honored to make your acquaintance. I hope we will get to know one another better."

"How long have you been here on Dilawe?" M'Kenna demanded.

"Scarcely a day," Thomas said, rising to meet her eyes.

"And this is the soonest you came to see us?" M'Kenna asked, impatiently, poking him in the chest with her forefinger. Allisjonil clicked his tongue and she stopped prodding. "We've been waiting forever! You couldn't just come here and talk to us right away? You don't know what it's like, being stuck here! We need to get out of this place! It's not good for our kids, or us." The buildup of chlorine finally got to her lungs. She stopped to cough.

The young man dipped his head apologetically.

"I am sorry to have made you wait. There are protocols to be observed. I am not in my own purview here. The Autocrat commanded our presence, and I needed to visit her. All I do is as a guest, no more. I can make no demands, only requests. I try to be as persuasive as I can, but it takes time."

M'Kenna waved away his apology. She was ashamed of herself for blurting out everything that was in her head.

"Yes, I knew that. Sorry. I'm just frustrated as hell being in here."

"I understand. But I want to assure you that I have thought about you all the time since you first wrote to me. I had no idea how difficult things were for you in here."

"I get that. But you wrote back. I want to thank you for that. It kept me from going crazy. Nobody we sent messages to even seemed to care about what was happening here."

"Well, I had no idea how bad it was. In fact, until I was informed of the situation, I did not know how many of you had been incarcerated." Lord Thomas tilted his head sideways and peered at her curiously. "You're the only one who sought out help. Tirelessly, from my understanding."

"Well, wouldn't you?" M'Kenna asked, furiously. "You know we're on trial for our lives, right?"

The young man's face went blank. "I beg your pardon?"

"This is a death penalty offense we're accused of! And we're innocent, but they might kill us anyhow."

"By heaven," Lord Thomas said, his eyes widening. "I had no idea there were such things as death penalties left in the galaxy for anything but identity theft."

"Well, there are! Didn't you listen to the laws they broadcast over and over as you enter Dilawe and Partwe systems?"

"To tell the truth, I turned it off," he admitted sheepishly. "It was rather dull, and endlessly repetitive."

"Well, *you* probably have diplomatic immunity, so probably none of those apply to you anyway."

Lord Thomas's face brightened. "I probably do. I never thought about it."

The taller man at his shoulder nodded his head very slightly. "That is so, my lord. You have full diplomatic privileges."

"Well, that must be good for something."

"For *you*," M'Kenna said, feeling herself getting angry, no matter how appealing her visitor was. "We have four children, and they're included in the indictment, even the baby!"

"I read that in your message," Lord Thomas said. He looked honestly concerned and angry. "They can't execute children. In fact, they should not even be threatening to execute you."

M'Kenna felt tears starting in her eyes. She was determined not to cry in front of him, but he really had come to see them, after such a long time when no one would listen to them or believe what she was saying.

"They can execute us, and they're sure trying. You know that they really are trying to kill us? Someone broke in here once. They almost got us then. Since then, we've been sleeping in shifts. I saw the guy again—it was an Uctu. And I wasn't hallucinating!"

"You mentioned that in your message," Lord Thomas said. "Tell me all. I'm curious as to why the first instance wasn't investigated more thoroughly."

"No evidence," Allisjonil said, shifting from foot to foot behind him. "The time-coded video didn't show any of the incident at all."

"Such things can be falsified," the taller man intoned. "It is not difficult."

"Yes, but no one is interested in checking how that could have been done," M'Kenna argued. "That orange bulb I found—!"

Lord Thomas made a calming gesture with one hand.

"Tell me everything that happened. Start at the beginning. I'd like to hear it all, just as you experienced it."

She closed her eyes to concentrate. It was getting harder every day. She didn't want Rafe or the kids to know, but her memory was going bad because the chlorine buildup was really getting to her. She had to make lists for herself on the tablet to remind her what to do every day. Lucky for her, the first attack was burned in her memory, better than those of happier times.

"I was reading on this tablet," she said, realizing that she had forgotten she was still holding it. "I noticed some movement in the kids' room. They were all sleeping. . . ."

Her mouth felt as though it belonged to someone else as it scrolled out details of the attack, how she had prevented the Uctu from touching her elder daughter. Listening to herself talk, she was surprised how heroic she sounded at taking on the assailant. Rafe added a few details to her description of running to tackle the Uctu and having the cell door slam in their faces.

"That's it," M'Kenna said, turning her hands up. "Guard Captain Oren took us into his office and ran the vids, but none of the video pickups caught the Uctu anywhere. And they said the wall he ran into was solid. It can't be. We saw him go through it!"

Lord Thomas listened intently, making a note to himself on his viewpad.

"Do you think the attack has anything to do with the cargo you smuggled into the Autocracy?" he asked.

"I don't know," M'Kenna said, throwing up her hands. She was so exhausted that even having someone care didn't seem to help much. "We *didn't* know it was there. We didn't smuggle anything! Neither did the others. I know them. They just don't do that. We're not getting rich on our cargoes, but we get by."

"Forgive me," he said, the planes of his handsome face turned down in apology. "I should have said 'allegedly' and 'brought inadvertently.'"

The tears returned to her eyes. "There isn't any *allegedly*. We didn't do anything. That's what I keep telling everyone, and no one listened!"

Lord Thomas's arms flapped for a moment, then he gathered her to his chest in an awkward hug. M'Kenna held herself stiffly, then let her body collapse. He patted her on the shoulder.

"We are listening, I promise you," he said, his breath stirring her hair. "I will do what I can for you and your family."

"And the others," Rafe put in, his voice hoarse. He sounded like that when he felt shy.

"Of course," Lord Thomas said, exuberantly. M'Kenna extricated herself nervously from his grasp. She couldn't believe he had hugged her. She felt strangely honored. "But I consider you my especial charges. You may continue to message me at any time. Let me give you the direct code for this viewpad. As long as I am within orbit, you will reach me easily. I'll do anything I can for you."

He picked her tablet up from the bunk and touched the small device to it. A rectangular contact icon appeared, filled with numbers and characters and a friendly three-dimensional image of his face, then shrank into the corner with the rest of her accumulated addresses.

"Where are we?" M'Kenna asked, suddenly. This man might tell her what no one else would. Allisjonil never talked about anything but their case. Lord Thomas's fair brows went up.

"Specifically, legally or physically?"

"Physically," she said. "They knocked us out to bring us here."

Instead of answering immediately, Lord Thomas looked back at the taller man, whom he had not introduced.

"That's rather rude, isn't it?"

"It is a matter of safety, my lord," the other man intoned.

Lord Thomas turned back to her as though he needed no other explanation. She wondered exactly who or what the other man was.

"Are you familiar with Memepocotel?" Lord Thomas asked. He said it perfectly, like an Uctu.

"We've been here a couple of times."

He smiled. "I envy you. This is my first time in the Autocracy. Well, if you know where the Autocrat's palace sits in the south central part of the city, this place is about forty minutes by flitter to the northwest. We are in the foothills of a mountain range, just inside the curve of a river with nice rapids. Back home those would be full of my cousins on watercraft."

"Hem!" The taller man cleared his throat.

"But I digress," Lord Thomas said, with a disarming smile. "Forgive me. I am a little nervous. This is only my second assignment as a diplomatic attaché, and there are so many mistakes I am capable of making! But, the confines of this prison are largely underground. On approach, I spotted the bald, gray egg of a dome protruding among the beige rocks. This was our destination. I spotted a smallish town on the south bank, which I assume is where the service personnel live. We set down inside a security cage woven of wire filaments. My guess is that they are electrified. Doubtless, there are many other protective features that are hidden from the naked eye. Apart from this corridor, all I have seen was an office occupied by a worried bureaucrat, and a host of brave-looking guards and some servicebots roaming the confines. Does that set the scene for you?"

"It's a thousand times more than we knew before," M'Kenna said gratefully. "Thanks. That really helps. You don't know what it's like, feeling like you're sealed inside a rock. It's horrible for all of us, but mostly for my kids. All of them were born in space. This is the longest any of us have been groundbound. I just want to get back on our ship. Can you get us out of here, even for a while?"

Lord Thomas's handsome eyes were sad.

"I am afraid not. Can I help you with legal representation?"

"I've got that under control, your lordship," Allisjonil said, shifting back and forth. "Everyone on this corridor is my client."

"Good to know."

"Look, you haven't asked it," M'Kenna blurted out, "but I'll tell you straight: none of us smuggled anything, especially not weapons. All we want is the truth to come out."

"We'll find it," Lord Thomas said. "My crew is astonishingly accomplished at discovering things no one expects them to find. We have already been gathering up information in other locations, but since your shipments were eventually meant to reach Dilawe, here is where we expect to find our answers. I will report back to you as often as I can."

M'Kenna's heart sank.

"So we can't get out until then?"

"I'm sorry. I am afraid not. I will do everything I can for you, I promise. And trust Parsons," he added, with a glimpse back at the other man. "He knows how to get things done. I have a pretty high opinion of myself, but a higher one of him."

M'Kenna glanced at the other man. He must be really something, if Lord Thomas thought that highly of him. She nodded.

"Thanks."

"Is there anything else I can do for you?" he asked. "Anything I can bring you?"

"I don't know. We just miss the little things. I mean, the food here is all right, but it's not our food, if you know what I mean. And they never bring the kids candy or snacks. The kids are being really good about this whole situation. I wish I could make it more normal for them. Not that anything around here is normal. It's kind of nice to have company."

Another glance at the dark-eyed man. "Well, I can spend a little more time with you, if you wish. Ask me anything. I'll tell you what I know. I'd like to get to know you better. How do you obtain your cargo? Who are your favorite distributors?"

Just like that, he led them into discussing shipping routes with Rafe, talked what sold best where with M'Kenna, all the while sitting on the floor with the little ones. He paid Nona outrageous compliments on her beautiful eyes and hair, and let Dorna crawl into his lap. Even from where she sat on her bunk, she could tell Dorna needed a change, but Lord Thomas didn't say anything.

"And what do you think your parents would like to have? Do they have favorite foods? I mean, your stay here is temporary, of course."

"Fruit jellies," Nona said, promptly. At once, M'Kenna felt her mouth water, craving that tart sweetness. It had been months since she had tasted any. "And Daddy likes champagne artichokes."

"Um, so do I," Lord Thomas said, his eyes dancing. "And what about the rest of you?"

"We're going to die," Lerin said solemnly. "We don't have to have anything."

Akela gasped and burst into tears.

"No!" he sobbed.

Lord Thomas picked the little boy up and put him on his other knee beside Dorna. He shook his head.

"Now, I can prove that's not true." He reached into the pocket of his beautiful jacket and took out a deck of old-fashioned playing cards tied with a ribbon. "Have you ever had your fortune told? No? Well, I am honored to be the first. Will you help me shuffle the cards?"

Carefully, patiently, the nobleman showed her elder son how to hold the halves of the deck in each hand and flip the edges together. M'Kenna found herself holding her breath. Lerin, uncharacteristically calm with a stranger, looked up at the tall man and smiled.

"You are very good at this," Lord Thomas said. After a few tries, Lerin managed a rough shuffle. Eager for his turn, Akela seized the deck but dropped all of them on the floor. Putting out his lower lip, he looked at Lord Thomas to see if he was getting a scolding.

"Now, you're just going for the easy option," Lord Thomas said, with a laugh. "Watch." He turned all the cards face down and mixed them together with both hands. "Now, gather them up."

The boys picked up the cards and handed them to him. He shuffled them once with a mighty *snap!* like a poker hustler, and fanned them out in the air. Akela laughed, his fright momentarily forgotten. Lord Thomas gathered the deck together, then dealt three cards in a line face up.

"Now, you see here? We have the queen of hearts, the six of clubs and the ace of diamonds. Help, wisdom and truth. There is not one bad card here. If I had dealt the nine of spades, that might mean death. But these are all good cards."

"You hid some of them!" Lerin insisted. Thomas held up his hands, protesting innocence.

"You can count them. There are 52." Lerin boldly went through Thomas's pouches and pockets, but came up empty. He sat back on the floor, his arms folded mulishly. M'Kenna wanted to laugh at him. Lord Thomas tied up the cards in their ribbon and gave the deck to him. "Here, take these. You can try it yourself. This is the chart showing what each of them means." He showed them his viewpad. Lerin scrambled up and ran for the children's tablet. Lord Thomas transferred the file and gave it back. He studied the other three children with a serious expression. "Hmmm. Now, I can't just give Lerin a gift. I owe all the rest of you present."

"Pwesent," Dorna piped up, her brown eyes shining. She hadn't followed most of what had just happened, but that word always got her attention. "I want present. Got me one?"

"Yes! I hope you like these."

From his pockets, Lord Thomas came out with a small cuddly unicorn-bear, a model of an Uctu carnival ship for Akela, and a box of face paints for Nona. Dorna leaped upon hers and cuddled it fiercely. Nona accepted the last with nervous excitement. All of her makeup was still on the ship, and she missed it. M'Kenna did, too. She almost wished Lord Thomas had given her one, too. She noticed that all of the items were marked with the Hotel Raffles logo. He must have picked them up in the gift shop on his way to see them. She was grateful to him for even thinking of bringing the children gifts.

"Say thank you," she chided them.

"Thank you," the children chorused obediently.

"Thank you, sir," Rafe added. "That was really nice of you."

"You may not know it, but I am an experienced uncle," Lord

Thomas said. He dislodged the two small children from his lap and rose to his feet.

"I can tell," M'Kenna said. "You know kids." She hesitated. "You're not the complete idiot we thought you were, sir. My lord, I mean. No offense, but what we saw on the vid, well, it worried us a lot." She tilted her head toward Rafe, who shrugged his shoulders in apology.

"Oh, appearances can be deceiving," Lord Thomas said, with a self-deprecating smile, as the three of them watched the children enjoying their presents. "I am an idiot but in ways that you cannot imagine. But I do try, really, I do. I must go now. You don't know it, but it's the middle of the night outside."

M'Kenna rose to her feet.

"Thank you for coming. I really appreciate it. It gives me some confidence that we can get through this mess."

"I am sure you will, you know. You are strong." Lord Thomas cocked his head and looked thoughtful. "You know what you need? You need a talisman against the loss of hope." He took a tiny device from another pocket. Bright colors twinkled from the miniature lights studded on gold wires. "This is my lucky circuit. I will send you one."

Nobles had weird ways. M'Kenna held up the tablet.

"You gave me your direct number, and you promised to get us out of here. That's as much of a talisman as we need for now."

"Oh, you'll like them," Lord Thomas said. "They'll help cheer up this dreary temporary domicile of yours. I'll send it along with those fruit jellies."

M'Kenna felt abashed. The children shouldn't have said anything.

"You don't have to get us anything. But, maybe, will you come back? That would help more than any sweets or little lights."

"I will come back," Lord Thomas promised.

A siren sounded in the corridor. Captain Oren appeared at the door. The guards chivvied the guests out of the cell, but Lord Thomas looked back at her and winked. M'Kenna cherished the warm feeling for as long as she could.

CHAPTER 36

"What more can I do for them, Parsons?" I asked, as we flew away from the prison complex. "They have touched my heart, especially the children. They are in a terrible fix." The compartment of the transport shuttle was large enough that we sat at one end of the cabin, well out of earshot of the other passengers returning to the capital, including the large, white-furred attorney, Mr. Allisjonil, as well as Ms. Metcalf from Ambassador Galeckas's office, who had been my escort from the city. "Every one of them professes their innocence. I cannot help but believe them. The Coppers were convincing, but it was the outrage of the Wichus that really make me believe that they have been used in some dastardly fashion."

Parsons had no more outward expression than usual, but I felt that he had been moved by the sight of all of those decent people locked up in cells smaller than my walk-in wardrobe.

"It is distressing, my lord. All the more because the evidence is mounting that they are innocent."

My heart, which had been heavy throughout my visit to that depressing place, lifted up and sang.

"You are certain?" I asked. "You were a trifle late meeting me at the prison, so I hoped there would be news." I put my chin in my palm and looked up at him in expectation. "By the crackling energy around you, it must be good. Let me hear it."

"I must confess, it merely added to the mystery," Parsons said. "Far from finding a solution, we have a new enigma."

"Tell me all!"

He hesitated a moment, then brought out the dull gray cube. I felt the air seal around us like an arm thrown reassuringly over my shoulders. Parsons closed his hand upon it.

"I do not wish to jump to a conclusion I cannot support, sir, but it would seem there was extensive tampering to the vessels of all of the accused. All of the nanites that run the purification systems on board each ship have vanished. To have one ship so swept clean could be explained by a programming error, but to have all in the same condition suggests an underlying cause. My tardiness came because we wished to reinspect each ship to make certain we had not missed any pockets of nanomachines. They are indeed all void."

"What do you make of that? How does that connect with the weaponry found in the waste tanks?"

"At present all we have are theories. It is possible that the nanomachines worked on a molecular level to open the tanks, hold back the contents, make it possible for the contraband to be introduced, then reseal the tanks to look exactly as they did before. Nanites have been used for microsurgery and many other actions that require absolute precision. Then the nanites were evacuated from the ships, so no one could determine how the trick was done."

"Those nanites would also have had to interfere with the cameras watching the landing bays," I pointed out. "No one saw anything. As Ms. Copper just explained to us, someone or something is tampering with video pickups to conceal their nefarious deeds."

"Indeed, sir. It was a most complex plot to place those items into the ships and must have included compromising the cameras. However, in this case, a trace was indeed left. The process seems to have taken *all* the nanomachines from the ships, not just the ones involved in the subterfuge. The smugglers caused the ships to gradually cease to function. In fact, two of them would not have made it all the way to Dilawe from Partwe without loss of life. It is a good thing that the ships were intercepted upon arrival in the Autocracy, or several people would have died."

I gulped.

"That's very odd. Surely the crews would have noticed the air was getting bad."

"It is possible that the change was so gradual that it had not yet come to their attention, sir. Most of these ships are very old. The crews would be accustomed to odors and noises. But I fear none of them would have survived a return trip to the Imperium in that state, sir," Parsons concluded. "Therefore, I must assume that they were unaware of the deficiency. None of them seems to be suicidal, not in previous examinations, nor in the opinion of the Uctu court service, nor my own observations just now. Otherwise, having accomplished the delivery of the illicit goods, they would complete the job and take their own lives. All the merchants that we visited this evening are eager to survive."

"But negative evidence is not evidence," I said, drumming my fingertips upon my cheek. "You can use it to speak to their state of mind in court, but naturally, we don't want it to go that far, and it might be misinterpreted by an Uctu magistrate. How infinitely frustrating." Still, I felt the stirrings of hope. "Are any of these pilots capable of visiting this odd plague on the others? Could one be responsible for all of them?"

"It would seem not, sir. It would require an advanced knowledge of engineering and resources that appear to be out of reach of simple merchant spacers. While several of them have degrees and experience in many fields, I saw no biographical history that suggested any of the prisoners are responsible. If one is working with the culprit, we have yet to determine that. I must also stress that opportunity to introduce the programming could not have been done in advance of arrival on Way Station 46, and the responsible party would not know if they would reach the station before all of the others. The insertion must have happened there."

I brought my fist down and pounded upon my knee.

"Then who is responsible?"

Parsons made the merest suggestion of a head-shake.

"That I do not yet know."

"How was the hostile programming introduced?"

"I do not know that yet, either."

"Well, I shall design circuits for all of them. One to a cell, I think, except for the Copper children. I think they would like one each, don't you?"

Parsons nodded austerely.

"Yes, indeed, sir. Once you have designed them, you may send the schematics to the repair facility that is attached to the impound station. I am certain they would enjoy the change from the day-to-day maintenance on ships and station. I have spoken to one of the fabricators, and they are in danger of job burnout, sir. You would be doing them a service by giving them a task that may be seen as pleasurable."

I beamed at him.

"By heaven, what a grand idea. What is the name of your connection? I will send my designs to him or her."

"Why not give me the file, my lord? In your name, I will be able to coax a more rapid response from the workshop than even if you were to ask yourself. I must go there in any case, to accompany the crew on further investigation of the impounded ships. I will also see to it that they are delivered with your compliments, along with whatever other goods you see fit to gift them."

"Comets, that's a good notion," I said. I worked while I talked. "You take another burden off my shoulders, Parsons. You always do. But don't forget the fruit jellies. I want Ms. Copper to have those as soon as possible. She has been a rock for those children. I think it's a great pity that she has been too frightened to undergo the habilitation therapy. Whatever cleared the nanites out of her ship has taken them from all the merchants as well. That is another reason that the magistrate must find them innocent."

"We will have to learn the protocol for providing gifts to those under detention, my lord."

I glanced across the cabin and caught Ms. Metcalf's eye. Like any good diplomat, she read my intent to converse. She rose from her place and made her way to us. Parsons subtly returned his small device to his pocket. Both of us stood to receive her. I took her hand cordially.

"Ms. Metcalf, I wish to thank you again for aiding me in visiting the prisoners. I warn you that I will want to go back again in a day or so. My responsibilities to them will not be discharged until I see them all set free."

"Of course, sir," she said. I offered her a cushion on my couch, and she settled onto it. Once she was seated, Parsons and I resumed our perches. "It's natural for you to take an interest in them. Unfortunately, we have to accede to local laws and customs. The trial is scheduled for three days from now, the day after the accession feast."

"Then I will be there," I declared. "They're innocent. If I may testify as a friend of the court, I will. In the meantime, I would like to provide them with some small gifts, some home comforts that they might have been missing." I brought out my viewpad. "For example, Captain Nuro of *Sword Snacks IV* has not had any beer since his arrest."

"We can't give them beer," Ms. Metcalf said, openly horrified.

"Why not?" I asked. "What harm can it do?"

"Well, it makes them noisy," she said.

"They're Wichus," I said, reasonably. "They are already noisy. Ms. Metcalf, these citizens of the Imperium are under threat for their lives. A little leavening of the mood will go a long way toward helping them to be in the best possible state of mind when they must go to court. I know that my emotions would be in turmoil, and at worst, madam, this may be the last beer they are able to enjoy."

I knew I was cruel to employ such dire emotional tactics, but it worked. Her face went still, but I was accustomed to trying to read the concealed screen that was Parsons. I could see the wheels turning in her mind as though her thoughts were printed in large type on her face.

"Very well, sir," she said at length. "If you will arrange the gifts, I will make certain that the prisoners will receive them."

I seized her hand and shook it with great vigor.

"You are most kind, Ms. Metcalf."

She retrieved her fingers.

"It's nothing, my lord. We wish to render you any service we can." She rose, and we with her. "I must send an inquiry to the Bureau of Corrections to learn how to bring in such presents. Let me get back to you."

"You have my connection," I said.

She went halfway up the ship, to an empty seat, and began to speak urgently into her pocket secretary. Parsons and I resumed our places.

"How did you progress with Her Excellence?" Parsons asked.

"Oh, we are going to be very good friends," I said. "We talked of countless matters, cabbages and kings, and whatnot."

"Did you inquire as to the reason for limiting ships coming into the Autocracy?"

"No," I said. "She was rather resistant to answering any questions of import, but perhaps in time. My hours were not wasted, though. My heaven, I had no idea as to the smouldering resentment that still exists within the Autocracy for the Imperium. The memory of the last battles still persists. And she has only been on the throne two years. Shojan still seems a bit raw around the feelings, and he has reigned in the Imperium for twelve years already. The friendlier I can persuade the Autocrat that we are, the better it will be in the long run for relations between our two peoples."

"That is a most penetrating insight, my lord," Parsons said, and I could not find a trace of irony or sarcasm in his tone. "But what of the matters at hand? The sooner that the embargo can be lifted, the better. And the well-being of those whom you have taken under your wing is in jeopardy."

I sighed.

"I will continue to try to ask Visoltia, in between reading her stars and the lumps on her head. But, Parsons, I feel that my answers will not come from her, at least not directly. As you are undoubtedly aware, the person with the greatest power is often not the one whose title is the most grandiose or lofty, but a more humble toiler. In that person, you will find the one who actually Gets Things Done." I did my best to make the capital letters audible.

"Her secretary?" Parsons asked.

"No." I fetched a deep and regretful sigh. "The very angry gentleman whom I recognize as being my mother's opponent in the last space war."

"Yes, the High Protector. I recall him from years past. He looks remarkably unchanged."

My eyebrows rose upon my forehead.

"Were you aboard my mother's ship in that final battle?" I asked. "I don't remember her telling me that."

"No, sir. But I was involved."

"I will bet that you were," I said, glancing out of the window of the shuttle as the sound of the hover engines changed from a smooth hum to a meaningful rattle. "But I will await the unfolding of that story on another day. I see the landing pad of the Raffles ahead of us."

CHAPTER 37

As Janice had foretold, the Autocrat did indeed command my time at her first available opportunity. I felt a gentle tap on my shoulder before the sun had actually risen. Excelsis was there, with a warming cup of tea in his mechanical grasp.

"Her Serenity wishes you to breakfast with her," he said. "The shower bath is running, at your preferred temperature. I have laid out the amber-colored suit, as the shade is one that she likes. The ambassador will be by in thirty minutes to pick you up. Do you prefer I shave you, or will you depilate your own face?"

At that unwholesome hour, even the sight of the nearly-empty streets in the more forgiving light of false dawn was not enough to wake up my poor, sleep-starved brain. I covered a wide yawn with one hand.

"I do beg your pardon," I said, with a half bow to Janice at my side. The skimmer that conveyed us toward the palace flew by means of a robotic pilot. She accompanied me out of courtesy.

"No problem. We get these calls all the time."

"I had better limber up my legs, if we are to spend forty minutes walking the maze."

"You don't have to worry about that," Janice said, with a grin. "We're going in the back way."

"There is a back way in?" I asked, knowing that I blinked stupidly at the notion.

"Of course there is," she said.

As if to underscore her assertion, the skimmer banked to the right, foregoing the avenue upon which we had walked the day before. Instead, it circled over humbler quarters and touched down in a garden that was as far from the playground of the idle as it was possible to get. Instead, Uctu gleaners in rough cloth smocks were digging roots and plucking bulbous fruit from the rows of food plants and trees. We touched down near a huge unadorned doorway. The stone step before it had been worn U-shaped over the ages.

I pulled myself from the air car and offered a hand to Janice.

"Why didn't we go this way the first time?"

A twinkle lit the blue eyes behind the protective spectacles.

"Because everyone has to go in the front way the first time. You have to pass through the Room of Trust. But the servants would never get to work if they all had to go through the maze every morning. It was tried during the days of the Eighth Autocrat, when the maze was first constructed. Since then, well . . ."

"The person who first saw reason regarding subsequent visits has my eternal gratitude," I said. I followed her into the building, and found ourselves in the kitchens.

We entered through the small door at the rear of the great chamber. Several ministers and servants clustered around the enormous divan with tablets and viewpads. The Autocrat, almost doll-sized in their midst, tapped a screen here, scrolled down a list there. The clamor was polite but insistent. As I knew from my occasional visit to my cousin's office, the stream of matters demanding input was never-ending. Rimbalius was among them, but no amount of effort on my part could cause him to make eye contact with me.

"Thomasin!" Visoltia said. She set down the tablet she was reading and held out both hands to me. I approached and put my palms together. "Oh, don't do that. We are friends now." I took her hands. She squeezed them, her jaw dropping with pleasure. She patted the divan beside her. I removed my boots and hopped up. Janice retired to the corner with Ema and Tcocna. "I hope you are ready for breakfast, because I am *so* hungry!"

A gray-clad female set footed trays across our laps, and set up waist-high mobile trays at easy reach to the advisors around us. Mechanical servers brought in covered dishes. Each was offered to her first, then to me as the guest. I took small portions of each one. Everything was delicious. Not sure what most of it was, but when my hostess ate it, I felt obliged to do the same. I know the ministers were watching me, especially High Nourisher, who looked pleased when I praised the flavor and quality of the food.

Visoltia pushed aside a bowl now empty of slivers of sweet yellow fruit, and pulled a dish containing a white, quivering substance like an egg-white omelette onto her tray. The mechanical server brought me an identical dish.

"Tell me my fortune for today, Thomasin," she said.

The plate before me provided me with the ideal field.

"Do you eat that unadorned, or with a sauce of some kind?" I inquired, indicating hers with the fork in my hand.

She gave me an odd look, and gestured to the line of small, clear glass bottles at the top of the tray waiting like soldiers to do her bidding. She picked up one that contained purple liquid.

"I can use any of these, but this is my favorite."

"Very well," I said. "I have invented a divination of my own, called condimentomancy. Put the purple sauce onto your food as you would normally do."

She followed my instructions. Having had a good deal of experience with Imperium-born Uctu aboard the *Bonchance*, I was ready with interpretations I thought that I could tweak to fit the physiology. But she made it easy for me. Two lines of evenly-sized purple curlicues spanned the omelette from bottom left to top right, touching the plate on either edge of the food.

"You're fair and methodical," I said. "I believe you have confidence in your surroundings, if not yourself. It would seem to me that you should continue to think so."

"That is wonderful!" Visoltia—Visoltiara—said. "I will keep that in mind today." She cut the white substance into small squares, careful to have a bit of the purple sauce on each.

The ministers around her seemed to breathe a sigh of relief at my words and her reception of them. I soon understood why.

We were on the fourteenth course of breakfast when a gray-clad servant came to announce the arrival of Lord Toliaus. The High Wisdom burst in, clad in bright gold, a gleaming ball of fire in his hand.

"Your Serenity," he said, swooping down upon us. He suddenly noticed my presence, and favored me with a haughty glare. I returned it with a smile.

"How are you today, High Wisdom?" Visoltia asked, with nervous respect.

"The fates have given me another day on which to serve you, dear lady." He brandished the ball at her, making her recoil onto the base of her tail. "I have your luck and guidance for today."

"But, what a nice change," Visoltia said, indicating me. I noticed that her hand trembled slightly. "Lord Thomas has given me my luck already."

Lord Toliaus turned a full and unreserved glare on me. I emulated the absent Parsons and regarded him with a blank stare.

"How could he know what the fates hold for you? He does not understand Uctu culture. Who knows what utter nonsense he is telling you?"

"Well," I said, the coldest of cold eyes fixed upon the minister. "I know what I am saying is utter nonsense. Do you?"

The rest of the cabinet stirred silently behind him. I guessed that most of them would have liked to talk back to him, as I had, but they did not dare, all but Lord Rimbalius, who looked faintly amused. By the frightened expression on Visoltia's face, he had an unbreakable hold on her. I expect that he managed to get revenge upon those who crossed him by manipulating her.

"Please, do not argue, my friends," she pleaded.

"Of course we won't," I said, lifting the tray off my lap. "We both care deeply for your well-being, don't we?"

"I care about Her Excellence and the well-being of this entire nation," Toliaus intoned. He thrust the flaming ball toward us again. "The state of business will be precarious today and for the foreseeable future. It is best to hold the reins tightly in your hands!"

"Yes, High Wisdom," Visoltia said. "High Finance, please give me your report now. Do you see signs of what Lord Toliaus has predicted?"

A thin-faced female with an unusually high crest on her narrow head stepped forward and gave her tablet to the Autocrat.

"As you see, Your Excellence. And the reports from High Production will show growth that might lead us to a better financial forecast, if you will permit loosening bonds on certain commodities?"

She beckoned forward a stout Uctu with almost gray-red scales. He glanced at Lord Toliaus as though requesting permission. Other ministers came forward with their tablets, pleading for attention, both from the Autocrat and Lord Toliaus.

High Wisdom wore smugness like another robe. He made certain of his power over the others before swirling his long skirts and striding out of the room. Once the door closed behind him, the entire party of ministers surged forward.

"Your Excellence!" "Your Excellence, the governor of Dneucia needs permission to undertake full infrastructure repairs on the eastern continent of Balawe Five." "Hospital supplies are low in the flood zone in Nendoma City."

She began to read tablet after tablet, all the time looking over at me. There were so many other matters awaiting her attention, and I was distracting it.

"With many thanks for an excellent meal," I said, slipping off the divan, "I must remove myself from your august company and check upon my cousin and her friends."

"Oh, don't go, Thomasin," she pleaded.

"I cannot in good conscience interfere with the sailing of the ship of state," I said. "But I will come back later."

"Join me for lunch!" Visoltia said. She glanced at Ema, who nodded vigorously. "Our food is your food."

"I am honored. May my cousin and her friends return to you? Jil so enjoyed meeting you."

"Oh, yes, yesterday was the Day of Grace, but today is ordinary. Come at noon."

"Oh, this is so much better," Jil said, stretching comfortably on the divan beside Visoltia. She and her friends had dressed to the nines and beyond in their new friend's honor. They had also brought chests and bags of their own jewels for Visoltia to try on. Jil helped the Autocrat fasten a complicated chain anklet through her round-tipped toes while we waited for the fifth course to be served. "I would have been too exhausted to eat if I had to walk the maze again! Although passing through the kitchens was much closer to food preparation than I normally get. But your garden is just drenched with light! My goodness, do you ever get enough of that marvelous sunshine? I long to bask in it."

"Truly, I don't get much time to sit out in the light," the girl said, admiring the glittering aqua-colored gems studding the gleaming gold chains around her slender legs. "I have so many duties."

"You are a darling to be so *responsible*," Jil said, "but it rots your brain to do nothing but work!"

"I don't work all day and night," Visoltia admitted, with a sly look at me. "I do watch *Ya!*, for example. Usually at night, after Ema and the other night servants put me to bed."

I clapped my hands.

"I thought you must be a fan," I said. "I am delighted to know it."

"I cannot help it," Visoltia said, her eyes full of mirth. "My ancient ancestors were the basis of the royal family," she said. "But based only. It is scandalous that today's viewers think that what they see is true history."

I leaned close, to impart the special knowledge that I possessed.

"I have recently acquired the first three seasons in a boxed set," I said, in low, thrilling tones. "The genuine article. A real collectible."

"The first three?" Visoltia almost whispered, awed. "I have never seen those!"

Jil's eyes twinkled. She knew what that usually meant, from a high official or an honored guest. I fetched a deep breath, but personal possessions were fleeting. The honor of the Imperium was forever. I placed my palms together under my chin.

"May I offer you the set, Your Serenity? It would give me great pleasure if you would accept it from me. I will find another. Allow me to send someone to our ship to retrieve it for you."

"Oh, I could not, no," Visoltia said, with a laugh. "It is too grand a present. But we must watch the episodes together, while you are here. That would be a greater gift to me."

I must admit, I emitted a deep sigh of relief. Jil laughed, knowing what was in my mind. But I took her generosity as an opportunity to broach another matter close to my heart.

"I wish you would reconsider your attitude toward my friend, Redius," I said. "He is also a devotee of *Ya!*, and he is not responsible for having grown up outside the Autocracy."

"That is his parents' sin, but it could be corrected by positive measures," Visoltia said, her small face tensing. "Will he return and swear allegiance to me?"

"I very much doubt it," I said truthfully. Her eyes were sorrowful.

"Then, I am sorry, my dear Thomasin. I cannot forgive him."

The mood had fallen to the floor and was trying to mine its way through the colorful tiles. I hastened to retrieve it. I reached into the pocket of my amber-colored jacket and brought out a small bundle.

"Your Serenity, I have brought a very special family relic of my own to share with you. One of my mother's distant ancestors was renowned for having the second sight. These are her Tarot cards."

"What is 'second sight'?"

"Natural intuition of a strong type. She was believed to be able to see the future. And to do that, she used these." I untied the cloth and displayed the contents. Visoltia looked at them in delight.

"Truly? But how pretty!"

Visoltia put the cards between her palms and closed her eyes. " These cards have been in many hands. I feel . . . personalities."

Jil peered at her, seeing if she was shamming, but I did not think the Autocrat was that accomplished at subterfuge. Her emotions were on her face for all to read.

"I believe you do," Jil said, in awe. "She's much more in tune than you are, Thomas."

"Billions are," I agreed. I admit that I was likely less sensitive than a girl for whom nuance could affect the lives of countless subjects. I had no more explanation for aura-reading as I did for psychic phenomena. "Would you like me to show you how to read them, Visoltiara? It is a most entertaining pastime."

"Oh, yes!"

It was the matter of a moment to put the interpretation manual through a translation program to render it into formal Uctu. I set my viewpad on the divan between us and showed her how to lay out that most common of interpretive readings, the Celtic Cross. I encouraged her to deal out ten cards in the traditional pattern.

The ladies gathered around us, complimenting the Autocrat on her gift for reading the symbols on each card. Not surprisingly, Uctu mythology had similar interpretations of common, everyday objects that both of our species used, such as cups and swords.

"What is this terrible one, Thomasin?" Visoltia asked, turning up the Tower card. "What a terrible and violent image!"

"Well, that is in your environment," I said. "Something is preparing to come to smash. You just need to make certain you are not caught up in it. Does that bring something to mind?"

"Like what?" the girl asked.

I shrugged wildly.

"I have no idea. It's just a picture, you know."

I caught a summing glance from Banitra and Sinim. It would be best not to appear too competent. Our journey would come to an end soon enough, and I did not want them seeing me as a strong and reliable helpmeet. I greatly preferred to have them as friends, or distant acquaintances, once we returned to Keinolt, not permanent love interests.

Jil was not fooled.

"Oh, Thomas, I am sure you have the entire manual memorized. What should Visoltiara beware of?"

I never expected her to have my best interests at heart. I sighed.

"Well, what are you fearful of losing? What would upset you if it ended?"

"The love and well-being of my people is the most important thing in my life," Visoltia said. "If it is destined that I should fail in their protection, that is the worst thing I can think of."

"The next card depicts your hopes and fears."

To my everlasting relief, she turned over the Sun.

"Marvelous!" I exclaimed.

I heard the door open behind us. Before I knew it, Lord Toliaus had appeared to loom over us. Disliking his arrogant attitude, Jil and I stared balefully at him, but he ignored our disapproval. Jil recoiled slightly when he did not retreat. She still did not quite understand our lack of influence. But Visoltia was eager to show him her new game.

"Oh, High Wisdom, look at this! Lord Thomas brought this Tarot deck for me to see. It is full of such interesting pictures that my mind is quite filled with ideas!"

He made the same hand sign that Visoltia had on our first visit, and made a great show of averting his eyes.

"Cast these from you, Autocrat!" he boomed. "Terrible things are associated with this artifact. Contact with it will bring you evil!"

"That's a bit melodramatic, don't you think?" I asked. "They are only a storytelling device. They are useful in helping to unlock one's natural intuition, of which Her Excellence seems to have a sufficiency.

She could find a great deal of wisdom in exploring her own thoughts through their assistance."

His eyes crackled with hate.

"Give them to me!" he said. "I know what you say they are for, but it is a lie. They will brainwash her! She can be harmed!"

He was doing his best to undermine my efforts to give her a tool that would aid insight. Clearly, if anyone intended to brainwash the Autocrat, it was the High Wisdom himself. I knew a fellow charlatan when I saw one. He had the Autocrat convinced that his way was the only way. That concerned me deeply. The Autocracy was our nearest neighbor and, for several years, had become our closest friend. Visoltia was so young, not only in years, but in experience. She needed a buffer between them so she could grow up, but now was not the time to fight this battle.

"If you wish me to take them from your presence, Your Serenity, I shall," I said. I rose and bowed, keeping the deck against my chest. The Autocrat put out a beseeching hand.

"Oh, don't go yet!"

"As you please, dear lady," I said. I sat down again.

"Then I will take the cards," Toliaus said, swooping down upon us. "They are too dangerous to her presence. She is the sun and stars of our nation!"

But I was not a reigning champion of tri-tennis for nothing. Before he could touch them, I snatched up the cards and held them behind me, out of his reach unless he actually jumped up on the divan with us. His hands closed on empty air.

"No, I am afraid you can't have them," I said. "But you can watch me enchant them so they will never hurt the lady."

I shuffled them before his eyes. Since she had never seen the skill before, and I was curious that such an advanced people had never created pasteboards for entertainment and gambling, it did look very impressive.

"There is no magic here! You are just flipping them around in your hands," Lord Toliaus said.

"No magic? Then what do you call . . . this?"

I took my hands away, and the deck kept dancing. The tiny devices I had added to the Tarot cards would not harm the ancient relics, and I could remove them easily later if my mother insisted.

Banitra put her hand over her mouth. Her eyes twinkled.

"That is indeed great magic," she said. She turned to the High Wisdom, whose eyes were all but starting out of his head. "Lord Thomas is known as a wizard among noble circles."

"Very pretty, Thomas," Jil said, dismissively. She had seen it time and again on the *Rodrigo*, of course.

The High Wisdom was beaten and he knew it.

"Well, you have control over them. I will trust you," he added grudgingly, "to put them where they can do no harm to the high lady."

I inclined my head a polite degree.

"Thank you."

"The High Wisdom can do wonders like that, too," Visoltia said. "Perhaps you will favor me with one at the accession feast, Lord Toliaus?"

"As Your Excellence wishes," he said. He was so angry that I would not have been surprised to see his scales leaping from his body to get away from the heat.

"I look forward to seeing what you can do," I said, my tone halfway to a sneer. He could not have missed my implication.

Gathering the skirts of his robe about him, Lord Toliaus skulked out of the room.

I was glad to see him go. I did not like him. I vowed to take him down a peg or twelve. Not only would it benefit Visoltia and the Autocracy in general, but it would feed my sense of justice. I had no idea yet how I would do it, but I vowed not to leave the planet until I had. Plans began to percolate in my mind, each one more diabolical than the previous one. I believe that I snickered out loud.

"Thomas!" Jil exclaimed.

My attention came back to the discussion just as it reached a subject that I knew well: current fashion.

"Will you help me to choose a costume for the accession feast?" Visoltia asked them in excitement. "It is my second year as Autocrat, a great celebration."

"Why would you wear human-style clothes on such an occasion?" Jil asked. "That is very important. It sounds like it ought to be all about *you*."

"Because you are my guests for the feast," Visoltia explained. "It is an old custom, to exchange one's outer shell for that of your visitors.

We remember that it is the person inside who is important, not how they look, and we will come to understand more about one another in that fashion."

"In that case, we should all go shopping together," Sinim said. "We look to you for advice on what we should choose in Uctu fashion."

"Oh, I would love to!" Visoltia said, beckoning to her servants. "Ema! Tcocna!"

The ladies appeared at her side.

"It is all arranged, my darling," Ema said, smoothing the Autocrat's gown as if she were a small child. "Flitters will await you at the palace door. They are programmed with the locations of the best shops."

They immediately began to discuss what to look for, and what colors and fabrics were appropriate.

I cleared my throat, my deeper voice cutting through the soprano twittering.

"I beg your pardon for interrupting. I wonder, Visoltiara, if you would mind if I joined you midway into the shopping expedition? I have an appointment that is to the benefit of all of us."

Visoltia nodded gravely.

"I give you my permission, but do not leave us waiting too long, Thomasin."

I dipped my head in gratitude.

"I will be there just as soon as I can."

I escorted the ladies to the palace doors and assisted them into the floating litter whose arched canopy would protect them against the fierce sun. A humbler vehicle bobbed along behind, carrying Tcocna, several more servants and containers filled with refreshments and iced beverages. The Autocrat, as was appropriate to her station, traveled in comfort as well as style.

Once they had gone, Ema showed me to a room with a looking glass, where I changed from the soft fabric of my warmly-hued suit to my naval dress uniform. I smoothed every seam and combed my hair until every strand lay in the necessary direction.

"You look terribly official," I told my reflection. "I hope you can be as effective as you look."

CHAPTER 38

Janice's aide, Donal Nirdan, had confirmed to me by message the time and place of my appointment with the High Protector. At the very moment of that designated hour, I presented myself at the bronze-bound doors in the corridor. The two Uctu soldiers, one old enough to be my father, the other with light blue spots on his face indicating his extreme youth, took my name and repeated it to an audio pickup point in the lintel. I offered them a friendly smile and a compliment on the day's weather, but apart from making certain they were pronouncing my name correctly, they returned neither to me.

I waited, my back straight and my feet at the precisely correct parallel, until the door opened to me eighteen minutes later. I stayed where I was, until I heard an impatient bark.

"Come in now!" The voice was that of Rimbalius himself.

I marched forward and stood just inside the doorway. To my surprise, the office was a private one. It was no wider than three times the length of the desk behind which Rimbalius hulked. No one else was present, not a secretary, nor any mechanicals. He looked up at me with the same glaring impatience that most senior officers employed when faced with one Thomas Kinago.

"I am very busy," Rimbalius said, waving to an unpadded bench that stood at the side of the desk. "State your business and be gone."

I slid onto the bench, keeping my eyes on him.

"Thank you for your time," I said. He lifted a lip impatiently.

"It is at the Autocrat's behest. What do you want? What matters do you wish to discuss with me that you won't with her?"

"There are several topics of importance that I have been sent by my cousin the emperor to inquire about," I said. "I have tried to bring them up to Her Excellence, but it occurred to me that I would probably get more action on the matters if I laid them at your feet. It is not lost on me, or anyone else who has had to deal with multiple layers of bureaucracy, that the person at the top of a pyramid of authority is not necessarily the one who can or will act upon a situation."

"Perhaps in your *Imperium*." He said the word as though it was a curse. "But here the Autocrat is the ultimate authority. We advise. She decides."

"May I put my concerns to you, so that you may advise her? You are accustomed to setting topics in a fashion that she will comprehend most easily."

Rimbalius almost quivered with fury. His nostrils flared in and out. "Are you insulting the Autocrat?"

"Never, sir," I said. "I have read her Infogrid file. I know that she is but seventeen summers old. If you had set *me* on the throne when I was seventeen, by my eighteenth birthday everyone in the Imperium would have been speaking Kail. I have no doubt that she is intelligent and is working as hard as she can to take on the mantle of a ruler."

"You may take your patronizing attitude and . . ." I strained to understand the phrase that followed, but considering his expression, the harsh sound of the words and the hand gesture, the context was inescapable.

Well, abject admiration and humility weren't working to break down the barriers. Where diplomacy failed, flippancy and daring sometimes succeeded.

"It is clear that you don't like me, Lord Rimbalius," I said. "I can't say I blame you. Naturally, you hold my parentage against me. You don't know me, but you faced off against my mother. She is a formidable enemy, but a truly wonderful friend. I hope one day you will come to know her. You must respect her, or you would not continue to fear that memory."

"Now you accuse me of cowardice!"

"Far from it," I said.

On impulse, I drew my sword. Instantly, a pulse pistol was in his hand. I tossed the blade into the air so that it came down blunt side against my forearms. I offered it to him, hilt first.

"What is this?" Rimbalius demanded.

"This is my sword, a yard of steel with a basket handle. It's been repaired recently, after a rather unfortunate encounter with a Solinian. It's a family heirloom, though it descends to me through the paternal line instead of the maternal. Mother still carries her own sword, of course. But I offer you my own weapon to run me through, if you think it will help the cause of peace between our two nations."

He looked tempted for a moment, then he threw the blade away from him. It clattered over the desktop and skidded across the hard floor to the wall. It would not break the steel, which had seen worse use, but I would undoubtedly have to sharpen the blade again. Rimbalius stood up and loomed over me, his hands on the desk. His knuckles flexed like bodybuilders.

"No! You are trying to trick me into starting another war."

"I am not, I assure you. I merely put myself at the greatest disadvantage, to tell you how very seriously the Imperium takes the questions they have sent me to put to you."

Rimbalius's eyes narrowed.

"Ask them. I do not promise to answer."

"Very well, then," I said. "The first concerns the merchants who are currently being held in your lockup facility on the outskirts of this city. As far as I can discern from their pleas to me and the statements of their counsel, law enforcement has not taken seriously their assertions that they are innocent of knowingly bringing contraband into the Autocracy. I am concerned that justice may not truly be done, and that they will bear the brunt of a system that, er, shoots first and asks questions later. The Imperium acknowledges that you must defend your borders, but you must also defend the rights of travelers to proceed unmolested unless proven guilty. These people have been locked up without even knowledge of where they are, let alone being free to assist in their own defense."

I was quite taken aback at the words coming out of my mouth. I had never known myself to be so eloquent. Perhaps Parsons was rubbing off on me.

Rimbalius listened, but the expression on his face did not change.

"We have no choice but to react strongly to the appearance of dangerous objects." He pounded the top of his desk with a broad fingertip. "The Imperium winks at these smugglers."

"Not at all," I said. I rose to retrieve my sword from the floor. I offered it a silent apology and placed it back on the tabletop, still with the point facing me. "Criminals must be punished for offenses of which they are convicted by a fair trial. As a private citizen I am upset that the fate for such crimes in the Autocracy is always death. I may also say that the laws put off many more importers and visitors traveling to the Autocracy than you will ever know. Because rumors spread, as rumors will, travelers fear that they can be imprisoned and condemned to death through simple inadvertence. We thought that your system of justice was as ours, based upon the presumption of innocence, but the treatment of the prisoners suggests otherwise."

Rimbalius's jowls shook with fury.

"That is not true! Our trials are thorough examinations of fact, beginning at a point of neutrality. No one is arrested without due cause. We *have* evidence. The fighter craft could not have been brought here by accident. I find it difficult to believe that the family of humans in whose ship it was found had no inkling. We must be more careful, not less. Our court proceedings are scrupulous in their intent."

"That may also be true. Publishing the transcripts of the trials in both Uctu and Imperium Standard on an Infogrid file might help facilitate the idea that the Autocracy is open to trade and will be fair to those who engage in it."

The High Protector seemed openly taken aback by the notion.

"We do welcome trade. The exchange of goods and ideas is vital to the Autocracy. You cannot say that we have not been good customers for the Imperium."

"It behooves you to battle the perception that it isn't, though. You can't help but notice that over the last several years, imports from the Imperium have tailed off to an historic low."

"Yes, I have noticed that."

"With that in mind, my imperial cousin is very troubled that you are limiting our imports still further. Soon they will fall below unsustainable levels."

"I know! But we cannot allow goods to be brought in that undercut industries that are just beginning to grow. The prices, even with shipping and transfer costs, of certain rare earths and emerging technology, are less than we can afford to make these goods. Our exports must exceed or equal the value of our imports, or we become a subject nation."

"That part is too deep for me," I admitted. "But there is a more immediate concern. At the risk of adding fuel to a fire I can already see burning, the problem is exacerbated by the bottleneck at the frontier jump points where our ships are trapped for sometimes months on end awaiting permission to enter the Autocracy," I said. "The matter is not yet well known across the Imperium, but news cannot help but trickle out, thanks to the Infogrid. The outrage will become greater. I would hate to see the relationship between our peoples suffer because of a custom we do not understand. Perhaps if you gave me an explanation of why so few ships are permitted into the Autocracy at any time, I could convey that home to my cousin, and he can assuage the critics. I am sure that there is a good reason that perhaps I will not understand, but I am not trained to deal in the greater secrets of government. You may even send it under seal, if you feel I cannot be trusted with the knowledge directly."

He glanced at me. Even though he was not of my species, I recognized the desperate vacillation by one who wished he had someone in whom he could confide. Then he realized with whom he was speaking, and shut down again. I felt sorry for him.

I brought out the cube that Parsons had lent me, and activated it. Like all Uctu, Rimbalius had incredibly keen hearing, and sensed the change.

"We cannot now be overheard, High Protector. No listening device or other pair of ears can perceive what we are saying. If they don't read lips, that is. It does not record. If you don't believe me, then I offer it to you to destroy at the end of our discussion."

His eyes widened.

"Are you a spy?"

"Not in the way you'd define one—I hope. I'm an emissary. You may or may not believe it, but my main function here is to facilitate cooperation between our two nations."

"Very well. I will take you at your word. But fear me if you are lying!"

I tapped the sword on the desk.

"I would, but I am not."

He nodded his head sharply once. His eyes fixed upon me as if he were trying to read my thoughts.

"All of the matters that you raise are at the pleasure of the Autocrat.

She has absolute power to decree her will. So it has always been. The lower houses of government can only advise, but we serve at her pleasure. The death penalties were introduced during the time of war, as a means of protecting ourselves against the black market that sprang up. You don't know what it was like, finding that you were considered vulnerable by everyone around you. And so many took advantage of us during that time that draconian laws were the only answer. The Autocrat was a changed male during the last years of his life, and would not listen to reason. When he died . . ."

He was a brave man, but even he quailed at stating the most uncomfortable of truths. I cleared my throat and pressed onward. My sword blade gleamed on the desk, as if reminding me how sharp was its point. I had a few sharp points to make myself, none less painful for not being made of steel. I offered him a grave smile, one I had cribbed from Parsons.

"I have heard, and you may chide me for speaking out of turn, I had heard that at the end of his life the late Autocrat was not in his right mind." Rimbalius glared, but he did not contradict me. "I speak as one who knows what it is like to deal with one who has been altered. My father returned from a long-ago battle a grievously changed man, and he has never recovered his wits. It has been difficult. One still loves and respects him, but it would put one in an impossible position if one had to live by his rule. Luckily, my father is retired from the world. Visoltia's father could not remove himself from office and hand rule down in order of succession, since his daughter was so very young at the time of his . . . indisposition. I expect he wanted to make a trusted ally like yourself her regent, but such things undermine the power of the throne, don't they?"

Rimbalius almost looked grateful not to have had to say anything himself. When he finally spoke, his words were tentative, as though he had to force them from the deepest recesses of his heart.

"I agree that such laws calling for death for so many infractions are wrong and outdated, but Her Serenity is afraid to change anything that her father did, no matter under what circumstances they were initiated. She seems to have taken a fancy to you, in spite of your maternal line. You have broken down her reserves and made yourself her friend. She has few in whom she confides.

"It is only in the last few months she has ordered me to constrict the number of ships entering from outside. When I dared to inquire why, she told me of her fear of spies and invaders. If a strict control is kept upon the numbers, then they will never achieve great enough strength to attempt to overthrow her."

"But you would never let that happen," I said, alarmed.

"No! Of course not! She is well protected, and her people love her. There are defenses she will never know of that can be activated at a moment's notice."

"Then," I paused to assemble my thoughts within this new language, "it is a whim of some kind? Based upon her fears?"

"It would seem so." He peered at me again. "You seem to understand such caprices."

"Whims are my stock in trade," I said. "I represent an entire subculture that is almost entirely driven by spur-of-the-moment decisions. I assure you that at the time they begin they seem to make sense to us, but if they are allowed to persist, the initial logic gets lost. Why, I could tell you of fashion trends that were started almost entirely by mistake, and it took the outcry of thousands on the Infogrid to bring them to a halt."

"These are not so simple as fashion," Rimbalius said severely.

"Lord Protector, there is nothing simple about fashion," I corrected him.

"Do not waste my time!"

I subsided at once, recalling that it had not been many minutes since he had hated me and my entire family line with an earthshaking passion. Our alliance was fragile to the point of shattering at a breath. I placed my hands together under my chin.

"I apologize, sir. I will help you in any way I may, toward our mutual benefit."

The gesture seemed to mollify him. He nodded. "If you can move the Autocrat to dismiss these fears, then you will do us all a service. She is learning, but in the meantime people suffer from her inexperience. I expect her to make mistakes. Those who see that forget that her father was the same way, and her grandfather and great-grandmother before her at her age. All must learn, then the Autocracy will prosper. But if you can teach her to take greater chances now, it will be for the better of our nation. We are still rebuilding after the punishments the Imperium visited upon us."

I blanched. I knew of the reparations that the Autocracy was forced to make, but I had no idea it had hurt them to pay.

"I'll try. Truly, I will. Thank you for your time, High Protector. I will go now." I held out my hand for my sword.

"No," said Rimbalius, and I almost saw him smile. He closed his hand on the hilt. "I will hold onto this for a time. I may take you upon your offer."

I bowed, warrior's son to warrior. "So be it. May I count upon your help in swaying the Autocrat from the way things were to the way, perhaps, that they ought to be?"

Rimbalius's eyes were wary but hopeful.

"You may." I offered him the gray cube, but he waved it away. "You might need that again. I have work to do."

"I will show myself out," I said.

I returned to the handy cubicle to change clothing and freshen myself up. I caught a glimpse of my own face in the mirror under the hook as I swung my jacket down. No visible change there. I was glad. I did not want anyone to see the weight of the matters of state that I was now carrying within me. I folded my uniform away into the carryall and hoisted it by its strap onto my shoulder.

My viewpad vibrated, indicating a live call. I thumbed the screen, expecting Parsons. I was rather proud of myself for the way that I had handled the interview with the High Protector, and looked forward to the microscopic crumb of approval with which Parsons would greet my news. Instead, Sinim's small face peered up at me from the viewpad. Her dark eyes were huge with worry.

"Oh, Thomas! Where are you?"

"I have just finished with my appointment," I said. "I will be along shortly. I am going to stop briefly at the hotel. May I bring you anything from there?"

She stuttered over her words, but finally got them out.

"Thomas, you must come here quickly! Lady Jil is terrified!"

"Terrified of what?"

"A man! She is hiding in a shop and we cannot get her out. Please come at once."

"I am on my way," I said. A man? What man?

With the floor plan on my viewpad to guide me through the labyrinthine tunnels, I strode in the direction of the kitchens, where my vehicle awaited. I negotiated a difficult series of turns and jumped down a flight of three metal stairs. A door opened, and a robed figure emerged, directly into the path of my leap. I threw myself toward the right wall as if diving for a difficult lob in tri-tennis, but my boot still impacted with the newcomer's tail.

"Ow!" bellowed the High Wisdom.

There is a nerve above the base of the tail of an Uctu that causes unbelievable pain when depressed. Normally it is protected by a five-way meld of scales, but Redius assured me that in the way of small children everywhere, every young Gecko swiftly learns how to cause his siblings or friends wholly avoidable, crippling agony. I knew from the contortions of his face that I had struck that nerve."How clumsy of me!" I babbled, catching him under the arm as he started to sag toward the floor. "I am so terribly sorry, Lord Toliaus. I was not looking where you were going. May I obtain assistance for you?"

He struck me in the face with the back of his hand. I blinked. It hurt, but nowhere near what he was suffering.

"Don't touch me! Oh! You assassin!"

"I am so very sorry," I said. My face stung. "I did not mean to injure you. How may I help?"

"Go! Get away from me! Get out! Get out of my sight!"

I liked nothing more then to absent myself from the scene of my faux pas. I remained facing him as I backed down the hallway. At the very next intersection, I turned and basely ran toward the exit. I was sorry for having assailed the High Wisdom, but my deep and secret self had longed since our first meeting to kick him in the backside because of the haughty way in which he intimidated Visoltia.

I had not thought that karma would take a hand so rapidly.

CHAPTER 39

I felt it to be a good thing that the embassy had seen fit to program the air car in which I rode, because it would have taken me hours to locate the shop that Sinim had mentioned. The canopy was only a lightproof fabric thrown like a tablecloth over the framework of the vehicle, so I had an unobstructed view of the countless shops on the brilliantly sunlit streets by which I passed, and the passersby and shoppers had an unobstructed view of me. I waved and smiled as though I was in a parade, all the time worrying what kind of trouble my cousin had managed to find in a store thousands of light years from home. I was grateful that the call had not come while I was still in delicate negotiations with the High Protector. My guess was that she had tried on something appalling, couldn't get it off again, and was too embarrassed to be seen in public. As to why she simply did not pay for it and cut it off at her leisure back at the hotel, I had no idea.

The console at the front of the car began to beep insistently. I prepared myself for landing and began to look around for the name of the shop in question.

The air car settled. I leaped out.

"Please wait for me here," I instructed it.

"As you please."

There was no need to parse the unfamiliar Uctu script on the various storefronts. The one I was looking for had to be that before which the Autocrat's canopied vehicle waited. Visoltia was inside it, conversing with a couple of small children who were leaning over the sill. Her servants were pouring bright red juice for all of them. She spotted me over their heads and beckoned to me.

"Thomasin!" she cried.

"Are you all right, Your Excellence?" I asked.

"I am fine, but I believe your cousin is in some distress."

"Where is she?" I asked.

Visoltia pointed toward the entrance.

"Still inside. She said she would not come out until you arrived."

How very odd, I thought.

Sinim jumped out of a display of furniture as I entered the shop. She seized my arm and pulled me along a shining strip of tesserated floor to the left.

"This way! She is in the fabric department."

"What happened?" I asked.

"Shhh! Don't speak so loudly. He might hear you."

"He? Who is he?"

"It is so strange," the young woman said. "We were looking at robes for the feast, going along the racks of clothing up on the second floor, when we bumped into a couple of humans who were also shopping. I thought he was going to strike Jil! Banitra stopped him. The woman pulled the man away, but Jil ran off. All of us went looking for her. Hopeli and I finally found her, but he is still here! I don't know how we are going to get her out without him seeing her."

"I will protect my cousin," I vowed. "Take me to her."

The blonde Hopeli browsed from stack to stack of colorful folds of cloth, all the time casting a wary eye upon the doorway. As soon as she saw me, she beckoned to me to join her.

"Where is she?" I whispered.

Hopeli slewed her eyes to the left. My gaze followed in their direction.

At the rear of the room was a dais, illuminated by a skylight in the ceiling. On it were mannequin forms swathed with shimmering cloth in brilliant patterns. One of them seemed unnaturally broad around the base. It quivered ever so slightly. I sidled through the department as though looking for just that excellent bargain that I could not do without, and stopped to examine the warm crimson fabric adorning the dummy just to the left.

"Jil?" I murmured.

She burst out of her cocoon and threw her arms around me.

"Thomas! Oh, Thomas, get me out of here!"

"Of course I will," I promised. "But what happened?"

"It's him!" she cried. "He is here!"

"Who?" I asked.

"Nile Bertu! The man I slapped on Sparrow Island!"

I felt as though I had been slapped, too. I drew back so I could see her face.

"He is on Memepocotel? Are you sure it was he?"

"Yes! I never expected to see him again in my life, and suddenly he bumped into me. I . . . well, he recognized me."

"Naturally," I said. "You make an indelible impression."

"Oh, Thomas!" Jil said in exasperation. "Well, he demanded an apology. I was so startled to see him that I . . ." She hesitated, her face red with shame.

"Yes?" I urged her.

"I slapped him *again*."

"Oh, Jil," I said. "And you think I am the impulsive one."

"That is because you are!"

I heard voices nearby, angry ones arguing.

"Shh!" I said. Jil grabbed my arm.

"He's coming back! What will I do? He must not find me. Oh, help me!"

"Hold still," I said, pulling her onto the dais and squaring her shoulders. "Be as motionless as a statue, as if your life depended on it."

I took a bolt of fabric from a display to my right and propped it against her legs to approximate an Uctu tail. Then I stripped the swathe of red cloth off the mannequin and wound it around her, careful to envelop her head.

I backed away again, and began to browse the sewing notions along the shelves in the wall.

Footsteps erupted behind me and chattered over the tiled floor. I used my viewpad to spy behind me. I beheld two humans and a Croctoid charging into the room. I kept my back turned to the entrance to the department. The humans were speaking Imperium Standard, arguing at the top of their lungs.

"I *saw* her come in here," the woman said.

"Where?" the man demanded. "There's only one woman in here."

They eyed Hopeli up and down.

"Miss, excuse me. Have you seen a pretty human lady in a green outfit? Long hair, a lot of jewelry?" the woman asked.

"No," Hopeli said, her face innocent. She was an admirable liar.

They looked around the room, but found no other way out. Jil stood on her dais, though I knew she longed to flee.

The Bertus glanced my way, but as I was a man in uniform, not an attractive woman wearing a few wisps of green cloth, they kept looking. Their search proving fruitless, they hurried out of the chamber.

As soon as I was certain they were gone, I unwrapped Jil's disguise. She fell into my arms, trembling. Hopeli patted her on the shoulder.

"Are you all right?" I asked. Jil brushed errant strands of hair out of her eyes.

"Yes! That was unexpectedly . . . quick-thinking of you."

Wounded, I put a hand to my chest.

"How can you say that? Am I not the reigning king of Sardines at home? Who has *never* been found in over fifteen years of playing every year at the feast of the Imperial Union? Who always has the greatest number of fellow sardines at the end of every game? Do you not remember sitting down on the couch in the Blue Parlor? There were four of us concealed in it. I was disguised as the back cushion. You never twigged at all."

"Oh, well, you needn't rub it in," Jil said crossly. The rest of her retinue came into the room. They surrounded Jil, reassuring themselves that she was all right. "But it was clever. I don't feel like shopping any longer. Take me back to the hotel," she said to the ladies. "Are you coming, too, Thomas?"

"No," I said. "I want to give that wretch a piece of my mind. How dare he demand an apology from you, then pursue you like a cat after a mouse?"

"That is a very good idea, my lady," Banitra said.

She and the others bracketed Jil like battlements about a castle keep, and hustled her outside to the Autocrat's vehicle. I caught the attention of a passing clerk.

"Have you seen a pair of humans around here?" I asked. "A man and a woman, with a Croctoid?"

"Oh, yes, sir," she said, pointing down a long corridor toward a glass door bursting with sunlight. "They asked me how to get a hire car to take them back to their hotel."

I strode as swiftly as I could and pushed my way out of the door. I was just in time to see a hovercar lift off and pass out from under the canvas awning and into the brilliant sunshine of the street. I made a note of the number and ran back to my conveyance. The Autocrat's car was gone.

"Are you in touch with a central computer?" I asked.

"Yes, sir," the vehicle said.

"I must find hire car number 871. Can you find where it is going and follow it? Please, it is a matter of importance."

"Yes, sir. It shall be done."

I hopped into the passenger compartment, and the car lifted off.

My curiosity radiated in waves like the heat bubbling off the pavement. Why would any man, in a fit of whatever desire, ever wish to come as far as this to demand an apology of my cousin? I would not cross the street if Jil had offended me, but I had been brought up with her, and we had quarreled more times than we had had hot dinners. Perhaps to a stranger the offense would rankle deeply enough to go to such lengths—but I recalled that this man was not a stranger, he was an Imperium citizen, and as such was personally inclined to affection toward the noble class. He must be extraordinary in some fashion to have retained resentful feelings regarding Jil. More logically, he ought to have had a kind of crush on her. All the same, he could have approached her in a more respectful fashion, and for that he deserved a dressing down.

My conveyance must have connected with the central traffic computer and received information, for we turned immediately right and began to follow a major thoroughfare. It was crowded with all manner of covered vehicles, most of them goods carriers. As I had noted on our first visit to the palace, most people enjoyed walking in the shade under the canvas drapes. They would certainly reach their destination sooner than I would.

"Are we close to them?" I asked the vehicle.

"They are ninety-seven meters ahead of us, sir," it replied. The information screen before me, which up until then had been airing cheerful public service digitavids about the scenes to see in

Memepocotel, changed to a heads up display of the street, with arrows indicating blips in the traffic pattern that represented me and my quarry. On my right, the hire car passed the Raffles. For a horrible moment, I thought it might stop there. Did they know where we were staying? The man had seemed surprised to encounter Jil. Or, even more terrible yet, were they resident in the same place? But no, the taxi went beyond the entrance. I hoped we might catch up before they got too much further.

To my annoyance, it negotiated a tight squeeze in between two larger vehicles and made it to the nearest intersection. It turned to the right. I waited, almost bouncing up and down with impatience, until we reached the same intersection. My body surged forward as though urging my vehicle to greater speed.

Around the corner, the neighborhood changed rapidly. From the elegant shopping district studded with expensive hotels, it became more modest, then almost run-down in character. The stone walls that had been so lovingly painted in bright pigments on the main thoroughfare were peeling here. The Uctus walking underneath the cool arcades wore fewer high-fashion items and more utilitarian garb. This must be the district where those lived who worked in the elegant shopping district.

A six-story building heaved up on my left. I read the name across its brow: the Home of Deep Welcome. Its façade bravely resisted the decay of its fellows. Carvings on the corners and the doorposts were just as beautiful as those on the palace. I suspected this area long predated the neighborhood in which I was staying. It might even have been a contemporary of Visoltia's home.

Hire car number 187 pulled away from the steps of the tall building. I all but drummed my heels on the floor until my conveyance pulled up to the entrance. I prepared to emerge, when my viewpad hummed in my pocket. I pulled it up and thumbed the screen. It was Parsons.

"Where are you, my lord? Lady Jil has just returned in a disturbed state."

"Yes, the fellow whom she assaulted on Starling Island is here. He must have followed her from the Imperium. The nerve of the man is overwhelming! I am about to alight and tell him what I think of his behavior."

The voice in my ear was as soothing as a lullaby.

"He could not have followed Lady Jil. He arrived before us, my lord. It is possible that he anticipated your plans, but the chances are greater that he has a different purpose for his presence on Nacer."

"What?" I demanded, not believing my ears. "You know Nile Bertu is here?"

Parsons's countenance might as well have been a still picture as a tri-dee transmission, so little did it move.

"Naturally. I have the records of every ship that passed through Way Station 46 up to six months before the regrettable incident on Starling Island."

"Why didn't you tell me?" I asked.

"It was not important enough to tell you, sir."

"Important?" I echoed explosively. "My cousin is terrified! I am going to demand satisfaction for her."

Parsons's voice became preternaturally calm. "Where are you, my lord? Precisely."

I sent him the coordinates from my viewpad.

"Dismal location," I added, turning the video pickup of my viewpad toward the hostelry. "We have by far the better view, and a much nicer neighborhood. Tell Plet to bring the crew here. I will summon local law enforcement!"

"You cannot, my lord."

"Why not?"

"Because as distressed Lady Jil is at his presence, he has not done anything yet to require the presence of the authorities. Do not invade the premises."

I was frustrated. My soul demanded I rush into the building and turf out the ruffian for the honor of my cousin. How dare he frighten her while she was innocently shopping?

"Then what should I do?" I demanded.

"For now, my lord, I think it would be politic to withdraw."

"But he is here, now!"

"For *now*, my lord," Parsons repeated, with emphasis. "Later, it might become useful for you to strike up an acquaintance with the Bertus. As fellow humans in a foreign locale, you may have an opportunity to befriend them. Offer to tell their fortunes, perhaps. But not at this moment, while your mind is not in a fit state."

I could not express the outrage I felt, nor the idea that I was battling through webs and swags of impenetrable obscurity that would have put the Room of Trust to shame.

"Parsons," I said, with ineffable calm that belied the turmoil underneath, "it is not lost on me that I spent some time in the *Bonchance* pokey because you asked me to tell the fortune of a crewmember whose intentions you doubted. I found that she was more harm to herself than to others, but the captain obviously did not know of your kind intent toward her, whatever that may have been. In other words, I believe that you set me up. Would it serve any purpose for me to ask you why?"

"None at all, my lord. At this time."

"As I thought. In the way of what manner of harm am I placing myself by communing with these common criminals?"

"For information and a personal connection. Does it seem reasonable to you that they have come all this way merely to interfere with your cousin? It required of us six jumps plus the combined efforts of the Imperium Navy and various resources to come here, and our mission is on the emperor's behalf."

It made sense. I ordered my car to retreat to a point out of sight of the hotel windows.

"When you put it that way, I suppose not, though a close cousin of the Emperor is a valuable prize. But all he had to do was wait for Jil to make an appearance at a public event, which she is prone to do. Jil, as they say, would attend the opening of an envelope. But what would be gained by having me lower myself to offer them a peek at the infinite?"

"This would give us a means to discern the direction of their efforts here. Your reading of them would provide valuable information. Should the opportunity avail itself, of course."

I knew my eyes shone. "When you put it that way, it is hard to refuse."

"I thought so, my lord."

"But it would seem too obvious to approach them with that offer."

"Leave that to fate, my lord."

"Fate?" I asked, astonished to hear the word from his lips. "You believe in fate?"

"I believe in inevitability. There are few humans in the city. An opportunity will surely arise when you will be thrown together. At that time you can make use of your unique talents to allow us to interview them."

"And why would we want to do that?" I asked.

"Do you recall what the crew of the *Moskowitz* said to us?"

"In great and memorable detail. Why . . . ? Ah," I said, as enlightenment dawned. "The Bertus are responsible for that unusual shipment of food concentrate that was installed in the dispensers on Way Station 46. This can't be a coincidence."

"Quite right, my lord. I believe in light of the Bertus' presence here that the sample merits further investigation. It would be illogical not to assume there is a connection."

"Shouldn't we keep a closer eye on them?"

"That matter is under control, sir. We do not have the power to investigate in this venue."

"Have you not called in the local constabulary? Is there an Uctu equivalent of Mr. Frank?"

"Not precisely, sir, but I have informed Lord Rimbalius as to the Bertus' presence. The Autocrat is not in any immediate danger that he knows of. His agents will study our dossiers upon them and any contacts that they have made while they are here. Action on *our* part requires more evidence. But you have been active as well. May I ask, how did your meetings go?"

I described the meeting with the High Protector, and the conclusions I had come to regarding that conversation.

". . . Therefore, somehow I have to convince the Autocrat to loosen up the regulations, Parsons. I believe that by making use of our shared enthusiasm I may help her to let go of her many superstitions. She is afraid, Parsons. She is so young to be a ruler. She needs a mentor, and is frightened of trusting anyone, so, I believe, she trusts everyone. I believe I can be that mentor."

A tiny wrinkle appeared on Parsons's brow, which for him meant deep concentration.

"Parsons?" I asked. "You have the air of someone who is listening to more than one conversation at the same time. Is someone else there? I can return and speak with you in person."

"No, sir. It is not that. A thought has struck me, though. I wished to inform you that the lucky circuits were well received by the prisoners . . ."

"Were they?" I felt a warm glow in my heart. "I am glad."

". . . Though not so well as the beer and other offerings."

"Well, that's to be expected," I said. "The circuits' beneficial working grows upon one. They will come to love them in time. In the meantime, beer and other more ordinary comforts will have a salutary effect. I will visit the prisoners again to ascertain other needs. But back to the Autocrat and . . . my other conversation, I believe that I can come to influence her toward what it is everyone needs."

The gimlet eye fixed upon mine.

"Do you not believe that behaving in such a manner is just as bad as what she has experienced?"

I smote my forehead in contrition.

"You are right, as always. In that case, I will use my specialized knowledge to try and help her see reality on her own. But she doesn't want to, yet."

"Few like to release the comfort of preconceived notions, my lord."

At that moment, I received a ping on my viewpad. The seal of the Autocrat herself opened in a corner of my screen.

"Will you hold a moment, Parsons? The Autocrat is summoning me."

Parsons nodded.

"Of course, sir."

I switched over to the message. The pleasant, ridged face of Ema looked up at me. She crossed her palms under her chin.

"Lord Thomas, Her Serenity requests your presence. Will you join her at the Second Levee and stay for dinner?"

"It would be my greatest honor," I said, returning the gesture. "Will I be required to change?"

"No. Please come as you are."

"I will be there as soon as my conveyance can bring me," I said. "Please give Her Serenity my compliments."

Ema dropped her jaw. "Of course."

I switched back to Parsons.

"I must go, Parsons. The Autocrat commands my presence once more."

"All else is well, sir. I will speak to you later, sir. Her Excellence must not be made to wait."

"I agree. Be seeing you." The epicene image vanished behind the disconnection graphic. I put my viewpad away.

"Very well, then," I said. "Driver, please take me to the palace. The kitchen entrance, if you please."

"Yes, sir. It shall be done."

The car lifted and smoothly moved into a gap in the traffic.

With regret, I watched the House of Deep Welcome recede over my shoulder.

CHAPTER 40

Skana heard the squeak of the window frame. She glanced up from the fruits of her shopping spread all over the broad green divan just in time to see a band of Uctus in dull brown robes and trousers leaping into the hotel suite one by one. They spotted her and strode toward her, hands out. She leaped to her feet.

"Who the hell are you?" she demanded.

When they didn't answer, Skana reached into her shoulder bag and came up with the pulse pistol she never traveled without. She let off two bolts. One took the leader right in the forehead. His face collapsed inward. The second bolt missed and burned a hole in the window frame. She rolled over the couch and came up running.

"Nile! Tuk! Invaders!"

The nearest bedroom belonged to Nile's girlfriends. She threw herself inside and slammed the heavy, white-painted paneled door. She slammed the latch down, regretting that she had had her bodyguards disable the other locks so the ladies couldn't barricade themselves in the room. The two women, wrapped in white silk bathrobes until they had to dress for dinner, looked up from their own shopping in alarm.

"Get into the bathroom," Skana ordered them. "There are intruders in the suite." They sprang up and rushed through the second doorway. She picked up the nearest pocket secretary and flicked it on. "Nile, where are you?"

There was no answer. Instead, she heard the stentorian bellow of her brother's voice in the sitting room.

"Dammit, what's the matter with you? Don't you lay a hand on me!"

The sounds of struggling were followed by a loud hissing noise. Skana started back from the door in alarm. Wisps of pale tan smoke came wafting underneath the door. She had just enough time to register its presence when her knees buckled and her mind went blank.

Her eyes flew open. It seemed as though it was only a second later, but the ceiling she was looking up at was not in the ladies' bedroom. Under her fingertips, the surface she was lying on was covered with rough, nubbly cloth. Her knees and jaw felt bruised. She sat up. Enstidius stood beside the couch. Behind him, Nile's girlfriends huddled together. A big Uctu with pumpkin-red skin and a pronounced ridge on his head menaced them with a knife as long as Skana's arm.

"What the black hole did you do to us?" she demanded.

"An emergency," the male said, helping her to swing her legs around. "You came to the attention of our enemy. We had to remove you from Memepocotel before you could be questioned."

"Why did you have to drug us?" she asked. "How about just coming to us and telling us we needed to get out of town?"

Enstidius shook his head. "No time, when the moment of our liberation is so close at hand. You might have questioned. Or argued with my emissaries. Now we are all safe."

"Safe from what?"

"From exposure." He wrung his hands together. "Oh, why did I have you come here to see? Now I have jeopardized the entire coup. Toliaus told me that it was foolish to take humans into my confidence."

"Whu—? Where—?"

Skana recognized Nile's voice and looked around for him. He was lying on a heap of cushions close to the couch on which she had woken up. She jumped down. Her bare feet landed on a sand floor. She picked her way to her brother's side.

"They took us out of the hotel, Nile," she said. Tuk was on the floor, already awake and glaring. Four Uctus stood in a circle around him with their pulse rifles aimed at him.

"Why?" Nile asked.

"Because our movements could be detected by following you," Enstidius said. "You made contact with other humans, friends of the Autocrat."

Nile looked embarrassed.

"How do you know that?"

"It was reported by the High Wisdom's spies. You were seen. Lord Toliaus has decreed. Those other humans will be present at the accession feast, so you must stay here until the power of our enemy is broken. We can't risk drawing attention. No one must know until the moment of the attack. I will make certain you can watch our triumph from the nose camera of my craft."

"You're not keeping us away from that feast," Nile said, angrily. "Especially if *she* is going to be there. I can't let anything happen to her."

"Her?" Enstidius blinked. "The Autocrat? I will spare her, of course."

"No! Lady Jil Nikhorunkorn. The lady I talked to."

"She is your loved one?"

"He wishes," Skana said, in exasperation. "I'm with him, but for a different reason. There is no way that you are keeping us away from the dinner when all hell is going to break loose. We didn't come all this distance to watch the action on digitavid."

"It's been decreed by the High Wisdom," Enstidius said. "It will be safer for all of us if no one can connect you with us. If they find us, the coup will never take place!"

"How can they?" Skana asked, reasonably. "We've never been seen with you."

"But what excuse will you give for appearing at the accession feast?"

"We're big businesspeople in the Imperium, with lots of connections. We're in town to talk trade with influential importers. We heard about the party and wrangled an invitation. How can they connect that with your patron taking out his rival?"

"Anything might create a chain of events in their mind. The High Wisdom reads the portents, and he is worried that you might tip the balance against him. We will have no second chance."

"Whatever is going through that spooky mind of his, we're on your side," Skana said. "All he wants to do is remove his rival. Obviously, the other guy is too well protected for an ordinary assassination. We provided you with the means. We're on your side."

Enstidius was clearly torn. "We are likeminded souls, you and I. You will understand that the attempt might have unforeseen effects? I do not wish you to be injured or even killed. I will do my best to avoid harming the lady, or our ruler, but I make no promises."

"Listen, my friend," Nile said, his eyes burning. "'No promises' is insufficient assurance. We are going, and your High Wisdom is going to have to deal with that."

"I am sorry. You're not. When it is over, if nothing goes wrong, we may permit you to return to your lands, with our thanks, of course. There is nothing more that you can say."

A bitter look from one of Nile's girlfriends told Skana she was thinking 'see how you like it?'

"The irony is not lost on me, ladies," she said. "I'll keep my word."

"You are so wrong if you think we're done negotiating," Nile said. He plunged his hand into his pocket. It came up empty. Skana felt for her own pocket secretary and her other electronic devices. She turned desperately to Tuk, who shook his head.

"Where are our devices?" she demanded.

"We had to leave them in the city. Your location must not be traced. We are far out in the desert, away from the city." He smiled. "I couldn't risk you activating the destruct codes, either. I knew you would be displeased."

"You must think that we were born yesterday," Skana said, folding her arms.

Enstidius blinked at her.

"You are not newborns, that I know."

Skana exploded in exasperation.

"It's an expression! Look, I'll lay it out for you. You're afraid we'd talk. We won't. But we get to see our goods in action, or there will be no coup. I can activate the destruct codes on your ships from here."

The master looked aghast. "But you have no device! There is no signal here! How could you possibly do that? You would not dare."

"Are you kidding? We imported five warships to this planet. We'll dare a hell of a lot."

"We will kill you, then you can't activate your codes," Enstidius said.

"They're set with a failsafe," Skana said. "And not the same one every time. If we don't do certain things at certain times, they'll activate, and you'll have a pile of dust. You need to get us back to our personal electronics or our ship, and you have just about two hours to do it before the first combo goes into effect. Do you think you're the first people ever to threaten us with torture or death? You amateur. You don't really know who we are, do you?"

The Uctu master vacillated, shifting from foot to foot in worry. He stared at Skana and Nile, trying to decide if they were lying or not. She gave him a smug smile, which made him even more nervous. He threw up his hands.

"Very well. You leave us no choice. I will ask the High Wisdom for his decision. You will stay here. My people will make you comfortable."

"Hurry up," Skana called as he scurried away. She sat down on the couch. Nile put his arm around her, chuckling to himself. She was heaving mad, but also shaking with reaction.

The girls came up to her.

"What?" she demanded, more sharply than she intended.

"Ma'am?" said the cost analysis specialist, her face shining with shy admiration. "Some day, I want to be just like you."

Skana patted her on the hand. "Thanks for the compliment, honey, but no, you don't."

CHAPTER 41

I returned from having breakfast with the Autocrat the next morning. I had been trying to teach her to meditate as I did, learning the skill of mindfulness. Alas, every time I got her settled and relaxed and thinking of an empty room or the sound of non-zebra hoofbeats, the High Wisdom would bully his way back into the State Bedroom with some excuse or other. He did not like what he saw as my growing influence over Visoltia. I couldn't blame him. The more independent she became, the less he would be able to frighten her into acceding to his will.

At the Second Levee the day before, he hovered at her elbow while she signed requisitions. To the annoyance of the High Nourisher, he persuaded Visoltia to divert the export of crops to a distant system and divert them to a nearer one. I would have wagered that he had some kind of financial interest in the matter, but could not even imply aloud that was what I thought.

I was accustomed to seeing courtiers maneuvering for advantage. In fact, I would have thought it strange not to see it. But he was outrageous in his behavior. If he were human, I would have said he was a man on the edge of madness. Something was going to break soon, and if I were truly in touch with the infinite, I might have seen a glimpse of what it was. He was dangerous. I worried what more he might demand of her. Visoltia was so afraid of displeasing him that she sent me home immediately after breakfast. He sensed my suspicions, and could not hide how much he disliked me.

The feeling was mutual. I was on the sharp lookout for a means of discrediting him for once and all.

I stopped in their sumptuous suite to visit with Jil's ladies, all of whom had remained behind in the hotel in solidarity with my cousin. I tapped upon the door to Jil's bedroom in the sumptuous suite.

"Go away!" came a cry from within. I turned to Banitra, who stood beside me.

"Lady Jil," she said. "It's Lord Thomas. I am looking right at him. Turn on your pocket secretary." She held up her own device and aimed the pinhole pickup in my direction. I struck a pose. "Do you see?"

"I am not coming out, Thomas," Jil said.

I decided not to make the appeal on my own behalf.

"Visoltia kept asking for you. She misses you. I hope you will not allow one arrogant human to interfere with your friendship. No one else in our entire family can claim the intimacy you have struck up—if only you don't let it fade away!"

"I can't come out!" she wailed.

"But there is so much more shopping to do," I reasoned. "You haven't bought your outfit for the feast. You can't be the only one of us who has nothing new to wear."

"I don't care. I am not going to the feast."

"Don't be silly. You love a good party. Visoltia told me that there will be a hundred courses, all exotic and delicious. And entertainment! Ten concerts, played by virtuosos from all over the Autocracy."

"Go away, Thomas. Please."

Banitra shook her head. "I will keep trying."

"Thank you," I said.

I went back to my chamber and found a message on the house system from Anstruther. I cast myself into a comfortable chair while Excelsis divested me of my boots, and summoned her up on my viewpad. There I found several messages from Plet, Anstruther and Redius. I had forgotten to turn it back on once we were finished with the meditation exercise. How unmindful of me.

"Good afternoon," I said cheerily, as Anstruther's image appeared. "How may I help?"

"Thomas," she replied, beaming. "Is Commander Parsons with you?"

"No, he isn't," I said. "He went off on a matter of his own

concern last evening. I haven't seen him since. Have you tried his own unit?"

"I did, but there is no reply. He must be off-grid somewhere. I really need to speak with him."

"You sound so excited," I said. "What is it you need to tell him? It must be good."

"It's about the merchant ships," she said, and her usually shy face took on a sly smile. "And it's funny. But I shouldn't talk about it on comm."

I sat up at once. Excelsis had clad my feet in soft-soled shoes, suitable for wearing around the hotel, but not outside. I signaled him to return to me in case I needed a change in footgear.

"Where are you?" I asked.

"In our suite. Fifth floor. Room 57."

I sprang to my feet. "I will be there in a moment."

The set of rooms assigned to my crew was on a humbler floor than my own, but palatial nonetheless. A central sitting room led off to four bedrooms and a rather grand bath. This common chamber had become an offshoot of the *Rodrigo*, since the crew had moved a good deal of useful equipment into it and laid out stations that approximated their own specialties.

"I knew it had to be a fantastic discovery," I said, the moment Anstruther let me into the room, "because you didn't blush at using my name."

"Oh, I'm sorry!" she said, clutching the tablet in her arms close to her chest. She looked up at me. "I don't mean to offend you."

Redius and Oskelev, standing beside a high table with some very advanced-looking computer equipment on it, laughed aloud. Oskelev pounded the Uctu on the back, making him stagger. Nesbitt, perched on a stool beside the table, let out a big guffaw. Anstruther did blush then.

"I am teasing you," I said. "Tell me your discovery."

Her embarrassment vanished in a twinkling.

"I know how the programming made it into the victimized ships, and it's not what we thought."

"Really? Show me!"

She led me to the table, pushing Redius aside as though he was a pesty younger brother which, in a way, he was. He made way for me to a binocular scanner half a meter high.

"I think I can prove that the crew had something to do with putting the nanites on board. They conveyed a number of the nanites into the tanks themselves."

"They *did* smuggle them?" I asked, looking from one eager face to another with growing horror in my soul.

"Not in a conscious sense," Oskelev said. "You remember the symptoms that the merchant crews said they were suffering from?"

"Intimately," I said.

"Do you remember the therapy to prepare you for the Uctu worlds?" Plet asked.

"Do I not?" I exclaimed. "What a load of disorientation! I have written a monograph on it, and the insights I gained from my days of disproportion. You should read it. I think it's one of the best things I have come up with."

Plet shrugged.

"Maybe later, my lord. But that is at the heart of the matter."

"What? Disorientation?"

"No, sir. *Nanites*. Just like us, the crew was injected with a load of them so they could deal with the difference in sunlight and the chlorine in the atmosphere." I looked at each of them in turn, still puzzled.

"Yes, but those were medical devices. And they were all gone from their bodies by the time the ships reached the Autocracy."

"Their programming was hijacked by other nanites," Anstruther said.

I felt my eyes widen.

"But where did those nanites come from?" I asked. Oskelev showed her sharp white teeth between bright pink lips.

"Remember what Anstruther discovered in the residue that Redius scraped off the internal spray valves, the food samples that we took out of the vending machine?"

"How could I ever forget it?" I said. "We all smelled like porridge for hours, especially Redius."

"Unappetizing," the Uctu agreed, blinking his large eyes.

"Well," Anstruther said, her own eyes dancing. "My analysis showed that it had a pretty high level of inedible material within it, such as iron, silicates and so on."

"Yes." I nodded. "I supposed that it was just meant to save

money on actual nutrients. A large measure of what we eat has no value but bulk."

"That's true. That's how they disguised them."

"Nanites?" I asked, in disbelief.

"Loads of them," Nesbitt burst out, unable to contain himself any longer. His big face was spread with merriment. "They ate a ton of them. Maybe literally."

The penny dropped, and with it, my jaw. I regarded four gleeful faces and felt laughter bubbling up inside me, desperate to get out.

"And *how* did the nanites get into the waste tank?" I asked, although the grin that spread across my face made it a rhetorical question.

"I think you know already, sir," Anstruther said, her eyes dancing. "Bit by bit."

I couldn't help it. I began laughing helplessly.

"Do you mean . . . ?"

I mimed the progression thereof vaguely with both hands.

"Yes, my lord. I mean, Thomas. Every bite they took of station food contained a large proportion of nanos along with the nutrients," Anstruther said. "Each nano was coated with a more palatable-tasting substance, but since the coating is designed to come off in the digestive tract, some weren't completely covered to begin with."

"So you could have a chocolate-covered spaceship? My cousin Nalney would love that. He would eat anything as long as it had enough chocolate on it. But, all of it? There were only six people on the Coppers' ship, most of them very small. Although children seem to emit a great deal of extraneous matter, they could not possibly have produced all of it."

"Well, they were there for three months, sir. That's a good deal of input."

"That's fantastic!" I shouted. "Oh, where is Parsons when we need him?"

We all cackled and hooted. But when I paused to wipe tears of merriment from my eyes, a thought struck me.

"But they didn't find any nanites in the waste tank," I said. "They found a warship. A solid craft. Nanites work in a group, not as a single unit, millions of tiny machines all doing their own assignment."

Anstruther beckoned me to the microscope.

"Take a look, sir. I only did a spectrographic analysis on the sludge before, but after we examined the merchant ships, I took a really close look at it. There are nanites in the sample, but they're not all individuals."

I peered into the eyepieces. I had seen nanites before. At minor magnification, a group of them looked like a handful of silver sand. At a much greater amplification, they resembled neat little globes studded over with tools so small that they ended in pincers or cutters made from single molecules. Instead, what lay under the scope looked like a box of broken toys.

"But these create shapes," I said, in amazement. "They are still as tiny as a miser's heart, but these look like pieces of something."

"They're made to go together," Anstruther said. "Form things."

"As in a stray one-pilot fighter?" I asked.

"Yes."

Plet cleared her throat. "That's probably why all the nanites were missing from the ship's systems. In order to form the patterns that were programmed into them, they would have sought out any other nanites nearby. They had the transit time to form into the fighter craft and those weapons."

"But why did they form before the checkpoint?"

"I think it was a mistake," Anstruther said. "Otherwise we would never have known. The program malfunctioned in some way."

"Do you know how the program worked that tells the nanites to become a specific object?"

"Not yet, sir," Anstruther said, her pointed chin set firmly. "The navy's development arm is working on parallel practices. I'm trying to read the coding against the programs we use, but they're a lot more primitive than what these people, whoever they are, have already accomplished. I'm running dozens of programs on different samples, trying to unlock their system. Once I can read the original code, I'll be able to trace the programmer and find out who commissioned the program. In the meantime, I can wipe the nanites' memories and reinitialize them with the system we have. Want to see?"

"Absolutely," I said.

Nesbitt plunked a pulse rifle on an electrically charged plate on Anstruther's table and stood back.

"This is from the stash the customs agents found," he said.

Anstruther pulled a dish of gleaming powder and sprinkled some of it on the gun. Then she activated her tablet. The rifle promptly collapsed into a long, narrow pile of silver. I was enchanted.

"Could you do that to the war skimmer?" I asked eagerly.

"I already did," she said. She brought me to the side of the room where a utilitarian plastic barrel stood and lifted the top. Light gleamed upon the contents.

"This silver powder was a fighter craft? Fascinating!" I ran my hands through the mass.

"They are not silver," Plet corrected me. "They're made of a dozen elements, but mainly iron, boron, silicon and platinum."

"What fun!" I exclaimed. "I'd love to play with them. I never got to have any fun with the ones on board the *Bonchance*. We were always working. What can you make them do?"

"There's nothing you can't make out of these."

She tapped at her tablet. The contents of the barrel seemed to quiver. The surface seemed to curl up and bead together. Before my eyes, figures of animals formed, perfect in every detail. They melded together and became a ball. The ball flattened out and elongated into the shape of a sword. I reached for it.

"Careful," Redius said. "Truly sharp."

I withdrew my hand. Anstruther tapped her screen, and the knife became a ladle.

"Watch this," she said. She picked up the ladle and scooped up a pile of the powder. "Hold out your hand."

I turned up my palm to catch the silver stream. Instead of piling into my cupped hand, they shimmered right through my skin and sifted back into the barrel.

"That's amazing!" I said. "I never realized they were that small. How did Ensign Dee keep his in their box, if they can fall through other structures?"

"Their programming," Anstruther said. "Individually, they're almost indestructible. They can lift a thousand times their own weight." A mischievous look crossed her face, and a silver ribbon of the nanites streamed out of the barrel. It spread over the floor and formed a translucent mat underneath my feet. I felt myself being pushed upward. I windmilled my arms to stay upright. Anstruther blushed with pride as she brought me down again. The silver square liquidated and retreated up the side of the barrel once more.

"I would play with this all day," I said. "But games aside, the nanites were shipped here to form weaponry. What other destructive items were brought in in this innocent fashion?"

"We don't know," Nesbitt said.

"The Bertus own the company that sent the shipment to Way Station 46," Plet said. "Therefore, we must assume they're responsible for the hijacking nanites. We have inspected their ship, the *Pelican*, but it looks like the Bertus already made a delivery here on Nacer. Their ship's holds are empty. Their manifest passing into the Autocracy said they were carrying ingots and metal chips."

"All made up of nanites. Lord Rimbalius needs to know that," I said.

"He does. Since I couldn't inform Commander Parsons, I brought this information to the prime minister myself," Plet said.

"I'll bet he did the Uctu equivalent of tearing his hair out," I said, picturing the choleric minister reacting to the phlegmatic lieutenant unfolding her tale.

"He . . . was openly upset," Plet admitted. "He said that his agents always hear rumors of planned coups or attacks against the Autocrat's rule."

"Against Visoltia? Who could possibly want to harm that adorable little girl?" I asked, horrified.

"The High Protector confesses himself baffled. He told me that he has suspected that there was some kind of attack being planned, but until now, he had no idea how weapons were being smuggled across the border. Anstruther demonstrated the process to him. This new technology means that an arsenal can be built up anywhere. It caught him by surprise, to be honest. He doesn't know what they haven't caught, and what is already in system. It would suggest that an insurgency is imminent. Now he wants to interrogate the Bertus to see how much of this nanite material they sent in, or brought in."

"They're in the House of Deep Welcome," I said. "Parsons knows that."

"Yes, sir, that is where they were staying, but they have vanished."

I felt as though the platform beneath my feet had been swept away, precipitating me onto the floor in a heap.

"What? When?"

"Commander Parsons sent me over to their hotel to put some listening devices into their rooms," Nesbitt said. "They're empty. The desk robot said that six humans, a Croctoid and a couple of Bluts were checked in, but they left the hotel and didn't come back."

"Where did they go?" I asked.

"We don't know," Plet said. "It is possible that Commander Parsons left to find them. I wish I could reach him."

"Can't you trace their devices? Their pocket secretaries and other electronics must hitch into the local Infogrid just as ours do."

"We could, but they left them behind, sir," Plet said. "The Bertus must have had an idea they were being watched. All of their personal electronic devices are still in their rooms. The High Protector's staff is trying to break the encryption on them. Only the people themselves and a few pieces of clothing are missing. As no tracers have ever been planted on their persons, we can't locate them. They're not on their ship, and the crew hasn't seen them in weeks."

I was downcast.

"So we have no way of knowing when an attack might come. Does the High Protector have an inkling as to where or when they might strike?"

"None at all."

I struck my palm against the table, making the nanites jump.

"The obvious time is at the accession feast! Her Serenity has to call it off."

Plet shook her head. "Lord Rimbalius tried to persuade her, but Her Serenity insisted that it will go ahead. In the meanwhile, our ships have joined the Uctu forces scanning the immediate area for any more fighter craft. But it is vital we locate the Bertus."

"Life and death, but it is likely that we won't see them again until it's too late." A thought occurred to me, one ray of hope in the utter darkness that was falling. "This new information ought to give credence to the merchants' assertions that they did not know they were carrying contraband."

Plet's face wore a sympathetic cast.

"I'm sorry, sir. Our discovery shows that ingesting the nanites did make the weapons appear on their ships, but it doesn't prove they didn't know about it."

"I am certain they didn't!" I insisted. "You have only to talk with them to hear it."

"Even guilty people say they're innocent," Nesbitt said, his voice hoarse. He hated to argue with me. I regarded him with sympathy, but I knew I was right.

Plet shook her head. "Only the people who planted them in the food dispensers can tell us that. We have to find the Bertus. The High Protector's staff has offered to let us see the images from the video pickups placed around the city. We may be able to trace the Bertus' steps from the time you last saw them at the hotel. We'll be working with the Uctu armed services from now until we find out what's really happening." She nodded to the crew, who switched off equipment and prepared themselves to go.

I approached Anstruther, who tucked her tablet into a shoulder pouch, along with a fist-sized stunner.

"Are you coming with us?" she asked.

"No," I said. "I promised to visit the prisoners this afternoon. I can at least bring them this good news. But I have a favor to ask of you."

"I'd be happy to," Anstruther said, her face flushing again. "What do you need?"

I ran my hand through the mass of nanites on the table. "These give me an idea. I have a notion that will surprise and delight the Autocrat. I can't and wouldn't shield her from knowledge of the potential threat, but at least I can help lift her spirits. Will you help me to make it work?"

"Of course . . . Thomas!"

"Keep it under your hat in the meanwhile," I said, keeping my voice low. Plet was already standing by the door of the suite, about to bark the order to fall in. "We will talk later. I want this to be a surprise for everyone, including Parsons. I like our relationship always to be infused with a sense of the unexpected."

"I promise," she whispered, then hurried to join the others.

CHAPTER 42

The contents of the parcels I brought in on a floating sled were thoroughly vetted by Captain Oren and his guards before I was allowed to take them into the lockup. The Uctu guards seemed bemused as to why I was bringing foodstuffs when the prisoners were being fed adequately. It wasn't a case of my vocabulary being inadequate, only my ability to sway them. In any case, Captain Oren allowed everything to pass but the yarn and knitting needles that Etta Rissul had asked for. I supposed at a stretch they could be used as weapons, but so could everything else, if one were creative enough.

I stopped in each of the cells, greeting the prisoners and offering reassurances and pleasant conversation. They were all grateful for the gifts and the news. The Wichus grabbed the carton of beer before I could hand it over. Accustomed to Oskelev's rough friendliness, I didn't take offense. They needed to cope in their own way. I told everyone what my crew and I had discussed. They all steeled themselves, working the knowledge into the defenses that they were mustering for the upcoming trial.

I saved my visit to the Coppers for last. Ms. Copper seemed pleasantly overwhelmed by the fruits of my shopping, but even more by the information I brought her.

"There was *what* in the food?" she asked again and again. She shook her head in disbelief. "No wonder the disposers in the landing bay were shut off! They wanted to make sure that, uh, that everything got into the waste tank. That is the sneakiest thing I ever heard of."

"It does speak of a long-laid plot," I said, trying not to watch directly as Nona, the elder daughter, tried on the magnetic earrings I had brought her. A quick run through the shopping precinct I had been forced to abandon the evening before had borne charming fruit. I wished that I could have brought them clothing, to replace the appalling green jumpsuits everyone was forced to wear, but no amount of persuasive talk could move Captain Oren to allow that exception.

Nine-year-old Lerin had received the adventure book-game unit I had brought him with a look of dismay for my stupidity.

"You know we sell these, right?" he said. "I bet you paid five times our cost for this."

"But those are all on your ship, and this one is here," I pointed out, in a friendly fashion. He couldn't argue my logic. He retreated with his brother to play with the game in the children's room, but not before fingering the lucky circuit hanging around his neck, all gold LEDs but the single blood-red light at the center.

"Thanks for this, though," he said.

"My pleasure," I assured him.

"We have to talk to our lawyer about the nanites. He knows we didn't have any knowledge of them," Rafe Copper said, his odd-colored eyes intense. His long back was straighter than it had been since I had met them. My news perked him up. I was glad to see the change.

"Mr. Allisjonil has the files," I assured him. "The clerk of courts has already been in touch with him. This speaks of a deeper and more complicated situation. In light of the new information, your trial may be delayed."

"No!" M'Kenna Copper said, running her hands over her hair. I noticed that it had been neatly braided and fastened at each tip with wine-colored beads. "Can't we get released on our own recognizance, or moved to some other facility, one with more room? We can't get off this planet, but I have to get out of this cell or I'm going to go insane."

"I am sorry to deliver more disappointment," I said. "I spoke to the ambassador. She has been fighting for that, but the High Protector is unwilling until they can lay hands on the real culprits. You are safer in here than you are out there."

Her eyes lit with wild fear.

"No, we're not. What you tell me just means we're in more danger than ever. They've tried to kill us more than once already, right here in this jail!"

I cudgeled my brain to think of a solution.

"Perhaps Captain Oren can be persuaded to put a guard on each cell until the trial? After that you will be free to go."

"They'll tell you they don't have the staff," Ms. Copper spat. "Not when they're bringing in even more so-called smugglers."

My ears perked up.

"More smugglers?" I asked, horrified. "The authorities intercepted *another* shipment?"

Ms. Copper aimed a thumb at the wall. "On that side. They brought in a man last night. He was yelling his head off that the stuff in his ship wasn't his. Rafe's been talking to him through the wall. He's furious at being arrested. Just like we were." She looked dismayed, even lost. "He hasn't had time to lose hope."

"I will have to visit him and see if there is anything I can do for him," I said. I rose and shook hands with the Coppers. "I wish there was more I could do for you. But please, don't lose hope."

M'Kenna Copper stood up to see me to the cell door.

"We're grateful for what you've done already," she said. "I'm sorry for the harsh things I said to you before. What you are doing is helping. We just have to hang on and hope they see we really are innocent."

"I have faith that they will," I said.

The guard waiting with my now empty sled let me out of the cell.

"I would like to meet the new prisoner," I said.

"Allowed," the guard said, a mature male with narrow shoulders and a long face. "But from outside. He is violent."

"I understand," I said. "Perhaps I can persuade him to calm down. You are not his enemy. Whoever put him here is."

Almost afraid of what I might see, I peered in the cell door. A lanky figure in an ill-fitting green coverall sat hunched on his bunk, his face buried in his hands. The leg of the jumpsuit was split, revealing the man's knee. Stains on the legs and shoulders spoke of the struggle that the guards had had getting him into the cell.

"Excuse me, sir. May I speak with you? My name is Lord Thomas Kinago. I am an emissary from the Imperium. I will give you all the help I can."

Slowly, the human raised his head, revealing a long, narrow, unshaven face full of trepidation and anger. His thick black hair was disheveled. I was horrified and fascinated at the same time.

It was Parsons.

I swallowed, gathering my wits together and enjoining them to do the best that they had ever done in my life. There had to be a good reason why Parsons was occupying a cell in the Uctu holding facility. I must under no circumstances allow it to be assumed that we knew one another. Still, my sense of humor got the better of me. A smile spread across my lips. I could not have restrained it if I tried.

"Well, fellow," I said. "It seems the authorities at last have you where you belong."

To my surprise, Parsons seemed to approve this line of badinage.

"That's not true, your lordship," he said. I noticed that he spoke in a rough accent, and his voice had taken on a peculiar nasal tone I associated with those brought up in the Ramulthy system.

"Do you know this human?" the guard inquired.

"I do," I said. "At least, I have seen his image on the tri-dee broadcasts. He is a famous shipper in the Imperium. I always wondered how he seemed to have grown so rich on such ordinary cargo."

The man in the cell smirked at me. My jaw dropped. Parsons smirking! I did not know his face was capable of forming an expression so crass.

"You don't know a lot," Parsons fleered. "Most nobles don't have a thought in their heads."

"Careful, fellow," I said, waggling a forefinger at him. "The single thought bumping around in my brain is that I was inclined to offer you my assistance, but you are fast driving it out with the thought that you are too annoying to live."

Suddenly, he became sober. The flint-black eyes fixed upon me.

"I'm innocent," he insisted. "Look, sir, you need to get me out of here. All I came to do was drop off cargo, and they threw me in here. I don't want to die!"

I turned up my hands in a gesture of relative helplessness.

"I'll do what I can, but that isn't very much. My standing is purely symbolic. But I will try. And I can bring you a few home comforts, anything that the prison system will allow."

Parsons bowed his head in abject apology.

"That's all I ask, sir. And my friends over there, other side of the wall. They're being pretty nice to me, a newcomer, you know. I just hate being accused of something I know I didn't do!"

"Well, I suppose we are all in this together. I intend to do my very best to help you, captain."

He sprang up off his bunk and came to prop his elbows up on the frame of the door. He moved with such feline grace and implied power that the guard pulled me a few meters away, out of reach.

I glanced into the Coppers' door. From where I stood, I could see into several of the cells, though they could not see one another. Loneliness must have added to the feeling of helplessness. Ms. Copper's dark eyes were always on me.

"You're good to want to help, sir," Parsons said. "No one else seems to give a crater. Will you come back again?"

"As often as I can."

I had to hurry out of the corridor before I started asking awkward questions. Parsons would let me know his reasons in good time.

At the very least, I could inform Plet and the others that I had found him. It was a relief to know we had not just lost track of him. In fact, it was the most certain I had ever been as to his whereabouts that I had ever been.

M'Kenna sat with her heels against her bottom and her wrists balanced on her knees on the floor with her back to the edge of the bunk. She was taking first watch while Rafe slept.

After Lord Thomas left, the new guy spent the whole time until lights out alternately bellowing about being locked up and whining that he was innocent. She heard banging and the rending of cloth coming from the cell next door. The guards must have seen something they didn't like on the surveillance monitors, because at one point a full half-dozen of them and the medic went past her. Their appearance set off another round of yelling from the man. The doctor returned, shaking her head, her white smock stained with red blood.

The shouting had really frightened her babies. Dorna refused to let her mother out of her sight. After a while, Rafe had wedged himself as close to the next cell as possible and struck up a conversation with the man, who called himself Steve. The talk went on for some time, but

Steve's voice lowered from a shout down to a whisper. Rafe had detached himself and shot M'Kenna a look of triumph. Their new neighbor was quiet after that, apart from a snore or two.

She checked the tablet on the floor beside her. Half an hour until she could wake Rafe up to take over. The kids were breathing softly. It was the most soothing sound in the galaxy. It made her want to lie down and just listen. She would have been asleep in no time. In fact, she was already yawning.

Something plastic made a soft clicking noise. She thought it was probably a beer container nudged by the foot of one of the Wichus next door. But instead of rolling noises, she heard a slithering sound. She listened more closely. It wasn't coming from the side near the Wichus. Maybe the newcomer was moving around his cell. It was never really dark in the cells. Dull orange security lights and yellow pinpoints indicating where the video pickups were embedded made a constellation if she squinted and really pretended. Unlike the stars, though, they never moved.

Until that moment. A shadow momentarily eclipsed the pinpoint at the far end of the corridor. M'Kenna rose softly to her feet and moved to the front of her cell. She stood with her back to the wall just beside the door and tried to look out. She knew she had not imagined the flicker. If it had been one of the guards, he or she would have been carrying a greenish handlight. The LAIs were covered in their own lights. Instead, whoever or whatever was out there was working in the dark. Her eyes were accustomed to the dimness. She scanned the arc of the corridor visible from the door. She saw nothing, but it didn't mean there was nothing to see.

She sidled back to the bunk and put her hand over Rafe's mouth. She could just glimpse the gleam of his eyes as they sprang open. He started to sit up, then recognized her silhouette. She uncovered his mouth but put a fingertip to his lips. She felt his head nod. They had already discussed what to do if there was another attack. This time they would catch the guy. No matter what he tried, he wasn't leaving their cell until the guards saw him. M'Kenna thought of waking Nona, but she had had very little martial arts training. Better to have all four of her babies out of the way.

Rafe turned on his side so he could see the door, but pretended to be asleep. Under the uncomfortable blanket, M'Kenna knew he had his slipper wound over his knuckles. She slipped back to stand beside the door, ready to jump on the intruder.

Her heart pounded so hard she had to strain to listen over the thudding in her ears. The chlorine in the air caught at her throat. She wanted badly to cough, but swallowed again and again until the feeling passed.

Outside, the shadow shifted one more time. She was sure the intruder was going to take them out first, then move on to the other prisoners. After all, she was the one making the most noise about getting them released. From what Lord Thomas had said, the people who had set her up couldn't risk having her and Rafe testify in court. The Uctu judicial system required live testimony to convict, and dead humans told no tales.

It took so long before something happened that her attention was beginning to waver. The shadow changed again, and the door of their cell began to slide into its recess. M'Kenna tensed her muscles, ready to spring on the male. She wanted to beat his scaly head into the floor. She leaned forward, hands ready to strike.

A black mass rose up almost against her. Startled, M'Kenna stumbled backward. The mass seemed to be her assailant, draped in dark-colored cloth to prevent the cameras from seeing him. He grabbed her around the shoulders with one arm and closed his other hand on her throat.

"Rafe!" she shrieked.

He jumped up from the bunk to help her, but more shadows poured into the cell. At least three of the dark figures threw themselves at him, bearing him down.

"Nona, run!" he bellowed. "Take the babies. The door's open! Go get help!"

Their elder daughter appeared in an instant, Dorna on her hip. The two small boys stumbled behind her. They made for the door, but more black-clad assailants came in. Nona grabbed for the only thing she could, the tablet computer. She struck at the nearest assassin. It brought its hand up under the drape and knocked the light rectangle flying. The tablet clattered to the floor. The assailant pushed Nona against the wall with one hand. The cell door slid shut. The Coppers were trapped with a half-dozen killers. Where were the guards?

"Help!" M'Kenna gasped.

"Mama!" Akela shouted. Two more Uctus picked the boys up. Akela and Lerin squirmed and kicked, trying to get down.

"Mama!" Lerin called. "Papa!"

M'Kenna choked, trying to drag air into her lungs. She stepped on her attacker's feet and kneed him in the belly. He was much stronger than she was. His face was covered, but he must have been able to see through the cloth. She tried to ram her forehead into his nose, but he tilted his head back out of her way.

"What's happening?" Nuro bellowed from the other side of the wall. "Hey! Who the hell are you?"

They weren't the only ones being attacked! M'Kenna grabbed for her attacker's hand and tried to drag it from her neck.

From under the black robes, his hand, pale gray in the security lights, rose up. Something was clenched in his hand. It looked like the kind of orange bulb the first assassin had tried to use on her. He brought it to her face. M'Kenna strained back, doing her best to avoid its touch. Her head hit the wall behind her.

A long, pale hand pushed in between them. Suddenly, the attacker wasn't touching her any longer. The draped figure went flying backwards, followed by a lanky figure in a prison jumpsuit. The Uctu met the newcomer with four limbs up, but it wasn't quick enough. The newcomer brought a solid foot down in the middle of its stomach. It went limp long enough for the human to leap over its body and bring his foot down just below the outlined head. M'Kenna heard a terrible crunch, and the attacker went still. She felt her gorge rise. She swallowed it. Her babies were still in danger.

In a flurry of limbs, the man spun from one attacker to another, delivering blow after blow with hands and feet. She had never seen a human being move so fast. The three figures holding Rafe dropped and didn't rise again. The attackers holding Lerin and Akela dropped the boys and threw themselves at him. He went into a crouch, a fearsome scowl on his face. M'Kenna suddenly realized it was their new neighbor, Steve. The Uctu had not taken two steps before he spun, lifting one foot in the air. He caught them both across their masked faces, knocking them back. M'Kenna ran to the boys and pulled them away into a corner with her. Rafe lowered his shoulder and cannoned into the figure holding Nona. When it tried to hit him with its tail, Rafe caught it by that appendage and flung it staggering out into the middle of the cell. Steve grabbed it around the neck with one arm and twisted its head with the other. Another horrifying crunch, and it fell.

Only one assassin was left standing. As if they had rehearsed it, M'Kenna, Rafe and Steve moved toward it. It shifted from foot to foot, then made for the door. The portal slid open, but Steve was on top of the masked figure before it could run out. He grabbed it by both arms, then reached down to a place near its tail. It let out a terrible scream and fell to its knees. Steve heaved it upright and it back toward Rafe.

"Keep him here. We need one alive."

He slapped the door with his open hand, and it rolled open. He dashed out, leaving M'Kenna goggling. Rafe grabbed the blanket off the bunk and rolled the writhing attacker in it. Then he sat down on it.

In a moment, they heard more horrible sounds. M'Kenna embraced her children and kept a fierce hold on them. Dorna sobbed against her chest. The other three were wide-eyed with shock.

Suddenly, all of the lights went on. Dozens of guards poured into the corridor. M'Kenna blinked at the pulse rifles pointing at her. She looked past them, and saw a rectangle of black at the end of the hall.

"I told you they came through the wall!"

She sat in Captain Oren's office with Dorna on her lap. The rest of the Imperium prisoners were jammed into the small room as the senior guard ran the video recordings back and forth.

"It is as you said it was," Captain Oren said. "The video does not show anything from the moment you say it began, but the cells are full of bodies."

"I told you so," M'Kenna kept saying. She couldn't stop herself, and saw no real reason to. She glared at him. "I told you so. I told you so!"

"Yes, yes," the Uctu said, impatiently. "I apologize."

"It would seem that the assailants had access not only to the video system, but also the physical plant of the prison," Steve was saying. M'Kenna stared at him. He might still be bruised, stubbled and wearing a torn green jumpsuit, but his manner had changed from a petulant, hard-bitten trader to someone who talked to people from a position of infinite authority. She peered at him, picturing him with a shave and a haircut.

"I know you," she said. "You're Lord Thomas's . . . what did he call you? Aide-de-camp. I forget your name."

"Commander Parsons," 'Steve' replied. "Lord Thomas has insisted all of you were in danger, as has my ongoing surveillance of you."

"You were spying on us?"

"Steve" lifted an eyebrow, and it stopped her dead.

"If I had not, I wouldn't have been here this evening," he said. "To be honest, we did not believe the attack would come as soon as this. I expected it to be the night before your trial."

"You were willing to spend that much time locked up because he asked you to?" M'Kenna asked.

"That and because there was no other way to ensure I would be here at the necessary moment," he said. He nodded to the Uctu guard. "Captain Oren cooperated most fully with our plans."

"Happy to," Oren said. "Thought it was lies. I apologize again."

"Well," M'Kenna said. The words came to her lips grudgingly. She was still mad that they hadn't believed her to begin with. "Thank you for saving my babies."

Commander Parsons looked deeply into her eyes.

"We will save all of you," he said. "This is not hyperbole. More proof has just been added to the balance on your side."

"The High Protector will get information from the survivors," Oren said, his expression bleak.

"I hope they have some," Parsons said.

M'Kenna was all too glad to go back to their cell, accompanied by a guard who stood at their door the rest of the night. Not that she could fall asleep, but she finally felt as if she was safe to do so.

CHAPTER 43

I was delighted to greet Parsons when the crew met to confer the next morning. He had sustained a small bruise on the temple. I also spotted some discoloration on his wrist that his cuff did not quite conceal. His description of his exploits after I had left him, however sparing of detail, was as exciting as a blockbuster digitavid. I could imagine the cool efficiency with which he had disposed of all but a few of the attackers.

"I accompanied the two surviving assassins to the High Protector's station," he said. "The fruits of the interviews with them were few. As I feared, they were rogues for hire, admitted to the premises by means of electronic keys supplied to them at a dead drop along with an initial deposit on their fee. They do not know the source of either. After the interrogation, I spent a few hours with the High Protector discussing the potential for an attack."

"But upon whom are they planning this coup?" I asked. "Surely not the Autocrat herself. She is a child. Her people love her. Everyone who stopped to chat with her in the shopping precinct was thrilled to have her there."

Parsons visited a look upon me that was patient and even kindly.

"Her policies are not popular with all of the Autocracy," he reminded me. "But her removal does seem unlikely. The next in line for the throne is just as amiable and inexperienced and as likely to continue the rules left in place by Visoltia's late father."

"Then who?" Plet asked. "Why would an attack be made? Who would benefit? What change could possibly come out of a coup?"

"Well, if I could change anything," I said, "it would be the annoying holdup at the borders. Everyone is affected by that."

"Has the High Protector said why such an irregular trickle of ships is being allowed in?" Plet asked Parsons.

"The numbers are on direct orders from the Autocrat," Parsons said. "He feels that it is based upon her superstitions. He cannot persuade her to change the quantity even by a single digit."

"That sounds really childish," Nesbitt said.

"She *is* a child," I said. "Did you know that the favorite lucky number here is seventeen?"

"Yes, sir, I did," Parsons replied. "Have you made any progress in dealing with these protective measures she employs?"

I ran my hands through my hair.

"I am doing my best," I said. "Every time I think I have persuaded her that it is all right to think for herself, the moment I turn my back, any good I have done is undone by Lord Toliaus. He doesn't like me. I tell better fortunes than he does."

"Could he be preparing to bring down an attack on her?" Plet asked.

"Oh, no," I said, waving a dismissive hand. "If the Autocrat were deposed, Lord Toliaus would be out on his nonexistent ear. No one else likes him. He would defend her safety to the death. She is the source of his influence. She does everything that he tells her to. Yesterday was another Day of Grace, and the number was eleven. She was highly agitated to hear that it's considered an unlucky number in the Imperium."

I stopped, surprised by a thought. Parsons eyed me.

"What struck you about that last visit, sir?"

"It wasn't just the last, but the first as well, Parsons. Toliaus! He came in to tell Visoltia that it was a Day of Grace."

"The Days of Grace is a very old superstition, my lord," Parsons said. He sounded dismissive, but he did not have my specialized knowledge.

"Yes, it is. Very old." I turned on my viewpad and pushed it into the center of the table so it could display the graphics I had discovered. "I had to unearth some ancient stone carvings before I found a mention of it. I think that Lord Toliaus resurrected that tradition for a purpose. He said that the number of grace for that day was five. Jil had to send away two of her ladies so the number remaining was five. But the Autocrat also summoned the High Protector. She told him five, also."

"What about five?" Redius asked.

I smiled.

"I would wager my tent and all of my divining equipment that the border stations were allowed to admit five ships at each way station on that day."

Plet checked a list on her own viewpad. "You are right, lieutenant."

"Good observation," Redius said.

"So someone is controlling the entry of all ships," Oskelev said. "To get bribes?"

"To control resources," Parsons said. "The Autocrat is very young. She does not realize how much power devolves upon those who control supply and demand. I would wager that her influence lies upon many other sources of wealth than shipping. The Autocracy ought to have prospered more than it has since the end of hostilities with the Imperium. It has not, in part because of these artificial limitations. I had suspected it was the High Protector. He has reason to sustain a grudge against the Imperium, but the stricture is not imposed only on ships that originate from the Imperium, nor as we have just seen, it is he who determines how many ships can enter."

"No," Plet said, enlightenment dawning on the pale oval of her face. "He's just being told what to do. The Autocrat has absolute authority. But who has authority over her?"

"Well, Lord Toliaus does," I said. "He's the only one who knows how many ships would cross into the Autocracy and when. All he has to do is declare a Day of Grace. I bet he has some kind of financial interest."

"But is he the mastermind behind a military takeover?" she asked.

"I would hate to think so," I said. "He is so jealous of anyone else's authority. It seems completely illogical to attack the Autocrat when she's the only reason he has any power to begin with."

"If he is the instigator, he has a different target in mind," Parsons said. "The High Protector must be informed. But Lord Toliaus cannot be working alone. He must have a network behind him that is planning this attack, led by a trusted ally or allies. The Bertus are the key to finding those others and whatever weapons they brought in. We must confer with Lord Rimbalius."

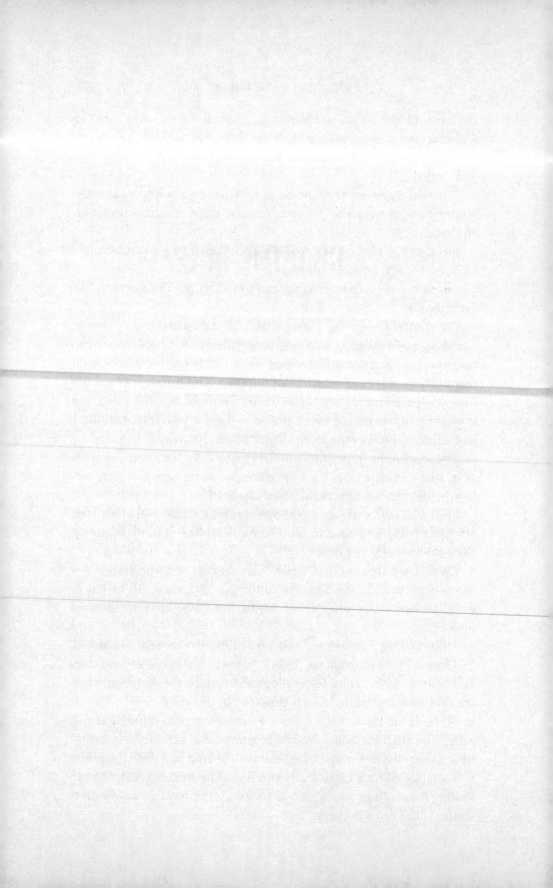

CHAPTER 44

"No, the Autocrat will not call it off," Lord Rimbalius said, all ten circular fingertips pressed against his desk. "I have tried many times to persuade her to wait. She points out, with some justice, that she has been in danger since the day she assumed the throne. This is a celebration of the second anniversary of that date. She will make herself seen by her subjects and by her guests."

"You can't fault her courage," I said, with a resigned shrug. "I got the same answer from her at breakfast."

Security at the rear entrance to the palace a day before the anniversary festival had become much tighter. Parsons and I were only allowed to enter after personnel wearing the livery of the High Protector had scanned not only our persons but our gear. I had readily surrendered my viewpad and bag of rune stones for examination. Even the air around us seemed suspect. The guards seemed unusually nervous. I could not blame them. They would have two days' difficult duty going through parcels, bags, boxes and crates containing the food and decorations for the next day's feast, not to mention examining every guest lest they were carrying a device of mass destruction.

"I am inclined to agree with the Autocrat," Parsons said, sitting beside me with a nonchalant air that suggested he had not spent all night wrestling with assassins. "The perpetrators cannot remain hidden forever. Leaks of information or sightings become more likely the longer they wait. It would seem logical that if you wish to draw forth the attack, a well-publicized, well-attended showpiece event is a worthy target."

"This is the Autocrat's life we are discussing! Not a carnival parade!" Lord Rimbalius glared at us. "You cannot dismiss her as though she is less important than one of your own citizens."

"I'm affronted, High Protector," I said. "The lady Visoltia and I are soulmates now. I would never betray one of my best friends."

"And you!" Rimbalius turned his ire toward me. "Playing upon the very whims that are holding back the Autocracy from maturing! You are as bad as . . ."

". . . As Lord Toliaus?" I suggested.

"You are certain of his involvement in the border blockade?" the High Protector asked, his expression shifting to one of incredulity.

"I think so. You permit only so many ships to enter the Autocracy based upon what she tells you. Is that not so?"

"Of course it is. She has absolute power."

"But do you know where the numbers come from?" I pressed.

"No. I presumed it was a whim of some kind. She has many. Most of them are harmless. I have been unsuccessful in trying to convince her that this one is not, but she will not be moved."

"I think I can prove that it was no whim. She was manipulated, as you were."

If thunderclouds had ever gathered over a red sandstone rock, it would have resembled the face of the High Protector at that moment."

"What do you mean, Loche Kinago? How could she have been? How would Toliaus have accomplished such a thing?"

"I'm not at all surprised that you didn't know," I said. "He was probably incredibly careful not to voice his demands where you could hear them, and none of the Autocrat's personal staff would think anything beyond it being one of his magical ramblings. They were accustomed to the Autocrat taking his word seriously. She has entire wardrobes full of trappings, not to mention songs, poems and prayers for each 'Day of Grace.' A lucky number is associated with each of those days. That day was five. And I sat there while Visoltia told you that the number was five. I will bet that he had five ships sitting on the other side of the border, waiting for permission to enter. I have no idea if it is weapons or contraband, or simply people of influence in other sectors that were on those ships, but it was he who fed Visoltia the number for you to act upon. I would imagine her servants and the other ministers felt sorry for you having to play along, but I doubt they would connect it with the border crossings. After all, few of them have anything to do with imports."

"All these months!" Rimbalius growled. "I will kill him!"

"No, don't," Parsons cautioned him. "Her Excellence would only see his death as martyrdom, and probably try to follow his teachings in her own way."

"But what else can I do? I have held this government together by the scales on my head after the late Autocrat's passing," the High Protector said, running his pliable fingertips over those eponymous items. "The system governments all think that the Autocrat must be slightly mad. I have felt for some time that there might be an attack to remove her. It troubles me even to have to think such a thought could pass the minds of her subjects, but I am a realist. People can only be pushed so far from the center of their comforts before they rebel."

"Now that you have this knowledge, you can use it to your advantage," Parsons said. "The next time a Day of Grace is declared, find a reason to lower the number that Lord Toliaus expects to see executed, and see how he handles the matter."

"That is good sense," Rimbalius said. "I would welcome further insights, but I am very busy with logistics for the feast tomorrow."

Parsons and I stood up.

"I will do more if I can," I said. "At the moment, she is so excited about tomorrow that even my attempts to get her to find a place of mindfulness when we meditate are failing. Perhaps the day after tomorrow, when the party has passed, I can get her to see the situation from the other side of the border, so to speak."

Rimbalius looked weary.

"So much of this would be solved if she would only grow up," he said.

"Oh, what fun would that be?" I asked. "I must go back to her now. I'm going to teach her how to manipulate a Ouija board to say whatever she wants it to."

I sat beside Visoltia as she passed down judgements and approved or denied requests from the ministers. I had long ago determined that Visoltia was only called upon to intervene when exceptions needed to be made to longstanding processes or budgets. She had a surprisingly good grasp of economics for such a young girl. The High Educator tried to slip an item in the Autocracy-wide expenditures for what sounded like an experimental program, and Visoltia caught it before he could explain it away.

"I cannot determine whether this is a good program or a bad program by a number, no matter how many zeros it has," she said, fixing the minister, a much older male Uctu, with a fierce gaze. "I want to see an explanation of what it will accomplish for this outlay. I approve the rest of your budget, though." Visoltia slashed her thumb across the tablet and handed it back.

Looking sheepish, the High Educator backed away. The High Nourisher caught me looking at him, and dropped her jaw slightly in amusement.

I heard some bustling at the rear of the room. Ema and a gray-clad servant brought lunch to us. To my amusement, the main course was a flat green patty that filled the plate, with an assortment of sauces on the side. She seized one and decorated her meal with it.

"Read my fortune to me, Thomasin," Visoltia said.

"My pleasure, Your Serenity," I said. I peered at the design, which I would have described as a modified Imperium Standard numeral two. "I see a high measure of excitement, which interferes with your thought processes."

She laughed at me.

"It takes no connection to the infinite to know that," she said.

"I am reading the sauce," I said. I held out my viewpad, on which was displayed the chart that I had made up of Uctu-oriented squiggles. "Do you see? This is exactly what I would expect."

"How dare you pollute the mind of the Autocrat with your outworlder sorcery?" Toliaus demanded, swooping down upon us. To my everlasting annoyance, I had not heard him come in. He picked up Visoltia's plate and held it out of her reach.

"Do you know, that is the second time today I have been accused of that?" I asked, carefully keeping my face blank. "I dare because she asked me to. Perhaps I should read your luck for the day. All predictions for amusement purposes only."

"You treat the infinite as though it were a game," Toliaus said. He glared, but I thought I detected a measure of fear in his expression. Perhaps I was having an effect upon Visoltia's grasp of self-determination.

There would never be a better opportunity to push the envelope. I grasped the figurative flap and applied pressure.

"The infinite, as you call it, can be fun," I admitted. "Although most of my correspondents on the Infogrid think much the same way you do. I think their discomfort is through a lack of knowledge. What is your excuse?"

"Condimentomancy appears to be a graspable science, High Wisdom," Visoltia piped up from beside me. She proffered a bottle. "Try it!"

"I will not!" Lord Toliaus boomed.

I brought forth the greatest expression of astonishment I had in my quiver and launched it.

"Are you telling the Autocrat that you will not obey her?" I asked.

Every other sound in the room died away at once. They all turned to look at Lord Toliaus. He turned up his glare. I admit that I deserved it, but I wasn't yet finished with him. This might be the very opportunity for which I was hoping. I held myself as still as a cat at a mousehole. Or, in this case, a lizard's lair.

Impatiently, the High Wisdom held out his hand for the sauce container. I held out my as-yet untouched luncheon. Very reluctantly, Toliaus took the tube and upended it over the field of green. In jerky movements, he produced a furtive line up and to the left, zigzagging down and to the right, with a sharp cedilla at the bottom, then he put the bottle down.

I studied it, then raised my eyebrows. I turned to the Autocrat with deep solemnity.

"You should dismiss this gentleman from your personal service, Your Excellence," I said. "At once."

"What?" Visoltia asked, shocked. "Why?"

"Because he is not trustworthy. He serves another ideal above you. He is afraid of exposure, but he has exposed himself!"

Toliaus hissed with laughter.

"He is not showing genitalia," the Autocrat said, puzzled. I cursed inwardly at having to communicate in a foreign language, particularly one that I had known well only a short time. I suspected Redius might have played a practical joke on me while he was teaching me colloquialisms. I would talk with him later. Of all the times not to be able to make use of a translation program!

"His private intentions, Your Serenity, not his private parts," I said, correcting my speech in haste. "Lord Toliaus has been misleading you. He doesn't believe in any of the things he says to you. They're just window-dressing for his own purposes. Do you see?" I presented my viewpad and brought up a portion of the chart that showed a similar design. "Read the indications listed below."

The High Wisdom glared at me. If he could have projected laser bolts from his eyes, I would have been a black spot on the coverlet.

"Is this true?" Visoltia demanded, her face drawn with woe. Toliaus hastened to reassure her, his tone as oily as suet.

"Of course not, my dear, cherished child. All that I do, all I have ever done is for you. I lead you through knowledge of the infinite. What the universe reveals to me is for the good of the entire Autocracy. What wisdom I have, all the power I possess, all my knowledge of the stars and the unseen, is at your service."

"What wisdom?" I said, in the most scornful tone I could muster. "What tosh! He has no more magic than a food synthesizer."

His eyes glittered. "Are you calling my skills false? You have no claim on the higher wisdom. I am a greater magician than you!"

"You don't know who you are dealing with," I said. "I am a powerful wizard in my own home. My *science* tells me that you're ineffective. Visoltia could do better for daily guidance by writing random words on slips of papers and picking one out of a jar."

"You? You question me?" Lord Toliaus was so furious he was gasping. I had guessed that no one else had ever insulted him twice. Behind him, Ema was gesturing frantically at him. I paid no attention to her. Toliaus was not yet at the stage where I needed him.

"If I am the first ever to tell you the truth, then you've lived a long time in ignorance," I said. "If you were a member of the imperial family, we would speak kindly of you. In hushed tones. In case you would hear us." I shook my head sadly.

Toliaus had at last reached the boiling point. Hot words bubbled out of him at a furious rate.

"*You* would treat me like an idiot? How could you ever hope to understand the depth of wisdom that I have attained? Your kind doesn't seem to understand what true intelligence is! I read the Infogrid files. I know how feckless the imperial family is. The lord of your domain keeps countless useless relatives on the public purse, and for what reason? Is it that he is so feebleminded that he cannot look wise without a covey of fools to surround him? He must be as great an imbecile as you!"

"What did you call my cousin?" I asked, allowing horror and outrage to dawn upon my face.

"Lord Toliaus!" the Autocrat exclaimed, standing up on the broad divan. With its added height, she could look him directly in the eye. "You impugn my imperial brother?"

"Your Serenity," Lord Toliaus said, a placating expression hastily taking its place upon his ruffled visage, "indeed, no! I was drawing an inference about this . . . this human, this pathetic fool whom your regal sibling chose to send here, into our midst . . ."

"In spite of my limited intelligence, I fully understand your implication," I said. "I cannot allow the insult to my cousin to stand." I had no gloves available to deliver the statutory blow, so I emptied the rune stones from their bag and grasped it by the drawstrings. It made a satisfying smack as I slapped Lord Toliaus across the face. "I challenge you, sir!"

"What?" Toliaus sputtered.

"Am I not clear?" I asked, rhetorically, I hoped. "You must pay for your insult. Therefore, I am challenging you to a duel. You may defend your words, but I will have satisfaction! The lady," and here I bowed low to Visoltia, "will witness our fight to ensure that it is fair, and that the outcome is just."

"I shall perform that office for you, Thomasin, and for you, High Wisdom," Visoltia said, her eyes wide and solemn.

I smiled inwardly as Toliaus squirmed, twisting his lizardlike body into a grand impression of a serpent practicing reeling, writhing and fainting in coils, as one of the great writers of Old Earth had once written.

"A fight?" he said weakly. "Physical altercation? Over words? You must have misunderstood me, Lord Thomas!"

"I doubt that, sir," I said. I appealed to the others in the room. "Did you hear what he said? Was my understanding mistaken?"

If Toliaus had never appreciated how few allies he had in court, he had ample proof at that moment. All of them, to the lowest servant in a gray smock, signaled no.

"Very well, then," I said, sliding off the State Bed and retrieving my boots. "I will confront you with the truth. As the challenger, the time and place are at my option. But the choice of weapons . . ." I did my best to avoid a smile, because I could almost see his brain working. ". . . Is yours."

I marched out of the State Bedroom and into the High Protector's office. I was glad to see that Parsons had returned. Plet had joined him. They were scanning an infinity of images projected upon the wall. I could hardly wait for them to pause and turn to regard me.

"I have done it," I said. "I am going to discredit Lord Toliaus."

"How will you do that?" Lord Rimbalius asked. He seemed to be alarmed at my appearance. Perhaps I did look a trifle excited, with my nostrils flaring and my face red with excitement, not to mention the fact that I was in my stocking feet.

"I challenged him to a duel! I provoked him into insulting the emperor. He left me no choice. We shall meet on the field of honor."

Parsons allowed just the corner of his mouth to turn up.

"Well done, sir."

"Thank you, Parsons," I said.

"I thought that you said to kill him would be counterproductive," Lord Rimbalius said, his heavy brow lowered almost to his eyelids.

I waved a hand.

"I don't plan to kill him. He needs to be discredited, and that is just what I will do. I must defeat him on his own ground, and I will get the Autocrat to disown him."

"But he'll attack you," Plet said.

"Not physically," I said. "He's a terrible coward. He only strikes at those who cannot strike back. He will only fight where he thinks he can win, using a weapon that he thinks only he can wield. As the challenged party, he chose the medium in which we will compete. I am skilled in numerous martial arts, starship racing, sword-fighting and marksmanship, which he could learn by checking my Infogrid file. As he is a terrible coward, I knew it wouldn't be a physical fight.

"Magic," I said, with deep satisfaction at the expression on their faces. "We are to have a duel of wizards at the Autocrat's accession feast."

"But you are not a wizard," the High Protector pointed out.

"Neither is he," I said. "But I will pit my technical trickery and superstitious folderol above his any time. He has had an audience of one. I have plied my trade with hundreds, even thousands. And I have an idea."

"Once I have made him foolish in Visoltia's eyes, when that gap in influence opens up, it is up to you to fill it."

"Oh, I will, human lord, I will. But perhaps you should stay here tonight. He will try to have you killed before the duel."

"He can try," I said, "but I posted news of the upcoming contest on my Infogrid file right there in the State Bedroom. If anything should befall me between now and then, you know what the public opinion will be."

"That is not a bad plan, my lord," Parsons said, "but the High Protector's information services have picked up rumblings of activity close to Memepocotel. Ground forces are gathering. Whatever the Bertus have brought in is likely to be used during the feast. We have been examining scans from all over the region. Power surges and unusual movement have been noticed. You could provide a distraction for the wrong reason."

"I think it's an excellent plan," I argued. "Dignitaries are coming in from all over the system. Her Excellence is very excited about the guest list. If I have sufficiently provoked Toliaus and he is indeed the instigator of the coup attempt, he will almost certainly strike during the feast, so as to rid himself of as many enemies as possible at once."

"In that case, I insist that you delay the duel, my lord," Rimbalius said. "We cannot risk the Autocrat's life like that."

"No," I said. "High Protector, I can meet his coup with great force, from within and without."

"You?" Plet asked, scoffing.

I ignored the scoff.

"Of course. I am the greatest weapon that you have. I can lift the embargoes on all the ports singlehandedly! Lord Toliaus will be actively trying to kill me, and all I have to do is humiliate him. Expect fraud galore, my friends. I must go back to the hotel to prepare."

I bowed deeply, and marched out the door, swinging my boots in my hand.

Upon returning to the hotel, I made immediately for Jil's suite.

Ignoring Banitra's curious gaze, I strode past her and rapped upon Jil's door.

"Go away!" my cousin's voice wailed.

"Do come out," I said. "It's been days, and you're not having any fun. The Autocrat misses you."

"I am not coming out!"

"But, Jil, I need you." I turned my most pleading gaze to the painted door. "I am making such interesting plans, and I need a trusted ally to help me with them."

The door was obdurate.

"It's not *safe*, Thomas. That Lieutenant Plet of yours told me that no one knows where Nile Bertu went."

"They will find him, Jil. Maybe sooner than you think. But you like Visoltia, don't you?"

"Yes. Of course I do. She's a darling."

"And you dislike Lord Toliaus, don't you?"

A notable pause ensued, before a tentative voice said, "Yes. Why?"

"I plan to take the High Ego to a humility lesson. Don't you want to help me with that? Hasn't he spoiled enough of our fun this trip?"

The door was thrown wide open. Jil beckoned me inside. Her friends, with grateful looks, followed.

"What do you have in mind?"

The six of us sought out Anstruther. We found her bent over her microscope. She became very shy in the face of my cousin and her coterie, but I commanded her gaze.

"We have a change in plans," I told her. "We will need to provide a much more showy exhibition." I pointed to the barrel of gleaming dust. "How much of that can I possibly carry around with me without rupturing both meniscuses?"

CHAPTER 45

Skana wore Lord Toliaus's embroidered outfit over a lightwe
undergown of her own. She accepted the puzzled glances and outr
gazes of admiration from the other guests as they entered the S
Dining Room.

She, Tuk, Nile and his two girlfriends had been transported f
the oasis before dawn in an unmarked flitter and deposited at the
entrance of the palace. Enstidius had dressed them up in h
voluminous robes with fake tails attached to their waists and ho
that pulled down to their chins, concealing their faces. He war
them not to talk to Lord Toliaus at any time. The Bertus didn't ca
long as they got to attend the banquet.

One of his underlings who had traveled with the Bertus made
they were scanned by one particular guard at the entrance. After t
he guided the five of them through the bowels of the palace to a
room where they stripped off their disguises and waited. And wa

Skana had to admit it was worth waiting for. The gray-clad ser
who had finally come guided them into this enormous, high-ceilir
room filled with long tables and a dais at one end. The chairs at
head table were ornamental but not too fancy, except for the on
the middle. It was molded of twisted bronze rods as thick as her
but mottled as though they had scales. Two uprights rose high on
back of the throne and braided themselves into a complicated k
with a bright orange gem the size of her head embedded in its he
Skana began to design the dais for when she and Nile took over.

designed two more chairs to either side of the throne. Not as fancy as hers, of course, but equal in size. She wasn't totally in love with the local style, but she could always import whatever she wanted, once the borders were open again.

She was filled with admiration and not a little envy. It was like being inside a rainbow mosaic. Not one square centimeter of the walls or ceiling, or floor, for that matter, was unadorned. On three of the high walls were enormous stained glass windows whose images twinkled with their own light.

"Do you think those pictures are history or mythology?" she asked Nile's two girlfriends.

"I don't know enough about Uctu culture to have an idea," said the cost analyst, whose name Skana had finally retained as Cenide. The three women had really gotten to know each other during their desert exile. With limited Infogrid access, there was little else to do but talk. "They're just gorgeous."

The other, Pemelle, could hardly speak, she was so overwhelmed. Both of them wore light green Uctu gowns with gold embroidery and flat oval gems around the neck and hems. They looked beautiful.

They were the first to arrive. A quintet of musicians with two stringed gizmos, a drum and two wind instruments looked curiously at them as they arrived and set up quietly in a corner. They began to play gentle, floaty airs. A few Uctu guests in fine Imperium clothing peered nervously into the hall, spotted the Bertus, and made their way timidly to an empty table. More followed, two or three at a time. The room had been set up to seat at least five hundred.

"When do you think she'll get here?" Nile asked.

Skana had no illusions as to who "she" was.

"Later. They'll make an entrance, just like they always do."

The five of them were by no means the only Imperium visitors. At least two dozen humans, all dressed with equal elegance, filtered in, along with a few Croctoids and a couple of Solinians, all in local dress. The rest of the guests were Uctu, who looked uncomfortable in human attire that wasn't really made to accommodate tails.

"You think we're gonna be able to tell who it is?" Nile asked, watching servants in bright yellow seating guests at the tables.

Skana shook her head.

"Not until the last minute."

Enstidius and his people had been remarkably careful not to use the name of the target. She and Nile didn't even know if Toliaus's enemy was male or female, only that it wasn't the Autocrat herself. Skana had looked her up on the Infogrid. Visoltia was a little girl. Skana and Nile had speculated for hours on who among the guests was worth importing fighters and arms. But no amount of reading the political or economic digests gave them a clue. All they knew was what was going to happen some time that evening.

Nile, Tuk and Skana all wore shield belts under their voluminous robes. When the action started, all they had to do was switch them on and enjoy the fireworks. Nothing the Uctu insurgents were packing could get through the multiple protective waves. The power packs only lasted about forty minutes, but the attack shouldn't take more than ten. How hard could it be to target one person and blast them?

Nile grabbed her arm.

"There she is!" he hissed into her ear.

Skana glanced at the crowd. Among the horde of coral-skinned Uctu, the human nobles stood out like golden statues. Lady Jil had on a translucent turquoise gown covered with golden embroidery like the mosaic designs on the wall. The tall man who was Lady Jil's cousin on her father's side towered above the group. He was dressed in a black robe covered with stars. Behind them was a group of women, a couple of whom looked like they could be nobles, but she wasn't sure. They all wore floaty dresses with light hoods clinging to their upswept hairstyles. Unconsciously, Skana touched her own coarse, rusty hair. Never mind. It was what was inside that counted. The Imperium ambassador and her partner who followed the nobles in were more in her own mold, their long blond hair modestly coiffed, and their Uctu gowns calculated to compliment their hosts instead of drawing awkward attention.

Nile stared openly at the procession. Skana rolled her eyes at him.

To their amazement, the lord caught sight of them, and spoke to Lady Jil. She startled openly, but her cousin bowed to the ambassador and detached himself from their party. He dragged Lady Jil toward them. Skana could hardly believe it. He seemed to be having some trouble walking, but they were definitely coming their way. Nile sprang to his feet.

"Well, hello!" the tall man said. "How nice to see fellow Keinoltians this far from home. I believe you are acquainted with my cousin, Lady Jil Nikhorunkorn. I am Lord Thomas Kinago."

"Sort of," Skana said, presenting her hand. Lord Thomas bowed over it. "Skana Bertu. This is my brother Nile. My assistant Tuk."

Tuk bowed deeply. Nile just gaped at the lady. Skana poked him hard with her elbow.

"Uh, yeah. This is Pemelle Dubarov, and Cenide Pollan."

"I say, Jil, it looks as if these ladies got the memo," Lord Thomas said, cheerfully. He hadn't missed the resemblance. He would have to have been blind to. "How very nice you all look. Don't they, Jil? Say good evening to the good folks."

"Good evening," the lady echoed.

"Nice to see you," Skana said.

"Thank you." Skana thought the girl looked like she might faint. Nile cleared his throat.

"Look, Lady Jil, you don't have to be scared of me," he said. The lady just quivered. She had to be feeling bad about how she had behaved. Skana changed the subject. She turned to Lord Thomas.

"So, what are you supposed to be?" Skana asked. "We had to buy *local* outfits for this party."

Lord Thomas smiled at her, and she felt as though she might swoon. Maybe there was something in Nile's obsession.

"I am dressed as a local," he said, leaning down and dropping his tone to a confidential whisper. "One of the Autocrat's ministers. Lord Toliaus."

Skana felt a shock at hearing his name, but thought she controlled herself incredibly well. "We don't know any of the ministers. We're just here to do business. You look like an old-time wizard."

"We wizards are eternal," Lord Thomas said, putting on an austere expression for a split second. He was a lot nicer than most of the nobles that Skana had met. "But I would be happy to tell your fortune." He slid into the chair next to Skana and spread a deck of fancy cards on the table. "Pick one. It will act as your significator."

Skana was so dazzled to have him close by that she chose the first card and turned it face up on the pristine tablecloth. Deftly, Lord Thomas spun a circle of cards around it.

"The Chariot is your card, Ms. Bertu. Two strong personalities pulling side by side. That's both of you, isn't it?"

Lord Thomas babbled on, talking about deep secrets and long journeys. Behind him, Lady Jil obviously couldn't wait to get away. She embedded herself in her circle of friends so there was no chance of Nile getting close to her. It didn't look like she was going to deliver the apology Skana thought she owed them.

Lord Thomas gathered up his cards and rose.

"Well, we must get to our place," he said. "It was a pleasure to meet you, Ms. Bertu, Mr. Bertu, ladies and sir."

Skana realized she hadn't been listening to a thing he said.

"Thank you so much, your lordship. It's so nice to meet you."

The nobles sauntered away.

"We have to tell them to leave," Nile growled. "They shouldn't be here now."

"It's their lookout," Skana said. "Did you notice she still hasn't told you she's sorry?"

"Thomas, I will never forgive you for that!" Jil said in Uctu, as I escorted her away. She clung to me, her chin on my shoulder. "How could you make me face him after I slapped him?"

"It was necessary, Jil, I promise you," I said, patting the hand that rested upon my elbow. "It's all part of the joke we are playing."

"They're part of the joke?" she asked.

"It's being played on them, too," I said. In more ways than one: now that the Bertus had surfaced, the Uctu security service would quietly take them into custody and get the information that all of us so desperately needed to prevent a crisis. I bowed to an Uctu male wearing a very fancy Imperium naval uniform that dated from two centuries back. "You could have apologized. That would have made it far less awkward."

"I couldn't. I just couldn't get a word out." Jil glanced over her shoulder at the brother and sister. "When does it begin?"

"After dinner, I believe," I said. I glanced around the room. Lieutenant Plet, in a handsome dark green caftan that was a formal ground-based army uniform of the equivalent rank, chatted a bit uncomfortably to a female Uctu wearing a very low-cut ballgown in an eye-watering shade of puce that clashed abominably with her scales. I tilted my head in the direction of the so-called merchants. She lowered her head in the merest suggestion of a nod. She lifted her wrist and spoke into her cuff. In the rear of the chamber, near a small five-piece musical ensemble, Nesbitt and Oskelev chatted as though they were ordinary guests. Parsons, as yet, was nowhere to be seen. I smiled at the knot of Uctu reporters at the center of the room, videoing everything for media broadcast and the Infogrid. "Yes, that is when the fun will start. Can you hear me, Anstruther?"

"Yes, sir," said the dulcet tones deep inside my ear. "How are you doing?"

"Well enough, though I feel as though I am sloshing like a mobile water tank."

"I have over two billion nanites supporting your knees and back, sir."

"Gratified to hear it," I said. "That will prevent the most immediate danger. Everything else ought to work exactly as we rehearsed it."

"Just to remind you, Thomas, don't let the stream get interrupted. If you do, the controller you're carrying will lose contact with it."

"Acknowledged," I said.

The rest of the reception was uneventful. The Bertus, having had a taste of my charm, did their best to run into us again and again. I was happy to pass the time of day and discuss our visits. Any means I could use to keep them in the hall and under the watchful eyes of the High Protector's agents was worthwhile. Jil excused herself and fled to the Autocrat's personal retiring room to regain her composure.

The crowd was elbow-to-elbow by the time the Autocrat made her appearance. The musicians in the corner stopped playing, and a tuneless *blat!* played upon some misshapen brass instruments sounded out in the corridor. The flattened fanfare continued. Into the room processed the Autocrat's entourage, beginning with a host of soldiers and spacers from all the military services. These wore ordinary Uctu uniforms and carried serviceable if formal weapons. Behind them came Visoltia's own servants. Ema and Tcocna caught sight of me and smiled. I gave them a small wave so as not to cause a commotion.

The next contingent to enter was the brass band whose official noisemaking had already been heralded. Eight rows of instrument players in sand-beige robes strode in. They kept accurate tempo, the only accession to music I was willing to grant them.

Once placed where they could perform damage upon the greatest number of eardrums, they struck up a grander marching tune to announce the advent of the ministers.

Visoltia's cabinet entered the room one at a time to polite applause by the assembled guests. The High Nourisher gave me a friendly look when I caught her eye. The ministers took their places on the dais behind their assigned chairs.

Most of them. Neither Lord Rimbalius nor Lord Toliaus had yet made their appearance. A pause ensued. Over the abominable band, I heard raised voices in the corridor.

Eventually, wearing an expression that would have shattered glass, Lord Toliaus made his stately way into the chamber. Once he had stepped up to the chair at the left hand of the Autocrat's throne, Lord Rimbalius entered. The High Protector looked annoyed instead of triumphant, which rather endeared him to me. He was wearing my sword on a baldric that stretched tight across his broad chest. The adapted Imperium uniform looked good on him. I would never have dared to say so to his face, of course. It was a shame that they were on opposite sides of an old grudge, because he and my mother could truly have been good friends.

At the very last, looking quite small and even more childlike than ever in a long white dress and a lovely but simple necklace that had been a gift from my mother's own jewelry box with my finest and most beautiful lucky circuit twinkling on the chain, her tail steady and without a single nervous twitch, came Visoltia.

Two guards jumped forward to help her mount the dais steps. I smiled as she wriggled in between the arms of the chairs to either side. She stood proudly before the throne, but did not sit down. Not yet.

"My dear people, my friends, my protectors, my providers and my teachers, I bid you welcome. Two years ago today, I stood here for the first time, following the untimely death of my father."

At that, Ema lowered her head and blubbered unhappily into a handkerchief. Tcocna patted her arm.

"You have all been with me and generously given me your help and support over those last two years. I was so proud to reach the first anniversary, and grateful to have lived to see one, the second anniversary of my accession. Thank you all for coming to celebrate this day with me. I have been provided with so many symbols of support. I know how fortunate I am to be among people who love me."

She sat down. I burst out into loud applause, until I realized the Uctus tapped their round fingertips together in acclaim. I patted my palms together much more gently. Visoltia beamed in my direction, and raised the lucky circuit to show me. I bowed.

The seating had been arranged deliberately to place me where I would annoy the High Wisdom the most. At a table for ten; six of whom were me, Jil and her entourage; I was closest to the head table and facing Lord Toliaus. Over the course of the excellent meal that followed, I performed condimentomancy for my tablemates, with Jil offering her own comments on my divinations. I trotted out my dancing cards, my laugh, and all the other forces I could bring to be as unbearable as possible. Lord Toliaus clearly wanted to ignore me, but I did my very best to make that impossible. Still, his attention was not entirely on me. I watched him as best I could out of the corner of my eye.

Toliaus offered extravagant compliments to Visoltia. She still seemed to be perturbed at him. For a male who was usually in control of his emotions, he seemed almost reckless. He threw insults at other ministers on the dais, especially Rimbalius, as if he felt he wouldn't have to answer for his behavior later on.

Enlightenment dawned on me, as it must have on the High Protector. Our eyes met briefly. I gave him a very brief but significant nod to show I understood. The plot was about to unfold. Everyone was in place. I was more than ready to poke holes in that monstrous ego. All the stars were in their appointed places, so to speak.

"It's almost time," I said in Imperium Standard, with an apologetic glance at the dignified Uctu guests. They smiled uncomprehendingly.

"I don't want to do it," Jil said suddenly, seizing my arm with a death grip. I felt her nails dig into my skin through my robe. "Thomas, I can't get up there."

I believe I blinked once. "Are you certain?" I asked. "Banitra has offered to come up with you."

"We can do it," her companion said, jumping in like a champion. I became aware that I would be deeply in Banitra's debt, but there was too much else at stake. "It will be so much fun. You know that! Come on."

"I can't," Jil said. Her eyes were huge with fear. I could see that she felt genuine distress. "I don't want to . . . be undignified in front of *that man*. I feel as though he will steal my soul or something. And there are reporters! My image will be all over the Infogrid in moments!"

It was no good to remind her how often we had ended up as trending news back home in the Imperium. It was also too late to train another magician's assistant. Plet had refused to play-act as one of my "victims," or to allow me to make use of any of the rest of my crew, as it would end up on their Infogrid pages, and subject to review, not to mention the derision of their peers. Jil's other companions were too shy to perform in public. I threw a glance at Banitra, but she tossed it straight back to me. It was up to me to be as persuasive as possible. I took Jil's shoulders and looked deeply into her eyes.

"Jil, this moment is very important to me. I am counting on you to help me with this. In fact, I need your help so badly that if you keep your word and go through with it . . ." I took a deep breath, for it was a heavy sacrifice. ". . . I will give you my *Ya!* boxed set."

Jil stared at me as though she couldn't believe her ears. Then a tiny smile turned up the left corner of her mouth. She laughed, although it sounded strained.

"You must want to perform your magic act in the very worst way, Thomas!" she said. She put out her hand and I took it. "You have a deal. I'll do it."

"Very well," I said, deeply relieved. "Then there's no point in delaying any longer."

I rose from my seat and approached the dais.

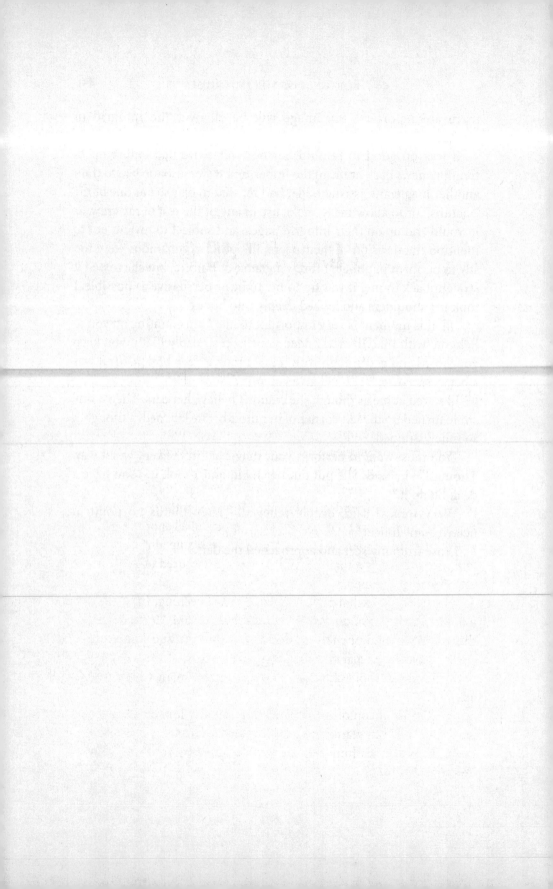

CHAPTER 46

My movements were more ponderous than usual, all the better to ensure that every eye was upon me. I still could not see Parsons, but I felt his presence close by. When I reached the dais, I bowed low. I almost overtoppled, but managed to catch myself.

"Your Serenity, it is my great honor to greet you on behalf of my government, my emperor and my mother. I hope that relations between our two peoples will be closer than ever from now on."

She dropped her jaw in a charming smile.

"Thomasin—I mean, Lord Thomas, we are honored by your presence and your friendship. We thank you also for the gift of wine and sweets to complement our feast. I am sure we will all appreciate them."

In a gesture of good will, I had had Angie box up almost all of the vintages and treats remaining in the *Rodrigo*'s secured hold. Alas, the caviar was long gone.

"Since we are exchanging garments for the evening, I thought you would enjoy some of our prized comestibles," I said. "It is but a small thing to have strengthened the bond between Uctu and Imperium."

She gave me a regal nod.

"I promise to work closely with my brother, Shojan, to deepen our alliance."

Lord Toliaus could not restrain himself any longer. He snorted audibly. Rimbalius glared at him. He glared back.

"It does you no honor to treat with humans, Your Excellence," Toliaus said.

"I have already noted your derision," I told him. "In fact, I have come to Her Serenity to ask permission to carry out the challenge that I set you yesterday. My wizardry against yours."

Toliaus stood up, causing his heavy chair to keel over backward. It landed on the dais with a boom. Everyone who had not already been looking our way before focused upon us now.

"I will show you my power," he snarled. "Here! Before the Autocrat's very eyes! I will show her that you are a fraud."

I looked down to examine my fingernails. They seemed unusually shiny. I admired them for a moment.

"If you think you can beat me, try," I said. I buffed my fingertips against my robe front. "You claim to be the greatest prognosticator and sorcerer in the Autocracy. I doubt it."

Toliaus stormed toward the steps of the dais. A couple of the gray-clad servants ran to right his chair. He waved them out of his way. I waited. He thundered toward me, but stopped a dozen paces away. He pointed a hand at me, the sucker-shaped tips of his fingers waving in a threatening fashion.

"I curse you with death, human!" he growled. "A plague eat your bones and leave your scales scattered upon the ground!" He carried on in that way for some time, his voice rising in intensity and volume until it was virtually ringing off the inlaid ceiling. When the sound died away, I clapped my hands slowly, to indicate extreme derision.

"Very weak," I said, mustering pity on my face. "Because, honestly, my brother and I used to throw worse imprecations at one another when we were six and eight years old. Is that all that you have?"

I think Toliaus must have evoked some psychosomatic heart attacks with his string of curses, and was somewhat put out that it hadn't worked on me. Visoltia eyed me worriedly, searching my face for any signs of impending doom.

"You will begin to feel it soon," Toliaus assured me. "You are to be pitied for what will soon befall you."

"Sticks and stones," I said, spreading my arms wide. "Your words have no effect."

"No?" he asked. "Then, feel this!" He thrust his hands out toward me.

I should have been ready for a genuine trick, but until that moment I had not been sure that he could do any. Lightning shot up from the floor through my shoes. Pain lanced through my body. I staggered from one foot to another, but every step brought fresh agony. Toliaus cackled. Electricity crackled all over my body and struck light from the silver filaments in my underrobe. Tiny bolts shot from my fingertips. I dropped to my knees, holding on to the nearest bench seat. The Uctu on it stared at me in open horror.

"Thomasin!" the Autocrat cried. "High Wisdom, stop this!"

"Not unless he surrenders, Your Excellence," Toliaus boomed. "It is his challenge to withdraw. If he does not, he will die."

I concentrated on a tiny spot of color just in front of my nose. It took everything I had to force out three words.

"Anstruther, help me," I gritted.

"Hold on, sir," came the dulcet tones in my ear. Suddenly, I felt as though I was growing taller. The lightning withdrew. I could breathe again. "I think he's got the whole floor electrified, but he can operate it in segments. I'll insulate you. Is that better?"

"Yes!" I took a deep breath and stood up straight. I felt heavy as a neutron star. I could still sense sharp pings striking the soles of my feet, but they were easily ignored. Summoning calmness to my visage, I turned to confront the High Wisdom.

"That was a good one," I said, with a friendly smile. "I didn't think you had it in you. Now, it's my turn."

I seized a pitcher of water from the nearest table and held it aloft. From my chest issued an almost invisible silver stream. It flowed up my arm, into the pitcher, down my body and across the floor, where it spread out around the High Wisdom. I waited for the faint gray arch to form over him, then I flicked my fingers toward Toliaus. He cringed backward, then down as the nanites began to precipitate droplets all over him.

"After lightning comes rain," I said. The assembled guests stared for a moment, then burst out laughing. "And following rain, a rainbow. We of the Imperium consider the arch a lucky sign." The nanites turned their silicon sides outward to catch the light. A cascade of color surrounded the High Wisdom. The guests applauded.

Furious, Toliaus shook his jowls, spraying water all around and dispelling my rainbow. He brought his hands together in a mighty thunderclap. I gasped in pain. It felt as though the walls had closed suddenly, squeezing me between them. I thought my chest would turn inside out as I struggled to breathe. I gasped. I was battered over and over by an invisible force.

"Sonic bursts, sir," Anstruther said. "I'll try and counter."

Blackness crept in from the edges of my vision.

"No," I croaked. I gazed haughtily at Toliaus. "These are all tricks." Though the battering bruised my ribs, I turned to face the Autocrat. "If you wish, I'll tell you how he does it."

"I touch the power of the infinite!" Toliaus shrieked.

I smiled at him sweetly.

"Then show us the future," I said. "Surely that would be easy for you."

He clapped his hands again, and the pounding stopped. I almost staggered at the relief of it. He put his fingertips up to his temples. He closed his eyes, tilted his head back, and began to intone in an impressive voice.

"You will have a long life, Your Serenity," he said. "Prosperity comes from every corner of the Autocracy! Wait—I see betrayal. These humans threaten your people's safety." Visoltia looked alarmed and frightened. He opened his eyes and glared at me. "You should not be here to sully the celebration of Her Serenity's accession."

"You're the one spoiling the party," I said. "But how unimaginative! I could have come up with more impressive predictions after an all-night bender. Let me show you the future, Your Serenity." I bowed to Visoltia. I spread out my hands.

Nanites flowed from the inside of my hand into my palm. I threw those into the air. I could not see them, but they climbed over one another's backs, holding on with microscopically small filaments to form a whisper-thin tri-dee screen. It turned to be out easy for Anstruther to reprogram the captured devices to the Imperium's program. Redius and I had put together a stream of digitavid clips from the Infogrid, all heartwarming images like Uctu and human shaking hands, playing together, children of all species dancing in the sunlight. Toliaus fumed. Visoltia watched them raptly, her jaw lowered with pleasure. I clapped my hand, and the nanites forming the screen dropped to the floor.

"My power is at your service," I said. "Would you like to see more?"

"Oh, yes!"

I beckoned to my cousin and her friend. Jil kept glancing toward the back of the chamber where the Bertus sat, but she rose and came forward.

I hoped that I would be able to accomplish this trick without making a fool of myself—that is, not more of a fool than normal. Anstruther was ready. She would carry out her instructions without regard for whether the process hurt me or not. When she was not feeling nervous, Jil had adored the idea of our act. The problem was to keep her from doing anything before I "enchanted" her.

"These are my subjects," I said, taking each lady by the hand. "I have made them my servants. They will obey my every command, even if it seems impossible." I touched their foreheads. They closed their eyes and swayed slightly.

"What is your will, my master?" Banitra asked in a breathy voice.

Jil looked put out, as though she wished she had prepared dialogue for herself in advance. But my cousin has always been ready for any jape, and threw herself into the part.

"I command you . . . to dance upon air!" I said.

"Mercy, master!" Jil pleaded.

I tore open the neck of my robe. Nanites poured forth from my chest in a silver cloud. They filled the air around the two women. Slowly, Jil and Banitra dropped backward and floated upward. The audience gasped.

Jil, I knew, had as a girl had tightrope lessons with the same teacher of acrobatics that I had employed. She had been an excellent pupil, as had been proved the night when at the age of fifteen she sneaked into the empress's wine cellar one evening by tottering along the top of a wall that had neither sensors nor cameras incorporated into it, and brought us back two bottles of regal brandy over four centuries old. But I digress. As the ladies achieved a height of three meters, she rose to her feet and began to gyrate in the air. Banitra was less graceful. She fell over several times, but was borne upright again by a silver cluster that supported her in the middle of her back. She lay limp in a balletic arch on the top of it, pretending to be still under my spell. I turned to the Autocrat.

"Don't you agree that my spells are superior to your minion?" I inquired, with insulting emphasis on the last word.

"Oh, yes!" she said. "Lord Toliaus, can you do anything as spectacular?"

The spots on the High Wisdom's head flared angry red.

"It is a trick! I know he is using machines!"

"Of course I am," I said. "Just as you were. I'd be happy to explain how I do it. Won't you? We're both a pair of frauds. Why not admit it?"

Rimbalius couldn't help himself. He began to chuckle. The chuckle grew to a laugh, then graduated to a guffaw.

"He has you there, High Wisdom," he said, banging his big hand on the table.

"Do not seek to undermine me," Toliaus shouted. He waved a hand into a fist. I heard a shriek behind me. Jil was falling. Toliaus must have brushed aside the umbilical connected to the stream of nanites that held them up. I rushed to catch them.

I caught Jil and placed myself so Banitra landed on my back.

"Can you fix it, Anstruther?" I asked.

"I'm working on it, sir," her voice said in my aural implant. The ladies were unharmed. I set them down and made a few magical passes. Nothing happened. I looked at my hands to see what was wrong with them. Small pieces of metal began to protrude from my skin. My throat began to close. I clawed at it, and felt more smooth metal. The nanites were resuming their previous shape! Jil regarded me with horror.

"Program override," I croaked.

"I'm working on it," Anstruther said.

"Hurry." I gasped for air as I was twisted into a backwards hoop. Toliaus, not to miss a chance, postured and made gestures above my body as though he was responsible for my agony.

"Do you see, Your Serenity? His own tools turn against him, because my truth is too much for him."

I had to give the old show-lizard credit. The Autocrat was wavering. I was almost out of breath when . . .

"Got it!" came a cry of triumph in my ear so loud I feared the rest of the room could hear it. The silver components shivered into powder and fell from my limbs. I rose to my feet.

"That's better," I said, settling my robes around my shoulders. "My technology bests your technology. And my truth . . ."

"My lord," said Parsons's voice in my ear.

"Parsons!" I exclaimed, pleased. "Where are you? You are missing a grand contest."

"I have been with the High Calculator's forensic accountants, sir."

"Well, that sounds dreary. I thought you might be out extracting confessions or uncovering an unsavory plot."

"I believe that we have done both, my lord. We have been examining the cargo manifests of the ships passing through every frontier crossing on the Days of Grace dating back almost two years, and found some interesting correlations. Ask the High Wisdom how, if he dislikes outworlders so greatly, that he has allowed himself to profit from Kail merchants importing inexpensive skanana seed, a staple in a third of the Autocracy. The funds passed through three shell corporations, but the same sum landed in Lord Toliaus's accounts."

"Really?" I turned to the High Wisdom. "It would seem that not only are you a wretch, but a greedy wretch. But I knew that. It seems that your coffers have been filled by your very manipulation of those so-called Days of Grace!"

"What?" Visoltia exclaimed, horrified.

I went to take his arm.

"Come and confess to the Autocrat. All you have ever offered is some form of trickery and base superstition. There are no Days of Grace, are there? It's all a plot to profit from her gullibility—all apologies to Your Serenity," I added with a bow. "The Kail have been quietly taking over a large portion of the market on skanana seed, all with your manipulation of the numbers of ships that could pass within the borders, always ensuring that your cronies were among those who could enter."

The Autocrat might have been a child in age, but she was eternal in her outrage.

"You betrayed me, High Wisdom? I trusted you to guide me! You . . . you have been using me to earn a profit on the backs of my subjects? Is nothing that I came to believe in real?"

"It is his fault!" Toliaus shouted. He shook me off and pointed at Rimbalius. "He is strangling the Autocracy with his limits and rules! But this is the end of his days!"

The High Wisdom spread his arms wide.

I could not fault his showmanship. At that moment the gorgeous stained glass windows and the walls surrounding them burst inward. Five silver arrows screamed into the room. I realized that they were single-pilot fighter craft, exactly the same as the one that Uctu

Customs had impounded. They were made to be nimble, little more than an enclosed pilot and a pair of pulse cannon on the stubby wings, plus the propulsion engine behind. They flew in formation around the enormous room. The crowd of guests shrieked in terror and ran for the door, but it burst apart as pulse missiles reduced it to rubble. Shards of wood, stone and metal peppered us all. I pushed my cousin and her friend to the ground and shielded them with my body.

Rimbalius leaped to pull Visoltia out of her chair and down underneath the table. Guards and servants swarmed to surround her. One of them activated a sonic shield that would dispel pulse fire. The High Protector rose up and leaped over the table. He drew my sword and made for Toliaus.

The High Wisdom grinned ferally. This was the moment that he had been waiting for. None of us needed the confirmation that Rimbalius was the target that Toliaus had planned to destroy all along. He backed away, putting guests, furniture and servants between him and Rimbalius.

"Enstidius!" he bellowed, pointing magnificently at the High Protector. "Kill him!"

Before Rimbalius could run him through, two of the fighters turned in mid-air and made for the High Protector. They peppered the ground with slug fire. He hit the ground and rolled behind Toliaus, making the craft veer off to come around for another pass. With their hand weapons, Plet and Oskelev provided covering fire for the crowd of guests as they scrambled over the wreckage to escape. A couple of bodies lay on the floor, never having made it to the door.

I wanted to help, but Jil's safety was my first priority. I put my arms around Jil's shoulders and pushed Banitra in the direction of the servers' door.

To my horror, Nile Bertu popped up beside me. He reached for Jil's hand and a stud on his belt.

Instantly, he lay flat on his face with Banitra sitting on his back. Hopeli appeared at our side. From somewhere within her filmy costume, Hopeli had produced a long and lethal firearm, pointed at his head.

"What are you doing?" I asked them.

"We're professional bodyguards," Hopeli said, tossing her long hair out of her face. "Commander Parsons engaged us to look after Lady Jil."

"Well done, Parsons!" I exclaimed. "I never saw that coming. Not that this fellow has proved much of a challenge."

The fighters zoomed over our heads. We ducked low to the floor.

"I don't want to hurt her!" Nile Bertu protested, kicking his feet. "I want to protect her! My belt's a shield! State of the art repulsors."

I made a decision. I pulled Banitra off.

"Go with him," I told the two women. "Don't let anything untoward happen. I need to help the Autocrat. Take Jil to safety." Bertu stood up and thumbed the button on his belt. The force field it generated shoved me backward.

"Thomas, no!" Jil shouted, as Banitra pulled her toward the door, but I had already turned back to the fray.

The silver craft were laying criminal waste to the State Dining Room. The huge chamber filled with smoke from burning tablecloths and liquefied metal and stone. In the midst of the wreckage, Toliaus stood untouched. I scanned the room for the High Protector.

But Rimbalius, too, had been prepared for an attack. Several of the guards pulled large pulse rifles from behind arrases, and under tables, and from behind statues. They shot at the flyers, but they were sadly outgunned. More soldiers poured into the room, armed with antiaircraft weaponry. They returned fire, blasting out large chunks of the ceiling. Pulse fire from the fighters struck into the midst of a group, sending the soldiers flying, but they were protected by shield belts. I had nothing but my robes and an idea.

"Anstruther, can you make me a suit of armor?"

"I'm not sure that's in the profile, sir."

"Nonsense. I can't believe no one ever tried."

Anstruther, like everyone else, always responded well to a challenge. Within seconds, my hands shimmered with silver, and I found myself looking at the world through a gleaming haze.

"Leave the room, sir," Parsons instructed me. "Let the military handle this matter. Our craft are coming down from orbit to join them. Those are mark six fighters."

"Parsons, they came from the same place as the one that Anstruther destroyed," I said. "They, too, must be made of nanites. Anstruther, can you disintegrate these, too?"

"Not unless they make contact with the ones I have reprogrammed, sir," she said. "That's how the merchant ships were contaminated. They transferred their program by touch."

"Then I need to touch them," I said. I stood up from my place of concealment.

A pair of fighters zipped past me. I caught sight of the Uctu pilots. They looked shocked at what must have seemed to be a silver man walking among them. I was too late to touch either craft. I had to attract their attention. I waved my arms up and down.

Rimbalius put his head up over the edge of an overturned table.

"Get out of here, you fool!"

Toliaus spotted him and pointed in his direction.

"There! Kill him!"

A fighter detached itself from the others and turned in a tight circle. It came in low, strafing the already-damaged floor. It was only a few meters off the ground. I waited until it was a heartbeat away, then leaped.

I missed my jump, falling onto the ruin of the dessert table. As I righted myself, brushing off ribbons of cream and jelly, another fighter craft followed in its wake. It shot at me, hitting me in the side. I flew meters into the air, and found myself in the path of yet a third fighter. I crouched and sprang.

To my surprise and delight, I managed to grab hold of the undercarriage. The fighter went zipping dizzily around the room, but I was an experienced skimmer pilot with numerous agility wins to my name. The only difference was that I was not steering and did not know where he was going to turn next. My insides were battered against my ribs, pummeling them into rags. I regretted my second glass of wine and the third helping of dessert.

"I've got one, Anstruther!" I shouted.

"Just hold on, Thomas," Anstruther said. I could tell she was gritting her teeth. Suddenly, I went plummeting to the ground in a cloud of silver dust. An Uctu in a helmet fell on top of me. Before I could register it, guards grabbed him and put him in restraints.

The other craft saw their fellow's destruction and promptly retreated into the upper reaches of the chamber. I threw handfuls of dust from the powdered ship upward, hoping to hit one of them.

But they couldn't avoid me forever, not if they wanted to kill their quarry. Rimbalius must have been watching me. He understood.

He climbed out from behind his shelter and held my sword up to the heights.

I applauded his courage, even as I wondered at my ability to keep him from being blown apart.

"There!" Toliaus shrieked. "Kill him!"

The four remaining craft homed in on Rimbalius from all directions. I raced toward him, prepared to spring. I would have only one chance.

"Anstruther, are you ready?" I asked.

"I've got them set to disperse, sir, but you're going to lose your armor."

"I'll be fine," I assured her, though I was certain of no such thing.

As the four small craft converged on the High Protector, their guns stitching the floor from every direction, I leaped into the air in their midst.

My protective shield sluiced away from me in ribbons, filling the air with filaments of silver that streamed upward. I landed on top of Rimbalius as a barrage of fire exploded over our heads. We tumbled together over and over, landing up against the foot of the dais.

I lay on my back with his foot on my chest. A silver rope led upward from my belly and spread out over the entire room like the crown of an enormous snow-covered tree. The four fighters seemed to be caught in its branches. They zipped outward, as though preparing for a return sally to strike their victim.

Then, one by one, the silver craft each burst in mid-air with an audible *poof!*

Naturally, gravity being what it is, once deprived of their ships, the pilots descended rapidly. I curled into a ball to avoid being struck by any more falling Uctus. They fell to the ground amid the wreckage and lay there moaning.

"Nooooo!" wailed Toliaus.

His dreams of vengeance dashed, the High Wisdom sought to escape over the wreckage of the grand doorway. I struggled to my feet to follow, but an Uctu in uniform broke loose from the fighting force and tackled him from behind. He twisted a claw up under the shield of scales at the base of the minister's tail. Toliaus gasped audibly.

"Walk," he said. "You shall confess to Her Serenity all that you have done."

In spite of the pain, the High Wisdom still tried to pull rank. He turned his head to glare at the soldier.

"You, a subject of the Autocracy, dare to lay hands on one of her ministers?"

Redius grinned up at him from under the helmet.

"I am not your subject," he said. "I serve Her Serenity out of friendship."

The reporters seemed to come out of the very enamelwork to point cameras and microphones in our direction. I straightened my robes and prepared to be interviewed.

Toliaus was dragged away into custody, still raging at Rimbalius. The pilots and their cronies had been arrested. At a word from Anstruther, the nanites mustered themselves into a cleanup crew and cleared away the broken glass and the shattered pieces of wall and door.

Visoltia gave a statement to the press, but her confidence had been shattered. She returned to the dining hall, but stayed in the shelter of Ema's arms.

"How could he do this to me?" she said over and over again. "He was my guide! My sage!"

"He wasn't a prophet, Your Excellence, but a profit," I quipped.

"Power corrupts, Your Serenity," Rimbalius said, simply. "You will learn that."

"But it did not corrupt you, my friend," she said, with a smile for him. "Thank you for guiding me even when I did not see where you were going."

He bowed deeply.

"I, too, was blind," he said. He turned to me. "I respected your mother, even when I hated her. I thought she had sent you to taunt me about our shared past. It was hard for me to see that the gift was presented in an open hand. You risked your life to save me today."

"It's what the maternal unit would have wanted," I said. "Now, if you can open the borders again so there is no holdup for our trade vessels, she will feel well recompensed."

"It shall be done," Visoltia said.

I could feel that I still had some kilos of nanites clinging to my tissues and bones. I held out my palm.

"Anstruther, make me a flower," I said. It formed in my palm, and

I presented it to Visoltia. She smiled and tucked it into the neck of her white gown.

A small hubbub erupted at the rear of the ruined hall. The servers's door opened to admit my cousin and her now-extended party, and Parsons.

"Oh, Thomas, are you all right?" Jil asked.

I patted my chest.

"I am intact. I will feel a good deal better when I have returned to my normal weight. Carrying sixty kilos of nanites around makes me feel deep sympathy for explorers of heavy-gravity worlds." I essayed a curious glance in the direction of Nile and Skana Bertu. "And you?"

"Oh, he was a perfect gentleman," Jil said. She kissed Nile on the cheek and squeezed Skana's hand. "Thank you for looking after us. And I am sorry for all the trouble I caused."

"Now, that's a lady," Skana Bertu said, looking more satisfied than if someone had given her a country manor.

At a gesture from Rimbalius, a host of guards moved in on the Bertus and their Croctoid secretary. In a twinkling, restraints were snapped on their wrists and ankles.

"Now, wait a moment," Nile exclaimed. "What's this?"

"I arrest you in the name of the Autocrat," the High Protector intoned. "For smuggling weapons of war over our borders. For the violation of no fewer than sixty-two laws that protect our state, you are hereby remanded into custody. You will be permitted legal counsel and decent creature comforts throughout the proceedings."

"No way!" Nile exploded. "Let us go! We just helped save this lady's life! We'll tell you everything about Enstidius and Lord Toliaus!"

Rimbalius tilted his head in the direction of the door. The guards hauled the Bertus away, still shouting to be set free. My feelings were torn between justice and mercy.

"But they will die, Parsons," I said. "All these regulations, all with the same harsh penalty. That's indecent. They did protect Jil."

"My lord Rimbalius," Parsons said, turning to the High Protector. "I must state on behalf of the Emperor that those persons need to be returned to the Imperium for prosecution. They also *exported* weapons of war without a license. We have first jurisdiction on them. Once they have served their sentences under our laws, we will see to it that they return to stand trial here."

What was unspoken was that by then, the death penalties would no doubt have been overturned. I let out a sigh of relief.

Rimbalius let his jaw drop just a trifle, and he emitted a throaty chuckle.

"Very well, my friend. We have the main perpetrator of this outrage. These humans may even see a lessening of their punishment for acting as witnesses against him. Once they have served their time in your prisons, of course."

"Of course," Parsons said.

"Since it is clear that they are not guilty," I said, with a deep bow to the Autocrat, "wouldn't it be a kindly gesture to free the other prisoners, Your Excellence?"

CHAPTER 47

"Will you ever come back to the Autocracy?" I asked M'Kenna Copper. She and her family had practically overwhelmed me with their demonstration of relief and gratitude upon their release from prison. My knees were still recovering from being leaped upon by all four children. I was pleased to accompany Parsons to shuttle them back to their ship. The *Entertainer* had had all its nanites restored to their proper functions. Ms. Copper, too, was scheduled to undergo her restorative therapy that very day.

"Once they change their laws," she said. "Up until the restrictions, this had always been a good run for us."

"I believe the change is already under way," I assured them.

The children, free for the first time in months, raced around the interior of their home ship, touching everything and shouting for joy. It did my heart good to watch them. M'Kenna gave me a shy smile.

"Thank you. Thanks for all you did."

"It was my duty and my pleasure," I assured her.

"One thing, though," Rafe Copper said. He tugged on the filament holding my gift to him around his neck. "You know these little things?"

"My lucky circuits?"

"You know, they're really cute. Mind if we have them manufactured and sell them? We'll cut you in on a percentage. But I think we could make a lot of money. Stars know we could use that right now."

"Our lawyer wasn't cheap," M'Kenna added.

"Why not?" I said, heartily. "I'll donate my portion to charity. Why not provide good fortune for everyone? You have just proved I was right all along, that those circuits were lucky."

Parsons removed a handful of twinkling lights from his pocket.

"I believe, though, that you would like to exchange the ones you have for these," he said. "There is a fault in the original ones. These have been checked for safe use."

"Sure," the Coppers said. They made the trade without question, but I was left full of curiosity.

"Why, Parsons?" I asked, once we were on our way back down to Memepocotel. "What is wrong with the lucky circuits I gave them?"

"I had them made to transmit sound, sir. It is why I became certain of their innocence. I was able to listen to their conversations while in prison."

"I still hold that the circuits are lucky," I insisted. "Without them, you might have been nowhere near these fine people when they needed you."

Parsons never sighed, but at that moment he came close.

"If you insist, my lord."

Now that the object of her terror was in custody, Jil lost no time in making up for the shopping that she had missed. She caught me as I returned to the hotel to pack for our own departure.

"Thomas, I'm afraid you're going to be the tiniest bit squeezed when we go home," she said, her voice falling into a wheedling tone with which I was intimately familiar.

"And why is that, my dear cousin?" I asked, though I could already guess.

Jil gave me a very sweet smile. It portended worse than I had initially assumed.

"Well, I have just purchased a new summer house in Ultin," she said. "It just cries out for up-to-the-minute décor. And there is a designer in the next street," she pointed out of the door, "with whose work I have just fallen in love."

I sighed. "How many rooms' worth of love?" I asked.

"Only eight. The house has just three bedrooms. The rest is for entertaining. They will deliver it to the ship, if you will give me the entry code for the hold."

"No can do, cousin of mine," I said. "Security, you understand."

She pouted. "But I thought it was your ship!"

"And so it is, within the good graces of the Imperium Navy, under the lordship of my mother. But Nesbitt will arrange to meet your delivery at the ship and bestow the cargo therein."

She stood on her tiptoes to kiss me. "You are splendid," she said. " I'll have my other purchases sent at the same time."

I admit that I blanched.

"*Other* purchases? How much of the Uctu economy have you supported since the last round of must-haves?" I asked, assuming a long-suffering expression.

"Oh, Thomas," she said, striking my arm with her fingers. "You know I came here to shop. And I have. You encouraged me."

"More fool I," I said. "Very well. It is a small price to pay for peace."

"I knew you would see it my way!"

The *Rodrigo* was stuffed full of goods, arranged into the smallest possible space by Banitra's deft hand. Still, Nesbitt informed me that even my quarters had several coffers bestowed therein, if only to get them out of the corridors that needed to be kept clear.

Visoltia called for a meeting with the royal correspondents from the press to express her gratitude to my crew and Lord Rimbalius's staff. She had commissioned medals with twinkling lights not unlike my lucky circuits and pinned them on each of us in full view of the cameras. At the end of the line, Redius waited with trepidation, but she stood on tiptoes to embrace him just as she had the rest of us.

"I will do my best to understand why some of my people left our realm," she said. "But I am grateful for your friendship and your aid."

"It is my gift to you," Redius said, much gratified. Visoltia grinned almost mischievously.

"We will correspond about *Ya!* in the future."

"I look forward to the conversation."

I was deeply gratified. Wherever she had come by it, the Autocrat had her own version of high wisdom. With Visoltia beaming our midst, we all posed for the cameras. I took the lead reporter aside and was assured of copies for my Infogrid file.

I took my final leave of Visoltia with deep regret.

"I will miss you, Thomasin," she said, when we had read my Tarot cards just one more time together on the broad divan in the State

Bedroom. She hugged me tightly, her small face nestled against the front of my robe.

"And I you," I assured her, patting her on the shoulder. "But we can keep in touch."

"Oh, we will!" Visoltia said, letting go and plumping back on the divan. She still seemed to be the eager child that she had been when I first met her, mere days ago, but I could at last see the shape of the adult to come. I regretted the loss of innocence, though it was not a total alteration. "Your reading says that we will always be friends."

I bowed to her. "If the cards say it, then it must be true."

"Well done, my lord," Parsons said, in a tone of voice that almost admitted to a trace of emotion as we departed through the privy door and out into the corridors. The servants smiled at us.

"I think it was," I said. The full story of the High Wisdom's perfidy gradually came out. In spite of the growing burden of proof and the terrible betrayal that it revealed, the Autocrat preferred to believe only a portion of it. "She still prefers her superstitions to real life. She misses her fortune teller."

Parsons looked sympathetic.

"You can do only so much, sir. The Lady Visoltia needs to have time to grow up. Thanks to your efforts, she will have it."

I sighed. "I know. In the meanwhile, I had Anstruther program a number of nanites for her. They will occupy the fissures and spaces within that marvelous crystal ball of hers. If she asks it whether someone is lying, they will measure temperature, respiration and pupil size and put the answer in the ball. And if someone won't admit the truth, they will tweak the pain nerve above the tail. She absolutely loves it. In time she'll learn to read people herself. A wise man from Old Earth once said, 'Trust, but verify.' Not a bad way to govern."

"No, indeed."

I straightened my back as we walked. It was time to essay a difficult matter.

"I have a favor to ask, Parsons."

"My lord?"

"Yes. In future, I would rather not take my cousins along on missions. You may say it provides good cover, but it inhibits my normal exuberance."

Parsons inclined his head less than a millimeter.

"As you please, sir, although you must admit that Lady Jil and her associates were more than useful to your activities. It is not every noble that would permit herself to be used as a stage prop."

"Oh, you would be surprised," I said, waving a dismissive hand. "We'll try anything if it sounds like fun. That's why I do this."

An eyebrow climbed his epicene forehead.

"The only reason, sir?"

I smiled blandly.

"No, of course not, Parsons. I also enjoy the pleasure of your company."

"You do me too much honor, sir."

I smiled, and ushered him through the kitchen doors before me.

"I saw it in one of the old books: Fortunate is he who has good friends."